K

DANIEL EASTERMAN

HarperCollins*Publishers*

HarperCollins*Publishers*
77–85 Fulham Palace Road,
Hammersmith, London W6 8JB

This paperback edition 1998
9 8 7 6 5 4 3 2 1

First published in Great Britain by
HarperCollins*Publishers* 1997

ISBN 0 00 651001 9

Set in Meridien

Printed and bound in Great Britain by
Caledonian International Book Manufacturing Ltd, Glasgow

To Beth, Eddie, Giles, John, and Patricia,
my Five Musketeers, for acts of friendship
far above and beyond the call of duty.

ACKNOWLEDGEMENTS

More than ever, I'm grateful to the skill, judgement, and thoughtfulness of my editor, Patricia Parkin, for steering book and author safely home. Behind the scenes, Malcolm Edwards provided support with flair, imagination, and thoughtfulness. Mary-Rose Doherty did remarkable things with her eagle-eyed copy-editing, as she always does. Up in Edinburgh (and not infrequently in London), my ever-astonishing agent Giles Gordon proved an inspiration and a more substantial pillar of strength than he knows. Warm thanks are due to my researchers, Elizabeth Murray in London and Claudia Caruana in New York, for dealing so efficiently with so many weird and wonderful requests. To my very dear friend, Paul Luft, profound thanks for his Germanic interventions. First and last, how could any of this have been written without the most gorgeous wife in the world? To Beth, not just thanks, but all my love.

PART 1

Kamp 17

CHAPTER ONE

Monday, 1 October 1940

The barbed wire stretched for miles and eternity. Everything it contained, everyone who lived behind it, was finite, trapped, condemned to die, even the guards with their deaths-head uniforms and sub-machine guns, even the camp commandant with his expensive tastes and sophisticated vices, even the dogs with their sharp teeth and vigilant eyes.

Concentration camp. The name trapped them all as effectively as the electrified wire or the guard towers or the guns. There were prison camps, labour camps, transit camps, even camps for the euthanasia programme, but nothing quite resembled this place. It had its own stench, its own sounds, its own mingling of light and shadow.

Ten thousand inmates, and more arriving daily, all crammed into a few square miles. The death rate had trebled in the past year, from all causes. Today would see it climb again. Today the inmates were being gathered to witness a mass execution.

They had been waiting on the parade ground for five hours now, weak, exhausted, and cold. The last meal had been thin soup at lunch time. Dinner – some potatoes and cabbage – should have been served up three hours earlier, but there was no sign of it. It had grown dark, and everywhere lights had been put on: the perimeter lights in the distance, and arc lights that lit up the entire parade ground. A battery of spotlights shone on the platform where the executions were due to take place, as though it was a stage. Guards moved among the prisoners, some with whips, some with cudgels, all armed, watching for someone to fall or try to slip away. If they fell, they were beaten till senseless. If they tried to break from the ranks, they were gunned down.

Daniel Horowitz tried his best to ignore the hunger pangs in his stomach. He'd grown used to them in the three years he'd spent in the camp, they'd become part of him, he understood them better than any pain he'd ever known. Above all, they meant he was alive, and that was the important thing.

He strained to make out the figures of a party of women on the other side of the parade ground. The camp was divided into east and west sectors, men and male children to the east, women and girls to the west. They saw one another at times through the long dividing fence, men eager for a glimpse of their wives, women to see their husbands. But anyone caught within two yards of the fence would be shot, so the most anyone could hope for was a moment of recognition from a distance. And days or weeks of anxiety and fear until the next. If there was a next. No news passed between the two halves of the camp.

Except on execution days. If it was a multiple hanging, as today's was going to be, they brought the women in to watch as well. As often as not there'd be women among the victims. They'd stand on the far side of the parade ground, patrolled by female guards, some of them more brutal than the men. Anyone caught trying to communicate would be hauled out and added to the roster for execution. There were no exceptions.

Daniel needed new glasses, but in the world of the camp such things were an unheard-of luxury. He took every possible care of the pair he wore, knowing they would not be replaced if stolen or broken. More than once he'd seen other men, their glasses smashed by a

12

spiteful guard, stumbling half-blind through the ranks at roll-call. The half-blind did not last long in the camp, just like the infirm, the old, the emotionally weak.

It was seven weeks since he had last seen Rosa, her hair cropped and her body pitifully thin in its shapeless grey sack, herded with other women towards the line of laundry sheds at the north end of the western sector. She had not looked up or seen him, but he had known it was her. It was three years now since they had last spoken, three years since they had been split apart at the camp entrance and taken to their separate fates. He did not know how much longer she could survive. If she was among the women on parade tonight, he would not see her.

It was important to Daniel to know if Rosa was alive or not. As long as she was alive, he knew he could survive. And he needed to survive, because of the vow he had made, the vow to remember and record, the vow to stand up afterwards and testify to what had happened. Throughout his three years in the camp, he had memorized everything, however small, however trivial. Faces, names, dates, incidents. The names of victims and the names of guards, the faces of the dead and the faces of their killers, executions, casual beatings, random shootings, deliberate cruelty – and, as rare as hope, small acts of kindness, droplets of water in hell.

The door of the commandant's office opened. Daniel watched him come to the front and ascend the steps to the platform. He took his place with the casual ease of someone who has done this before many times. At that moment, there was a movement at the front, and a guard detail dragged the condemned forward, pushing them one at a time to the steps and up to the gallows.

There had been a small rising in the camp two days earlier, and this was the consequence. The leaders had all been members of the resistance. About one hundred inmates had been shot, and fifteen 'ringleaders' caught. Now, here they were, their faces bloody and bruised,

13

their eyes unfocused, limping, wheezing, and, in one case, dragged by the hair to the foot of the gallows. Twelve of them were Jews. Three were women. One was a boy of fifteen. Daniel knew all this, because he had made a point of asking. Their names were inscribed on the record he kept in his head. He'd taught himself how to remember, just as he'd taught himself how to survive.

The commandant watched in silence as the guards dragged their victims to the gallows and pulled the nooses over their heads. None of them resisted. In the crowd, a low murmuring had begun – the combined sound of male and female voices whispering prayers. 'Hear, O Israel' was repeated over and over. Suddenly, one man's voice rose above the others, singing the Hatikvah, the Jewish anthem. Another voice joined in, then another. Defiantly, a woman's voice rose in unison with the men's, followed by others.

The commandant gestured at an officer standing beside him. Next minute, a burst of machine-gun fire rattled into the air across the parade ground. It lasted about three seconds, and when it stopped, the singing voices faltered. A terrible silence fell.

Seconds passed while the commandant allowed his gaze to travel over the shivering mass of humanity huddled before him, grey and shaven, the men in plain striped shirts and trousers, the women in sacklike dresses, divested of dignity, utterly exposed to his smallest whim. He stepped up to a microphone that had been set up at the front of the platform. When he spoke, his voice was relayed through the camp by a system of loudspeakers.

'If there is another outbreak of singing,' he bellowed, 'the next shots will not be aimed into the air. You have my word.'

Daniel expected him to step back again and order the hangings to begin. He kept his eyes fixed on the condemned, imprinting their pale faces and emaciated limbs on his mind, sharing their despair, holding on to the little hope he had that one day there would come a reckoning.

But the commandant remained at the microphone, as though daring his victims to yet another act of defiance. Daniel had seen him supervise countless executions, had watched him more than once as he shot or strangled or bludgeoned to death a helpless inmate. In his mental record, the man's face bore an expression of exultation. He shuddered as the speakers crackled into life again.

'You all know why we're out here tonight. Two days ago a group of your companions made a very stupid attempt to stage a break-out from this camp. They didn't get very far, and I hope you'll appreciate just how pointless it is even to think of escaping from here. Tonight, the leaders of the attempt will be hanged as punishment.

'But I didn't bring you all here just to watch them hang. I brought you here to learn a lesson. It is a simple lesson, and I intend you to learn it well. In the course of the rebellion, seven of my men were killed and eighteen injured. For each of those injured, one of you will die. For each one killed, four of you will die. Before they are hanged, those responsible for this plot will watch with their own eyes the consequences of their actions.

'Since they chose to rebel, they may also enjoy the privilege of choosing who is to die with them. Each one will choose three others. I will choose the last.'

He gestured again to the officer beside him, a tall man known to Daniel only by his surname, Landau. Landau strode up to the first of the condemned men, removed his noose, and pushed him forward. The man, Zahar Kaplinsky, shook his head, refusing to cooperate. Landau slapped him hard on the face, but Kaplinsky still refused to select anyone. The commandant's voice boomed out again.

'I should have explained that any refusal to cooperate will simply result in unnecessary bloodshed. If you do not select three of your fellows, I shall have my men shoot ten for each man killed and five for each man injured. The choice is yours.'

Kaplinsky seemed to struggle for a moment, as though straining against invisible bonds, then slumped and let himself be led from the platform, down to the parade ground. Daniel remembered him as a happy man, always grinning, his spirits somehow rising above the camp and its torments. He had brought others through weeks and months of suffering, now he too had been brought low.

Two minutes later, Kaplinsky was brought back, leading three men from the ranks below, all from his own barracks, from whom he had been forced to make his choice. Kaplinsky was taken back to the gallows and again garlanded with the noose. The commandant had the three other men led before him. Taking a knife from his belt, he cut their throats while Kaplinsky watched. When it was done, he nodded, and the stool on which Kaplinsky stood was kicked away, leaving him dangling, choking to death slowly.

As Kaplinsky struggled to die, the man beside him was brought down and led into the crowd. The process of culling continued.

Daniel watched, recording everything. What he would have given to own a camera, to be able to put everything on film. Better on film, he thought, than in his thoughts, burning him day and night, awake and dreaming. But a camera was out of the question, so he watched and remembered.

They came to the first of the women. She was escorted to the female sector and set to work. Weeping, she selected three of her barracks companions, and they were taken together up the steps. Daniel felt his heart grow cold as he watched them, straining to see their faces. Rosa was not among them. He felt his chest relax, then tighten again as the commandant's knife flashed.

The second woman was already being taken on to the parade ground. Minutes passed while she made her selection. On the gallows, her companion was writhing at the

16

end of the rope. Daniel waited in agony. He looked up as the four women were led up to the platform, and his heart tumbled like an acrobat who slips in the last somersault. Rosa was the last to stumble up the steps, waiting in line like a lamb who knows at last it must face the butcher's knife. He would have recognized her anywhere, without glasses, in darkness or in fog. She shivered, and he called her name aloud.

'Rosa!'

He saw her turn, questing, desperate to find him. Again he called, and he tried to move, to signal to her, but his arms were pinned by the men on either side of him.

Jakub Rosenberg whispered to him, 'Stay where you are, Danny. Let her go. There's nothing you can do.'

He struggled, but Jakub had him hard by the arm on one side, Yankel Lob by the other.

'Danny, I love you!' Rosa's voice echoed across the vast expanse of the parade ground, drowning all other sounds, all other loves. For a moment, there was silence. Then Daniel looked up and saw the commandant snatch Rosa by the hair and pull her head back to expose her throat. He closed his eyes, and when he looked again, they were hanging the woman who had chosen Rosa. And he whispered the Shema for her and for Rosa and for all the dead until he felt himself pulled from the parade ground, unresisting, without hope or heart. In the distance, as he stumbled back to his barracks, he heard a man's voice raised again in song, the words of the Hatikvah thrown against the darkness.

That night he did not sleep. All through the dark hours, he remembered. He remembered Rosa's face, and her voice, and her smile, things she had said to him, the shape of her naked body, the look in her eyes after lovemaking, the sweet smell of her breath, the softness of her skin. And he remembered her name and all the things pertaining to her, the things he would hold in record until the time for reckoning had come. Over and over again he repeated them: Rosa Shulman, born 3 February 1912, Baltimore, Maryland, the daughter of Hirsh and Havivah Shulman, died 1 October 1940, Howard County Concentration Camp, Florence, Maryland, the wife of Daniel Horowitz, the mother of Reuben and Hanna Horowitz, both deceased, killed by Major Jim Jackson, governor of the camp. Rosa Shulman, born 3 February 1912, Baltimore, Maryland . . .

From Heinrich Ritter's *Judenverfolgung im Dritten Reich und der Neuen Amerikanischen Republik* – The Persecution of the Jews in the Third Reich and the New American Republic, (Leipzig, Max Werner Verlag, 1975, Appendix One)

Concentration, Extermination, and Labour Camps in Greater Germany, Europe, and Russia	Concentration, Extermination, and Labour Camps in the United States of America
(Part List)	(Part List)
Alderney (Channel Islands)	Abbeville AL
Armersfoot	Abbeville GA
Auschwitz	Abbeville LA
Auschwitz-Birkenau	Abilene VA
Auschwitz-Monowitz	Adamsville AL
Baltoji-Volke	Afton NM
Belzec	Agua Nueva TX
Bergen-Belsen	Alamo TX
Birkenau	Albuquerque NM
Blechhammer	Andrews IN
Blizyn	Atchison KS
Bobrek	Augusta GA
Bor	Augusta KY
Börgermoor	Ayers WA
Brandenburg	Barney IA
Brauweiler	Basinger FL
Buchenwald	Bassfield MS
Budzyn	Baton Rouge LA
Chelmek	Bird City KS
Chelmno	Bowden GA

Concentration, Extermination, and Labour Camps in Greater Germany, Europe, and Russia	Concentration, Extermination, and Labour Camps in the United States of America
Columbia-Haus	Bracken TX
Dachau	Branford FL
Dora (Mittelbau)	Brookston MN
Dürrgoy	Burgdorf ID
Dziadlowo	Burnsville WV
Esterwegen	Burr Oak IA
Flossenbürg	Butler AL
Fuhlsüttel	Byron IL
Gesiowka (Warsaw)	Caledonia MI
Giado	Calhan CO
Gransdorf	Calico Rock AR
Gross-Rosen	Calistoga CA
Gurs	Campbell NE
Hammerstein	Cape Canaveral FL
s'Hertogenbosch	Casa Grande AZ
Heydebreck	Catasauqua PA
Hindenburg	Cedar Butte SD
Hohnstein	Century WV
Jawiszowice	Central SC
Jaworzno	Chadron NE
Josefow	Clarksville TN
Kaiserwald(Riga)	Clay City KY
Kampinos	Colfax NM
Keilis	Conway SC
Kemna	Corpus Christi TX
Koldyczewo	Coxsackie NY
Konin	Creedmoor NC
Kopernik	Dawson Springs KY
Les Milles	De Leon TX
Lichtenburg	De Ridder LA
Lowicz	Des Arc MO
Lublin	Duluth MN
Majdanek	Dumfries VA
Maly Trostenets	Elk Park NC
Mauthausen	Epes AL

Concentration, Extermination, and Labour Camps in Greater Germany, Europe, and Russia	Concentration, Extermination, and Labour Camps in the United States of America
Minsk Mazowiecki	Fay OK
Mohringen	Firesteel SD
Muhldorf	Florence MD
Myslowice	Fort Laramie WY
Natzweiler	Frenchtown NJ
Neu Dachs	Gabriels NY
Neuengamme	Garland NE
Neumark	Genesee MI
Neusalz	Germantown MD
Neustadt-Glowen	Gibson GA
Niederhagen	Glendale WV
Nordhausen	Goshen UT
Novaki	Grand Rapids MI
Nowogrodek	Greenfield TN
Oranienburg	Halligan Reservation CO
Osthofen	Hamilton GA
Papenburg	Hamilton OH
Piasnica	Harrington WA
Plaszow	Harrisburg SD
Poniatowa	Harrison NE
Portet Saint Simon	Heber Sprints AR
Quednau	Hermansville MI
Ravensbrück	Hodges SC
Récébédou	Hoffmann NC
Rivesaltes	Honey Island TX
Sachsenburg	Ida Grove IA
Sachsenhausen	Illmo MO
Saint Valentin	Indian River MI
Schwenningen	Isabella CA
Sobibor	Iva SC
Sonnenburg	Jamaica VT
Sosnowiec	Jefferson City TN
Stutthof	Jewell OR
Szebnie	Johnstown PA
Tasmajden	Junction UT

Concentration, Extermination, and Labour Camps in Greater Germany, Europe, and Russia	Concentration, Extermination, and Labour Camps in the United States of America
Trawniki	Kabetogama MN
Treblinka	Kane WY
Vaivara	Keatchie LA
Vulkanwerft (Stettin)	Kidder SD
Warthebrucken	Kimberly WI
Wustegiersdorf	Kirkland IL
Werden	Kline SC
Zaslaw	Kramer ND
Zezmariai	Krotz Springs LA
	La Belle MI
	Lake Charles LA
	Lake Hattie Reservation WY
	Lake Park GA
	La Mesa NM
	Lawrenceburg IN
	Lebanon KY
	Leon WV
	Limestone ME
	Little Meadows PA
	Londonderry VT
	Lone Pine CA
	Long Island WA
	Macon MS
	Marion AL
	Marion NC
	Miles City MT
	Missouri Reservation ND
	Mobile AL
	Montpelier ID
	Morgan GA
	Mount Vernon AK
	Mystic GA
	Nauvoo IL
	Navarro Mills Reserv. TX

Concentration, Extermination, and Labour Camps in Greater Germany, Europe, and Russia	Concentration, Extermination, and Labour Camps in the United States of America
	Newark NY
	Newport IN
	Newport NC
	No Mans Land Island MA
	North Charleston SC
	Northport WA
	Norway MI
	Oakdale LA
	Oconto Falls WI
	Old Glory TX
	Oneida NY
	Orange VA
	Oxford KS
	Palmyra NE
	Paradise MT
	Pendleton SC
	Perry FL
	Petersburg VA
	Pine Island MN
	Plymouth NE
	Port Angeles WA
	Port Bolivar TX
	Portsmouth NH
	Providence RI
	Quarryville PA
	Quincy OR
	Rainbow City AL
	Randolph VT
	Red Bluff CA
	Richfield UT
	Richmond KY
	Rio Tinto NE
	Riverdale ND
	Robbins NC
	Rochester NY

Concentration, Extermination, and Labour Camps in Greater Germany, Europe, and Russia	Concentration, Extermination, and Labour Camps in the United States of America
	Rochester TX
	Rockville SC
	Russell PA
	Sacramento CA
	St Joseph MI
	Salem NY
	San Diego TX
	San Francisco CA
	San Rafael NM
	Scranton ND
	Seven Springs NC
	Sharon TN
	Sidney OH
	Sleepy Eye MN
	Smithville GA
	South Fork CO
	Springfield MA
	Stamping Ground KY
	Summerton SC
	Tamarack ID
	Taylor AZ
	Temple OK
	Three Rivers NM
	Thornburg VA
	Torrington WY
	Turners Falls MA
	Union OK
	Upper Tract WV
	Valdosta GA
	Ventura CA
	Vicksburg AZ
	Virgil KS
	Wachusett Reservation MA
	Walton IN

Concentration, Extermination, and Labour Camps in Greater Germany, Europe, and Russia	Concentration, Extermination, and Labour Camps in the United States of America
	Warren MT
	Wellington UT
	West Branch IA
	Willard NM
	Winchester TS
	Windsor SC
	Yonkers NY
	Yutan NE
	Zanesville OH
	Zephyr TX

PART 2

The Refugee

CHAPTER TWO

Pamlico Sound
Off the North Carolina Coast
Monday, 22 October 1940

The conning tower of the *Torque* rose above the waterline like the keep of a small fortress, a thing of darkness set against a dark sea and a dark sky; from the shore it would have been invisible, but for the small red light that had been set to blink at intervals of thirty seconds. The pick-up position had been chosen carefully: the nearest coastguard station was several miles away, there were no large townships or holiday homes. Just a beach and a dirt road leading away from it.

They had slipped into Pamlico Sound under cover of darkness, creeping through the narrow Swash Inlet at periscope depth, running silently on electric motors grouped down. There was a storm out at sea, but here in the sound the waves were lower.

A man of medium height stood in the conning tower, listening to the waves as they broke against the hull of the submarine. He was already dressed in the clothes he would wear ashore, everyday clothes that did little to protect him against the weather; he shivered in a high wind coming off the sea. His small suitcase lay at his feet like the battered baggage of a refugee, and the sudden thought stabbed him that that was exactly what he'd become, for he carried no hope of return in him.

He could barely see over the parapet, nor did he need to. Wherever he looked was blackness. The night, like the position, had been well chosen. The moon was past full, and, as though the elements themselves worked at the Special Operations Executive's bidding, it and the stars were covered by thick clouds. The shore was barely audible a mile away, unseen waves breaking against unseen rocks.

'We dive in five minutes,' said Peter Bosworth, the ship's commander. He glanced at the luminous dial of his watch. 'If your man isn't here by then, we go back out to sea and return tomorrow night. You don't have any choice in the matter.'

'I'm not arguing.' The agent shivered again. He knew Bosworth hated him, that he and every member of his crew regarded him as an albatross they longed to discard.

There'd been an incident two days earlier, when they were still due east of the Pan-American Neutrality Zone. The sub had picked up a mayday message from a British ship, the *Hyperion*, a merchantman out of Liverpool carrying seventy-four crew and twenty passengers. The message said the ship had been hit by torpedoes and was sinking fast.

Peter Bosworth had given orders to surface and make for the coordinates given by the sinking vessel. The agent, whose codename was Victor, had countermanded Bosworth's orders, and the *Torque* had resumed its original course. The atmosphere on board the submarine after that had been terrible. But even Bosworth knew that Victor had the authority to override any decision made by him or his colleagues. Victor's orders came from the very top. There'd been a private interview in an underground bunker beneath Whitehall, in the course of which it had been made abundantly clear that the submarine and its crew, indeed the entire British navy came a pretty poor second to Victor and his mission.

The *Hyperion* had gone down while the *Torque's* Wireless Telegraph operator picked up its last signals. Seventy men, twenty-four women and children, and a single lifeboat that could not be launched. No-one had spoken to Victor after that. He'd carry it with him for the rest of his life, his own anguish and the knowledge that he might have saved ninety-four lives and in the process destroyed thousands more.

Up here, the roll of the boat was much more noticeable than it had been below. In spite of the fresh air, with its taste of salt and its queer, inexplicable scent of land, he wanted to be sick. He'd never made a particularly good sailor, had hated his father's sailing parties, and had always loathed the transatlantic crossings his family's way of life had imposed on him almost from birth. Basic navigation and sailing had been the only real terrors for him during his two months' special training at 101 STS in Lochailort. The waves tonight were high, and the boat coming to meet him – if it ever came – would be little more than a dinghy.

'He'll be here,' he said, gritting his teeth, though he'd no idea why he felt so confident. His contact could be dead for all he knew. Picked up by the FBIS, interrogated, and shot. If he'd talked before they put a revolver to his forehead, the entire crew of the *Torque* might be awaiting the same fate. He stood on tiptoe again and craned his neck to look down on the sea. It was in an angry mood tonight. He shuddered again at the thought of taking a small boat out in that.

Suddenly, a white light appeared ahead. Bosworth unfastened the catch on his side holster. The sailor next to him drew back the bolt on his Lee-Enfield rifle and aimed it in the direction of the light. Below, on the deck, another sailor swivelled the four-inch gun that was the submarine's only surface weapon.

The light vanished, followed moments later, by the bump of oars being shipped, and a grating sound as a light boat grazed the hull of the submarine. Victor held his breath. Bosworth tossed a line from the tower. It lay slack against the hull for a few seconds, then grew taut as the man below

31

made his vessel fast. A voice spun out of the darkness, a man's voice, heavy above the plash of waves.

'Hi, there! We're ready for your consignment.'

It was an American voice, mid-Western, solid, with something implacable about it. Hearing it gave Victor the shivers, just the ordinariness of it. He knew where he was finally. The thing he'd been planning for all these weeks was suddenly stark reality. That wasn't Scotland out there in the dark, that was America. And this wasn't another training exercise, this was the real thing.

'We need your code,' shouted Bosworth. Victor noticed that his hand fidgeted with the butt of his gun. He was not at ease.

'Gaspee,' replied the boatman. Victor suppressed a smile. Someone in London was trying to be witty. The *Gaspee* had been a British revenue cutter burned in 1772 at Namquit Point by a band of men from Providence, one of the first acts of insurrection that had led to the American War of Independence.

'Spell that.'

Obviously Bosworth had not gone to the sort of school where they taught American history as a regular part of the curriculum. The boatman spelled the name out letter by letter, and Bosworth looked it up in the Confidential Books that contained the signalling ciphers and codes for the mission. There were only two copies of the Books: one in a safe in the wardroom, kept by the *Torque's* Navigating Officer, the other in a locked file at Special Operations Executive headquarters.

The codeword system was as watertight as the sub itself. The signal 'Gaspee' would have been transmitted from London earlier that night, heavily coded, chosen at random from two hundred possible codes, each linked to a second password. Bosworth was now running his fingers down twin columns of codewords, looking for 'Gaspee' and the word printed next to it.

Using a separate code, the second password had been

transmitted shortly after the first to a resistance radio operator called Moshe Rosen in Washington. Rosen had then transmitted it to a second operator, one of five within a radius of fifty miles from the landing-site. It had been the task of this operator to rendezvous with the boatman on or near the beach, to make sure all was well, and to pass him the link-word just before he set off. The chances of the FBIS intercepting and decoding both transmissions were infinitesimal. The likelihood of their connecting the two messages as components in a single mission was negligible in the extreme.

'Link-word?' Bosworth barked his question, startling Victor from a reverie. He'd been back in school in Boston, listening with rapt attention to Mr Bradenton telling his fifth-grade class the story of Captain Abraham Whipple, leader of the party that had lured the *Gaspee* to its doom.

'Thunderbolt,' came the answer.

Bosworth nodded.

'Get ready to receive some packages,' he said. Ten boxes, narrow enough to pass up the conning tower ladder, were brought out one at a time and gently lowered into the boat, where the American stowed them carefully.

'All secure,' he shouted when the last box was lashed down. Bosworth turned to the man he'd travelled all this way to deliver.

'You're on your own now,' he said.

The agent held out a hand and took Bosworth's in a firm grip. This would be the last time he'd be called Victor. He'd taken the name from *Old Possum's Book of Practical Cats*, which he'd bought for his niece Jessica the year before, just after its publication. 'A cat must have THREE DIFFERENT NAMES,' Eliot had written, and now he had his three: his real name, John Makepeace; his temporary codename, Victor; and the name he would inhabit the moment he stepped into the boat now waiting for him, John Ridgeforth. Up there in Scotland, they'd made damn sure he never forgot his new identity for a moment, not even in his sleep.

'John Ridgeforth' had taken a lot of inventing and even more stitching together. A rag doll was no use to the men behind John's mission. He would have to stand up to close scrutiny without coming apart at the seams.

A team of back-room boys at Beaulieu had worked round the clock to forge papers to match his identity – not just the ones he would have to carry round with him, but dozens of others that would be smuggled across the Canadian border into America and later slipped by resistance agents into files in government offices, schools, and businesses. By now, John prayed, his ghostly alter ego had bodily substance in all the places he had never lived. He even had friends and relations ready to vouch for him. Some of them were people in high places.

He paused with his foot on the first rung of the ladder.

'Captain,' he began, 'if it makes any difference, I'm sorry about . . .'

Bosworth cut him off.

'We're all sorry. Being sorry doesn't help. Blame it on the war. By the time it's over, we'll have a lot more to be sorry about.'

He handed him the suitcase.

'Good luck all the same,' he said.

He only looked back once, about three minutes after they had cast off. There was a brief sound of engines above the surge of waves, but when he looked the *Torque* had already dived. It was as if it had never been there, as though the darkness to the east went on for ever, beyond Ireland, beyond England, beyond a war-blighted Europe, until it encompassed the globe.

CHAPTER THREE

He never learned the boatman's name, not then, not later.
In the short time they were together, they exchanged no
personal information. The boatman had few instructions
for him: most of what he needed to know he had been
told in London. Maybe he should have mentioned the gas
tank. It was a small mistake, but it was to cost lives.

They left the boat a few yards above the waterline. The
tide was going out, and there was no need to anchor it.
John saw the other man's face briefly, as they made their
way to where he'd left the pick-up vehicle, a Duesenberg,
parked on a grassy slope above the beach. The boatman lit
a flashlight, explaining that he just wanted to check what
part of the beach they'd reached – coming in like that in
pitch darkness, off a rolling sea – and John caught sight of
him then, his ordinary face, his ordinary eyes; he'd have
passed him in the street without a second glance. What
made him different to all those other millions out there,
that he was willing to take such a chance, that he'd risk
his life to land an enemy agent on an open beach?

John climbed into the driving seat and wound down
the window. The top was already up. The boatman shone
the flashlight across the dashboard, and he saw his face
again, dimly outlined. It seemed to him that, in spite of
his seeming coolness, he was under great strain.

'Know how to drive one of these?' he asked.

'My father had a Duesenberg,' John answered. He saw
the other man's eyebrows lift a fraction, and guessed he

was surprised by his accent, American, not English. 'And I drove a roadster like this when I was at college.'

'You've told me too much already. I don't want to know nothing about you, mister. That way I can't tell nobody nothing if they ask me.' John thought he sounded like a farmer, but he'd handled the boat with real skill, brought it in on a heavy sea the way he'd seen canoeists navigate the rapids of the Housatonic. It occurred to him that he knew next to nothing of the people among whom he had done so much of his growing up.

The boatman paused. 'Go on up this dirt track 'bout a mile, mile and a half. Keep your lights off till you reach a road. Either way you turn, you'll wind up on US 17. You can get most anywheres from there. Left turn'll take you down to Wilmington, right'll get you up to Portsmouth, Virginia. You'll find a couple of route maps in the glove compartment. Don't tell me where you're headed, 'cause I don't need to know, and I don't want to know. You could be making for Alabama or New York, hell, you could be heading right across to San Francisco or Seattle, makes no difference to me.'

John opened the glove compartment, and the boatman pointed the flashlight so he could see inside. There were several maps. He took out a brand-new Esso map of the middle-Atlantic states, one inch to eighteen miles, 50c, the sort you could buy anywhere. On the front cover, more prominent than the publisher's name, was a flaming cross and the legend: 'Approved for Publication by the National Klan Censorship Office.'

He put the map back. As he did so, the boatman reached across and pressed the side of the compartment. A flap fell down, revealing a shallow space. Inside lay a pistol.

'It's loaded,' said the man. 'A Colt automatic, just like I was asked to get. Come outa government stores. Can't be traced. Got a new history attached, and been converted to full auto. Magazine takes ten rounds.'

John nodded and closed the flap, then the compartment.

'Extra ammo's further in. If you need more, don't go to a store, get in touch with our people. Once you get on the highway, watch out for police patrols. They got checkpoints on all the main roads. Stopped me twice on my way here. Don't worry, though – I changed the licence plates soon as I got off the road. Massachusetts plates.'

'Why the patrols?' John spoke nervously, thinking there might be an alert, that word of an agent's arrival had somehow leaked out.

'Hoover announced a new regulation yesterday. Has the full backing of the President and Klan headquarters. No Jews or coloureds on the road after sunset, not 'less they've got a permit from a white man they're workin' for. Police are on the roads tonight, all looking out for any poor bastard ain't got no permit. Jailhouses gonna be full to bustin', you'll see.'

'What about Hoover's own people? Are they on the roads tonight too?'

'FBIS? Hell, no. They'll stay at home tonight, leave all that stuff to the police. Themselves, they're way beyond that now. Kickin' some poor black boy's head to putty ain't their style. Lacks what some folks call finesse. Mr Hoover and his crowd ain't ordinary flesh. Klan from birth, some of them. They don't act like us, they don't think like us, and they sure as hell don't dream like us. They got through lynching niggers in seventh grade. What they want for themselves is high-class entertainment. Sort they'd get from folks like you'n me.'

John shuddered. J. Edgar Hoover's grey-coated agents had long ago lodged themselves in his imagination as fallen angels of the darkest breed. The Klan, in its white robes and pointed hoods, was chilling enough, but it had become ubiquitous, and he knew that, beneath the bedsheets lurked nothing more truly sinister than ordinary citizens bent on mischief. The Klan hierarchy that now ran the country was something different again, far from innocent and far from ordinary. But the agents of

the Federal Bureau of Internal Security, Hoover's dark
and unfettered creation, were the very elite of America's
undersoul. If John or the boatman had anything to fear,
it was, above all, from them.

'You'll find a permit for the gun in there, too,' the man
said. 'A flashlight and papers for the automobile. Better
check 'em 'fore you go. I ain't so much as looked at 'em.'

John opened the compartment again, and the boatman
handed him the flashlight. When he'd scrutinized all his
papers and passed them as correct – meaning that they
corresponded fully with the false identity set up for him
in London – there seemed nothing else for it than to start
the engine and head off. The man took back the flashlight
and switched it off. Around them, the darkness was old
and black, with a quality beyond that of ordinary night.

'Can I give you a ride?' he asked. 'At least as far as the
highway.'

'It's good of you to ask, but I've got to row the boat back
to where it came from,' the man said. ''Ain't much of a
night for it, but I got no choice. Best nobody finds it here
in the morning.'

John started the engine.

'Remember, keep those headlights off till you hit the
highway.'

'I'll remember.'

He reached a hand through the window. He took it and
found it hard and rough to the touch, a hand made what
it was by years of work. He thought of his father's hands,
soft and uncalloused, caressing his cheek as he bent to kiss
him goodnight in a world that seemed not only long ago,
but impossibly kind. But even then the kindness had been
slipping away, almost unnoticed, all around them.

'Watch out for yourself,' the boatman said. Next thing,
he was gone, swallowed up, like the *Torque*, in that infinite
and terrible darkness.

He knew by heart the route he had to take, he'd rehearsed

it often enough on mock-up roads near Beaulieu. But until tonight, it had always been a game, just like the weapons training and the explosives instruction and the radio lessons – something you learned to do, but told yourself you'd never need in real life.

They'd driven him hard, shouted at him when he made mistakes (about fifty times a day), pushed him when he thought he couldn't run another inch or decipher another word or pump another round into the target; but it had remained at the level of a game. After all, they'd pushed him hard enough at school and college, and most of that had been pointless, or so it now seemed. It was how he got through it all. 'This is just make-believe,' he'd told himself, 'it'll never really happen.' And now it was happening, and he was doing in cold blood what he'd been trained to do, and he was more scared than he could ever have imagined.

But the fear wasn't the worst. None of his preparations had prepared him for the simply overwhelming sense of loneliness that poured over him as he sat hunched over the wheel, straining to see through the blackness.

He remembered what Sammy Bright had once said to him, while he put him through his paces one cold evening at Lochailort. He'd worn him out with questions, tricking him, trapping him, forcing him to understand just how hard this was going to be. He'd protested, and he hadn't said anything at first, just sat and looked at him. Outside, a red sun had been slipping down into the Sound of Arisaig.

'You'll be on your own out there,' he'd said at last. 'Nobody's going to bail you out. A single mistake could be fatal. You can't afford to trust anyone, not even members of the resistance. Relations, old friends, teachers, anyone you ever had dealings with before – none of them can ever be contacted. John Makepeace doesn't exist: never forget that. You're John Ridgeforth now.'

They'd given him photographs of people he was supposed to have known in a former life he'd never actually lived, total strangers who would claim to have known him as a child.

'Who's this?' Sammy had continued, turning over a shot John had never seen.

'Abe Hines. We used to spend our holidays near his cabin outside Ashley Falls.'

'Not your "holidays". Your "vacations". What was his wife called?'

'Ann.'

'With an "e" or without?'

They'd gone on like that into the small hours, and up again at dawn, day after day, night after night. He'd memorized their faces and names and habits until he could name them without any slip of the tongue. In reality he was an actor preparing to go on stage with a cast who'd been rehearsing without him.

No-one from his real life even knew he was here, or ever would. His parents, his sister Connie, his aunts and uncles, his best friends all thought he'd been posted to carry out sensitive work for an overseas unit of the Ministry for Economic Warfare in Palestine. Letters sent to him were re-routed to a basement office at Ministry of Economic Warfare headquarters in Berkeley Square, where a girl called Valerie typed banal replies on blank sheets bearing his signature. If he was killed or went missing, his parents would receive an official telegram. There'd be no explanation, no body, no funeral.

The darkness seemed immeasurable, as if God in a moment of anger had stripped His creation of landmark and sense. Suddenly he felt the tarmac slide beneath his tyres and knew he'd come to the highway. Braking hard, he turned left and switched on his headlights. Like a lightning rod in a storm, the sudden road pulsed into life ahead of him, and for another moment he was lost entirely, as if all roads he had ever known had coalesced abruptly into this one, inevitable road. He pressed down slowly on the gas pedal, and the Duesenberg gathered speed.

CHAPTER FOUR

Washington DC

The three men and one woman seated round the table in Moshe Rosen's kitchen did not have the air of conspirators. A casual observer would have taken them for four friends playing poker, smoking cigarettes, and drinking whiskey and black coffee. Strictly speaking, the whiskey was illegal, but drinking it hardly constituted a federal offence. The worst you might get was a public whipping, same as for adultery or listening to black music. There was nothing here to attract the Federal Bureau of Internal Security. Unless . . .

Well, for one thing, the cards belonging to each player weren't exactly moving. They sat face up on the table, in exactly the same positions they'd been in for over an hour. For another, none of the money had actually changed hands in all that time. To make matters worse, the whiskey in two of the glasses had not even been tasted. It was good quality bourbon – the real thing – taken from a stash in a shipment of jazz records from down south in Georgia; but only one of the players was a devoted drinker.

'I still think London should tell us more. It's enough we've agreed to help the man they're sending, but what if his mission compromises our own operations?'

The speaker, Moshe Rosen, was the communications officer and radio operator for the cell, a violinist who had become a silversmith when Jews had been banned from playing in orchestras. He was a thin man of thirty or more, cautious, circumspect, a troubled soul whose life revolved around his wife Miriam and his daughter Anna.

'London has promised us support, support we badly need. We can't afford to turn them down at the present time. I'll be in constant touch with their agent, and I'll make sure he does nothing without keeping me informed. There has to be give and take. It's too late for us to pull out now.'

Miles Vanderlyn was a law professor at Georgetown, spectacled, bow-tied, a little overweight. His tired gaze and slumped posture betrayed late nights, worry, a life cut in half by a regime that had turned its back on law and justice and the disappearance of a wife whom he'd loved beyond measure.

'When does he arrive? Have they decided?'

Miles hesitated.

'He could be here tonight. The submarine makes contact somewhere south of here. The plan is for him to drive to Washington and head straight to my rooms.'

'This guy's English or what?' Charlie Benson was the cell's political officer. The underground was a loosely connected amalgamation of discontents united solely by their opposition to the regime, with no one group or philosophy dominating. That called for some subtle coordination between potentially conflicting interests: Jewish groups, black resistance cells, Communist and Labour sections, and Catholic activists. It was Charlie's role to liaise with each group in order to use its talents and manpower in the most efficient way possible. By day he taught English in a high school at Quantico, by night he plotted the overthrow of the Aryan Alliance and the government of the United States.

Vanderlyn shook his head.

'I don't think so. They won't pass on any details about him, but they did say he's half-American. He can carry it off.'

42

'As your student?'

'My former student. I think they've got somebody who really studied law; there'd be too much risk putting anybody else in. His front story is that he's a lawyer from New England.'

'I'm still uneasy. Does he have to get that close to the President?' Mary Laverty drained the last of her whiskey and put the empty glass reluctantly back on the table. She was fifty years old, halfway through her third failed marriage, three-quarters of the way through her one and only liver, and one hundred percent in command of one of the sharpest brains in America. She was the group's coordinator of women's sections. Her office job was out at Washington Airport, where she worked as a flying instructor. Before that, she'd been a professor of philosophy at Harvard. Until philosophy had become a taboo subject, unless you were willing to teach the views of Klan thinkers like Nash and Holbrook, men who could scarcely write English, had never read Plato, and thought Kant was a county in England.

'I can't answer that,' said Miles. 'If they think that's where he needs to be, I don't see why we can't just go along with them. They're fighting a war, for God's sake, same as we're doing here. A lot of their people have died already. German planes are bombing London every day. We share the same objectives.'

'We share *some* of the same objectives,' interjected Mary. 'Just as we share some of the same language and some of the same religion and some of the same history. Sometimes the sameness gets in the way.'

'Who would you rather we were collaborating with, Mary? The British or the Germans?'

She shrugged.

'You're perfectly right. I just wish they trusted us more, that they let us in on what this is about. It's like the whole thing's being run from London and we're just the junior partners.'

'They're supplying the agent.'

'We're supplying the back up, and we're putting some of our own people at considerable risk. That earns us some respect. Why don't you tell them that when you're next in touch?'

'I shall, don't worry.'

'Will he need weapons?' Charlie asked.

'Vernon's taking care of that.'

'Who's arranging the pick-up from the submarine?'

'Five or six groups are on standby. We won't actually know where the sub's expecting to rendezvous till an hour or two beforehand. Moshe, you'll be expected to monitor their radio signals and relay the position to the appropriate group.'

'What about the guns they said they'd deliver?' Mary asked. Her eye wandered repeatedly to the whiskey bottle. Recently, she'd been seeking comfort in it a little too often. Life in the New Republic would have driven a nun to over-indulge. The thought sobered her. She'd known nuns driven to suicide by the brave new America of the Klan and the Aryan Alliance.

'They'll be unloaded from the submarine and taken ashore by whoever picks up their agent.'

'Hell, we need guns here in the capital,' exclaimed Charlie.

'Don't worry, we'll get our share.'

'Can't this guy drive ours up?'

Vanderlyn shook his head.

'Too risky. He has to get through the Hoover Checkpoint. The guns have to come in separately. Vernon's taking care of that, don't worry.'

'What if he fucks up?' Mary's voice had grown harsh with the alcohol. 'What if he threatens to put us all at risk?'

Vanderlyn fanned the cards on the table in front of him. A royal flush, a winning hand if they'd been playing a real game. He barely knew how to play poker, had never considered himself cool or self-contained enough for it. And here he was playing a much more deadly game for much higher stakes.

'We won't let that happen,' he said. 'He'll meet with a fatal accident. It happens all the time.'

He turned over the next card in the pack. It was the ace of spades. He put it back face down like a man who, visiting a fortune teller, prefers not to know the future after all.

PART 3

The Road to Xanadu

CHAPTER FIVE

Monday, 22 October

He drove slowly, without lights, without thinking. Behind him, the coast was already a memory. The sound of waves crashing against the shore lingered in his brain, but it quickly dimmed and was replaced by the humming of his tyres. After the perpetual light of the submarine, the darkness beyond his windshield calmed and soothed him.

The darkness continued without apology for the half hour it took him to trace the dirt track back to the highway. US 17 as far north as Windsor, then across country to US 301. That would take him up into Virginia, to Petersburg, where he'd take US 1 the rest of the way to DC. Until tonight, it had always been a game, just like the weapons training and the explosives instruction and the radio lessons – something you learned to do, but told yourself you'd never need in real life.

The road stretched out in front like a long finger, beckoning him on. Without encouragement, the Duesenberg handled like a dream, and he almost imagined he was back in England, driving home late at night after a college ball in Cambridge. Or in Massachusetts, coming back from his first date.

It didn't take much to disturb his reverie. As he left the coast behind, the world began to build itself around him. He passed his first car, a Ford V-8, just outside Askin. From then on, traffic was thin, but constant. His lights picked out signs of habitation everywhere: barns, fences, gates, road signs, and clusters of houses that rapidly became small towns. He kept a steady pace, well below the limit, but not too slow to attract attention. His original route would have to be altered. The boatman who'd picked him up from the submarine had warned him that police and FBIS patrols would be out on all the main highways tonight. As a result of the new curfew on blacks and Jews, John decided to travel on minor roads where possible.

His headlights picked out a straggling line of men ahead, shuffling in single file along the shoulder of the road. He thought it was a chain gang, then, as he swept past, realized they were slaves being walked home after a hard day in the fields. White overseers with bullwhips kept the line moving. As he passed, the white men glanced at his car, admiring it, but the blacks kept their eyes straight ahead where they'd been taught to keep them. He saw their faces, hollow and creased with pain, then he was past and there was nothing ahead but darkness again.

The first sign appeared about ten miles from Vanceboro, a long white gash in the darkness caught by his lights for a couple of seconds and seared into his brain for ever. 'Black Curfew 7.00 p.m.'. The second came about a mile after that: 'All Jews Must Register with their Local Board'. After that, he started to see them everywhere. 'No Catholics Beyond Greenville'; 'Craven County – Jew-Free since '39'; 'Commie Agitator – Get Out or Get Shot'.

Any lingering doubts he may have had that this was still make-believe vanished as he drove through the outskirts of a little place called Pinetops. A large billboard, lit by a single spotlight, proclaimed that 'Klan Justice is God's Justice', and was followed by a second bearing a Biblical quotation: 'Thou hast destroyed the wicked, thou hast put out their name for ever and ever'. He slowed down, seeing more lights ahead, then wished he'd kept on going.

The gallows had been erected on a four-foot high platform to one side of the road. It consisted of a beam maybe twenty-five feet long, supported at both ends and in the centre by high wooden struts. It had not been cobbled together hastily, but was skilfully made and built to last. Two lights with tin shades and naked bulbs stood atop the beam at either end. There were eight nooses in all, and six were in use.

He knew right away that this had not been the scene of a mob lynching. Nailed carefully to the beam was a hand-painted sign reading 'Edgecombe County Sheriff's Office'. The bodies hung in two orderly bunches, three on one side and three on the other. He counted four men and two women, all dressed in their everyday clothes. The wind was not strong enough to rock their bodies, but it lifted the edges of their clothing against itself like small, pitiful flags.

The women and two of the men were black. They wore placards round their necks, describing their crimes. The women had been hanged for 'Stealing Bread', the men for 'Looking at White Women'. The third man was dressed in the garb of a Catholic priest; the sign round his neck read 'Corrupter of Youth'. Next to him hung a young man of no more than twenty. On one arm he bore a Star of David with the letter 'K' inscribed in the centre, and on his chest a crudely-lettered and misspelled placard said: 'Unrejistered Jew'.

He swallowed hard and drove on. In the town, men and women were walking up and down the high street. A little girl smiled at John as he drove past; in one hand she carried a red balloon, with the other she clung to her father, a tall man in farming clothes. A small cinema was showing *Rebecca*. Photographs of Laurence Olivier and Joan Fontaine glowed behind small panes of glass like phantoms. The coming attraction was a dubbed version of the new German film, *Jew Süss*, starring Ferdinand Marian.

The beauty of his roadster drew mocking glances from some of the younger passers-by. This was pick-up truck country, and the Duesenberg, chosen for Washington, was

51

conspicuous. North Carolina had suffered badly during the Depression that had brought Charles Lindbergh and the Klan to power. There was still severe poverty here, as everywhere, and John had no wish to draw attention to himself.

Still distracted by the scene at the gallows, he took a wrong turning just south of the Virginia state line, and found himself on a back road that seemed ominously quiet. About to turn round in order to rejoin the main highway, he glanced in his driving mirror and caught sight of a blue light behind. The light drew rapidly closer, flashing rhythmically through the darkness. He held his breath. He knew he hadn't been speeding. Maybe he shouldn't be on this road, maybe it led somewhere he wasn't supposed to be. The new America was full of secret places and signs warning citizens to keep out.

The cruiser drew level with the Duesenberg, slowing down as it did so, and John's heart skipped several beats as someone in the passenger seat shone a powerful flashlight directly at him, forcing him to look away. Blinking hard, he slowed down. A moment later, the police car had picked up speed again and gone ahead. He saw its taillights flicker, then disappear round a bend.

When it had gone, he pulled in to the side of the road. He opened the glove compartment and took out a route map. Using the little flashlight, he traced the roads he had taken, and worked out which one he was now on. On reflection, it might not be so bad. If he stayed on this road, it would eventually rejoin a main highway on the northern side of the state line.

He eased the car back into gear and made ready to drive off. As he did so, a pick-up truck went past with a party of men in the back. He noticed that one or two of them were dressed in white. He drove another couple of miles without seeing anything. A couple of cars passed him, one of them at high speed, as though impatient. The road was flanked by tall trees, but every so often there would be a break through which he could see the edges of flat fields and row after row of tobacco plants. He wound down the window slightly, and at once there was a sharp scent on the air, a warm, heady smell that reminded him of roses past their time.

Suddenly, as he turned a bend, he saw the road ahead was lined on the left-hand side by cars and pick-up trucks, all pressed in hard against the bank. He went on past slowly, aiming to leave the scene behind and press on down to the main road, a mile or two further on; but as he reached the end of the long line of parked vehicles, a police-man appeared from nowhere and motioned him to one side, flagging him down to park in front of the end vehicle.

John wound down the window the rest of the way. His heart was fluttering. The policeman sauntered up to the car, lit from behind by the headlights of his own vehicle. The black uniform with its Klan flashes was an almost comical contrast to that of the London bobby John had seen on his way to the dock in Harwich. But as the man drew level with the window, he knew it wasn't in the least bit comical.

'Saw you coming backaways a piece,' murmured the policeman. He was very young, maybe twenty-five, twenty-six, and he swaggered even when he was standing still, as though he needed to make an ongoing statement about himself. The gun on his hip seemed to have a swagger all of its own. He was chewing gum – very casual, but alert. His eyes flickered over everything: the Duesenberg, John, the leather seats. 'Don't see many cars like yours in these parts. You left it a bit late. Reckon they'll soon be finished back there.'

John wondered what he'd driven in to. He felt instinc-tively that it would be better not to admit that he didn't know what the hell was going on 'back there'. And he had an idea that no-one would be driving down this road at this time of night who did not want to be involved in whatever it was. He smiled.

'Had a bit of trouble on the way here. Engine needs an overhaul.'

'Hell of a car, though, ain't it? You ain't from round here, are you? Couldn't miss a car like yours. Never saw one like this before in these parts.'

John realized that, even if the Duesenberg had been a good choice for the circles he planned to mix in in Washington, it had served to mark him out in a place like this, where most people didn't have four wheels, let alone leather seats to go on them.

'Just heading back to Washington. I heard about this and thought I'd make a detour.'

The policeman looked hard at him, as though weighing him up in a balance so delicate a feather might tilt it, or a look, or a thought.

'Better get a move on, then,' he said. 'Don't want to miss nothing.'

John opened the door and got out of the car. It was cold, and he regretted not having brought something warm to wear at night. He looked at the policeman questioningly.

'Which way?' he asked.

'Head on through that gate there. You'll go up a hill, then it's straight down. Just follow the lights. Ain't far.'

He shut the door and headed off in the direction indicated. As he walked, he could feel the policeman watching his back. All seemed quiet, and that was strange, given the number of cars and the press of people that must have come in them. He remembered the men in white he had seen earlier. This must be some sort of Klan meeting. But surely the Klan didn't have to meet under cover of darkness in back fields any longer.

The gate led on to a dirt track, barely visible in the light that came from a dim moon. The track went flat at first, then lifted steeply, going straight as an arrow up a sharp incline. It was not far to the top. From the ridge of the hill, John found himself looking down suddenly into a little valley. And as he looked, he began to understand,

and he felt sick and wanted to turn back. But he knew the policeman was back there, wondering what a dude in a smart motor car like that was doing out here in the backwoods of North Carolina.

CHAPTER SIX

The darkness closed in on the little cabin like a nightmare about a sleeping child. It wasn't an easy darkness, not a darkness a man would want to walk through alone. Sometimes there was silence, sometimes strange sounds rippled through the night and left an impression of foreboding in the air.

Abraham Smith looked at his wife, then at his daughter, then at his son. He sighed and got up from the table.

'You can't be planning to go out there, Abe,' said Louise. 'You know they got a curfew set from tonight. We can't none of us set foot outside till dawn.'

'I don't always reckon to do what I'm told to do. But I'm not intending to go out. I'm just restless, knowing I can't.'

Joey looked up from his book. He was reading *Moby Dick*, quite a few years ahead of his age. It wasn't easy going, but he was making progress with his father's help.

'Pop, you said you'd help me with my arithmetic tonight.'

'So I did, and so I intend. You give me some peace for a while, and I'll be with you. I want to talk to your mother some.'

They went to the bedroom and left the children to themselves. He sat down beside her on the rickety bed they'd inherited from her folks. She was shaking a little. She knew he had bad news.

'Honey,' he said, 'I had a letter this morning from Bob Stuttins. He says there's no legal way I can fight this order.'

Stuttins had been at Howard University with him. He'd studied law and gone on to join a firm of black attorneys in New York. Now, like Abraham, like professional black people throughout the country, he was reduced to a life of drudgery and hard manual labour. But he kept in touch, and used his legal knowledge to help out where he could.

'No legal way?'

'He says it'll make things worse for me if I keep on going against it. They could send me to one of them camps. They could put me in a chain gang.'

'But if you get relocated to Alabama, what happens to me and the children?'

'I already explained that. They'll keep you on here. You should move in with another family, maybe the Lees. You can pay a little rent, share their food. You're a strong woman, Louise, I know you can see this thing through.'

'Will they let me keep the children, Abe? I've heard they're taking black children away from their families, sending them out to work in fields and factories. I'm not strong enough for that, Abe. I couldn't see nothing like that through.'

'Hush. They won't take Lua and Joey. They're too young.'

'Joey's old enough. He's working already.'

'That's right. Which means he's needed here. What worries me more is, who going to teach him his lessons when I'm not here?'

'Abe, you shouldn't even have taught him all you have done. Black children aren't allowed an education. Just keeping those books in there is enough to get you flogged.'

'Louise, I've explained this. By the time Joey's grown, all this craziness will be done with. I believe that. It may be too late by then for me, but if Joey's unlettered, where's he going to fit in? It'll set us all another generation back. My daddy worked with his hands all his life, but he beat and kicked me so I could go to school. Joey can't go to school, and Lua won't be able to go. But I wanted to teach them both at home. You'll have to find a way to keep the books and look out for someone to teach them. Speak to Harris Grant. He'll help.'

'Harris is a white man.'

'Don't matter. He's a good man. There's a lot of white folks willing to take risks. They hate this thing as much as any of us. I've heard he teaches the Simpson boy. When you get fixed, have a word with him.'

She put her arms round him, knowing he was lost to her. It had always been hard for black people, and the further south you went, the harder it got. Now, it didn't matter how far north you travelled, life was harder than it had ever been. They could pick you up off the street and sell you to a passing farmer, and you'd never see your family or friends again. They could hang a man for looking sideways at a white woman, they could string up a woman for refusing the attentions of a drunk making his way home from a Klan meeting. It didn't make a peck of difference that drinking was against the law, or that sex between the races was banned: they'd hang the woman and tell the man to behave himself better in future.

A cry came from the next room. Louise pulled herself from Abraham's arms and hurried in to find Lua on the floor. She'd fallen while standing on the chair to take a cup down from the dresser. Louise took her in her arms and comforted her, and slowly her howls gave way to sobs, and the sobs diminished and became gulps of passing misery. The cessation of the child's cries made more apparent than before the strange silence that wrapped itself round the little wooden house.

'Shhh,' warned Abraham. He stepped to the door and opened it a crack, listening. Closing it again, he stepped up to Louise.

'What's wrong?' she asked.

'I'm not sure,' he answered. 'Hard to say exactly. I can't hear the generator down at the mill. But I can hear cars up on the road. There's a lot of traffic for the time of night.'

'Could be something to do with this curfew.'

He nodded, but that didn't seem to fit.

'Could be,' he said. And, stepping to the door again, he listened more carefully.

CHAPTER SEVEN

Most of the people down below were carrying torches. They were gathered in a semi-circle round a small shack, a poor man's dwelling in the middle of fields. Behind them, a low hill cut the sky, and on it someone had set alight a wooden cross. Beside it, on a tall pole, fluttered the Stars and Stripes, like an echo, the burning cross at the flag's centre illuminated by the real cross at its side. This was old-style Klan country, and this was the old Klan doing what it knew how to do best.

As John watched, a torch was thrown onto the roof of the shack, followed by a second and a third. Within seconds, the tinder-dry dwelling had taken the fire into itself and was burning insanely. He could hear it from where he stood, a manic cackling, as though the flames were tongues. And then another sound, a woman's voice screaming, and in its wake, other voices laughing, as though Charlie Chaplin had just shimmered into view.

It didn't take long. The door of the shack opened, and people came stumbling out, coughing, blinded by the smoke: a man, a woman, and two children. John didn't need to be told that they were black.

'Reckon we could get a little closer than this,' said a voice in his ear. He turned to see the policeman standing beside him, his uniform refulgent in the red light reflected from the blazing shack.

John said nothing, but he followed the man down the slope and into the milling crowd. Men and women moved about in a curious, ugly silence, and here and there John saw children as young as eight or nine trailing behind their parents, as eager as any of the adults to witness the cruelties to come. He also noted the uniforms – white and red robes for Klan members, black for state police, brown for Aryan Alliance militiamen. They hadn't come out here to hide, but to administer their brand of justice on the spot, like hunters who will go to the hills sooner than enter a butcher's shop.

The black family had run straight into the waiting arms of the Klan. This was their show, one they had long experience in running. The man and woman had clung to one another, and the children, screaming, ran for them, but men in red silk robes pulled them apart and dragged them separately to the hill on which the cross was still burning. Their faces were lit starkly by the flames rising from the little shack.

John was drawn into the crowd, pressed forward by the tidal pull of it, carried with everyone else towards the hill. The policeman had moved away, and was talking and laughing now with colleagues; but every now and then he would cast a glance in John's direction.

And now, as though released from a corporate vow of silence, the crowd began to bay. John knew that, however long he might live, he would never forget that sound. It seemed to start deep down in their chests, a low rumbling that might have emerged from the earth itself. It rose slowly in pitch and volume until the field rang with it, taking on shape and meaning. John had expected hatred, something raw, uncivilized, and pained, but this was different: it was sullen and cold, the calculated product of more than simple race hate.

'Hang them, hang them, hang them, hang them . . .'

The chant went on without ceasing, throbbing through the night like a great drum, or hundreds of drums beating with a single voice.

He looked at the faces and saw them contorted in

expressions of malice verging on joy. They were like the people he had passed not long before on the streets of Tarboro: shopkeepers, farmers, salesmen, clerks, just the sort of people who went to see films like *Rebecca*, who spent Saturdays at the ball game and sang in the choir at church on Sundays.

It happened very quickly, with what seemed practised ease. The black man and his wife were dragged to the foot of a leafless tree. The woman cried out in a sobbing voice, calling for her children, summoning God and Jesus to intervene, pleading with her persecutors to have pity. The children howled, neither God nor Jesus lifted a finger, and the crowd pressed in for the kill.

It was all done dispassionately, as one might slaughter an ox or dispatch a sheep. Men slipped rough nooses over their heads and dragged them the few remaining feet to the foot of the tree. It was a matter of moments to toss the ropes over branches and to haul the couple up into the tree, their arms and legs flailing, silently dying while the crowd watched approvingly. John turned his face away. He wanted to be sick, and knew he could not.

When he looked up again, the kicking had stopped and the bodies were turning lifeless on the bare branches. The crowd had grown silent again, and the only sounds were the voices of the orphaned children, bleak and uncomprehending at the foot of the hanging tree.

He thought it was over then, and thought of slipping away, but at that moment he realized the horror had just begun. The two men holding the children now brought them forward into the light of the torches, and John saw they were a boy of about seven and a girl even younger, perhaps three or four.

A man detached himself from the crowd, dressed in the red robes of a Klan dignitary, a plump man whose only dignity lay in his regalia. He wore spectacles that planted a surprised expression on his round face, but the hard lines of his mouth conveyed another impression to John, the image of a man who knows exactly what he is doing, and who will do it however much it may hurt somebody else.

The red-robed man stood just under the tree, flanked by the swaying bodies of the man and woman he'd just had killed for whatever crime or uncrime they'd been judged guilty of. The torches flung a lurid light across his face, his fat belly, his thick arms. He seemed a primeval thing, red and menacing, a creature of blood.

'Folks,' he called out into a silence created by his own voice. He sounded utterly unlike a killer: down-home, warm-hearted, concerned, a good citizen organizing a village show, ground-hog day in the backwoods, a good old boy among his neighbours. 'I want to thank you for coming out here tonight. I know some of you have come a long ways, and that you have a long ways to travel 'fore you get safe back home. But I know you wouldn't be here if it wasn't important.

'We hanged us two more niggers tonight. Back in the days before this country got itself right, there were folks who said hanging niggers was wrong. Hell, you couldn't even thrash a bad nigger for fear some Jew lawyer or some commie intellectual would sound off to their congressman, and say you weren't fit to be called an American. No, sir, because the Jews and Catholics and Masons and Communists had this country where they wanted it, and if treating blacks like human beings was going to further their interests, they'd make a song and dance about it from Chicago to Chattanooga and back again.

'But, as I say, that was before the ordinary people of America – people like yourselves – saw which way the wind was blowing and stood up and let themselves be counted. That's why we're out here in this field tonight with blazing torches, and we aren't hiding from the law.

'The miserable pair you can see either side of me didn't like the new America we're building. They didn't like to be told they could be bought and sold like hogs or chickens. The boy had gone to Howard University on a scholarship and gotten ideas. Got talking to lawyers 'bout what he called his constitutional rights. Ain't nothing worse than a black boy with an education. Argued the Bureau for Negro Relocation didn't have the right to send him back down to Alabama where his pappy come from. So some of us reckoned we had to teach him a lesson, him and all those other black boys think they're smarter than white folks just 'cause they've gone to a fancy college and learned to wipe their backsides like Christians.'

The fat man paused. John felt a shudder pass through him as he watched him preen himself, gratified by his own oration. Beneath the good old boy exterior and the homespun language, John could see the unmistakable lineaments of a clever politician working his pitch.

'Reckon it's getting late, and I know some of you lawmen have got more important things to do, so let's wind this up.'

The Klansman nodded, and to John's horror, the two black children were dragged to the front. Two more ropes were produced from somewhere in the crowd, and nooses slipped round their necks. The little girl whimpered, frightened, but not comprehending the reality of what was happening. Her brother, knowing what they meant to do, called out for help in a loud, despairing voice.

John could bear it no longer. Regardless of the disapproving faces surrounding him, he began to push his way back through the crowd, stumbling to find a way out of the nightmare into which he had walked. All the time, the boy's voice rang in his ears, pleading as his mother had pleaded, for life, knowing there was nothing else, that there could be no second chance. Then, just as John broke from the very rear of the throng, the voice was cut off. He looked round and saw the policeman staring at him.

With the child's voice rocking through him, echoing from beyond sudden death, and the smell of burning wood stinging his nostrils, John ran up the hill, and back down again to the track that led to the road.

64

CHAPTER EIGHT

The darkness was not great enough to hide the Duesenberg, but John, his eyes dazzled by torches and his mind crazed by the little boy's last cries for help, spent what seemed an age searching for it. Somewhere in the distance he heard the staccato sound of applause, like machine guns rattling, then a great cheer, as though a football crowd was up there, rooting for their local team. He found the door at last and collapsed into the driver's seat. His hand shook as he pressed the ignition.

As he drew away from the bank and eased the car out to the centre of the road, he thought of the submarine in which he'd been smuggled across the Atlantic. The *Torque* would be well into Raleigh Bay by now, dug deep down at one hundred feet or more, and heading fast into the open sea. He felt an obscure sense of redoubled shame, that he'd let them all down, even if they need never know. His presence could not have prevented the child's death, yet he felt a sense of blame. He felt as though a curse had been laid on him. Ahead, the darkness called him on to something unguessable.

He thought of the young couple whom he'd seen hanged, and was unconsciously led to think of his own parents. When he was sixteen, his father had told him about an execution he'd attended years before, at a penitentiary in New York State. The prisoner had been a client of his father's in the days before his arrest, and he had asked him to be present as a witness. He had taken over twenty minutes to die in the electric chair. The equipment had malfunctioned, and everyone in the room had smelled the odour of charred flesh.

'He was innocent,' John's father had told him. 'The real murderer confessed two years later, before he went to the chair in Sing Sing. My client's last words were "I didn't do it. You've got to believe me." But nobody did.'

The story had provoked in John a lifelong horror of capital punishment, and a revulsion against injustice in any form. That, in turn, had prompted his decision to study law at Harvard and, later, to do research in international law at Cambridge. He'd still been in Cambridge when a man from a secret department in Whitehall had come to recruit him.

His father, Anthony Makepeace, had told the execution story deliberately and with much forethought, in order to create precisely the effect it had done. Perhaps not the studying of law, and certainly not the recruitment by Britain's new sabotage organization – but certainly the horror and the revulsion. His own life had, in some measure, been characterized by a passionate belief in justice and the rights of the individual, and he had been determined to pass that passion on to his son.

Anthony Makepeace came from a long line of English radicals, with a string of reforming members of parliament making the family name synonymous with fair play, decency, and incurable bloody-mindedness. The Makepeaces had never been easy people to work with, live with, or marry into. In their time, they'd annoyed slavers, gunrunners, bombmakers, mill-owners, government whips, bishops, judges, generals, lords, prime ministers, Indian rajahs, hangmen, gin barons, opium traders, kings, queens, and – so some of them claimed – the Almighty Himself.

The Makepeaces themselves had the blessing of sufficient worldly goods and enough brainpower to stand up to anything the British establishment might choose to throw at them. The family had been Quakers since the days of

George Fox, even if some had served in the army, one had been an admiral who sank the Barbary pirate Abdoul Kader, and another – John's great-grandfather William – had knocked a man down in Pall Mall for insulting Gladstone.

John's father was a lawyer, a junior barrister at the Middle Temple who, in his mid-thirties had gone to Boston to act as advisor on British company law to Klein McLaren, a large bank with major interests in London. There he had met and married Rachel Pearlman, the only daughter of the city's leading reform rabbi and niece of the bank's Vice President. The couple kept homes in Boston and London, and John had been brought up between both worlds – half-American, half-English, half-Jew, half-Quaker, half-fish, half-fowl.

And now, what had he become? John Ridgeforth, a monster conjured up by the Baron Frankensteins of British intelligence from the bits and pieces of other men's lives.

The Duesenberg began to pick up speed. John was intent only on distancing himself from the scene of the lynchings as fast as he could. His contact in Washington would start to grow anxious if his arrival there was seriously delayed. He had his telephone number, but the chances of finding a public call box anywhere out here were slim. Better to press on and try to make up for lost time.

Something flashed in his mirror. He glanced up and saw a blue light turning lazily through the darkness behind. Each time he looked in the mirror after that, the light was closer. He slowed down, realizing he'd been driving over the speed limit. The last thing he needed was a run-in with the law, however trivial the reason.

The police cruiser passed and pulled in sharply in front, slowing to a halt and forcing him to stop a few yards behind it. The door of the cruiser opened and a familiar figure stepped out. As far as John could see, he was alone.

The young policeman stepped up to the Duesenberg, and

John wound down his window. He smiled. The policeman did not smile back.

'Step out of the car.' The friendly banter had been replaced by the harshness of barely limited authority. John noticed for the first time the cross on the man's lapel. Not just local police, then, but a member of a Klan unit.

'Is something wrong, officer? Was I speeding back there?'

'Don't make me ask you twice. Just get out of the car like I asked you to.'

John opened the door. His feet were barely on the road when he felt himself caught and spun and thrown face forwards across the car. No sooner had his hands hit the roof than his legs were kicked apart, leaving him off balance.

'Left the party in kind of a hurry, didn't you?'

'I'd seen all I wanted to see. No point in hanging around. I've got people waiting for me in Washington.'

'Ain't that nice? Look on your face back there, you weren't having a good time.'

The policeman frisked him, his hands moving with practised ease. What was he looking for, John wondered – a concealed weapon, or concealed beliefs?

'I didn't go for a good time. I went to see some niggers hanged. Hell, I took a detour just to get here. I'd never seen a lynching before.'

'How'd you know we were fixing to hang them niggers?'

John thought quickly, knowing the possible consequences of a wrong answer. The last sizeable township he'd passed through before the wrong turning had been Tarboro.

'I stopped for a coffee back a piece. Place called Tarboro. Man in the diner said there was going to be a hanging, told me which way to come.'

'So you just thought you'd have yourself a little look at the things these Southern folk get up to when the nights start getting dark.'

'I was told it was a public hanging.'

'You called it a lynching back there. I get suspicious, somebody calls a legal execution a lynching. I'd like to take a look at your papers.'

'They're in the glove compartment.'

'Get them.'

John straightened with difficulty and bent down to slip back into the driving seat. As he did so, he noticed that the cop had taken out his revolver and was holding it pointed at him.

'Just so's you don't try no funny business. If I see a gun coming out of there, your brains will be the latest luxury item in this fancy car.'

John fished out the ID papers he'd been given. He was wondering just how legal the execution back in that field had really been. At a guess, there had been no trial to convict the condemned. On the other hand, legal and illegal were more or less interchangeable terms in the new America. He handed his papers to the policeman.

'Stay there.' The policeman replaced the gun in its holster and pulled a flashlight from his belt. He read through the papers carefully, as though alert to the possibility of forgery. John tried to keep calm, but he knew it would take only one small error to turn suspicion into certainty.

'What's a lawyer from Massachusetts doing down in these parts?'

The policeman's manner had changed. Lawyers were a breed that had to be handled carefully.

'I was visiting relatives in Charleston. Aunt of mine died and left me some money. I felt obliged to go down for the funeral.'

'You headed on back there? Massachusetts?'

John shook his head. The policeman kept the flashlight turned on him, forcing him to look away from the beam.

'I'm heading for Washington. I mean to stay a week or so with family friends. They say there's a chance of a job in the Justice Department. Or maybe with the FBIS.

69

I'd like to work with those guys. Hoover's doing a ter-rific job.'

'Sure is.' There was a pause as the policeman handed the papers back. 'How come you ain't travelling on the interstate?'

'I thought I'd see some of the Carolinas. This is my first time down this way.'

'Ain't much to see at night.'

'I'm not so sure. I saw plenty back there.'

'Frighten you?'

'Some. I told you, I've never seen people hanged before.'

'Stay around. We hang niggers and Jews like other folks hang laundry. Leave 'em out to dry as well. You figuring to get to Washington tonight?'

'I'd like to.'

'You'd better get yourself back on the interstate, then. There are curfews on some of the side roads. When did you last fill up on gas?'

John thought quickly. He'd never been on the road north of Charleston. Only one place name came to him.

'Florence,' he said. 'Stopped at a little gas station just outside.'

The policeman stabbed the flashlight across the dash-board. The motor was still running, and all the indicators were lit.

'You like to tell me how in hell your tank's still three-quarters full?'

John looked at the gauge. The policeman was right. Damn the boatman – he must have filled the tank before setting out to sea, and forgotten to mention it.

'That gauge is broken,' said John. 'It always shows three-quarters. I've been meaning to get it fixed for months.'

The policeman didn't look like he believed him. He walked round to the front of the car, glanced down briefly, then came back to John.

'I'd like you to tell me your licence number.'

John froze. He'd never even thought to memorize it.

70

'How the hell do you expect me to remember a thing like that?'

The policeman hesitated only a moment longer.

'OK, mister, I want you to switch your engine off, then get your ass on out here again, where I can see you. And move real slow.'

John did exactly as he was told. The engine died, bringing a sudden, desperate silence marred only by the hum of the patrol car in front. The blue light swung through the night like a migraine, hitting John's eyes again and again as though intent on disorienting him. He blinked and turned, swinging his legs through the opening.

The patrolman was young and strong, and John could sense confidence wafting from him like a perfume. The police had trained him, and the Klan had polished and brutalized him, and he was capable of anything. His mistake lay in not even guessing the real threat. He had John down as some sort of liberal lawyer from up north, sneaking through the byways of North Carolina in search of incidents like the one he'd just witnessed. That sort of person could be a nuisance, but seldom dangerous, and never a physical threat.

John moved before the patrolman registered what was happening. He'd positioned himself precisely, using the doorframe as a brace. His right leg shot out, taking the policeman between the legs, a cruel, disabling blow that sent the man staggering backwards with a howl of pain. The flashlight flew from his hands, shattering on the hard surface of the road. The darkness pressed in tighter, and the blue light kept on turning, lighting the two men in a slow, strobe-like motion.

In spite of the overwhelming pain in his groin, the policeman reacted with an almost primeval instinct, reaching for his revolver in a desperate attempt to ward off danger. It was already too late. John already had his arm, and, twisting hard, broke it at the shoulder. The policeman screamed, dark, animal-like, his face contorted in the blue light.

The scream was broken off as John moved behind him, slipping an arm round his neck and breaking it in a single, practised motion. It was the worst thing he had ever done in his life, and the most necessary, and he knelt on the ground after it was done and threw up everything in his stomach. In Scotland, they'd taught him everything he needed to know: how to maim, how to disable, how to kill. But they hadn't taught him how to live with the consequences.

CHAPTER NINE

The others had gone, Charlie first, then Mary, their departures staggered in order not to draw attention. People watched. Neighbours noticed comings and goings, made note of anything out of the ordinary. You didn't know who was going to make a report to the FBIS, or when a knock might come at the door.

Miles would be the last to leave, as always. He'd let half an hour pass before setting out. Cell meetings drained him, gave him a feeling of unreality. He had to readjust to the world outside, give himself time to become a law professor again. Tonight had been particularly hard.

A young man, Lou Marangella, had been found selling guns belonging to the movement. He had contacts with organized crime, which was finding life hard under Klan rule. Gambling, alcohol, and prostitution were all strictly prohibited, and the law was severely enforced. The criminals still made a good living out of back-room casinos, bootlegging, and well-disguised brothels, but run-ins with the law were getting harder to avoid. That meant guns, and guns were hard to come by. Marangella had been a procurement officer for the underground, bringing weapons across the border via New Mexico. Then he'd got greedy and started raiding his own stashes, selling the guns on to gangsters for ten or twenty times their value. He'd made a lot of money, spent a lot of it on girls. One of the girls had been a friend of Charlie's, and she'd told him about Lou and his money. The underground had just sentenced him to death.

As always, Miles sat in the front room with Miriam, unwinding from the strain of the meeting. He tried to put Marangella and his fate out of his mind, but he found it hard. The kid had been likeable, a well-disposed, sensitive boy who'd been prepared to risk his life to overthrow a tyranny. It hurt Miles badly, not just that they'd been betrayed, but that tomorrow morning, when he got up, he'd have to make a phone call that would send another man to put a bullet through Marangella's head.

'You think too much.' Miriam leaned forward and shook him by the shoulder. He looked at her and smiled. If he'd been younger, he'd have fallen in love with her; maybe he had already, without admitting it to himself. She was beautiful, thoughtful, calm. She reminded him of his wife Helena. He put the thought out of his head immediately.

'I'm sorry. I think I should give this thing up. I'm getting too old for this cloak and dagger stuff.'

She smiled.

'How old are you, Miles?'

'I was sixty earlier this year. It's old enough.'

'You don't look fifty. You sound forty. Forget about getting old. They need you, believe me. Ask Moshe.'

'Does he tell you that?'

At that moment, Moshe came in.

'He's landed.'

'You're sure?'

Moshe nodded.

He looked on edge. He'd had to handle two transmissions from the submarine, and each one had carried a higher-than-usual risk of discovery. Even his brief recognition signals could have been picked up by the FBIS monitoring station at Arlington and traced back.

'The submarine sent out a "mission completed" signal a few minutes ago. He should be well on his way by now.'

Miles felt the weight fall on his shoulders again.

'Let's hope he doesn't run into any trouble,' he said.

And he thought of the darkness outside the city, and the

bleakness of it all: America and its burden of inhumanity, like a gauntlet they all had to run, each day until the end of their lives.

'Listen,' Moshe said, and as he opened the door they could hear the sound of a violin coming from the next room. Anna, the Rosens' daughter, was practising. She played for two hours every morning and two hours every night.

'She already plays better than I do,' said Moshe. 'I'm not exaggerating. She has a talent. Listen.'

Anna was playing the adagio from Bach's violin concerto No 2 in E major. Miles had heard her often before, but never like tonight. Tonight the music seemed raised to another level, as though a small crack had opened between this world and the next. Miles sat entranced until she reached the end. Moshe closed the door.

'You never had children, did you, Miles?'

Miles shook his head. He and Helena had always wanted at least one child, but it had never happened. It had always been a sort of compensation that he and Helena would at least have one another in their old age. But now . . .

'It doesn't matter,' he said. 'You grow accustomed to things. Gains and losses. You're lucky though: Anna's the child I would have wanted. Is she still playing with the orchestra?'

Miriam and Moshe exchanged glances. Miriam handed a cup of coffee to Miles.

'They sent her home from school a few days ago. All the Jewish children. There are no places for them. I have to teach Anna myself. The orchestra's a school project.'

'But she enjoyed it so much.'

'They were jealous. The other children, their parents. Here was this nine-year-old Jewish kid who could play like no-one else. It upset their system of values. We're a lesser race, it doesn't fit if we do things better.'

'What stupidity!' muttered Miles.

'It will change,' said Miriam. 'It has to. A situation like

this can't go on for ever. So we're making Anna keep up her practice. When things improve, she won't have to catch up.'

'If they improve,' said Moshe. 'If Lindbergh makes an alliance with Germany, they could win this war. It could take generations before there's even a chance of over-throwing them.'

'You mustn't give in,' Miles admonished him, suddenly forgetful of his own tiredness. 'Public support's only skin deep. If we can provoke them . . .'

'It only brings more reprisals. They're arresting people every day now. The camps are full, and still they're putting more of us in them. I'm scared, Miles. I'm scared for Miriam, scared for Anna. I've told Anna that she should go to you if anything happens. That you'll see she's all right. I lie awake at night, worrying about her.'

'You'll be all right. You're both careful.'

'Being careful isn't the answer. The only way to be safe is not to be black, not to be Catholic, not to be Jewish.'

'I'm none of those things, but I'm not safe. No-one's safe in this country any longer. Being careful is what counts. Not drawing attention to yourself.'

Moshe opened his mouth to say something, but the door swung wide and Anna came in to say goodnight. She hugged and kissed her parents, then crossed to Miles and planted a kiss on his cheek.

'I heard you playing, dear,' he said. 'Every time I hear you, you've improved out of recognition. I wish my singing was going as well.'

Miriam was giving Miles singing lessons. At his age, he was hardly going to become Caruso, but he knew the Rosens needed the money. Moshe had played with the National Symphony Orchestra until it was rendered racially pure. His new job didn't pay nearly as well.

'You're coming along fine,' said Miriam. 'You just need to practise more. Like Anna here.'

76

She went to her daughter and rubbed a hand over her head in a protective gesture.

'Get yourself ready. I'll be up in a few minutes.'

Moshe kissed Anna goodnight. She left the room, pausing to wave to Miles.

'When's her birthday?' he asked.

'January the fifteenth,' answered Miriam. 'She'll be ten. I can't believe it. My little girl ten already.'

Moshe glanced at Miles.

'Did you hear about Danny Horowitz's wife?'

Miriam put out a hand as if to stop him.

'Not now, Moshe. Anna could come back in.'

'I have to tell him, Miriam.'

'What happened?' asked Miles.

'She was hanged. In Howard County. It happened a few weeks ago, but word only got out today.'

'Poor man. I'm sorry.'

'She was picked out of the crowd. They made someone choose her. No reason, just for the hell of it.'

Vanderlyn looked tired again. He got to his feet.

'It's time I left. I've got classes in the morning. Constitutional history.' He snorted. 'The great irony of my life.'

'Would you like Moshe to give you a ride back?'

Miles shook his head.

'No, I'd rather walk. I'm upset by what you told me. About Rosa Horowitz. Helena and she were friends. Not close friends, but they saw one another from time to time.'

'Miles, I'm sure Helena's all right.'

Miles looked at Miriam and nodded.

'Yes, of course, I'm sure you're right.'

'Moshe shouldn't have said.'

'No, he was right. If they'd hanged Helena, there'd have been news. It's a good sign.'

He picked up his hat and coat, and wrapped a woollen scarf round his neck.

'I'll come back tomorrow, Moshe. We need to work

out the details for that transmission the day after tomorrow.'

'Take care, Miles.'

'You too. Both of you. Kiss Anna goodnight for me. It's because of her I'm doing this. Tell her that when she grows up.'

From Charles Maddox Crane's *A Brief History of the United States under the Klan Administration. Volume 2: The Lindbergh Years* (Arundel Academic Press, New York, 1991, pp 458–62)

The weather on 8 November 1932 was mild in most states, encouraging a healthy turnout of voters. A total of 41.7 million people voted, some forty-seven per cent of the electorate – the largest vote ever registered in the United States until that date. The vote for Charles Lindbergh was not altogether surprising, given that support for Hoover had almost entirely evaporated, while Roosevelt was tainted with what a great many people still perceived as reckless left-wing attitudes.

Most Republicans realized early on in the campaign that Hoover was a lost cause. They and other right-wingers saw their best – indeed, their only – chance in the Aryan Alliance of America, a coalition around the undeniably popular figure of Lindbergh. Moderate right-wing voters seem to have deceived themselves into thinking that, once in power, Lindbergh would break with the Alliance and with its core membership of the Klan, that he might even declare himself the Republican he was at heart. It was not too far-fetched a notion. Had the Klan been the fringe organization of the mid-twenties, it is hard to believe that a man like Lindbergh would have seen them as anything but a liability in the long run.

But the Klan of 1932 was a well-honed political machine that had shed much of its more bizarre elements and its redneck image to mount a genuine challenge to the bipartisan system of the past. Creating the AAA had proved a masterstroke, providing a much broader power-base than the Klan alone might have hoped to achieve.

The Depression was the catalyst that prompted most Americans to reassess their political stance. If Lindbergh had not agreed to stand, it is highly likely that another candidate from the same mould would have been fielded, though probably with less success. Hoover had effectively put himself out of the running by his poor handling of the devastation caused by unemployment and widening poverty. Roosevelt had practical solutions to the economic problems, but next to Lindbergh he seemed lacklustre. For a lot of people, there was no contest between a polio victim and a flying ace.

Even so, Governor Roosevelt came within a whisker of winning. In the end, it was an electoral college majority that won the election for Lindbergh and the Alliance. But, once in power, it was only a matter of time before America's new rulers took steps to dismantle the political system that had brought them to power. Within a year of voting Charles Lindbergh into office, the American people were to wake up one morning to find they had invited a Trojan Horse into their great and shining city.

PART 4

Xanadu

CHAPTER TEN

The road in to Washington was tangled with road blocks, mainly police, some FBIS. He came in on US 1, through Stafford, Quantico, and Woodbridge, and every few miles there would be flashing lights and dark cars straddling the highway, and everywhere men with emotionless faces and questing eyes peering through the driver's window, scrutinizing him as though he were an insect under glass. Behind them, half-hidden by mottled shadows, armed men stood watching, as though put there to carry out an ambush. The flashing lights would catch the dull barrels of their guns and turn them momentarily to bright wizard's wands.

His papers passed muster at each inspection, his face and the Duesenberg did the rest. When he gave the address to which he was going, he was waved on politely, sometimes with a salute; but each time he felt he was being sucked deeper and deeper into a trap.

The closer he drew to the capital, the more formidable grew the apparatus of the Aryan Alliance police state. The checkpoints ceased to be ad hoc arrangements of police vehicles and became fixed posts, manned exclusively by heavily-armed FBIS agents in grey uniforms. Passing Dumfries, he became aware of a long chain-link fence topped by barbed wire, and a mile later saw a tall gateway, floodlit and guarded by soldiers. A sign above the gate declared this to be the 'Prince William County Concentration Camp'. Armed guards looked out from towers on either side of the gate.

During his last visit to America three years earlier, John had heard of these camps, but this was the first time he had actually seen one. Modelled on the German camps of the same name, they were run by a division of the FBIS and manned by elite guard units trained by the Bureau.

From a spot just north of Accotink, the road was lined with flags: the presidential Stars and Stripes with the burning cross in its centre, Aryan Alliance Triple-A flags with three radiating A's like a windmill, set in a circle of stars, Klan flags with their four crosses set in the angles of a St Andrew's Cross, resembling old Confederate flags, all lit by spotlights set at the foot of each staff.

None of these surprised John, though he had never before seen so many in a single place. But he was startled to see, displayed prominently among them, long vertical banners emblazoned with the red circle and black swastika of Nazi Germany. They were a new development. Above them were pinned starkly-lettered boards carrying the words: 'German-American Solidarity Bund'. The days of American neutrality were clearly numbered.

The little boy's cries and the policeman's raucous scream mingled in his brain as he drove, neither one quite drowning the other out. He had dragged the policeman off the road into a field, and left the patrol car parked where it was, taking care only to extinguish the lights. Someone would find the dead man the following morning, maybe even later that night. But John was relying on the fact that only the policeman could have linked him or his car to the scene of the hangings or to his own death. He knew his licence number by heart now, and sang it out loud at every checkpoint.

As he passed the national airport, he saw on his left a giant floodlit cross that dominated Arlington Cemetery. And ahead of him, across the river, directly in front of the still-unfinished Jefferson Memorial, another icon looked down on travellers entering the city: the newly-erected Lindbergh Monument, Ernesto Begni del Piatti's massive bronze-sheathed tribute to the President's flight across the Atlantic in the Spirit of St Louis. It was entitled 'Flight to Freedom', and resembled a bird of prey about to soar heavenwards. A battery of floodlights chiselled its beak and talons into the night sky.

He had planned to turn at the flyover onto Mount Vernon, and then down to Key Bridge to cross over into Georgetown, where he was headed; but the turnings had been sealed off, forcing all incoming traffic over the Highway Bridge and so through into central Washington. The bridge was controlled by a permanent checkpoint manned by Marines. An FBIS man in a greatcoat approached the car. John wound down his window.

He'd been briefed on what to expect if the cross exits were shut. This was the notorious Hoover Checkpoint, expressly set up to filter everyone passing into the capital, and designed to trap members of the resistance. If he made a mistake here, there would be no second chances.

The man had close-cropped blond hair and a sharp, chiselled nose. His eyes had nothing in them, nothing at all. No love, no hate, no wonder, nothing. It was as if a transparent wall had slammed down between him and the world he scrutinized.

'Papers.' The voice was mechanical, yet it held no suggestion of a bored functionary going through the motions. John sensed intelligence and cunning. He passed his papers through the window, making a conscious effort to control the trembling in his hand.

Without hurry, the agent leafed through the papers, making careful notes on a pad as he did so. He kept them in his hand while he asked his next question.

'Destination?'

John gave the destination in Georgetown for which he was headed.

'Who lives there?'

'A friend. His name's Vanderlyn. Professor Vanderlyn.'

'Purpose of your visit?'

'Professor Vanderlyn taught me law at Harvard. He came here a couple of years ago to take a chair at Georgetown, and we lost touch. I said I'd look him up on my way back north.'

The inquisition continued, polite but unrelenting. John knew that his answers would be scrutinized later, and that, if anything did not match up, men in grey uniforms would be at Vanderlyn's apartment within the hour.

'OK, I guess that's all I need to know. Make sure you hand this sheet in on your way out of the city.'

The man handed back John's papers, together with a pink sheet that served as a sort of entry permit to the capital. He put everything in the glove compartment, smiled at the agent, and drove on.

Once over the river, he let the city take him to itself as if he was an offering and it a vast stone deity set above the nation. On public buildings, on boards erected in public spaces, on hoardings along every avenue, party slogans proclaimed the glories of the new republic. Everywhere he saw photographs of President Lindbergh – acclaimed as the Great Aviator, the Man of Destiny, The Liberator, and the True Patriot. As often as not he was to be seen standing shoulder to shoulder with Vice President Stephenson, dressed in the robes of a Klan Grand Wizard. And at every intersection there were stylized portraits of American soldiers, storeys tall, their arms raised in the universal Fascist salute.

He remembered many of the slogans from the early days of the Party's rise to power. 'A Single Nation, a Triumphant Race, a God-given Leader'; 'God's People, God's Nation, God's President – United in Victory'; 'One Party, One Klan, One Vision'; 'Race Purity: God's Gift to Mankind'.

And everywhere the letter 'K', on shop-fronts and garage roofs, on schools and libraries and hospitals. It was used to indicate complete Aryanization. No Jews or Coloureds were admitted to premises displaying the sign. They would not be served in shops, or employed in businesses, or taught in schools, or treated in clinics. John drove past like someone recently landed on a strange planet where anything may happen.

He drove up 14th Street, then made a left on Pennsylvania Avenue and followed it through to Georgetown. The address was the corner of Reservoir and 35th. When Georgetown University was taken out of Jesuit hands in 1938 and all Catholic staff and students dismissed, the Convent of the Visitation, which adjoined the campus, was also seized. The nuns had been forced to find shelter in private homes, while the convent buildings were turned overnight into faculty accommodation and renamed the Martin Luther Residence.

It was a series of red-brick buildings running along the west side of 35th from Reservoir Road to P Street. Miles Vanderlyn had a suite of rooms on the fourth floor. The government had been generous towards faculty who had agreed to be relocated from other colleges to fill the posts at Georgetown. The former convent had been transformed into something resembling an exclusive men's club. John gave his name to the desk clerk in the lobby and took the elevator to Vanderlyn's floor.

CHAPTER ELEVEN

The professor was waiting for him in the open doorway of his suite. He was in all respects identical to the man in the photographs John had been shown in England: a balding, avuncular, mild-eyed academic. The image was completed by the horn-rimmed spectacles and the stubby pipe that seemed to have grown from his mouth through some perverse yet entirely natural process, as though law professors were a species grown in bottles and decanted when mature.

Nevertheless, it was vital to observe absolute caution. If Vanderlyn had been exposed or compromised, this first contact could be a trap waiting to be sprung.

John stretched out his hand.

'Hi, Professor Vanderlyn. It's great to see you again. You're looking well.'

'It's good to see you, John. How was your journey?'

'Uneventful.'

'That's what I like to hear. It's been pretty uneventful here too. How's your mother?'

'Oh, she's fine. She sends her love.'

Vanderlyn, reassured by this exchange of coded phrases, indicating that all had gone well, stepped closer.

'Let's go inside,' he whispered. 'It doesn't do to hang around in the corridor.'

John, also set at ease, followed Vanderlyn into the apartment.

It was like stepping inside a time chamber, as though

the modern world had been all but banished by an act of arcane magic. No telephone, no radio set, no gramophone, no steel table lamps. Both lighting and heating units were skilfully concealed. The furniture was a mixture of late colonial and federal American – tasteful, elegant, and, if John's uneducated eye was any judge, original and extremely valuable. He was drawn almost at once to an extraordinary portrait of a white-haired man that hung above the mantelpiece.

Seeing him take notice of the painting, Vanderlyn urged him to go closer.

'His name was Adriaen Vanderlyn. My great-great-something grandfather. The painting's by Copley. It was done around the time he painted Paul Revere, a few years before he left for London.'

'It's a wonderful painting.' John hesitated. 'And this is a beautiful room.'

The professor smiled, gratified by John's honest appreciation of his home.

'I don't think the nuns would approve of what I've done to the place. But then no-one lets them approve or disapprove of anything any longer. Some of them have been sent to camps.'

John looked at him, shocked.

'On what charge?'

'Oh, the usual. "Parasites on society", "Vatican agents" – something like that. I don't pay much attention to the wording of those things. It's all such tomfoolery anyway.'

'Hardly that, if people are sent to those places as a consequence.'

Vanderlyn looked contrite.

'I'm sorry. I have my ways of coping with this brave new world I find myself in. You must excuse me if I seem flippant. Please, sit down. You must be very tired.'

John found himself ushered to a mahogany-veneered sofa in the Sheraton style.

'This looks very like a . . .'

'Phyfe? You're quite correct. Now, sit on it, boy, sit on it. It's survived generations of Vanderlyns, and I doubt very much if it's about to collapse because a Ridgeforth sits on it. In any case, it's the real article, whereas you . . .'

John sat down heavily on the sofa. It was surprisingly comfortable.

'Is it safe to talk here?' he asked.

Vanderlyn sat down opposite him on a klismos that was, no doubt, also a genuine Phyfe.

'My dear boy,' he said, 'I doubt very much if there's a single room or apartment in this entire republic that could be regarded as entirely safe to talk in. The boys in grey have eyes and ears everywhere. However, I have no reason to believe this room to be any less safe than, let us say, President Lindbergh's bedroom, so I think you may speak much as you please.'

'I just wondered . . . Do you think it's a good idea for me to stay the night here? I . . .'

'You're afraid someone may take us for a couple of homosexuals?'

John reddened, then nodded.

'Lord above, don't you imagine I've already thought of that? Our new rulers have a bee in their collective bonnet about that sort of thing. No-one in his right mind gives the least opportunity for gossip. That little tell-tale in the lobby earns as much from J Edgar Hoover as he does from the university. You're to spend the night in the faculty guest wing. I'll take you there shortly. But first there are some things we need to talk about. First of all, why did it take you so long to get here?'

The amiability had not left Vanderlyn's voice, but it had acquired a fresh quality, a note of astuteness and resolution that told John the professor was a lot harder than he looked.

'I . . . The man who met me told me there were police patrols on the main roads. I stuck to the back roads. And I got lost a couple of times.' John thought it best to say nothing about his visit to the lynching, or his killing of the policeman. It was an understandable mistake, but it compounded the boatman's error in not warning him about the gas.

'In future, stay on the state and interstate highways. The back roads go through too many small towns. Those are breeding-grounds for the hard-core Klan. Someone like you gets noticed in places like that. People start asking what you're up to, where you're going, where you've been.'

John remained quiet, knowing he'd already found that out the hard way. For the first time it dawned on him that any carelessness on his part endangered, not himself alone, but anyone he came in contact with.

'Is there any chance of getting something to eat?' he asked. 'I haven't had anything since I left the . . . Since I arrived.' He had not wanted to say the word 'submarine' aloud. It was remarkable how quickly a sense of paranoia took hold.

Vanderlyn frowned.

'I'm sorry. I should have asked. It's too late to get anything from the kitchens, but if you don't mind eating cold, I've got some bread and salami.'

'Sounds great. Back in England, nobody's even heard of salami. All the food's rationed anyway.'

'I've heard about that. It must be bad. And if we go into the war alongside Germany . . .'

'You blockade the Atlantic, you invade Canada, Britain loses its main lifeline, and the war ends a couple of months later.'

'The European war. There will still be Russia, then the Pacific. After that, who knows? There'll be a scramble for the old British and French colonies. We'll probably take most of South America. The war won't end, it'll just move house.'

Vanderlyn paused. He looked old suddenly, and spent, as though his inner vision had cracked like a mirror, from top to bottom. 'I'll fix that food for you,' he said, rising and slipping through a side door into his little kitchen.

Left alone, John felt abruptly dislocated from all sense of normality. He had left England fighting for its life and crossed the Atlantic to find himself at last in a strange room filled with antiques and portraits of the dead. Listening to the sounds coming from the kitchen as Vanderlyn prepared his food, he was reminded of the apartment he'd shared with Linda in his last few years at Harvard, while studying for his doctorate in law. They'd married in 1934, two years after the AAA came to power, and separated three years later, when Linda had realized just how much damage she could do to her career by being married to somebody half-Jewish.

She'd joined one of Boston's top law firms, McLellan Bryce, the year before, the first woman to do so, and she'd been ambitious to make her mark. Soon after that, the first anti-Jewish legislation had passed through Congress. Howard Bryce, the son of one of the senior partners, had taken her for lunch one day and mentioned – 'just in passing' – that there might be problems after all in her working on a case she'd recently been assigned to. Their client was most particular about avoiding Jewish association, however indirect. Howard was sure she'd understand. He'd been right. She spent twenty-four hours thinking about it and about two hours acting on it, moving all her possessions out of the apartment and writing a short explanatory note which John had found on getting home from the library.

He'd spent another year in Boston, finishing his doctorate, before making the move to England. Finding a job in the States would have been nearly impossible anyway. Linda had filed for divorce on the grounds of 'racial incompatibility', a new legal definition that had put an official end to their marriage within a month. She'd stayed with McLellan Bryce, been promoted, and seen a lot of Howard. For all John knew, they were happily married by now. He no longer loved her, but he thought of her often, mostly with regret, for he had loved her once.

The door opened and Vanderlyn appeared carrying a tray on which stood a pot of hot coffee, two cups, and a large plate of sandwiches – salami, pastrami, ham, chicken, beef, with liberal fillings of lettuce, tomato, onion, and mayonnaise.

'This is a feast,' said John. He hadn't seen food like this in years. Vanderlyn set the tray down on a low table and set everything out with an almost fussy precision.

'You've been house-trained, I see,' John remarked, taking a side plate and reaching for a sandwich.

Vanderlyn shrugged. 'I get by. I had to learn to do things after my wife . . .' His voice faded and he looked down.

'They told me she was dead. I'm sorry.'

'Actually, I don't know if she's dead or alive. They arrested her four years ago, took her off to a camp in New York state. She belongs to a Jewish family from up there. She's a scientist, a physicist. She did work on radioactivity at Chicago before we moved here. I believe she was on the verge of making a major breakthrough before they arrested her.'

'What was the reason for the arrest?'

'Helena was the local secretary for B'nai B'rith, got involved with some legal cases, made herself unpopular with the wrong people. There were never any formal charges. I fought it, of course, but then she disappeared. They said she'd been transferred to another camp, one near here, Howard County. I tried to get to see her, but they said she wasn't there any longer. I've been doing everything possible for years to find her, but it's no use, it's as if she vanished into a black hole. I make myself assume she's dead. It makes it easier.'

'But you don't really think so?'

Vanderlyn sighed. His face creased with pain. He shook his head.

'No. In my heart I'm convinced she's still alive out there,

that the system will bring her back to me someday, just like it took her away. Does that sound crazy?'

'No, of course not. When my wife . . .'

Vanderlyn looked at him sharply.

'You don't have a wife.'

'Sorry, I for . . .'

'You can't afford to forget. One unguarded remark like that puts us all in danger.' Vanderlyn paused to pour two cups of coffee. 'I think it might not be a bad idea if we spent an hour going over your story. Then I'll brief you on what happens next. You aren't too tired, are you?'

John shook his head. Since leaving the submarine, the freshness of the air had gone to his head, and he felt wide awake.

'No, I'm fine,' he said. 'Go ahead.' He marvelled at how smoothly Vanderlyn had taken charge. This might be an SOE operation, but it was already clear that the American resistance was not about to abdicate real control. They, after all, had more to lose than anyone if things went wrong.

Together, Vanderlyn and John went over his cover story, checking, crosschecking, criss-crossing names, places, dates, events.

'We have to be sure your version and our version match up,' said the professor. 'We aren't up against stupid people, believe me. They notice things. They're trained to notice, and they're good at what they do. Very good.'

It was like being back in Scotland, only this time his interrogator was a law professor with years of courtroom experience. John found himself being grilled like a murder suspect, his every statement subjected to a fierce cross-examination. At the end, Vanderlyn pronounced himself satisfied, and at once proceeded to list every point on which John had been vague, uncertain, or hesitant. John pushed away the sandwich he had been eating, his appetite eroded by anxiety.

'Tell me about John Ridgeforth,' he said.

'Ridgeforth? You know all there is to know about him. You are John Ridgeforth.'

John shook his head.

'No, I'm a simulacrum. What about the real man? Or is he just a fiction?'

Vanderlyn made a gesture of denial, a lawyer's gesture, as though to indicate that lies could form no part of his existence.

'No, he's a real person. Or was. He died earlier this year in a riding accident, while out hunting near Salem.'

'That was convenient.'

Vanderlyn looked back without blinking. A lawyer's look, intended, like the gesture, to defy his interlocutor to challenge what he said.

'Yes, extremely. He had exactly the right qualifications. Summa cum laude in law like yourself, a doctor's degree specializing in administrative law. I'm told he even had an accent just like yours.'

John returned Vanderlyn's look. He had not been brought up among lawyers without knowing how to interpret their gestures and their glances.

'How long exactly has this plan been under way?' He spoke the words calmly, as though talking about a road-building scheme; but inwardly he felt tainted. It was a man's life, after all. And not just that. It was a President's life, and so much depended on the whole thing that it took John's breath away just to think of it. Already, over ninety lives had been surrendered for no other purpose than to get him to the coast of the United States in utter secrecy.

Vanderlyn hesitated. He held his coffee cup in front of him, an exact match of John's. Carefully, he turned it on its gently curved saucer, as though seeking a point of equilibrium. The smell of fresh coffee wafted from it, dark, intense, almost violent.

'You mean the plan to kill Lindbergh?' He too was conscious of the enormity of what they were discussing. If anyone overheard them, they would be dead themselves before the night had ended. 'We first started on it three years ago. It never got anywhere until now.'

'Why not? It isn't that hard to kill a man, even a President.' But he knew that wasn't true. Killing the policeman had been the hardest thing John had ever done.

Vanderlyn took a mouthful of coffee, grimaced as though he found it too bitter for his taste, and put the cup down again. John noticed that his hand shook slightly, as though he was under strain.

'Lindbergh's just a figurehead, a dupe, a poor fool of a pilot who flew a bit too high and a bit too fast. If he's to be assassinated, there has to be a reason. Not just that he's President, not just that the AAA finds him useful. We had to be sure his death would serve a genuine purpose, that it would further our cause, or save lives, or expose the government. Alive, he's dangerous, but dead he could become the sort of symbol you can't wipe out.

'We'd more or less reached the conclusion that it was best to leave Lindbergh alone and concentrate on more useful targets, like Stephenson or Hoover, when your intelligence people contacted us. They said they wanted to assassinate Lindbergh and pin the blame on the Germans. That suited them, but when we thought about it, we reckoned it was OK by us too.'

'Us?'

'The resistance. Ordinary Americans who simply hate this monstrosity that's gotten hold of them. The folks down home.'

John remembered what some of the folks down home had been doing earlier that night, but decided to say nothing.

'How would it help you?'

Vanderlyn raised his cup and drained it in a single, long swallow, as though it was medicine.

'It would help us break up the Aryan Alliance. The AAA's nothing but a sham, a front that let the Klan take power. It's already split, but as long as Lindbergh's up there as its

96

leader, the public sees nothing much wrong. If he says it's OK to put people in camps or arrest them for being Jews or Catholics, most of them will just go along. They aren't interested in ideology or abstract politics. All they want is steady jobs and enough money to feed the kids.

'Things are different at government level. There's a real split between what you might call the patriotic AAA and the more hardline Fascist types. The patriots want to keep America apart from the rest of the world, the hardliners want to join Germany and Italy in creating some sort of Fascist world empire. Vice President Stephenson leads the Fascist camp, along with Hoover.

'Stephenson can't afford to get rid of Lindbergh. He doesn't yet have complete control of the country. Lindbergh's personal popularity still counts for a hell of a lot. Still, Hoover and the FBIS are doing their best to gain power where it counts. Given a year or so, they'll be in a position to move. That's when Stephenson shoves the President aside and proclaims himself Führer.

'But if Lindbergh is shot before then, and it looks like the Germans did it in order to bring America into the war, it'll make Stephenson's job a lot more difficult. The people will side with the patriots, and Stephenson's only choice will be war inside the Alliance. That could be our chance.'

The professor looked at John. This time, John saw in his face, not a lawyer playing with words or gestures, but a troubled man seeking some sort of hope in life.

'A lot depends on you,' Vanderlyn said. 'This country's running out of time. I hope they trained you well back there. I've made a few notes on the main constitutional problems Lindbergh's facing. You'll need to study them.' He took three or four folded sheets from his pocket and passed them to John.

'How soon before I get access to Lindbergh?'

'We can't guarantee it. The man you're to replace should have had an unfortunate accident last week.'

'There seem to be a lot of accidents lately.'

Vanderlyn shrugged.

'We had to time it properly. If we took you in too soon, it would seem like too much of a coincidence, raise suspicions. But if we waited too long, they could find someone else. Laura will know. She'll make the decision.'

'Laura?'

'Your cousin, Laura Cordell. Maybe you don't remember – you wrote her a letter a few weeks ago saying you'd be visiting Washington. Don't worry – you'll be given a complete briefing before you meet her.'

'Why wasn't I told about her before?'

'It would have been too risky. Laura's too important. She has to be protected at all costs.'

'I don't understand. What makes her so important?'

Vanderlyn steadied his gaze. A cloud passed across his eyes, then vanished.

'Laura is married to David Stephenson,' he said, his voice no more than a whisper. 'She's the wife of the Vice President.'

CHAPTER TWELVE

The German Embassy
Washington DC
Tuesday, 23 October
9.56 a.m.

Hans Geiger stood at the window of his office, looking down on the south side of Massachusetts Avenue. The street below was full of tiny people. There were moments when he almost thought he could reach down and scoop them up in one hand, like a giant or a god who plays careless games with other people's lives. Behind him, the prattling voices of Burns and Allen tumbled from the radio. Geiger did his best to ignore them. He was waiting for the 10.00 a.m. broadcast of the Furtwängler concert on NBC. There was to be a special performance of Pfitzner's *Kleine Symphonie* in Carnegie Hall, the first of a series to be conducted by Furtwängler as part of the burgeoning American-German cultural exchange pro-gramme. The new Cultural Attaché along the corridor had been working hard, and programmes of German music were now common on all American stations. They had plenty of gaps to fill, after the recent ban on the broadcast of all forms of jazz and negroid music.

Gracie Allen's voice grated on Geiger. He was not a Cultural Attaché, and in his opinion the very concept of American-German cultural exchange was nonsensical, given that it could only ever be a one-way street. Mentally, he added Burns and Allen to his list of American irritations. The list already included hamburgers, baseball, chewing-gum, air-conditioning, and the sight of Negroes in public places. He'd been in Washington a little over a year, since just before the outbreak of war, and every day had been a torment.

Geiger had learned his English in England, at a language school in Winchester. Pukka English, it was, the King's English, English as she was spoken. Even though they were now his enemies, he continued to have the greatest respect for the English. He considered them a cultured race, a people of genius, almost a match for their Teutonic rivals. It genuinely hurt him that the two countries should find themselves at war with one another.

These Americans, however – he cast a despairing glance down at the throng on the pavement – were Germany's sworn allies, days or weeks short of irrevocably declaring themselves fellow combatants in the great struggle for civilization. Yet he found them boorish, raw, at times infantile. He could not – or would not – understand their drawling accent or their neologisms. 'Hi'; 'howdy'; 'gee' – he shuddered at the thought.

George Burns bade the nation farewell. A pause followed, filled with gentle crackling, then a clock on the radio struck ten and a man's voice announced the symphony.

> 'This is Bill Munro speaking to you from New York. I'm here to welcome you to the first of our new series of orchestral concerts from the Carnegie Hall. These gala occasions are being hosted by the German-American Solidarity Bund. This morning's concert is Hans Pfitzner's Kleine Symphonie, a new work by one of Germany's leading composers of the present day. As you may know, Pfitzner . . .'

*   *   *

Geiger winced at Munro's mispronunciation of the composer's name, which had come out as something resembling 'Fizzner'. For all he knew, the man was a sports commentator drafted in to cover the concert. Fortunately, Bill Munro's knowledge of Pfitzner and his work dried up in half a minute. There was a brief pause. No doubt the commentator was thinking how he could describe the line-up of the orchestra. The sound of Furtwängler tapping his baton for silence relieved him of the responsibility.

The first bars of the symphony filled the room. Geiger relaxed and gave himself to the music. He put Bill Munro out of his mind and began to think benign thoughts of the New World and its Second Republic.

There was a sharp knock on the door. Sighing, Geiger turned from the window.

'Come in,' he said.

It was horrible Feder, his assistant, a clever man without a trace of culture. Geiger detested him as much as he needed him. He entered, saluted, and held out a sheet of yellow paper. Geiger frowned at it while he turned down the volume on the radio.

'Pfitzner,' he said, as though owing the other man an explanation. 'All the way from New York. His *Kleine Symphonie*. It's not bad, really, though I prefer his cello concerto. What do you think?'

'I wouldn't know, Herr Oberführer. Never been musical myself. Mind you, I don't dislike Orff. Very jolly.'

'Yes, extremely lively.' Reluctantly, Geiger turned down the volume of the radio. Orff indeed! 'What have you got for me?'

'This just arrived from the Sicherheitshauptamt, sir. I decoded it myself.'

Geiger grunted and took the paper from his subordinate. There had been no need for Feder to stress his own hand in the decoding. All communications for Geiger were transmitted to the embassy using an encryption system known only to him and his immediate underlings. Geiger's official posting at the embassy was that of Police Attaché, but this was no more than standard cover for the national station chief of the Ausland-SD, the branch of the SS security service – the Sicherheitsdienst – responsible for intelligence work outside the Reich. Unlike most SD representatives, Geiger reported directly to the head of the service, Reinhard Heydrich, and, on occasion, to Himmler himself. Communications from the Wilhelmstrasse headquarters of the SD were strictly off limits to regular embassy staff, not least the Military Attaché, Baron Friedrich von Schillendorf, whose responsibilities extended to supervision of the intelligence operations of the rival Abwehr.

Geiger sat down at his desk and scrutinized the sheet Feder had brought him.

> Reichssicherheitshauptamt Amt VI,
> Sicherheitsdienst Zentralabteilung III2
> Source: SD Radio Communications
> Interception Service, Station Biii
> Codename: Parsifal
> To: Oberführer Ausland-SD Washington
> 0917 hours 22 October 1940
> SECRET
> SD intercept and decoding station Biii reports the following communication from battleship *Von Eschenbach* to Naval Intelligence Atlantic: 'British T-class submarine sighted inside American coastal waters at coordinates 35° 14′ N 74° 04′ W, violating Pan-American Neutrality Zone, sailing due east. Please advise action.'
> At your discretion what use to make of this information. Permission to pass to US authorities if appropriate. Please report any outcome. Heil Hitler.

Geiger pursed his lips. He glanced up to see Feder still standing mute in his original position, awaiting orders, deferential to the point of obsequiousness. Feder was one of those young National-Socialist intellectuals who'd joined the SD after 1934 in the hope of combating the 'little Hitlers' who threatened to undermine the Party and corrupt the Reich. His devotion to the cause was absolute. He lacked common sense, initiative, and tact, but in Geiger's eyes his worst failings were bad breath and body odour. 'Horrible Feder' was more than just a nickname. He'd have dismissed the man long ago, if only to breathe pure air; but Feder knew too much about the Oberführer's personal life to make it worth the risk.

'Well, Feder,' he said, 'what do you make of this?'

'I've checked the coordinates, sir. They put the submarine a few miles east of the coast of North Carolina. There can only be one reason for a submarine to go sneaking about there.'

'Landing agents? You're probably right.'

Geiger mused for a moment. The muffled sound of the symphony, sounding tinny now, as though played by a Lilliputian orchestra concealed in the body of the wireless itself, formed a backdrop to uneasy thoughts.

'I don't think we'll tell our American friends about this yet. But if you'd be so good as to ask Sturmbannführer Werfel to step this way, I'd like him to look into it further. If British agents really were landed on the coast last night, it could prove providential.'

Feder gave him a puzzled glance. Geiger merely smiled. Feder did not know everything, not by a long chalk.

PART 5

Laura

CHAPTER THIRTEEN

Tuesday, 23 October

John arrived early at the Vice President's residence. David Stephenson had bought the Decatur House on Lafayette Square, barely a stone's throw from the White House. This had been the first centre of diplomatic and social life in Washington, and Stephenson's decision to open house there had been intended to provoke the maximum impact among those who cared about such manners. He was a parvenu who had crawled and beaten his way almost to the top, and he had no intention of taking a back seat.

John had been invited to lunch by his cousin Laura, with whom he'd spoken on the phone earlier that morning, telling her he was in town as promised and that he'd love to see her. She had gushed a little down the line, and he'd formed an impression of a mannered and confident society hostess, an impeccably coiffured Daughter of the American Revolution, statuesque, blonde, and cold.

He knew plenty of women like her. His parents had entertained them often enough in Boston, and he'd met them at college balls and graduations, at yacht clubs and polo meetings, at charity lunches and Kiwanis dinners – tall, lonely women in perfectly cut clothes, who moved like ghosts through a world of mirrors and cut crystal.

He might even have shaken hands with Laura Stephenson in person, assuming she'd been on the Social Register at the time. His father had taken him to Washington for the

January-February season of 1925. They'd attended the Judicial Reception and the Dinner to the Chief Justice and the Supreme Court, John's first adult evenings. He'd been fifteen and very gauche, and he'd spoken barely half a dozen words all evening.

An FBIS guard at the door asked for his name. He was expected. The guard showed him in to a high-ceilinged entrance hall where a West Point cadet relieved him of his coat and scarf. Moments later, a butler appeared through a concealed doorway.

'Mr Ridgeforth? Mrs Stephenson's expecting you in the library. If you'd be so good as to follow me.'

The English accent took John by surprise, and for a moment he was back in London, being ushered in to meet the Prime Minister. Every detail of that interview had left its imprint on his mind, above all the great man's parting words.

'Mr Makepeace, I wish to impress upon you, for your own peace of mind, that the mission you are being sent on has been sanctioned by the very highest authority.'

'Thank you, sir, I . . .'

'You mistake me, Mr Makepeace. I do not mean myself. The King has been fully apprised of the mission you are to undertake. He does not like it, but he understands its necessity. I say this to reassure you, for your moral comfort or what you please. But I have to tell you that, should you fail in your task, I shall say that I have never heard of you, never seen you, and never spoken with you. I hope you understand that. Now, good luck, and God bless you.'

The butler preceded him up a twisting flight of wide, delicately balustraded stairs in whose well a vast lantern of blue and white glass hung on a long brass chain. Everything here was on the grand scale, and John marvelled at his own temerity in setting foot in the house.

They reached a double door on the third floor. The butler showed John into the room and closed the door noiselessly behind him. John turned, but the butler had already vanished as quietly as he had come.

A woman sat at a long desk before a high sashed window. Her back was to him, most of it concealed by the chair in which she sat. Her hair was indeed blonde, and gathered in a chignon that left the bare nape of her neck exposed. He realized she had not heard him enter. Like a small boy brought to his headmaster's study to answer for a misdemeanour, he coughed gently. Caught among high shelves of leather-bound books, the sound seemed too muffled to be heard. But the next moment the woman at the desk turned and looked at him.

It was as if a small phial of crystal had smashed entire against bare marble tiles, or a mirror cracked into ten thousand silver pieces, each reflecting infinite mirrors beyond itself. Something broke or cracked or snapped in him then, something that could never be repaired, not in a dozen lifetimes. It was not a breaking of the heart exactly, but a fracturing of the spirit underneath, a splitting that separated past and future precisely, like the halves of a red apple.

'You must be John,' she said, and he watched her rise from her seat and come towards him, and he could not speak at first, because she was all things he had not expected. She was beautiful and sad and dark-eyed, and as fragile and doomed as fine-spun glass set on a narrow shelf above stone.

'I'm Laura Stephenson. Welcome to Washington.'

The timbre of her voice was utterly different from that of the woman he had spoken to on the phone, deeper, softer, less artificial.

'I expected . . . someone older. Or am I making a mistake? You're Mr Stephenson's daughter?'

She laughed, and for some reason the sound was not diminished by the dead weight of the books all around.

'That shows how well you know your cousin! I'm David Stephenson's wife. Our daughter's just three years old. But you should know that.'

He realized what a stupid mistake he'd almost made. Vanderlyn had told him about the child.

'How is little Shirley?' he asked.

'Much like her namesake. Precocious and inclined to simper. I despair of ever turning her into a human being. You'll meet her in due course.'

'I'm looking forward to it. Is she as beautiful as her mother?'

She reddened and lowered her eyes momentarily. When she looked up again, he caught for an instant that same sadness he had seen in her at the very first, but this time it had a quality of alarm in it. He thought he had been impertinent, and would have apologized had she not responded first, smiling.

'Are we to be kissing cousins, then, Mr Ridgeforth? You should be more careful with your compliments.'

He guessed her to be little more than twenty-five or twenty-six. Too young to have been at any of the dinners he'd attended fifteen years earlier.

'Why don't you come over here and sit down?' she asked. 'We have to talk. Lunch isn't till half-past one today.'

A wide, leather-upholstered sofa straddled the gap between two bays of book-crammed shelves. Above it hung a portrait of a middle-aged man in Klan regalia.

'My husband,' Laura said. 'You'll meet him at lunch. He looks a little ridiculous in that outfit, don't you think?' There was an edge to her voice that seemed in disharmony with the lightness of her manner. She sat down and patted the seat next to her. He noticed that her hand was long and very slender, the fingers pale against the polish on her nails. She was dressed in a Mainboucher suit that must have been cut in Paris before it fell to the Germans. It was fastened at the neck with a plain gold brooch that reminded him of one his mother used to wear.

'It's all right,' she said, 'we can talk safely here. This is David's private library. It used to be the salon, but David had everything changed round when we moved in. He wanted to make his mark on the place. So the salon went down and the library came up. This is where David meets his friends. Not even Hoover would dare to eavesdrop.'

'I hope you're right. I have to tell you, it came as one hell of a shock to find out my contact to the White House was Stephenson's wife. Everything I know about my cousin Laura stops in my teens. I think it's time somebody filled me in on what's been happening since then. Such as how my buck-toothed little cousin came to be Mrs Vice President.'

'Buck-toothed?' She pretended to be horrified. 'You were misinformed. That brace was purely cosmetic. What else did they tell you about me?'

He paused, collecting his thoughts. Back in Scotland, his cousin Laura had been just another character in the pageant of his fictitious life, and he'd paid her no more attention than any of the others.

'Your father's Norman Cordell. He lives in Newport, Rhode Island, in a house his father built back in the 1880s, he owns as many ships as some ranchers own heads of cattle, he belongs to the Newport Casino country club, and he sails yachts in competition. Am I right so far?'

She nodded.

'You forgot to mention one thing. He's also a liar, a cheat, and a bully.'

He half expected to see her smile, but when he glanced round it was evident that she was wholly serious. They had prepared him with facts, but not with the feelings to make sense of them. He felt disadvantaged, knowing how easily the wrong emotion might betray him.

'I'm sorry,' he said.

'Why be sorry? My father never beat me or raped me or scarred me. He was never drunk, he never swore in front of me, he never brought women home to embarrass my mother. I was fortunate. I had anything I ever wanted: clothes, ponies, parties. You remember the parties, don't you?'

111

He smiled, not knowing what else to do.

'Men like my father don't have to hit their children to make their lives hell. They have other ways of doing things. I thought all men were like that when I was small. My mother had a breakdown when I was eighteen. Did you know that?'

He shook his head. It was almost as though they were playing a children's game of make believe.

'She's in a sanatorium in Switzerland, in Lucerne. I visit her there once a year. My father never goes. He went once, six months after she was first admitted, but the doctors said she was uncontrollable for weeks afterwards.'

She fell silent, and her silence filled the room. He was imagining pain that had no description. With someone else he might have asked, 'What did your father do? How did he drive your mother insane?', but not with her. After a while, he broke the stillness as well as he could.

'They said . . . They told me you painted. That you were very talented.'

She seemed far away, then brightened and smiled.

'Painting? Yes, I used to paint. My mother encouraged me. Perhaps I was talented, I don't know. It was a hobby, really. My father thought it was a harmless diversion. It made me more interesting. And then I asked to be sent to art school, to Moore College, or Philadelphia, or maybe even Paris – I wasn't sure, I would have gone anywhere. He didn't say anything, but the next day all my paintings and all my equipment were gone. My mother told me to say nothing, or she'd be in trouble.'

She looked round at him.

'Why am I telling you all this? I hardly know you.'

'You're my cousin. You're bringing me up to date.' He sighed and looked down. 'I'm sorry. I need to know these things. They never told me details like this. I wasn't prepared.'

She nodded.

112

'It's all right. You're risking your life. You have a right to know.'

'What happened after that? How did you meet David Stephenson?'

'David?' She seemed to slip away from him again. There was a place he could not follow her, very near at hand, yet inviolable. 'David was – is – a friend of my father's. I'm not sure how they met, but they did business together at one time. For all I know, they still do.'

'Does your father visit David?'

'You mean does he come up to Washington? Sometimes. But you needn't worry. He's very busy right now. He hasn't been here in months.'

'It's important he and I never meet.'

'I know. Don't worry.'

'Was your father a Klan member when he first met David?'

She shook her head.

'I don't think so. No, I'm sure he wasn't, not then. He joined in thirty-two, like millions of others. Before that he just hedged his bets. He knew David well, though. I think he may even have helped him financially. David used to come to our house a lot in the old days. I never saw much of him, of course, I was only a child. You wouldn't have met him: father kept him to himself. Later, when his first wife died, I was twenty. He was already Vice President by then, of course, and wasn't able to visit as often as before, but my father fixed things so I was around every time he came.'

'Home from college, you mean?'

'No, I didn't go to college. I thought I'd made that clear. Art school, college – it made no difference. My father has . . . fixed ideas about women, what they should and shouldn't do, where they should and shouldn't go. I stayed at home, I went to lunches, I danced with the whitest, cleanest, richest boys at the stuffiest, most chaperoned dances. Until David took the bait. From then on, it was David every weekend, David and no-one else, David's

113

yacht or David's lodge and nowhere else. I married him in the end. Where else did I have to go? I was twenty-one. We have one child. But I've told you that, haven't I?'

'Yes, you've told me that. Her name's Shirley. She's three.'

She smiled, a cautious, enervated smile.

'Yes. She takes after her father. And Shirley Temple: he named her after her.'

She broke off as the door opened and a man entered the room, followed moments later by a second dressed in the uniform of a German military officer. The door closed, and the two men crossed the library floor in the direction of the window. Neither caught sight of Laura or John, shadowed as they were in the alcove formed by the bays on either side.

The strangers went to the desk and began to talk in low voices, their heads close together, as though to ensure that what they said could not be overheard.

Laura stood.

'David, I didn't expect to see you here. I thought you were still at the Treasury.'

The first man got up from the desk. John recognized him immediately.

'Laura. What a surprise. I thought you'd gone down to lunch already. I was going to join you there.' He paused, catching sight of John. 'This must be your cousin.'

John stepped forward, stretching out a hand.

'John Ridgeforth, sir. I'm honoured to meet you.'

'Call me David.' Stephenson took his hand and pressed it with a hard grip intended to show who was in charge.

John smiled and nodded.

Stephenson stepped back, bringing forward the stranger.

'Darling, I don't think you know Baron Friedrich von Schillendorf, the German Military Attaché. He and I have some business to discuss before lunch.'

The baron clicked his heels and took Laura's hand, kissing it. Very formal, very polite, very controlled. He shook

114

John's hand. The grip was not as hard as Stephenson's, but it threatened more.

Laura looked at her wristwatch.

'Goodness, it's past lunchtime. John and I got caught up talking about old times. We'll go straight down. I've told people you'll be there. Don't be long.'

Stephenson smiled. A long, meaningful smile that said he'd do as he damn well pleased.

Laura went ahead of John to the door. As she made to close it behind them, she saw her husband and the German, seated again. They turned their heads and smiled at her. She closed the door with a soft click and headed towards the stairs.

CHAPTER FOURTEEN

Howard County Concentration Camp
Florence
Maryland
Tuesday, 23 October

The smell hung over the camp like a miasma. As if by magic, it ended a few feet outside the electric fence. The guards said to one another that it was the stench of the inmates, but the inmates knew better: it was the stench of fear. They breathed fear every moment of their lives, waking and sleeping, they carried it on their skin and on their clothes, they ate it with their bread, and they drank it with their water.

Florence was a white camp. Blacks from Howard County went to Dayton or Carroll County at New Windsor.

Suggs, the red-haired guard from Pittsburgh, prodded him sharply in the base of the spine, making him jerk upright with a stab of pain.

'What you starin' at, Moses? Jew ass not good enough for you, you want some pussy as well? Pussy's out of bounds to kikes, so don't even dream about it. Now get the fuck movin'.'

Danny moved. His motion was the paced trot he'd learned at the cost of several beatings during his first weeks in the camp. Move too slow, and they beat you for wasting time, move too fast, and they whipped you for getting out of line.

He passed the first Catholic barracks, a long wooden hut with the markings 'KA1' stencilled inside a heart. There was a bizarre humour about the spelling and symbolism of the Klan universe, in which they all moved now. 'KA' stood for 'Katholic', just as 'KI' was the abbreviation for 'Kike', 'KO' for 'Kommunist', and 'KW' for 'Kweer'. They said that some wit in the Justice Department had introduced it into the anti-subversion legislation back in the early days after the Klan came to power. He glanced down at the tattoo on the back of his hand. Everyone in the camp had one. His was a Star of David with the letter 'K' inside and his number underneath. Rabbis earned two 'K's, standing for 'Krist Killer', so it was said. Catholics had a sacred heart with 'K', Communists were decorated with the inevitable hammer and sickle, inscribed with a 'K', and homosexuals merited a pansy likewise initialled.

Even within the camp, segregation of different kinds existed. Jews were separated from Catholics, Jehovah's Witnesses from Communists, pacifists from Kommon Kriminals, and everyone from the dreaded Kweers. The system was not entirely rigid, however. Concentration camps were labour camps, designed to extract the maximum effort for the minimum in food, clothing, and winter heat. Over-dividing the workforce would have been counterproductive, so the disparate groups who slaved at the different sections of the kyanite processing plant ended up shoulder to shoulder on the production line.

Danny was a kyanite polisher. He'd been a teacher before, when the world was normal. They'd put him and Rosa into the camp when they closed the Jewish high schools. He'd taught history. He thought he'd been a good teacher: popular with the children, innovative, willing to challenge received ideas. Some of the parents had been unhappy with his thoughts on the authorship of the Bible, but he'd never said anything in class that he hadn't been able to back up with solid scholarship, and they'd respected that. Now, looking round him at the dingy world of the camp, at the gaunt barracks, the watchtowers with their armed guards, the smoking chimneys of the processing plants, the parade ground, the shooting pits with their rows of wooden stakes, the punishment cells, the lines of shuffling figures in grey striped uniforms, new faces every day – he asked himself what all that was worth. Here, he had learned to admire the simple faith of the orthodox, their powers of endurance, their acceptance of all he could not bring himself to accept.

They came to a two-storey clapboard building painted white to distinguish it from the low grey slabs of concrete and nailed board that surrounded it. A flaming cross had been carved above the main door, echoing the cross in the Stars and Stripes that flew above the roof. A sign next to the door read: 'Federal Concentration Camps Administration: Camp Governor's Office'. A guard in CCA uniform opened the door, and Suggs pushed Danny ahead of him into the hallway.

He'd not been inside this building before. Self-consciously, seeing carpet on the floor and pictures on the walls – things he had not seen in years and had almost forgotten – he ran his hand over the stubble on his head, as he might in earlier days have run his fingers through his hair to straighten it. The gesture took him back to the day he'd gone to Rosa's house to meet her parents, and he felt again the anxious tightness in his stomach that had accompanied him throughout dinner. And he remembered Rosa's face when her father had said yes, and holding her on the porch afterwards, all anxiety gone, and kissing her, and longing for her. He had almost forgotten longing, it seemed an emotion from another world.

Suggs had come for him like the angel of death, barking his name and number out in front of everyone at his end of the processing plant. He'd set down his tools and climbed off his stool numbly, responding to the summons as he'd seen countless others do before him. His colleagues had gone on working, terrified even to look up. A look in the wrong direction at a time like this could condemn a man as readily as a curse or a blow. But as he had turned, he had seen one man glance his way, his friend Reuven Cantor. It had been a frightened, fleeting glance, but it had said a million things there had never been time to say before. People who were summoned in that way never came back.

Suggs barked at him, ordering him up the stairs. He climbed up slowly, his heart racing like a dynamo, wondering why he had been brought here and not straight to the execution pit. It had not occurred to him to ask Suggs what his offence had been. Guilt or innocence were meaningless terms in this place. But why the governor's office? Was there some new formality to death?

There was a door on his left, a black door that boasted a sign saying 'Governor Jackson'. Suggs banged on it. Danny did not understand. Why was he being brought to see Jackson in person? They had never met before. All Danny had ever seen of the man was at a distance, on the parade ground, making announcements, proclaiming the virtues of the New Republic to the degenerates he had been set above.

A low voice grunted something indistinguishable, and Suggs opened the door. He saluted.

'The prisoner you wanted to see, sir. Horowitz one nine seven zero seven two. Sir.'

'Thank you, Suggs. Leave him here. Stay downstairs. I'll call you when you're needed.'

Suggs saluted, pushed Danny into the room, and backed out.

Behind his desk, Jackson seemed larger than he had appeared outside, viewed across the vast expanse of the parade ground. He wore the uniform of an FBIS Major, well-tailored, cut from expensive cloth. His crew-cut hair was grey, and he wore a little grey moustache in homage to the German leader. Some of the guards had grown them in the past year: Danny reckoned it was a spreading fashion outside as well as inside the camp.

The governor smiled and gestured to a chair on Danny's side of the desk.

'Take a seat, Mr Horowitz. You needn't worry, you aren't in any trouble.'

Dizzy, his heart still pounding, Danny somehow managed to get to the seat and collapse onto it.

'Looks like this is your lucky day, Horowitz. Got a report here says you were wrongfully imprisoned. Schools Administration needs teachers, someone looked you up, found you should never have been here.'

Danny stared at him.

'Ain't you gonna say something?'

Danny gulped. His mouth and throat were suddenly drier than they had ever been.

'I've . . . been here three years,' was all he could say.

'I know, son. Says so right in front of me. No use crying over that. That's something your people are always doing. Book of Lamentations, that was written by one of yours. Book of Job too. But a man's gotta make do with what he's got. You've learned some things during your time here. Just be grateful for that.'

Danny was speechless. Nothing in his experience had prepared him for this. Not just release, but the governor in person giving him the news and talking to him while he sat in a chair, almost like equals. His wife's killer and himself, facing one another across a space so narrow he might have killed him with his bare hands. Had something happened in the world outside? Had there been a revolution, a coup, a free election?

'You'll find a heap of clothes over in that corner, boy. Won't be much of a fit, but you can't go out of here in those rags. Minute somebody saw you, they'd shoot you as a runaway. Go on, get dressed, and I'll have Suggs take you out of here. You can have a few dollars to get you home. Where you from, boy?'

'Baltimore, sir.' Danny stood, fearing his legs would give way at any moment.

120

'Didn't know there were many of your people up that way.'

'Yes, sir, quite a few.'

'I'll be damned.'

Danny found it tempting to agree, but on the verge of freedom, he held his tongue. If he had learned anything in his three years at Howard County, it was that a moment's affability might turn as quickly to anger and violence. He started to strip off the camp uniform. For the first time, he became aware of how badly it smelled, of the sweat and dirt and dried urine that filled its fibres. And the fear. He wondered if he would ever be able to wash off the fear.

'Do they want me to teach, sir? Is that why they're letting me out? Will there be a job teaching?'

Jackson had got to his feet. He strolled across to some shelves and took down a file.

'What's that, son?'

'Will there be a job for me when I get back to Baltimore?'

'Might be Baltimore, might be somewhere else. How would I know?'

There was an edge of impatience in the governor's voice, as though this was something he wanted to get over with. Danny hurried to dress, afraid he might, by his slowness, lose the man's favour, maybe even lose his chance for freedom. They'd given him underclothing, a shirt, and a second-hand suit, dark blue, a couple of sizes too large. He kept his back to Jackson, conscious of his thin nakedness in another man's office.

Jackson slipped the file back on the shelf. Danny was pulling on his trousers. A thin belt served to hold them round his narrow waist. Someone had used foresight. He cinched the belt as tightly as possible and picked up the jacket. It was far from new, but it felt like the most expensive garment he had ever possessed. He felt his heart beating quickly, still, afraid of this thing he was becoming, this new person, this simulacrum of a human being.

'Let's see how you look, son. Turn around.'

Danny turned.

Jackson was smiling. Danny forced himself to smile too, then he noticed the gun pointing at his chest.

'Had to be done this way, son. Orders from above. Somebody up there wants you dead for some reason. That's how it is these days. Guess that's how it's always been.'

Danny went on smiling. It had to be a joke, a man like Jackson wouldn't waste his time making him dress in a suit just to shoot him. Sometimes if you smiled hard enough, they just put their guns away and laughed.

The smile faded from Jackson's lips.

'Reckon you think this is all some big joke. Well, if it is, I ain't been let in on the secret. I've just got one favour to ask of you, son. Seeing you're one of the Chosen People and on good terms with the Lord, I'd appreciate it if you explained to him that I'm a good man and just doing my job.'

He eased the trigger back gently.

'Just doing my job like my daddy told me I should.'

The shots vibrated in the still air. Far away, in sheds and outbuildings and barracks, a handful of inmates looked up. Most kept on working, eyes fixed on the task before them. It was all there was.

CHAPTER FIFTEEN

Lunch was informal yet restrained. John had expected a dozen or more people, but in the end there were only six at the table: Laura, Stephenson, Von Schillendorf, a rubbery-faced man from the State Department called Doonan, his skinny wife Mildred, and himself. Laura dominated the conversation, weaving threads to link one guest to the next, and everyone to herself. Stephenson himself said very little, and John thought he seemed tired and preoccupied. Perhaps affairs of state kept him up late.

Von Schillendorf's English was fluent. He responded wittily to Laura's leads, and John could see that, like himself, he found her fascinating. It was hard to imagine anyone not being entranced by her. He had not recovered from the shock of first seeing her, from the knowledge that he could not bear the thought of being parted from her, absurd as that seemed, and so without foundation. Throughout the lunch, he found his gaze drawn back to her again and again, as though one among the many threads she was weaving led to him above all others. And he noticed, or thought he did, that her gaze strayed to him more often than it should, and lingered there a fraction of a second longer than was proper.

In spite of Laura's best efforts, it proved impossible to steer wholly clear of politics. It seemed there were few other topics nowadays, even if one began with art or literature or the latest Broadway show. Everything had a political content. Paintings, books, and films were either decadent (and banned) or expressions of the true American spirit. There seemed to be no middle ground. Someone mentioned the new curfew laws, and that led to a discussion of a proposal for the compulsory sterilization of blacks, something for which Doonan appeared to have overall responsibility.

'I reckon we shouldn't stop at the blacks,' said Mildred Doonan. She stooped over the table as she spoke, like a spindly, long-necked bird of prey. Her clothes were black, and her thin face had the mournful intensity of a vulture or a crow. 'We should sterilize them all – the Jews, the Catholics, the crooks, the alcoholics, the down-and-outs. They're just parasites. We should clear them out, every last one of them. Make the air a lot cleaner for our children.'

'In Germany we treat this subject very seriously,' said the Baron. 'We have placed the entire question in the hands of our leading scientists. The biologists and the geneticists. Since 1933 we have been sterilizing the infirm, the mentally retarded, the criminally insane. In a generation or so we will be free of such defects. And now, since this war has started, we have a programme of euthanasia. Far better to give them a merciful death. In a time of war, there must be priorities. Logic must take precedence over false humanity.'

'I'm not so sure about sterilizing the blacks,' Stephenson put in, one of his few comments during the meal. 'We need slave labour, and it's cheaper to breed our own than import it every few years from Africa. As long as they're kept separate, it doesn't seem to matter to me if they breed like rabbits.'

John listened to the conversation with mounting disbelief. With the partial exception of pale and dreadful Mildred, no-one spoke with heat or passion. Everything, even the culling of whole races or the mercy killing of entire sections of the population, was discussed in a calm, matter-of-fact manner, in a tone that might ordinarily have been reserved for dinner-table talk about antiques or racehorses or golf handicaps.

124

'What about you, John?' Stephenson asked. 'You haven't said anything yet. Laura tells me you're a distinguished lawyer. You must have an opinion on this.'

'Well, not quite, sir. Eugenics is an aspect of the law I've never really studied. But I think what you said is right: it makes no economic sense to wipe out able-bodied workers. You'd likely have problems with the unions.'

There was a guffaw from Doonan, who sat facing John, fork poised to cram a wedge of steak into his mouth. He set down the fork with a clatter.

'Where you say you come from, son?'

Mildred sniggered.

'Reckon he just got in from Bechuanaland or one of them places.'

Stephenson glared at her, and she smiled uneasily, not having grasped fully the nature of the young man's relationship with the Vice President.

'Well, I don't really think we're likely to have much trouble with the unions over slave labour,' said Stephenson. 'Or over anything much else. You'll find we have the unions properly under state control. You're right, though – the niggra makes a good packhorse. But what about when he outgrows his usefulness? That's my problem.'

'Yes, sir,' said John, 'it is a problem. Like the Baron just said, maybe we need to consult expert scientific opinion.'

Stephenson snorted.

'Spoken just like a lawyer.'

John smiled, as if the Vice President had made a joke. But he had sensed the animosity behind the comment. David Stephenson despised lawyers. Or feared them.

Laura moved the conversation on to other topics. With politics forgotten, the atmosphere grew lighter. Stephenson retreated back behind his armour-plating. John and Laura exchanged reminiscences about their childhood summers. Von Schillendorf spoke with affection of a holiday he had spent as a child in Vienna. Doonan, whose first name nobody, not even his wife, ever seemed to use, waxed

125

lyrical about the house he and Mildred planned to move into after Christmas. It had belonged to a Jewish doctor, a surgeon who'd been dismissed from his post at Saint Elizabeth's.

'We bought it for almost nothing,' Doonan said. Like his wife, he appeared mournful, but he lacked her predatory look. He was a planner, a systematizer, who got where he wanted by logic, not instinct. His eyes were opaque, like shuttered windows. 'You can pick up Jew houses for next to nothing. There are Catholic houses too, but the Jews live in better neighbourhoods.'

'Not that we'd want one as a neighbour,' smirked Mildred. John wondered who would possibly want to live next door to the Doonans.

'What happened to the doctor?' asked John.

'Cohen? Shot himself. Or something. Shame in a way. They say he was a great surgeon. Steadiest hand in Washington. But his thing was gynaecology. Who wants his wife being cut open by a Jew? Not to mention . . .' Mildred shot a warning look at her husband, who refrained from expanding on the iniquities a Jewish physician might inflict on American womanhood.

Von Schillendorf and the Doonans left straight after lunch. John expected Stephenson to return to his office, or retire to the library upstairs; but instead he joined him and Laura in the drawing-room for coffee.

'I'm sorry, John,' the Vice President said as he sat down in an overstuffed armchair next to the fireplace, 'but these lunches come with the job. They give me a chance to meet people in an off-the-record sort of way. Loosens conversation, gives them a chance to relax, maybe lower their guard a little.'

A maid brought in a tray with the coffee things. She set it down on a low table. Laura thanked her and said they needed nothing more.

Stephenson glanced at Laura, who had sat down on a sofa to his right.

126

'Aren't Doonan and his wife something, though? Do you reckon they have to use some sort of padding when they do it? Do you reckon?' He burst into laughter, hugely tickled by his own joke. Laura smiled faintly and reddened visibly.

'Where the hell is Bechuanaland anyway?' Stephenson asked, wiping a tear from his eye. He mimicked Mildred Doonan. *'Reckon he just got in from Bechuanaland or one of them places.'*

'I think it's in Africa, dear,' ventured Laura. Stephenson glanced round at her, and for a flash John noticed something other than affection in the look. Upstaging the Vice President clearly was not considered good behaviour. He wondered if Laura Stephenson knew who her husband really was. Or, more precisely, what he was.

'Coffee smells good,' Stephenson said. 'You like to pour some, hon? Don't get much chance to get the family together, do we?'

He looked at John again.

'I'm sorry about that. Bechuanaland be damned. Hell, you're family. No reason you should have to sit through all that nonsense.'

'You thought it was nonsense, did you, sir?'

'Some of it, yes. You thought so too. I could tell. But Laura and I like to keep off politics at home. I get my fill of it at work, and she couldn't care less. If I'd known sooner you were coming, I'd have called it off.'

'I did mention he could turn up any day, dear,' Laura protested.

'It's all right, sir. I didn't mind in the least. In fact, I found the conversation most stimulating.'

'Will you quit calling me sir? You're my wife's cousin, and that makes us cousins-in-law. No call to go sirring me. Call me David if you have to call me anything.' He looked at Laura, as though he had only just heard her.

'I do believe you mentioned it, dear. You'll have to

excuse me, I've been so busy, it plum went out of my head.'

Away from his guests, Stephenson grew relaxed and voluble. The tiredness seemed to lift from him. Or had it been merely a ruse, a device to suggest he was being inattentive?

'You planning to stay in DC long?' he asked.

'Well, I'm really just passing through. I wanted to visit an old professor of mine who's down here now, and I thought I'd like to spend a day or two with good old Laura, catching up on things.'

He smiled at Laura, and she smiled back, as though they'd been exchanging cousinly compliments all their lives.

'How long is it since you and Laura last saw one another?'

'Must be getting on for five years, maybe more.'

'Long time. How come we haven't seen you before this?'

'I was out of the country when you and Laura got married. Paris, France. After that I got kind of involved with a woman. I'd rather not talk about that.'

Stephenson nodded, man to man. This was language he understood.

'Never been to Paris myself. Hear it's a great place. I can't go now, of course – be considered too political. But maybe later. I'd like to see – what is it? – the Moulin Rouge. You ever go there?'

John nodded.

'You'd enjoy it. Maybe we can go together some time.'

'I'd like that. Tell me, whereabouts are you staying here in Washington?'

'With that professor I told you about. There's a guest room in the Faculty Hall.'

'Where's that?'

'Georgetown. Professor Vanderlyn teaches a course in constitutional law there. He was famous for that at Harvard.'

Stephenson paused in thought.

'Vanderlyn? Name seems kinda familiar.'

'Couple of years back he was nominated for a seat on the Supreme Court.'

'That's it. Seem to remember he got turned down. Some sort of liberal.'

John realized he could be walking on treacherous ground.

'No, sir, I don't think so. Miles is a constitutionalist. If Congress makes amendments to the constitution, he'll go along with it. He believes in the rule of law. But that doesn't make him a liberal.'

'Reckon it doesn't at that. You some sort of liberal, John? You get tainted with fancy ideas up there in Harvard?'

'I learned law, sir – sorry, David – not politics. I go along with Miles. If Congress passes it, it's law.'

'What if the President made the laws?'

'That wouldn't be constitutional.'

'But what if it was necessary? What if there was a state of emergency, like we had back in '33?'

'State of emergency's different. Calls for drastic action.'

Laura broke in.

'For heaven's sake, can't you men talk of anything but politics?'

They both smiled sheepishly, and Laura passed round the coffees she had poured. There was chocolate to go with it, real chocolate imported from Belgium. John's mouth watered – chocolate was almost impossible to obtain in England.

'David,' said Laura, 'when we were talking earlier, up in the library, John told me he was . . .' She paused. 'No, why don't you tell him yourself, John? The thing about Washington.'

'Oh, that.' John shifted uncomfortably. 'Well, it was more Laura's idea than mine. She was saying how Washington is where everything's happening these days. I have to agree. You've got the best people down here now, some really sharp minds. I feel kind of . . . The truth is, I'm getting bored with what I've been doing back home, in fact I haven't been working for several months now. So I started thinking . . . I don't know, I'd like to be part of what's going on here. I thought, if there was work I could do, solid work that could do some good, I'd be tempted to make the move. Laura thought I should stay a few days longer, look around, talk to some people, see what's on offer.'

'You asking me for a job?' Stephenson looked directly at him. It was a disconcerting look, hard, questioning, without animosity, but also without encouragement.

'Hell, no, David. I never thought . . .'

'That's all right. People ask me for jobs all the time. Just so you know I almost never give them one.'

Laura leaned forward and touched the arm of her husband's chair. John noticed that Stephenson moved away slightly as she did so.

'David, what you're sitting opposite is talent. John has one of the best legal minds in the country, but he's too modest to admit it. He came top of his year at Harvard, graduated summa cum laude, won the Simonton award, went straight to graduate school, and was awarded the Randolph Forrest prize for his dissertation. He's a legend. The trouble is, he has no ambition.'

Stephenson's eyes narrowed as he scrutinized John more closely.

'What was this dissertation about, John? What special talents have you got to offer this great country of ours? You an expert on real estate, by any chance? Inheritance tax?'

John shook his head slowly.

'No, sir. Those are things I've never handled. My topic was administrative law. How state institutions function.'

'I know what administrative law is. How come you stayed up in New England, never looked for work in Washington?'

'I told you, I had some personal problems. I wanted to keep a low profile. Now I'm not so sure.'

Stephenson got up and went to the mantelpiece. He

took a large cigar from a heavy wooden box and clipped it. Without looking round, he asked, 'You smoke, John?'

'No, thank you.'

'Don't mind if I do, do you?'

'Why should I?'

The Vice President turned, cigar clamped firmly in his mouth, puffing smoke.

'Some people say I remind them of Mr Churchill. You see any resemblance, John?'

For a moment John's stomach turned over. How could Stephenson know he'd actually met Winston Churchill, that they'd spoken for over half an hour in private, and that he had received the orders for his mission directly from the Prime Minister? Then he remembered that anybody who'd ever set eyes on a newspaper knew what Churchill looked like.

'None at all, sir.'

'Damn right.'

Stephenson returned to his chair. Laura glanced at him anxiously. Everything depended on his response.

'Hell of a coincidence,' muttered Stephenson.

'What is, dear?'

'Did you ever meet Jerry Witkiewicz?'

Laura shook her head.

'Little guy. Polish. Wears glasses, very brainy. He's my advisor on administrative law.'

'Never met him.'

Stephenson turned back to John.

'You heard of Jerry?'

'Sure, we met a couple of times. He won't know me.'

'No matter. What matters is this. I've got a team of people to advise me on every damned thing. Jerry Witkiewicz is one of the best. He's important to me, stops me putting my foot in it, say I want to draft some legislation, whatever. Thing is, Jerry had an accident last week. Damn near got himself killed.'

'I'm sorry to hear that. What happened?'

'Damnedest thing. Jerry has a little place in the Blue Ridge Mountains, up near Marksville. Drives up there most weekends, does some fishing, a little hunting. He's an outdoor type. Doesn't look it, but he's keen as mustard. Friday before last, he was on his way there, driving west on the 211. That time of day, there was no other traffic, the road was empty. Then this truck appears, coming the other way, down the slope. Can you believe this? The truck's steering gives way just as it gets within a couple of hundred yards of Jerry. He's driving a Chrysler. Next thing, the truck swerves right across the road, hits Jerry, and turns him over. Poor bastard, lucky he wasn't killed.'

John whistled.

'He's on an empty road and a truck comes out of nowhere and ploughs right into him? What is that, fate or something?'

Stephenson shrugged.

'Beats me. They checked out the truck. Some pin or other sheared right through. The driver was shook up, but he came out of it a lot better than Jerry. Some freak accident, though.'

'I'm sorry to hear about this. Is Mr Witkiewicz all right?'

'He's badly smashed up and goes unconscious every few hours, but they say he'll live. His doctor wants to keep him in hospital for a couple of months minimum. That's my problem. This has come at a bad time for me. I'm working on some important legislation and I need an advisor. I have people looking for someone right now. And then you turn up. A dream come true. Maybe.'

He looked back at Laura.

'Honey, is he really as good as you say? I don't want some crap, just because he's your cousin. I've a lot riding on this, and I need an honest answer for once. Is he good or is he a schmuck? Could he take Witkiewicz's place?'

She looked back at her husband gravely, as though he'd just asked her to marry him, and she was weighing up her future.

132

'Yes, David, he's good. Believe me. Very good. And, yes, I believe he could do whatever Witkiewicz did for you, only better. I told you, he's a legend.'

Stephenson took the cigar from his mouth and jabbed it at John.

'You heard what the lady said, John. What do you think? You like to work for me?'

CHAPTER SIXTEEN

Tuesday, 23 October
8.05 p.m.

Larry Loomis could never get comfortable. His wife told his friends he was a martyr to piles. He'd told her to stop, but she went on regardless, as though the idea of being married to a martyr, any martyr, made up for any embarrassment she might have caused him. Larry knew things about her he'd considered telling her friends, indiscreet things, things that would have made her cringe; but he knew what she could be like when her feelings were hurt, or if she merely suspected they might be hurt. He preferred piles and embarrassment.

The hard seats at the ball game were torture to him. He brought his own cushion, but by the fourth innings or so, the seat always won. If he hadn't been such a big fan, he'd have taken up pool years ago.

When the discomfort grew too much, he consoled himself with the thought that his job with the FBIS gave him status. He'd never had status in his life before: he'd grown up in rural Virginia in a family of dirt-poor farmers, his father had been an alcoholic, his mother had worked off and on in a brothel, and he'd never held much of a steady job himself till he got in with the Klan.

That had been back in the twenties, when the Klan was just getting on its feet across the country. They'd looked after people like him, poor white folk who just needed a chance in life. He'd never stopped being grateful. He'd started at the bottom, but within a couple of years of joining up, his local Klan organization had fixed him a job in the sheriff's office. The sheriff, an old buzzard name of Hennessy, had objected to begin with, but by then the mayor and several leading citizens were making their own way up in the Klan, and old Hennessy had soon learned it was better to keep quiet.

When Hennessy retired in 1933, Larry had been given the job. Two years later, when J Edgar had set up his new Federal Bureau of Internal Security, Larry had been one of thousands of Klan members eager for a job in the agency, and he'd been selected for a post at FBIS Headquarters. Seniority in the Klan went a long way in those days. But Larry had more than just that going for him. Larry was smart. He'd used his pay at the sheriff's office to take evening classes at a local college, and by the time he'd moved to the FBIS, he knew more about criminal law than half the lawyers in Washington.

On the field below, the ball game had already reached the fifth innings. Washington were ahead, and Myer was coming in to bat. The arc lights picked out the tiny figures of the players, making them unreal, like projections on a screen. The Senators had last won the pennant back in '33. Larry had watched them all that season, and never missed a game since. He knew they could do it again. They'd won the World Series in '24, but he hadn't been around then. In '33, they'd lost to the New York Giants. Larry was hoping that would happen again. It was his dream match.

Larry knew he would never make it to the top. He was ambitious, but he'd been white trash too long to learn the social skills that oil a man's way into the key positions in life. He accepted that. A man had to take what life offered, and then see if he couldn't dazzle it up a bit. Larry did his job, took a promotion if one was on offer, and found ways of enhancing life on the side.

When he looked round that evening, Larry saw one of

life's little enhancements walking towards him, ready to be dazzled. 'Mr Baker' wasn't his real name, but Larry knew he came from the German embassy, and he knew he paid serious money in return for serious information. Larry flattered himself that he was the man's chief contact, maybe the Germans' top insider in Washington. It gave him a little status and a lot of money, and it helped take away some of the flatness of knowing he'd never achieve his real potential. More than that, the money was building into a substantial trust fund for young Bill. It would see him through law school, maybe there'd even be enough to set him up in a good law firm afterwards. Every little helped.

'Mr Baker. Nice to see you. You've missed a lot of the game.'

Some elementary digging – actually, it had been more like scraping – had informed Larry that his contact's real name was Werfel – Sturmbannführer Pieter Werfel – and that he worked for Hans Geiger, the current German Police Attaché and SD station chief in Washington. But Larry played the game that had been set up at their first meeting. He called Werfel Mr Baker.

'You're sure it's for all right, Larry? I don't want I should spoil your game.'

'No, no, it's fine. You talk, I'll watch Myer bat.'

'Myer? Which one is he?'

Loomis pointed him out. They often met at the game, but Werfel never got the hang of it, however hard Larry tried to explain. The Senators were playing the Cleveland Indians tonight. It was the rubber game of a three-game series. Davis was pitching. Not a great pitcher, but Larry knew he had a tough slider that could force Myer to commit himself too soon.

'Watch this,' he said.

Davis laid the slider on Myer, but the batsman had been expecting it. He connected hard, and the ball soared over the infield, right between the left and centre fielders. Myer dropped the bat and ran for first base.

136

'What can I do for you, Mr Baker?' Loomis asked, one eye still on the game.

'Someone I know would like some information. Police and FBIS reports for the east coast from Wilmington up to Atlantic City, and west as far as Appalachian Mountains. From last night through to this afternoon.'

Loomis whistled.

'Some friend. He must have a lot of money.'

'Yes, I think he has.'

The German took a slip of paper from one pocket, found a pen in another, and scribbled some figures. He passed the paper discreetly to the man beside him. Loomis glanced at it, and at once lost all interest in the ball game.

'Your friend must want these reports very badly. What sort of thing's he looking for? I can't just take everything in sight. Have you any idea how many reports get written in a single day?'

'Just so. You are to look for things out of the ordinary. Behaviour not so normal. Suspicious people, maybe one suspicious person. Especially, my friend interests himself in what is happening near the coast. Perhaps boats have been seen that should not be there. Perhaps there have been lights.'

All around, the crowd was intent on the game. Men and boys munched on hot dogs and drank Coke from slender bottles. Men in uniform moved among the crowd, some selling the official party newspaper, *The Aryan Banner*, others its more lurid counterpart, the viciously anti-Semitic magazine, *America Now*. Its banal catchphrase was 'Keep our Kountry Klean'.

Every game now, there were more uniforms. Klan Guard, FBIS, AAA Militia, and the brown and khaki uniforms of the youth movements, KidsKlan and Junior Klan. Larry never wore his uniform to the game, especially if he was meeting Werfel.

'How soon?'

Werfel shrugged.

'I know it is difficult. Perhaps by the end of the week.'

Loomis groaned.

'I can't promise anything. I'm not Kaptain Kondor, you know. How do I know how much stuff there's going to be? Last night was the start of the new curfew regulations. Can you imagine how many reports are being written right now? That's a hell of an area you want me to cover. Can't you pin it down a bit more?'

'Pin it down?'

'You know, keep things to a limited area.'

Werfel shrugged. He'd studied the map all that afternoon, making calculations based on the submarine's last reported position.

'Perhaps,' he said. He was reluctant to give too much away, but he knew Loomis was right. Why make the job harder than it need be? 'OK, you could start by looking at the area west of Pamlico Sound, then you look to all roads from there to Washington. See what comes up. If it makes interest, maybe you don't have to look no further.'

There was a roar as Myer skidded to the homeplate. On the field, the little figures dipped and bobbed. Music blared from loudspeakers. Larry moved his backside in an attempt to find comfort. A hot-dog seller came down the aisle.

'Let me get you a hot dog,' he said to Werfel. 'My treat.'

CHAPTER SEVENTEEN

Tuesday, 23 October
9.23 p.m.

John got back to Vanderlyn's place late that evening.
David Stephenson had insisted on taking him back to
his office and introducing him to the other members of
staff, from secretaries to other advisors. The Vice President
had surrounded himself with a carefully selected band of
men with brains and energy. John felt himself dwarfed by
them. They were the vanguard of the second phase of the
revolution. He could see it in their eyes and sense it in
their voices. These were men waiting in the wings of a
great theatre, biding their time, awaiting their moment,
anticipating the applause that would greet them when they
finally walked out on stage.

'Get to know the place. Speak to other people. Ask
around. See if you like it. If you need to, spend tonight
making your mind up. Let me have your decision first thing
in the morning. But if you like what you see and you think
you'd like to start work right away, just tell Masterson in
Personnel. He'll give you a pass.' Stephenson had whisked
his new protégé from room to room, scarcely giving John
time to shake hands or learn names and functions. And
then, introductions made, he had vanished, saying he had
an important meeting with the Secretary of State.

'Don't tell anyone you're my wife's cousin,' he whispered as he left. 'Can't have folks getting the wrong idea.'

John had nodded and gone through the motions, asking questions about the work, speaking at length with Witkiewicz's secretary, an attractive brunette called Diane Rivers. Diane had lamented her boss's absence and made it clear from the outset that John would be no substitute. That was fine with John: he had no plans on being around for long. As for making his mind up – he'd done that, or had it done for him – long before he ever arrived in Washington. He'd been sent to America for no other purpose than to take Witkiewicz's place as David Stephenson's advisor.

He left just after six, his mind reeling with facts and figures, having made, he hoped, a favourable impression on the gorgeous but cool Miss Rivers. Her scent still lingered in his nostrils. He remembered it well from his years with Linda, Worth's *Sans Adieu*. He'd make a point of picking some up for Diane when the moment seemed right. But thinking of it, his thoughts returned, as they had returned all day, to Laura Stephenson, to her eyes and mouth and long, white neck. And to that sad, troubled look he had caught in her unguarded eyes.

Vanderlyn took a long time to answer the door of his apartment. John had to knock three times before he heard the sound of Miles's footsteps. A chain was slipped audibly into a bolt, then the door opened partway.

'Who is it?' Miles sounded on edge.

'It's me, John. Is something the matter?'

For answer, Miles shut the door, unfastened the chain, and opened wide, almost pulling John into the little hallway as he did so.

'What's up?'

Miles was flushed. His bow tie had slipped, and his hair was tousled. John felt embarrassed, realizing he must have caught the professor in flagrante with a woman or, as he had begun to suspect, a man.

'I expected you back hours ago,' said Vanderlyn, like a worried mother.

'I had to go . . .'

'Never mind, never mind. Something has come up. I'm sorry about it, but I had no choice. When you knocked on the door, I thought you might be the FBIS.'

'FBIS? Why?'

'I'll explain. Come in here quickly.'

Vanderlyn hurried him into the antique-cluttered living-room. Seated on the Phyfe sofa was a little girl, nine, maybe ten-years-old. She sat perched demurely on the edge of the seat, her hands folded on her lap. Her hair was raven-black, luxuriant and long, and it curled across her shoulders like pitch, framing a pale, tense face. John could see that she had been crying. Her red eyes stood out against the pallor of her cheeks like smouldering coals cast upon snow.

'John, this is Anna. Anna's parents are close friends of mine.'

He turned to the child and soothed her, saying, 'Don't worry, Anna. This is John. He's a good friend. You can trust him.'

John smiled and tried to look as reassuring as possible.

Vanderlyn spoke to John again.

'Anna is Jewish. Her family name is Rosen. Anna's father is a violinist with the National Symphony Orchestra. Or was until a year ago. More recently he has been working as a silversmith, a trade his father taught him. His parents came from Lithuania around the turn of the century.

'Anna's mother is teaching me to sing. Isn't that right, Anna?'

The little girl nodded shyly.

'I'm not a very good pupil, I'm afraid. Not like Anna. Anna has a lovely voice, but, more than that, she plays the violin like her father. Beautifully. More beautifully than you can imagine, my friend. But perhaps you will hear her play some day.'

'I'd like that very much,' said John, smiling at the child. Then he turned back to Vanderlyn.

'What's wrong, Miles?'

Vanderlyn looked at Anna.

'My dear, will you excuse us for a moment? There's something I need to talk about in private with John. Don't worry, I'll be back soon.'

Vanderlyn steered John to the kitchen.

'The FBIS came for her parents two hours ago. She saw it happen. She was with a friend opposite: she'd just been to the grocer's for errands. There was a secret police car outside their house. She hung back and saw two men in leather coats coming out of the house, one holding her father, the other her mother. They bundled them into the car. Anna was terrified. She hid for a while. When she finally calmed down, she had the presence of mind to telephone me. I told her to come over.'

'How'd she get in?' John asked. 'Didn't the clerk see her?'

Vanderlyn shook his head.

'I told her how to get in through the delivery entrance at the rear. Some of the men here use it if they want to bring women back. There are stairs from there to all the floors. No-one knows she's here.'

'What are you going to do?'

'I don't know. She can't stay here. I have a cleaner who does the place twice a week. She'd be bound to find her. I need to get her out of here to somewhere safe. There are several hiding-places in the city for Jews and others at risk. I could get her to one of them, but I don't drive, and walking could be risky after the curfew.'

'You have to get her out. If she's found here, you'll be compromised. Stephenson already knows we're connected. It's too much of a risk.'

'I can't just throw her out, John. She's only a child, for God's sake.'

'Doesn't she have family she can go to? At least until her parents are released.'

Vanderlyn looked at John in astonishment.

'Good God,' he murmured. 'I never took you for such a fool. You've been away from this country too long. Don't you know what's going on here? Anna's parents are dead by now, or, if not, I pity them. If the FBIS find Anna, she'll go straight to a camp. Shall I tell you what happens to pretty little girls in those places?'

John looked at the older man in horror.

'How can you know they're dead?'

'Moshe Rosen worked for the resistance. He was the radio operator who handled communications for your mission. It may just be a coincidence. He handled a lot of other traffic besides. But they'll kill him and Anna's mother the moment they've got what they want from them. Or else they'll just shoot them out of hand. We must save Anna. I didn't exaggerate when I said she plays the violin beautifully. She's a remarkable musician, it would break my heart if anything happened to her. There was a case . . .'

He looked away from John, troubled. In the mundane surroundings of the little kitchen, surrounded by jars and plates and cooking implements, their conversation seemed bizarre.

'There was a man, a friend of Moshe's, another musician. I knew him a little. He played the cello. They took him to a camp in Virginia. The first thing they did when he told them his profession was to break his fingers, one at a time.'

Vanderlyn fell silent. John watched him, frightened of this world, so like the one in which he had been brought up, and yet so alien.

'How far is this house? The safe house?'

'A mile or so.'

'Tell Anna to get ready. I'll drive you there.'

143

CHAPTER EIGHTEEN

Tuesday, 23 October
10.14 p.m.

The safe house was in an apartment block just east of Rock
Creek Park. They drove there in silence, through streets
almost empty of people, although it was just past ten. The
car was stopped once, crossing the creek on Piney Branch
Parkway. A small checkpoint had been set up there by the
regular police. John showed the pass he'd been given to
get him into the Vice President's office the next morning.
Vanderlyn's papers were in order. Anna had been provided
with a fake ID by the professor, identifying her as his
grand-daughter. Under the floorboards of his apartment
he kept a collection of blank identity papers to cover most
eventualities. In the process, little Anna had become a pure
Aryan citizen and a zealous member of KidsKlan.

Once across the creek, they headed left, skirting the
park. There were a few cars, but no pedestrians. Everything seemed soulless, bleak, and dead. The street lights
obliterated the stars, as though they had been placed there
in order to wipe the sky as devoid of spirit as the city
beneath.

Vanderlyn advised John to park about a block from the
street they wanted.

'People see things,' he said. 'They watch, they remember,
they make connections. A car like yours stands out. It's
an appropriate car for someone in your position, it lends

144

credence to your story, but it was a bad choice. You need to look prosperous, not conspicuous. Leave the car here and pick it up later.'

They walked down the deserted footpath, conscious of the patter of their own footsteps and the echoes they raised on every side. A curtain twitched and fell back again. A light was extinguished behind a high window. Somewhere, an unseen door opened and closed.

'Will my parents be at this house, Professor Vanderlyn?' asked Anna. She was walking hand-in-hand with him, quite naturally, as though they really were grandfather and grandchild.

'Not tonight, dear. Maybe not for a little while. We have to find out where they were taken.'

'My aunt Rachel and uncle Ben were arrested by the secret police,' Anna said. 'They never came back.'

'I know,' said Vanderlyn. 'I heard about that.'

'I think they were killed.'

He did not answer her this time, and her remark hung in the air around them like a shroud.

Later, she asked if the people who lived at the safe house were Jewish.

'The couple who own it aren't Jewish, no. Is that a problem?'

She shook her head.

'It's just that we aren't supposed to spend time with people who aren't Jews.'

'Who told you that?'

'Well, there were seven of us at school, and when they said we had to leave, they told us we shouldn't mix with Christian children. And none of the kids in my street will play with me.'

'Well, child, you're mixing with Miles. He may not be much of a Christian, but he's not too particular about what company he keeps.'

Anna laughed; a little, anxious laugh that betrayed the fear underneath.

They stopped at a two-storey house at the corner of a side street cutting diagonally into the park. Vanderlyn pressed the bell and waited. Moments later, a man's voice answered, cracked and indistinct.

'This is Miles,' said Vanderlyn. He'd telephoned earlier, and was expected. A buzzer sounded, and he pushed the street door open.

'I don't think I should come with you,' said John. 'I'm already getting too involved in this.'

Vanderlyn took him by the shoulder.

'It's all right. There's someone I'd like you to meet. You're perfectly safe, believe me.'

Before leaving England, John had been given strict instructions to avoid getting mixed up with local activities. The resistance was there to provide back up and a communications network, that was all. But no-one had told him the correct procedure for a situation like the one in which he now found himself. His instructors were on the other side of the Atlantic; Vanderlyn was two feet away. He shrugged and nodded.

As he followed behind Vanderlyn and Anna, he glanced round at the naked, poorly-lit street. Cars were parked on both sides. A man went past, walking a small dog, his neck muffled against the cold. John turned and went inside.

Vanderlyn made the introductions.

'John, this is Vernon James. Vernon's our quartermaster.'

John raised his eyebrows. The man in front of him was a tall black man dressed in casual clothes, with a dog collar protruding above his sweater.

'You surprised because I'm black or because I'm a reverend?' James asked.

'I didn't think many pastors were involved in the resistance.'

James laughed.

'More than you'd imagine. Mostly they pray and take in

strays, just like I'm doing tonight. But I prefer to get my hands a little dirty. Jesus didn't exactly hold back when he laid into the moneylenders at the Temple. Tough situations call for tough decisions. This is a tough situation. Anyway, I haven't always been a reverend.'

'What were you before?'

'I played piano with a jazz band over in Chicago. Swing mostly. Played with Jimmy Dorsey a few times. Technically, that's my real profession, except nobody playing jazz no more. I consider myself in semi-retirement. Waiting for the good times to roll again. Like a lot of people.'

'So you're not really a pastor?'

'I'm a man of God, or so I'd like to think. I used to preach in church on Sundays, studied in Bible class some nights, took a diploma at Howard University. Now I'm a full-time minister at a Baptist church outside town. Don't God work in mysterious ways?'

John smiled. God and His ways had always puzzled him.

'This is my wife Mabeline,' James continued, introducing John to a slim woman of about thirty.

'And this is Anna,' said Vanderlyn, bringing the child forward.

Vernon stretched out his hand gravely and shook Anna's.

'So this is Anna Rosen. You don't know me, but I'm a friend of your father's. He ever tell you about me?'

She shook her head.

'Well, he told me a lot about his little girl. About how you play a mean fiddle.'

Anna looked discomposed.

'A mean violin,' Vernon corrected himself. 'You bring the instrument with you?'

She shook her head, on the verge of tears.

'Don't worry,' said Mabeline. 'We'll find one for you. You can practise here.'

'You sure you've got enough room for Anna?' asked Vanderlyn.

147

'For a few nights, till we can move her someplace more suitable. The cellar can hold a family. It's too big for Anna on her own. I'd like to get her fixed up with a Jewish family, people who can look after her properly. She looks like a smart kid. I have some ideas. But let's wait till things calm down.'

He turned back to Anna.

'Sweetheart,' he said, 'why don't you and Mabeline go fix us all something to eat? I'd like to talk to the professor. After that, Mabeline can show you where you're going to sleep.'

Anna let herself be led off meekly. She was growing tired, but her fear kept her alert.

The three men retired to Vernon's study, a cluttered space little bigger than the wardroom on the *Torque*. It was littered with books and papers, heaps of old church magazines, hymn books, religious tracts, and stacks of jazz recordings in brown paper covers.

For the next hour they talked about equipment John might require, and debated how best to repair the damage done by Moshe Rosen's arrest. Vernon kept a transmitter in his house, but he was unskilled in its use.

'What about the British embassy?' Vernon asked. 'If you had an emergency, couldn't you use their equipment?'

John shook his head.

'They know nothing about my mission. The ambassador isn't to be trusted.'

The former King Edward, now Duke of Windsor, had been appointed ambassador to Washington not long after his marriage to Wallis Simpson. His pro-Nazi sympathies had never been much concealed, and in America he had shown himself a staunch supporter of the new regime. Churchill desperately wanted to get rid of him, but the Foreign Office reckoned his popularity in America made him more of an asset than a liability, and so he stayed.

'We'll find somebody, don't worry,' said Vanderlyn. 'First, I'd like to find out what happened to Moshe. We both

148

need to know whether or not he was targeted because of your arrival. Now, I think it's time we were on our way.'

'Won't you stay for some food?'

'I have an early start in the morning,' said John. 'At the Vice President's office.'

They made their farewells. Anna had already eaten and been taken to bed in the concealed room in the cellar that served as a refuge for fugitives from the FBIS.

It had grown cold outside. John turned up his collar and started walking back to the car.

CHAPTER NINETEEN

Tuesday, 23 October
11.45 p.m.

David Stephenson had been Vice President now for eight years, eleven months, and fourteen days. Before that he'd been Grand Dragon of the Realm of Indiana, and even now he had the honorary title of Assistant Imperial Wizard. His superior in the Klan, Hiram Evans, probably had more say in David's decisions than the President. If there was such a thing as Klan blood, it ran in David's veins, bright red and certain of its destiny.

He was heavy-set and balding, not likely material for the nation's second-in-command. Small, perturbed eyes glanced out warily from beneath waxen lids, snatching brief glimpses of the world before returning to their patient vigil, like small, translucent animals cradled in skin. For millions of Americans, he was hope incarnated, a living flame to guard against the darkness of poverty and loneliness and distrust, a beacon against the forces of liberalism, Communism, and black assertiveness. For millions of others, he was the darkness in person.

It didn't really matter where they were. The car was its own universe, a warm capsule that moved through the night as a shark moves through unfathomed depths of ocean. David was growing alert. Von Schillendorf was coming to the point at last. The suave lunch guest of that afternoon had not lost his easy manner; but the topic he now pursued was rather more serious than any he'd skated over between courses.

Von Schillendorf had been the Reich's Military Attaché in Washington for the past four years, and during that time he had come to know David Stephenson very well. David had invited him and Leroy Carmichael to a game of golf out at the Fairfax Country Club just outside Alexandria. It had grown dark before they got halfway round. They'd retired to the club house after that, still talking of general matters: politics, and how to treat black slaves, and music, and science.

Carmichael was the President's Special Advisor on Scientific Goals, and widely regarded as the next American eligible for a Nobel Prize. His development of Pauli's exclusion principle had attracted attention both at home and abroad, and over the past few years he had acted as scientific advisor to a host of university and government committees. Stephenson had made him responsible for the general supervision of a project set up by him soon after he became Vice President, and it was in that capacity he now sat in the back of the cadillac exchanging pleasantries with two men he might otherwise never have met.

'David, I think you should know that our work is now finished. The German end of the project is complete.'

Von Schillendorf – a baron, according to the diplomatic handbook – was as sophisticated as Stephenson was vulgar, but underneath, the two men shared more than a taste for casual golf and good cigars. The baron's blood was considered too pure to be mixed with that of any but the highest Teutonic aristocracy; but it was just as red as Stephenson's, and just as certain of its destiny.

'Does this mean we can have your findings? It'll speed things up at this end if we can see how your people have made out.'

Von Schillendorf shook his head.

'That's out of the question, of course. We're willing to share certain items of information, as we've been doing

151

from the start; but it was always agreed that the two sides of the research could only be coordinated once they were both completed. My superiors are growing impatient. Some of their scientific advisors think they may be in a position to bring the entire project to a conclusion without further American involvement. I have to warn you that there is considerable pressure for such a decision. If your teams don't hurry up, you may miss the boat.'

Stephenson snorted. His eyes hooded themselves momentarily, then brightened again.

'We've been in this from the start, Friedrich. You couldn't have got to where you are now without us. We have an agreement.'

'I'm aware of that. But science in the Reich is politically driven. Nobody makes independent decisions. Even the military are subject to political compromise. And I can assure you that pressure to have this completed is coming from very high up.'

'Are you threatening us with a pull-out?'

The baron shook his head. He had fenced with bare sabres in his youth, but this was twice as perilous.

'Personally, I think it would be foolhardy for us to try to go it alone. We need your expertise and your access to the best equipment. It could take us another five years on our own. But we need you to speed things up. A few months could make an enormous difference.'

'But that's impossible.' Carmichael's glasses glinted as they passed a light hanging at a railroad crossing. They'd left the city behind fifteen minutes earlier and were cruising the black fields of Maryland, fanning the cold verges with their passing breath.

'I understood you were well advanced.'

The scientist shook his head.

'Advanced, yes. But it's a hell of a long road. We could ruin everything by rushing it. Science requires patience. It can't be dictated to by political demands.'

'I admire your sentiments,' sniffed the baron, 'but they're

really of no practical use to me, nor, I imagine, to David here. The politicians pay your wages, buy your raw materials, and equip your laboratories. My country is fighting a war, a war into which yours may be drawn any day now. We need this project to be completed. It's just a matter of the will to do it.'

Carmichael's head moved from side to side desperately.

'Will cannot replace knowledge. We need more time, and we need more funds. Operating this project in secrecy puts constraints on us. If you want to speed things up, then you have to go public. Tell the President what's involved, approach the House Scientific Commission for increased funding. I can't promise anything, but it might be possible to complete within a year.'

Stephenson shook his head.

'You know that's impossible. We've kept the President in the dark on this from the beginning. We agreed it was the best policy. He admires Germany and German technology, but he wants to keep American interests wholly independent. If he hears of the project, he'll shut it down.'

'I disagree.' Carmichael was growing vehement. For several years now he'd laboured under the strain of running a project that had to be kept concealed from his real superiors. 'Lindbergh's a reasonable man. He has a passion for science. If he knows the real nature of your work, there's a good chance he'll go along with it, recommend higher funding levels.'

'You don't really know him. If anything happened to him and I became President, then there'd be a real chance. But as long as Charles is in office, the project has to stay hidden.'

'I think I should be the judge of that. To be honest, I've been giving this a lot of thought lately. It's time he was told. Hearing what Baron von Schillendorf's just told us has helped make my mind up. I'm going to speak with President Lindbergh tomorrow. I'll tell him everything, in my capacity as his scientific advisor. He'll listen to me.'

153

Stephenson leaned forward and drew back the glass separating them from the driver.

'Randall, would you pull in here, please?'

They were in a vast emptiness. Blackness hemmed them in on all sides, and when the car slowed down and halted, and Randall switched the engine off, a silence descended that seemed ageless and without limit. The headlights remained lit, projecting a cone of illumination into the night, as though to form a bridge between the tiny world in which they travelled and the formless immensity beyond.

David opened the door beside him.

'Get out,' he said. His voice had lost its veneer of reasonableness. Something stark was revealed, something colder than deep water or thin ice.

'What are you talking about? What's this about?' Carmichael floundered, finding himself suddenly out of his depth, out of his imagination.

'I said "Get out!". Now, do it. Out of the car!'

Long accustomed to obeying masters whose orders were concealed in the garb of politeness, Carmichael was no match for someone used to having his smallest whims obeyed. He slid along the long leather seat and stepped down. The tarmac was hard and gritty. A smell of vegetation rushed into his nostrils, soft and sweet, but unnameable. He thought for a moment that the Vice President was going to leave him here, miles from anywhere, to walk through the night until he reached a farm or was picked up by a passing vehicle. But to his relief he saw Stephenson step out of the car on the other side and close his door. He wanted to talk in private, then.

The Vice President walked to the trunk and opened it. Carmichael waited, thinking he must have papers and perhaps a light to read them with. As Stephenson came round the side of the car, he could see he was carrying something, but he couldn't make out what it was.

'Why do little fucks like you always try to fuck me up?' Stephenson's voice had lost all civilized content. It rasped, it

154

sawed through the darkness, it contained no pity, no hope, no humanity.

'I don't understand. Why are you so upset?'

'You can ask me that? You think you can ask me that? You work for me, and you plan to talk to Lindbergh like some high-school buddy? Gee, Charlie, look what that rude Mr Stephenson's been getting up to?'

'I don't have to speak to Lindbergh, not if it's bugging you.'

'You don't have to, but you will. If you get the chance.'

He was a couple of feet away now, and in the instant before he made his first lunge, Carmichael saw what he held in his hand: a golf club.

The club struck Carmichael across the shins, almost bringing him down with a single blow. But he staggered backwards, raising an arm to fend off a second attack. The club whistled through the air, missing him narrowly, forcing him back, limping and whimpering, all down the length of the car. As he reached the front mudguard, Stephenson moved in closer and swung hard, striking him with the full force of the swing on the left cheekbone, shattering it. Carmichael roared with pain and fell backwards across the front of the car into the beam of the headlights.

Stephenson stepped into the beam after him. He was grim now, and silent, and dedicated to what he had started. He swung the club again, bringing it down hard on Carmichael's upper arm, breaking it clean in two. Carmichael screamed again, but with less strength this time. The club lifted again and came down on his nose, and was lifted, and came down again on his shoulder, and again on his forehead, and he was no longer screaming, but moaning, then grunting, and the club went up and down like a piston now, harder and harder, cracking, breaking, bludgeoning the splintered skull as though it was a watermelon. He went on hitting until Carmichael was no longer Carmichael, no longer even a memory of what Carmichael had been, but a battered, clubbed, ruined object, a mingling of bone and flesh, human only by testimony of the clothing it wore.

He stopped finally, not so much exhausted as bored, and walked back to the trunk, and replaced the club, and shut the lid. Back in the car, he told Randall to drive on. He reversed in order to drive round the thing that had been Carmichael, then drove on as though a pleasure drive had merely been interrupted by a minor obstacle. Von Schillendorf said nothing. He had long ago understood what manner of man the Vice President was. And he had seen worse things in Germany many times. As for Randall, he'd made a career out of discretion. Better a career than a fate like Carmichael's.

Stephenson sat down beside Von Schillendorf.

'I think it can be done,' he said. 'If I become President.'

From *A Child's Cyclopedia of the United States and its Symbols* by Randolph Bergman (Pennsylvania Children's Press, Harrisburg, Pennsylvania, 1939)

What do you think about in the mornings when you go to school and salute the flag? Or when you attend meetings of KidsKlan and recite your Oath of Dedication in front of Old Glory? Do you think about the stars, that stand for the forty-eight states of the Union? Or the stripes, that stand for the original thirteen states? Or do you fix your thoughts on the circle at the centre of the flag, and the burning cross at its heart?

The flag is the symbol of our nation, and the cross at its centre is the symbol of our faith and our trust in the God Who created us and brought our nation into existence. The cross stands in a red circle, to remind us of the blood that was shed in the First Revolution and again in our Second Revolution.

It's a burning cross, because this nation was born in fire and is being reborn in fire again. It's a white cross, because this nation was built by the white race, and because the Kristian faith is God's gift to His own people. And it's a plain cross, to show that America is a Protestant nation, standing up before the other nations and before God to accomplish its mission.

So the flag reminds us of our mission as Americans, as Kristians, and as members of God's chosen race. Remember the words of your Klan oath: 'I dedicate myself to God and my President, to work with my hand and my brain to build on this continent a nation above all others, to keep my blood pure from racial taint, to defend my religion and my race from all who seek to destroy them, and to live a life of purity, truthfulness, and honor in the sight of God and man.'

Why does the cross stand in a circle? Some people say it's a reminder of the days when white settlers rode across the great American plains, bringing law and civilization. They were surrounded on all sides by naked savages, savages armed with bows and arrows and tomahawks – if you've ever spent a Saturday afternoon being entertained by Hopalong Cassidy or the Three Mesquiteers, you'll know what I mean. And you've probably seen a band of settlers move their wagon train into a circle, to make a stand against a horde of whooping redskins.

Today, that circle is all that stands between us and savagery. It's a barrier against the liberals, the Kommunists, the Jews, the blacks, the Katholiks, the krooks, the bootleggers, the drug-dealers, the jazz-lovers, the fornicators, the panhandlers, the Freemasons, the racketeers, the dope-fiends, the bloodsuckers, the degenerate painters, the dirty-minded writers, the Negro krooners, the hucksters, the Socialists, the organized Laborites, the new-dealers, the gangsters, the sodomites, the perverts, the gutter journalists, the nigger-loving, Jew-loving, Katholik-loving Quakers and Unitarians, the pacifists, the pimps, the whores, the Ivy League intellectuals – all those legions of whooping, war-painted wild men who want to drag us out of our wagons and into the wilderness.

Next time you salute the flag, think of that circle and how safe you feel inside it. The circle is the Aryan Alliance of America. The cross is the Ku Klux Klan. As long as they are there, we will all be safe from barbarism.

PART 6

Long Live the King

CHAPTER TWENTY

Wednesday, 24 October

John woke early the following morning with a splitting headache. He had not slept well, anxious both about the events of the previous evening and his coming day in Stephenson's office. It was also worrying him that he'd soon have to start looking for a place to live: he couldn't stay more than a day or two longer as Vanderlyn's guest, nor would it be wise to do so.

While he showered and dressed, he listened to the radio. There was light music at first, then a diatribe by some Klan big-wig, directed against speculators and profiteers. Straightening his tie in the mirror, John glanced at his wristwatch. It was five past seven. The diatribe on the radio had been replaced by a cookery programme. A woman with a mid-west accent was going through a recipe for cherry pie. John listened idly, vaguely wondering what had happened to the seven o'clock news bulletin.

He was about to switch off the radio and go down to breakfast when he pulled up short. The woman on the radio had got to the end of her recipe and started summing up. What she said didn't make any sense.

'You'll find plenty of fresh cherries in the shops over the next month or so. Remember, the bigger and the blacker, the better. Good shopping and good cooking. I'll be back next week with another seasonal recipe, this time for strawberry shortbread.'

Cherries weren't around in October. Nor were strawberries. The piece must have been a recording. But why hadn't the station just held it over till next summer? John sensed something was wrong. The regular news bulletin was being held back and the gap hastily plugged with material snatched at random from the shelves. A recording of Mozart's string quartet in G minor had just begun.

He twiddled the knob that controlled the tuning, switching from station to station in the hope of finding news, but most stations were broadcasting music, and several had fallen silent. Something strange was going on, of that he was certain. No doubt he'd find out when he got to the office. He slipped on his jacket and made to switch off the radio again. But his hand froze halfway to the set as the music was interrupted by the voice of a male announcer.

'We interrupt this recital to bring you an unscheduled news bulletin. Please stay tuned to your set.'

There was a profound silence, then crackling that lasted about half a minute. It was replaced by solemn music that John did not recognize. But the mood of the music made it clear that the coming bulletin was likely to be bad news. He wondered if it had happened at last, if America had entered the war alongside Germany. It would be ironic if true, for the whole purpose of his mission was to prevent that happening.

A couple of minutes passed like this. John moved the needle along the dial again, but now every station was playing music of a similar kind, slow and sombre. He returned to NBC.

Moments later, the music stopped. There was a brief silence, then the voice of another male announcer, his voice solemn and unsteady.

'This is Harold Lamont of NBC News. It is with the greatest sadness that I have to tell you that our beloved President, Charles Augustus Lindbergh, was shot and killed this morning. Two gunmen, as yet unidentified, entered the President's bedroom a few minutes after five o'clock, and shot both him and his wife at point-blank range. The couple were declared dead by the President's personal physician at fifteen-minutes-past-five.

'The gunmen were encountered by Marine guards as they attempted to make their escape. When they refused to drop their weapons, a gunfight followed in which both were fatally injured. Details of their identity and possible motives are expected shortly. In the meantime, J Edgar Hoover, Director of the FBIS, has called for calm, promising his agency will leave no stone unturned in the hunt to discover whether the gunmen acted alone or as part of a wider conspiracy.

'Vice President David Stephenson was sworn in as the thirty-third President of the United States ten minutes ago. He is expected to address the nation within the hour.

'Just a minute . . .'

There was a long pause. John stood staring at the radio, barely able to believe what he had just heard. Was someone playing an elaborate game? Was this about to be announced to the public as a British plot, with himself as the fall guy? He'd come to America with the express intention of preventing Stephenson taking over the presidency: had the Vice President been one step ahead of him all along?

The radio burst into life again.

'We've just received that information I promised you earlier. The gunmen who were shot in the White House this morning as they fled from the President's bedroom have now been positively identified. They were Daniel Horowitz, aged twenty-seven, of Anne Arundel county, Maryland,

and Moshe Rosen, aged thirty-two, of Washington. Both were Hebrews and are believed to have had close connections with Jewish underground circles. An FBIS spokesman has informed us that further arrests are thought to be imminent.

'Now over to Walter Cronkite in Washington.'

CHAPTER TWENTY-ONE

America lost one President and gained another. The king is dead, long live the king. The transition from one to the next took place with remarkable ease. Outwardly, little changed. David Stephenson already had everything and everybody he needed in place, as though he'd been planning this moment for a long time. With few exceptions, Lindbergh's personal staff were given their marching orders. Stephenson's bright young men stepped out at last upon their stage. John Ridgeforth found himself a presidential advisor without having spent a single moment working with a Vice President.

On the day of the assassination, he went straight to Vanderlyn's apartment. The professor had not yet left for his classes – which would, in any case, be suspended.

'Miles, you've got to set up radio contact for me. I need fresh instructions.'

Vanderlyn shook his head.

'Can't be done. This is the excuse they've been waiting for. The FBIS will be picking people up off every street corner right this minute. Anyone with the slightest black mark against his name will be slammed in a cell or hauled off to a camp. We've just got to lie low till it passes.'

'You don't understand. I can't reach a decision on my own. I was sent here to kill Stephenson, to stop him doing what he's just done. Now he's President, it's only a matter of time before he declares war on the side of Germany. I have to know what I'm expected to do.'

Vanderlyn looked at John, his expression a mixture of horror and compassion.

'I'd rather you hadn't told me that. I want to know as little about your mission as possible. If you want my advice, sit tight till the situation calms down. Then I'll have you put in touch with London.'

John would not be put off.

'I need a radio. Just tell me where the nearest one is. I can operate it myself.'

Vanderlyn remained adamant.

'You're here with our agreement, not at our request. What you've already told me makes me regret our decision to collaborate with London at all. If you use one of our radios, you'll be putting God knows how many lives at risk. It's out of the question.'

'Your lives are at risk already. I didn't ask any of you to join the resistance. All I'm asking is that you behave like one. It's precisely because the situation has become so dangerous that I need fresh orders. It could save more than just your lives.'

'You are aware, aren't you, that one of the men shot in the White House was Moshe Rosen, the radio operator who was handling communications with your London control?'

'Yes, of course I am. The man they picked up last night. Hours before he turned up in Lindbergh's bedroom. If he ever did.'

'And what do you make of that?'

'It's pretty obvious. A set up.'

'Precisely.' Vanderlyn's attention was already shifting. He'd been thinking about the implications of Rosen's death ever since it was announced. 'A set up for what?'

John had been too preoccupied with his own situation until now to give the matter much thought. Now it seemed transparent.

'To pin the blame on the resistance.'

Vanderlyn shook his head.

'Perhaps. But the other alleged assassin was Jewish as well. It's more likely they want to blame the Jews. I don't like to think what's going to happen as a result.'

He paused. John noticed for the first time the ticking of an antique clock on the wall. The sound made him nervous, as though time was being speeded up.

'Very well,' said Vanderlyn. 'Give me time to think about this. If it can be done safely, we'll put you in touch with London.'

CHAPTER TWENTY-TWO

Monday, 29 October

Five days later, Charles Lindbergh and his wife were buried with great pomp and circumstance in Arlington cemetery. From across the country, mourners poured into the capital. Their grief was real enough, but the new administration milked it for all it was worth. Motor buses ferried wet-eyed Klansmen in from every state, and the funeral procession was dominated by column upon column of white-robed, hooded figures, stretching like a great snow-covered beast through the city's streets.

Stark against the robes of the Klan were the black uniforms of high-ranking German officials, who took precedence among the foreign guests. They included Hermann Goering, Hitler's deputy Rudolf Hess, foreign minister Von Ribbentrop, Heinrich Himmler, and a scattering of generals. A tacit agreement had been reached between Germany and Britain that neither side would attack the aircraft carrying their delegations to the funeral. Nevertheless, both Churchill and Hitler had deemed it prudent to stay at home.

The German ambassador, Count Julius von Drexler, formed a separate group at the rear with his staff, among whom John, watching from the sidewalk, recognized Baron von Schillendorf, the man he'd had lunch with the day he'd first met Laura.

*   *   *

The days leading up to the funeral were uncannily quiet. Vanderlyn had been mistaken. There were few arrests, no members of the resistance were picked up, and only a handful of Jews were killed or beaten up around the country. The Klan was biding its time. Reaction to the assassination was being orchestrated very carefully, and from the highest levels.

A diplomatic reception in the White House followed the funeral. John, who suddenly found that he ranked as a close relation of the First Lady, was invited. He would have preferred to stay away, but a refusal might have been misinterpreted. Laura and he had not met since their lunch together, and it was time they behaved like long-separated cousins again.

Ordinarily, the entire reception would have been held in the East Room, but the war in Europe dictated otherwise. No-one wanted to see the visiting belligerents glaring at one another from opposite ends of one room. The American party was divided between it and the smaller Oval Room, while the new President and his wife paid visits to each in turn, paying lip service to the concept of political neutrality. Had anyone been keeping a record, it would have been apparent that David Stephenson spent considerably longer in the East Room with the German delegation than with their British counterparts down the corridor.

John arrived just as Stephenson and Laura were progressing back to the East Room. Laura smiled and kissed him fondly on the cheek, but she seemed tense, and he sensed she was bothered about something.

'I have to speak to you,' she whispered as she leaned close. 'Later.'

Her nearness confused him, implying as it did an intimacy that had no basis in reality. And yet she was every bit as real as the agitation he felt on seeing her.

The President stuck out a hand and grabbed John's in a crushing grip.

'John, I'm sorry we haven't had a chance to talk properly. How are you settling in?'

'Fine. Everyone's been really helpful. Of course, these aren't ideal circumstances . . .'

'Tell me about it. But you're more essential to me than ever. They fix you up with an apartment yet?'

John nodded.

'Right away. On 16th Street. Just past the National Geographic headquarters. It's exactly what I'd have looked for.'

Stephenson looked pleased. He liked his boys to be happy. He lowered his voice.

'Got a woman to take back there yet, son?'

John reddened and smiled weakly.

'No, sir. Too much to do.'

'Well, don't waste time. Man's only young once.' He paused, conscious of his new-found responsibilities. 'John, you'll forgive us if we get back to our guests. Some very important people here tonight. Lot of hands to shake.'

The presidential couple were whisked away into the vast room, and John felt himself drawn in after them. He'd scarcely got through the door when he felt a hand grasp his upper arm. He swung round. Baron von Schillendorf was standing beside him. A tall man, he towered above John, a broad smile on his face.

'Mr Ridgeforth, how delightful to meet you again. A shame it has to be under such sad circumstances. Come, I must introduce you to some old friends.'

The old friends were standing in a group a little apart from everyone else. They had already been introduced to the President, and most of them would be seeing him again the next day. John's heart sank as he realized who they were.

'Herr Himmler, I'd like to introduce you to a young friend of mine, John Ridgeforth. John is the cousin of Mrs Stephenson, the wife of the new President.'

Himmler turned, clicking his heels, and for a moment

John thought he was about to greet him with the *Hitlergrüss*, but instead he shook hands, once, without warmth.

'Sorry,' he said, 'but my English is not so good.'

'*Es macht nichts,*' answered John. '*Ich spreche ein bisschen Deutsch.*'

Himmler's eyebrows went up a fraction.

'How interesting. An American who speaks good German. What did you say your name was?'

'Ridgeforth.'

'Your mother is German?'

John shook his head.

'No, I learned German at college. I wanted to study your country's legal system.'

The baron interrupted.

'Mr Ridgeforth is an eminent lawyer. He is the President's advisor on – what is it?'

'Administrative law.'

Himmler nodded.

'And your study of our legal system. Was this historical?'

John shook his head.

'Only partly. I made a comparison of the judiciary under the Weimar Republic and under the present system.'

'And what did you conclude?'

'That the new system is much more . . .' John paused. The temptation to speak the truth was almost irresistible. 'Efficient,' he said.

From behind steel-rimmed spectacles, Himmler gazed at him without blinking. With his weak chin and round, hamster-like cheeks, he seemed at first glance an insignificant man, but close up there was something profoundly unsettling about him. John felt himself stripped and subjected to intense scrutiny.

'Will you excuse me for a moment, Mr Ridgeforth?' The SS chief slipped away, only to return moments later escorting Hans Geiger.

'Mr Ridgeforth, I'd like you to meet a colleague of mine.

Herr Geiger is the Police Attaché at our embassy here. He has a very great interest in legal matters.'

John took Geiger's outstretched hand.

'Nice to meet you, Herr Geiger.'

'Likewise. I've heard excellent things about you.'

The conversation moved on to a discussion of how America and Germany could help each other in developing an international system based on a strict implementation of law and order. John, who had formed a clear picture of the National Socialist concept of justice in the past few years, did his best to discuss the issues without giving away his true feelings.

They had just started on theories about how best to solve the Jewish problem when John sensed a shift in the atmosphere. Several eyes turned to the door. John twisted and saw Laura standing by the entrance, arm-in-arm with a much older man. A little girl with blonde hair tied up in a huge ribbon held her by the other hand. The President had just left. Laura was looking in his direction, and when he caught her eye she smiled.

'Excuse me, gentlemen,' John said, 'but I think Mrs Stephenson would like to have a word with me.'

'Of course.' Himmler, Geiger, and the baron all shook him warmly by the hand.

'I'd like to speak again sometime,' said Geiger. 'Perhaps you can get in touch. This is my personal number.' He handed John a card with his name and a telephone number printed on it. John pocketed it with a little bow and made his departure.

Laura was still waiting by the door. She looked more nervous than before. He was about to say something, but she anticipated him.

'John, it's good to see you again. David's just gone back to the Oval Room. All this to-ing and fro-ing's getting to be a terrible bore.'

She paused, as though unsure how to continue. He started to speak again, but she broke in once more.

'John, this is my daughter Shirley. I remember you asking about her a while back.' She bent down and whispered to the child. Shirley smiled and put out her hand.

'I'm pleased to meet you, John.'

She didn't simper and she didn't lisp, and John thought her a perfect miniature of her mother.

'And I'm delighted to meet you,' he said, taking her hand and shaking it gravely.

'You know they shot the President, don't you?' Shirley asked.

'I'd heard that, yes. It's a terrible thing.'

'But they won't shoot my Daddy, will they?'

John felt himself go cold inside, but somehow he managed to get out a strenuous denial of the very possibility.

Laura drew his attention. She laid one hand on the older man's arm.

'John, you'll have to forgive me. I'd have introduced you before, but there wasn't a chance. This is my father, Norman Cordell. I've just been telling him all about you.'

CHAPTER TWENTY-THREE

The Sheriff's Office
Halifax
North Carolina
Monday, 29 October
7.10 p.m.

'Harkins! You there?'

Jim Harkins sighed and pushed back his chair. What did the old man want now? He went to the door and stuck his head inside the main office.

'Yes, sir.'

'Well, get your butt in here and close the fucking door behind you.'

Harkins shifted into the servant-master routine he adopted when Scarfe was in a swearing mood. The old man had been elected sheriff of Halifax county two years ago. It made no sense, but what the hell did these days? Scarfe was seventy years old, and it seemed he'd learned nothing else in life except how to order other folks around. Some people thought that made him the right man for the job. Jim Harkins thought it made him a fool. He stepped into the office and let the door close behind him of its own accord.

'You wanted me for something, sir.'

'Hell, I wouldn't have called you if I hadn't wanted you. You ever hear tell of a man called Loomis?'

Jim pushed out his lower lip and shook his head.

174

'Don't recall anyone of that name, no, sir.'

'Well, he seems to know you. Big shot. Works for the FBIS up in DC. Says you helped him with a case once.'

Jim thought for a moment, then his expression cleared.

'Loomis. Yes, I recollect him now. Virginian. Dirt-farmer who made good. I remember him.'

'Got a memo from him here. Well, sit down, boy. You're behaving like some girl taking dictation. This man Loomis wants to know did anything out of the ordinary happen in Halifax county night of the twenty-second October.'

'What night of the week was that?'

'Says here it was a Monday.'

'I know. Night the new curfew came into force.'

'Shit. I should have known. That was the night we hung those niggers down on the Freemont farm. You remember?'

Jim managed a smile. This was the sort of thing you didn't argue about, not these days. Jim had never joined the Klan, but he'd kept his nose clean by saying as little as possible and by being a good policeman, maybe the only good one in the county. He resented men like Scarfe. The sheriff knew next to nothing about police work, but he'd been the county Klan's choice for the post, so that was that. It was something Jim had to live with.

'That was the night Pete Slocum got killed. I guess that qualified as out of the ordinary.'

Scarfe looked put out.

'Guess it does,' he said. 'Can't be what this Loomis is after, though. We sorted that out, didn't we?'

Jim gave a wry smile. Lowell Scarfe's idea of sorting things out was to grab the nearest black man and string him up on the most convenient tree. They'd picked up three young blacks the night after they found Pete's body in the field next to his abandoned car. Scarfe had kept them in the county jail at Halifax for a couple of hours, questioned them in his quietly threatening way, sent in Joe Swaggart to beat them up some, and gone in again.

By then they'd have confessed to raping their mothers and sisters if he'd told them that's what they'd done.

There'd been a large mob outside the jail by then, most of them in white hoods, just like the old days. Not a lynch mob, though. There was no need for lynch mobs these days. Stringing up niggers was all taken care of by due process, according to the law. Scarfe had handed the boys over to the crowd one at a time, and they'd done the rest. The youngest had been twelve, the oldest fifteen. Jim had said nothing. But he'd forgotten nothing either.

'Those boys didn't kill Pete Slocum and you know it,' he said. 'Hanging them may have satisfied the folks out there, but this Mr Loomis won't be put off so easily. The truth is, we've got an unsolved crime on our hands. I reckon he should know about it.'

Scarfe snorted and turned his face away.

'Like hell he should! That case is closed, and don't you forget it. All the paperwork's been done, it's signed, sealed, and over. Bring a thing like that up with the FBIS and you can't tell where it's going to end. You want trouble round here, son?'

Jim shook his head, but he knew trouble was coming whether Lowell Scarfe liked it or not. Jim had been one of the first at the crime scene, he knew what they'd found. What he'd told Scarfe was true: those kids hadn't killed Pete Slocum. His neck had been broken clean through, by somebody who knew what they were about, or so it had looked. Nothing had been stolen, not even the cigarettes Pete had been carrying in his vest pocket. The kids they'd arrested had been petty thieves at worst, and none of them had possessed either the strength or the skill to snap a big man's neck like that.

Jim knew a couple of other things, things he hadn't passed on to his boss, because he knew Scarfe wouldn't understand what to make of them. But he reckoned Loomis might be interested. And he started wondering whether there might not be a chance of a job up there in Washington.

176

He was one hell of a good policeman, and he was being wasted down here. It might be a wrench for May-Ellen, but it would get him out of the Halifax county sheriff's office and out of sight and hearing of Lowell Scarfe.

The autopsy report on Pete Slocum had suggested a time of death that coincided with the hangings back up the road. Pete had been there, directing traffic and keeping an eye on things, to see nobody got hurt that wasn't supposed to get hurt, and Jim had made a point of interviewing anybody he could find who'd been in the field at the Freemont farm that night.

People had been happy to come forward, knowing a policeman had been killed. Quite a few had seen Pete, and some had spoken with him. They'd nothing unusual to report. The hangings had gone off smoothly, there'd been no trouble in the crowd, Pete had laughed and joked with his friends. Nothing to give a lead of any kind.

And then Jim had struck lucky. He'd been talking about the killing down in Bernie's Bar with Zach Hutchins. Zach and Jim had been buddies in high school, and they still downed a few glasses together at weekends. They'd married girls from the same year, dated them together. Every summer they still had a barbecue, all four of them, and reminisced about old times. Old Zach ran a barber's shop in town, but in his spare time he was a high flyer with the Klan. He knew a lot of people in Halifax county, and Pete liked to chew the fat with him, because he had the lowdown on just about anything and anybody.

Zach had been at the hangings. He still called them lynchings, said he liked the word, it made him feel nostalgic, gave him a warm feeling in his groin. No need to make a secret of it, watching somebody dancing at the end of a rope gave him a high, made him feel like he still had ten lives to live.

'You see Pete Slocum up there?'

'Sure I did. Couple of times. Passed the time of day. I liked Pete, he was one of the best.'

177

'See anything unusual?'

'What sort of thing?'

'You tell me.'

Zach stared into his whiskey glass. He seemed to be thinking something over. Jim didn't push him, he knew there was no point. If Zach meant to speak, he'd speak, if he didn't, nothing on earth would persuade him. By and by, Zach seemed to make his mind up. He lifted the glass and drained it in a single swallow; it had been all but full. He pushed it across the counter to Bernie, who refilled it without being asked.

'May be nothing at all, Jim; may be nothing at all. But Pete was a good man. You know he was seeing Betty Pearce up by Hollister. Pretty girl. Reckon they might have got married. Crying shame a man can't live his life without some niggers come along and kill him for the hell of it.'

'You reckon the niggers killed him?'

Zach took a mouthful of whiskey and let it massage his gums.

'You asking me? Your police force arrested them.'

'Zach, what did you see? Or did somebody tell you something? I've got to know. If the niggers didn't kill Pete Slocum, the killer's still out there.'

'You think they killed him, Jim?'

Jim did not answer, and Zach took his silence for no.

'I know I can trust you, Jim. I can, can't I?'

'Depends what you mean, Zach. If it leads to a court case, if it puts Pete's killer on the stand, it'll have to come out.'

Zach took another mouthful of whiskey. This time he swallowed it straight down.

'Let's say I had this from a friend. Real close friend. Seems he was the last person to see Pete Slocum alive. 'Cept for his killer. This friend went to see the hangings with a woman, a woman who isn't his wife, someone he's been seeing a lot of this past month or two. You following me, Jim?'

Jim nodded. He thought of Zach's wife, Peggy, sitting at home. She'd always wanted kids, but somehow they hadn't come along. Peggy had grown a little fat and a little dull and a little sad. Jim felt sorry for her: if this came to court, it would destroy her. He wondered if justice had to mean cruelty. The way he saw things, someone always got hurt in his line of business, and it wasn't always the guilty party.

'They didn't go up to the field in the end. Got kind of taken up with one another back down there in their car. Stayed there with the lights out when everybody else had gone up. Pete was still down there by the gate, keeping an eye on things. My friend says he saw a car drive up and pull in. Funny kind of car, not the sort you see round these parts. Out-of-state license plates.'

'You . . . your friend get the number?'

'Hell, no. He was kind of . . . involved with other things. Reckons a man got out of the car, though.'

'Black man?'

'In a car like that? No, this was a white man. Young man, about thirty. He went up to the field. Pete followed him. Stayed a while, then came back to the road, looking like he was in a kind of hurry. Got into his car and drove off. Next thing I saw . . . my friend saw was Pete coming through the gate and moving across to his patrol car, then taking off after the other man. From what I hear, he didn't go too far. Stopped a bit down the road.'

'That's right. Mile or so. What sort of car was this man driving?'

'Duesenberg. Can't tell you the model.'

'And you say it had out-of-state plates? You remember which state?'

'Sure. Massachusetts. Long way to come for a hanging.'

The other thing Jim knew he'd discovered for himself. Back at the crime scene, he'd scoured the area round Pete's body and up and down the road for about two-hundred yards in either direction, then through and under the car. He'd been looking for clues, but there'd been nothing. They'd swept the car for prints, but Jim hadn't expected much. One thing he did find out later, though – there were no prints belonging to any of the three hanged black boys anywhere on Pete's cruiser.

Just as he and the others had been about to pack up and leave, he'd pointed to a patch on the ground, a couple of feet from the car. He'd noticed it earlier.

'What the hell's that?'

Johnson, the runty little deputy from Heathsville, who'd been first on the scene, gave a shrug.

'Looks like somebody threw up.' He bent down, sniffed, and pulled back. 'Shit, they sure did.'

Jim had seen the significance of the pool of vomit right away.

'Get it scooped up and have Sam send it over to the lab in Raleigh.'

'Aw, hell, do I have to?'

Jim had flung a large specimen bag at him and told him to get on with it.

'Tell them to send their report to me personally,' he'd said before leaving.

The report had taken almost a week to get to him, and by then they'd hanged the blacks and closed the case. Pete was in his grave, the kids were in theirs, Halifax county had four more grieving families. But Jim had been troubled all the same. The report hadn't made a lot of sense. But it sure as hell fitted Loomis's requirement for something 'out of the ordinary'.

According to the lab, whoever had thrown up on that spot had eaten a meal about three hours earlier. Not much of a meal – some corned beef, peas, potatoes, and stewed apple, all of it from cans. In itself, that wasn't odd. But the meal had been washed down with something less common. Ersatz coffee, the sort that was made from acorns. As far as Jim knew, that sort of thing wasn't even on sale anywhere in the United States. The only place you'd be likely to find it would be Europe, where they had a war going on.

Whoever had killed Pete Slocum had either flown on a magic carpet straight from England or France or one of those places, or he'd been on board a ship a few hours before the crime. One way or another, Jim knew he had something of interest for Larry Loomis.

CHAPTER TWENTY-FOUR

Norman Cordell took John's hand and shook it enthusiastically.

'Pleasure to meet you, John. Laura's been telling me all about you. You're doing a great job.'

Grey-faced, Laura broke in.

'I thought it was best to let Father into the secret about the security angle. How people are supposed to think you're my cousin . . .'

John suppressed a nervous swallow. He wished he knew just what she *had* told her father. Norman Cordell had a reputation as a sharp thinker. He was the last person in the world John had wanted to see.

'Are you planning to stay in Washington long, sir?' he asked.

Cordell shook his head.

'Just came down for the funeral. I liked Charles Lindbergh. He was a good man, a good American. He and I had some fine times together. But I've got to get back to my desk. I'm leaving after lunch tomorrow. This war in Europe's more than doubled my workload.' He paused, glancing at the German delegation opposite, then leaned closer to John. 'What do you think, John? Will David take us in alongside those guys? Bring the whole shooting match to a conclusion? He say anything about that to you?'

John sensed he was being pumped for privileged information. He wished he knew the answer himself.

'No, sir, not a word. Things have been a bit hectic here.'

Cordell nodded.

'You're right. David must have a lot on his mind. I'll see what I can get out of him tomorrow at lunch. I believe you're going to be there too. Just a small affair, I understand, just family.'

He broke into a broad smile, as though sharing an old joke. John smiled back with as much animation as he could muster. The thought of a family lunch made him feel physically ill. Whatever story Laura had concocted for her father's benefit, it would hardly hold up under such conditions.

They chatted a little longer, then Cordell suggested that Laura introduce him to some of the high-ranking Germans.

'I particularly want to meet this Himmler character. They say he's built one hell of a power base for himself. I think he and I could do business.'

'I'd be careful,' said John. 'I'm not sure he can be trusted.'

'Believe me, son, if you'd been in business as long as I have, you'd know nobody can be trusted. But war's good for business, and what's good for business is good for America. You agree?'

John nodded sickly. He'd heard that Cordell had plans to ship black Americans to Europe as slave labour.

Shirley said goodnight. She'd have to go to bed soon. John bent down to kiss her. He'd expected someone spoiled and precious, and found instead a good-natured little girl who made no demands on those around her. She kissed her mother and grandfather, and an aide took her away, her tiny figure reflected in mirrors and the sharp crystal drops of massive chandeliers.

Laura watched her go, then turned and kissed John on both cheeks. Cordell shook hands again and followed his daughter to the other side of the room. As she left, she looked round at John, and he read panic in her eyes. Panic and something else. She'd said she wanted to speak with him later, but he could not see how there would be an opportunity.

He found himself suddenly at a loss, in a room full of people he did not know. Offered another glass of champagne, he declined, deciding it was scarcely worth his staying any longer. He was tired, and he had a lot of thinking to do. He slipped through a door in the west wall, and made his way back down to the basement. Moments later, he was back outside. He had come without a coat, and the sudden cold seized at his lungs. Shivering, he started to walk back to his apartment. The sky above had cleared, and stars were fighting for space within the swathe of darkness over him. As he passed through Lafayette Square, music came from an open window somewhere, sad music that matched his mood and the mood of the city.

At the corner with K Street, a woman in a red coat leaned against the wall. She smiled as he passed, and he noticed the desperation in her face. It reminded him of Laura's panic, of the sadness he had seen in her eyes on their first meeting. He paused, and the woman took it as a signal to move towards him.

'Cold night,' she said. 'Too cold to be walking about like that.' She spoke with a foreign accent, as though not long arrived from Europe. From the light of a nearby streetlamp he observed that her face was pale. She was young, somewhere between twenty and twenty-five, but her eyes seemed much, much older.

He nodded politely, too wrapped up in his own thoughts even to think of taking up her veiled offer. It was not comfort he wanted, or sex, or a mockery of love. What he sought was self-knowledge of some kind, and he knew she could never give him that. As he walked away from her, he saw her slump, all animation gone in a single instant. A few yards further on, he noticed a man skulking in the shadows of a shop doorway. Not a pimp, he thought, but a police agent engaged in some sordid game of entrapment.

Washington was a city of traps, he told himself, and very soon he would fall into one of them.

His apartment was comfortable, but bleak. He had preferred his bunk on board the submarine. At least there'd been other people. He listened to the radio for a while, then undressed and went to bed. It was just after ten.

He must have slept, for he became conscious of a jangling sound, and when he looked at his watch it read half past eleven. Someone was ringing the door bell. His pistol lay in the drawer of the bedside table. He took it out and slipped it into the pocket of his pyjamas.

'Who's there?' He pressed a switch and spoke into a little grille near the door. It crackled in response.

'John? It's me, Laura. Can I come up? I've got to speak to you.'

'Laura? What the hell are you doing here? You'll be . . .'

'I can't hang about down here. I'll be recognized.'

He pressed the button that operated the lock mechanism on the street door. His apartment was on the fourth floor. Half a minute later, he heard the sound of the elevator door as it opened and closed. He slipped on a dressing gown, then rather than wait, he opened the door and stepped into the corridor.

He watched her come towards him, her feet silent on the thick carpet, like a figure in a mirage or a dream. She was wearing the same dress he'd seen on her earlier, with a light coat thrown over it, still unbuttoned. He wondered what she'd done with her watchers and her bodyguards.

She reached him, and he thought for a moment she would kiss him on the cheeks again, but instead she swept past to the door of his apartment.

'I want to talk,' she said. The softness had left her voice and been replaced by something resembling steel. He realized he hadn't begun to understand just who or what Laura Stephenson was.

He followed her inside and closed the door. In the living-room she stopped and turned to face him. Her face was cold, and her eyes were no longer sad or panicky, but filled with barely controlled rage. He scarcely recognized her.

'All right,' she said, 'suppose you tell me exactly what the hell is going on. What do you think I am, some sort of moron?'

He lifted a hand and made to approach her, as though he could calm her down by gesture or mere intent.

'No, just stay where you are,' she snapped, and he stopped dead in his tracks.

'You've got the better of me,' he said. 'I don't know what you're talking about. You know what's going on. Who I am, where I've come from. I've kept nothing from you.'

'Like hell you haven't. I only know what people have told me, and I don't think very much of it is the truth. I don't have much time before somebody notices I'm missing, so suppose you make it quick. I'll ask a simple question, and I'd appreciate it if you gave me a simple answer. You were sent here to kill Charles Lindbergh. Is that right?'

He looked at her, bewildered.

'Lindbergh? Why the hell would you think that?'

'Why wouldn't I? Are you going to tell me this is all just a coincidence? A secret agent arrives on a submarine from England, he makes contact with the Vice President's wife, and a few days later the President of the United States is gunned down in cold blood. Some coincidence. So who's next? David? Me? Shirley?'

She had started to grow hysterical.

'Calm down,' he said.

'I won't calm down. This is my family I'm talking about. This is my life. Do you have any idea what's going on at this moment? Do you think, just because there haven't been any arrests, that David has forgotten about Charles Lindbergh's killing? They're going to kill a lot of people in revenge, John, there are going to be massacres up and down this country. And I just happen to be involved with the murderer. How do you think that makes me feel?'

186

'Laura, you're getting this all wrong. Why don't you just sit down and listen to me?'

'Give me one good reason why I should do that. You took advantage of me, you put my life in danger. Do you know what they'll do to me if they find out I've helped you?'

'You're married to the President. They won't touch you.'

'Which planet are you from? David will kill me. But first he'll kill Shirley, then my father. Then he'll send someone to Switzerland to kill my mother. And that will just be the start. Don't you understand anything about this country, about the people who are running it? Do you know anything about David Stephenson? He'll wipe out my family and then he'll kill my friends, anyone I've ever known from the age of two, anyone who ever said hello to me in the street. You don't know him, you don't know what he's capable of.'

'Laura, you're getting this out of proportion . . .'

'You think so? You think I don't know the man I've been married to all these years, what he can and cannot do? He's President now, there's nothing and nobody to stand in his way any longer.'

'Keep your voice down. If anybody finds you here . . .'

'I want you to leave. Leave Washington tonight. I don't care where you go. Canada, Mexico – it's up to you.'

He strode up to her, genuinely frightened someone was going to come and investigate the shouting. For a moment, he thought of slapping her, just to quieten her, but it was not in his character to do it. He half raised his hand, then dropped it again. Perhaps it was that gesture, perhaps the look of despair on his face, but something got through to her. She grew quiet and, looking round, found a chair to sit down on.

'Suppose you listen to me for five minutes instead,' he said. 'I agree we have a problem, but we aren't going to solve it by shouting or by my skipping out of Washington.'

He sat down facing her.

'Okay,' he said, 'what did you think I came here for? When you agreed to help, that is.'

'I thought you wanted papers, secret documents. I'd give anything to see this government put out of action, so I agreed to do what I could.'

'Which put your life at risk as much as this.'

She shook her head vehemently.

'Not like this. This is different. If I'd been found helping you steal a few papers, David could have handled it. There was a risk, but not too great. This is different. This is like being in a hurricane. Not even David can protect me from what's going to happen.'

Suddenly, her poise gave way. Her face crumpled and she bent forwards in her seat, like a scared child hunching herself against some expected blow. She began crying with deep, convulsive sobs. He watched her for a while, at a loss what to do to help.

'Laura,' he said finally, 'you have to believe me. I had nothing to do with Charles Lindbergh's assassination. If you want to know the truth, I did come here to kill someone. That's still my mission. But my target wasn't Lindbergh. I told Miles Vanderlyn that because it fitted in with his plans. But I was sent to kill someone else. You have to believe it, because if you don't you're going to get us both killed. And, yes, very probably the rest of your family as well.'

Slowly, her sobbing subsided. She looked up at him, her eyes red, her cheeks puffy.

'Who did you . . . ? Who were you sent to kill?'

She had guessed already, he knew that. There was no point in pretending any longer.

'David Stephenson,' he said. 'To stop him becoming President. To prevent him signing a pact with Germany and coming into the war against the Allies.'

She nodded, numb with fear and understanding.

'Don't you see?' he said, 'that's why I couldn't have been involved in the Lindbergh assassination. As long as Charles

Lindbergh was President, he would have kept America out of the war. That alone was an enormous help to Britain. Churchill knew he would never fight with us, but it didn't matter as long as he didn't go in against us. Your husband was the real threat. And now he's in the White House.'

She remained silent for a long time, and he said nothing, letting her think it through, letting the truth take hold.

'I don't understand,' she said after a while. 'The men who killed Charles. They were . . . One belonged to the resistance, the one called Rosen. The other was a Jew who'd escaped from a concentration camp. Why would they kill Lindbergh?'

'I don't think they did. In fact, I'm sure they had nothing to do with it.'

'Sure? How can you be sure?'

He told her what he knew about Rosen. She listened, frowning. What he said made no sense. But he'd been with the little girl, Rosen's daughter, he'd heard her story at first hand.

'Do you believe me?' he asked.

She hesitated for only a few seconds, then nodded.

'But if it wasn't the resistance, and if you weren't involved, then who . . . ?'

'It's not hard to guess. Who had the most to gain?'

'You mean . . . David?'

'David, yes, certainly. But I don't think he'd have moved on his own. It would have been too great a gamble. He had to know he had someone else to rely on once it was over. I'd put my money on the German embassy.'

Laura shivered. She remembered the man in the library that morning, the man David had wanted to speak with in private.

'Can you prove it?'

'Not easily. But if what you say is true, if there are going to be massacres, then we have no choice. We have to find evidence, and we have to make it public.' He paused. She

189

sat in front of him, shaken and bewildered. 'Will you help me?' he asked.

She stared at him as though he had made an improper suggestion. Her entire world had been turned upside down. All she wanted was to creep back to the White House and slip into her daughter's bedroom and watch her sleeping, all she wanted was to sleep herself and wake in the morning without fears, free from all danger.

'I don't know. I need time to think. Whatever I thought I'd got myself involved in, it wasn't this.'

'Laura, people are going to die.'

She went to him and put her hand over his mouth.

'Please. People are dying every day in this country. I need to think this all over. Give me a few days.'

She did not take her hand away. He felt the warmth of her fingers against his lips. He looked up and their eyes met, and he felt her hand move from his mouth to his cheek. As though with its own volition, his hand moved and covered hers. She did not try to pull away. Instead, she kneeled in front of him and leaned forward until her head was only inches away from his.

'I'm frightened,' she said. He could barely hear her, her voice was so soft. 'Please. I want you to hold me.'

He looked at her for a few moments, knowing that everything had slipped out of his control. She did not look at him as he leaned towards her, nor when he put his arms round her, but closed her eyes and let herself be held, and she did not move for what seemed a very long time.

CHAPTER TWENTY-FIVE

Tuesday, 30 October

Vanderlyn rang early the next morning. He wanted John over right away.

'I'm due at the office.'

'Make an excuse. This is important.'

'What's it about?'

'I'll tell you when you get here. Make sure you bring your diary.'

When John arrived, Vanderlyn was waiting for him in the lobby.

'Let's go outside. You look like you could do with a walk.'

'I can't be long. I don't want to draw attention to myself at the White House.'

'This won't take more than a few minutes.'

The professor seemed tired – no, more than that, burnt out – and John remembered the risks he was taking, not least in being here with him.

They walked down to the back of the university, and along Canal Road, skirting the river, dull and leaden here where it began to widen as it flowed down to Key Bridge and Theodore Roosevelt Island. A freight train passed, slow and noisy, cutting them off from the water for a while, and a light rain began to fall, as though baptizing them in a strange faith to which neither man had as yet given allegiance.

'This is for you,' said Vanderlyn, handing John a piece of paper. 'It came from London last night.'

'You've got a new operator, then?'

Vanderlyn shook his head.

'After what happened to Moshe, we're avoiding any direct radio contact. This came through New York. It was brought down by hand.'

John unfolded the paper. It contained a series of coded letters broken into groups of five. Vanderlyn's reference to his diary had alerted him to the need for a sheet from his one-time pad, which he kept hidden in his apartment. He took the sheet from his diary and decoded the message one letter at a time. It didn't say much, but it was enough: 'Your target remains as before. You have two weeks maximum to operation.' The sting came in the signature: 'Orator.' It was his private codename for the Prime Minister, assigned to him in person as a guarantee of the authenticity of non-routine instructions. His orders were being confirmed from the very top. It left him little room for manoeuvre.

John crumpled both the message and the decoding sheet and hurled them in a long arc into the river. The rain fell on them, and in moments they had gone for ever.

They walked on, heading towards Palisades Park. They spoke for a while about how John was getting on at the White House. He decided to say nothing to Vanderlyn about Laura's visit of the night before.

A white dog came scurrying out of nowhere, intent on unseen prey, hurtling across a forlorn carpeting of wet grass. Vanderlyn watched it until it had vanished beneath the chain bridge.

'It's time I came to the point,' he said. 'They've started picking up Jews across the country. It's kind of low-key at the moment, but it's gaining momentum.'

John had already seen that morning's newspaper headlines: 'Jewish Plot: New Names', and 'Further Arrests in Lindbergh Slaying Plot: Jewish Rats on the Run'.

'We know someone else was behind this. Can't someone

go public with what you know about Rosen? An anonymous letter to a newspaper.'

'We've tried that. You can bet every newspaper editor in town's just dying to be the first to say "The Jews Didn't Do It". Besides that, we have a problem. There was always a possibility that Moshe Rosen escaped that night, picked up Horowitz somewhere, and headed for the White House. We didn't think it likely, but we had to be sure. Now we know. Danny Horowitz spent the last three years in Howard County Concentration Camp. His wife Rosa was hanged there about a month ago. He had a good motive, but it wouldn't have done him any good. He was still in the camp the day before Lindbergh was shot.'

'You're sure of that?'

'Positive. We have direct confirmation from three of the inmates.'

'Then why . . . ?'

Vanderlyn shook his head.

'Don't be such a fool. They'll talk to one of our people, sure. But so much as a whisper of a hint that somebody was going public with that information, and they'd follow Danny Horowitz within minutes. Them and anybody they'd spoken to in the past week, and probably a lot more besides for good measure. Nobody's going to talk, John – believe me.'

'Then what are you going to do? You already knew this was a set up. How do you plan to find out who was behind it?'

'That's our problem. Horowitz was sent to the governor's office that afternoon. That's the last anybody saw of him. The governor knows who asked for a Jewish body. That's who we have to go for.'

'The governor?'

'We're going to kidnap him. Use some of his own techniques. Find out what he knows. We need your help.'

CHAPTER TWENTY-SIX

John arrived at the White House an hour later. His office was in the Executive Wing, about ten yards from the President's. No sooner had he settled at his desk than Sam Hoskins, Stephenson's private secretary, came in and said the President would like to see him at eleven o'clock.

'What's it about?'

Hoskins shrugged. He was an old Klan buddy of Stephenson's, Grand Scribe for the Realm of Indiana when the President was Grand Dragon there. The two men were very close. John guessed that Hoskins knew more about Stephenson than anyone, and that he derived considerable power from that fact.

'Couldn't tell you. Hope you haven't been up to anything you shouldn't.'

He left with a smile that could have been cut from a face on a cereal packet. John was connected, and Hoskins would never cross him openly. But the little secretary trusted no-one who wasn't Klan.

John spent the next hour in a state of apprehension, thinking he must have committed some faux pas the evening before. Maybe he'd offended Stephenson by leaving early. At eleven, he put on his jacket and a smile to go with it, and headed for the Oval Office.

Stephenson was standing at a window, looking out into the gardens. A man of medium height stood next to him, a heavy-set man in early middle age. As John entered, they both turned round. Stephenson stepped towards him.

'Nice to see you again, John. Come here, I want you to meet an old friend of mine. This is Ed Hoover. You know who he is, of course.'

John stepped forward nervously. He hadn't expected to meet the head of the FBIS in person. Hoover held out a smooth hand and took John's without warmth. His grip lacked energy, yet John felt invaded by it, as though some immaterial force in Hoover was seeking to penetrate him. He looked up and saw himself reflected in a pair of immaculate blue eyes, as deep as underground caverns that had never seen light.

'David's been telling me a lot about you, John. I'm much impressed.'

'Well, sir, I'm honoured to meet you. I've heard a lot about you as well.'

Stephenson laughed. John had noticed the laugh before, a restrained guffaw that seemed to say, 'We're all men together, we could laugh like hyenas if we wanted.' Stephenson wanted camaraderie, wanted something raw that political life could not offer him. There was a weakness in there somewhere, and John wondered if he could seek it out and use it.

'Ed dropped by this morning to show me his file on the Jewish plot. You know he uncovered one, don't you?'

'No, I . . . Well, I saw something in this morning's papers about a roundup.'

Hoover nodded.

'We're picking up Jewish radicals anywhere and everywhere. Expect to have about thirty thousand in custody by the end of this week.'

'Surely that many can't have been involved in the plot to kill Mr Lindbergh.' John wondered how far he could go.

'All depends what you mean by "involved".' Hoover flicked a piece of lint from his lapel. There was something fastidious about him. He seemed ill at ease even here, as though the President's office might harbour the unthinkable. 'The plot to kill the President was known to maybe a half dozen people. But that half dozen had to have support, and the supporters couldn't function in the New Republic without a wider network. It's that network we're looking to dismantle. After that . . .' He looked round at Stephenson, lifting his eyebrows.

'John,' said Stephenson, 'I'd like you to go over to FBIS headquarters this afternoon if you've got time. Ed has some people working on the Jewish problem. They'd like to speak to you, get some perspectives, chew over the legal position.'

John nodded. Hoover had turned his gaze on him, as though challenging him in some way.

'I'd be glad to talk to them,' said John. 'But what exactly do you mean by the "Jewish problem"? Other than in the usual sense.'

Hoover hesitated before answering, as though his choice of words might turn out to have a bearing on the legality of his actions.

'There are nearly five million Jews in this country, about half of them in New York. Another eight million in Europe, maybe another two million in other places. That's about fifteen million Jews too many. The Germans are taking care of their Jews, and from some talks I've had it looks like they know where they're going. Our problem is what we do with ours. A lot of them are in camps already. That helps keep them out of mischief, but it leaves a lot on the outside. Some of them we need until we can replace them with real Americans. The rest . . .'

He shrugged.

'We need to change the constitution, decide what makes a Jew a Jew. If it's his religion, that creates problems. If it's his race, we can find a way out. What we want is something like the Germans have got.'

'You mean the Nuremberg decrees?'

'That's it. That's what we need to talk about. Fitting something like that into the constitution. Just so's we don't upset anybody.'

'What will happen to the people you're picking up now?'

Hoover picked a fingernail. It was not noticeably grubby.

'They'll be charged, just like any other criminals. We'll charge most of them as subversives. If they're guilty, they'll hang.'

'You reckon they'll be found guilty?'

Hoover's plump face broke into a genuine smile for the first time.

'I *know* they'll be found guilty. We didn't go to all this trouble just to let them go again.'

The clock on the mantelpiece struck a quarter past. Hoover looked round.

'David, I've got to go. Since I've got your approval on this, I can get it moving a lot faster. I'll keep you in touch.' He smiled again at John. 'Don't forget our meeting. One o'clock suit you?'

John nodded.

'Fine. Call at my office. I'll take you round to meet the boys.'

As he reached the door, he turned.

'Don't bother bringing a copy of the constitution. We all know it backwards over there. Isn't that right, David?'

Stephenson smiled and the door closed, and there was a sudden intimacy in the room, as though a bond was being forged between them, the President and his appointed assassin.

'Let's sit down,' said Stephenson. John saw him glance at the clock as he did so, and guessed his next appointment was at 11.30. A White House staffer bustled in carrying a bundle of red Treasury Department files, and skipped away airily as though he, and not the President, was in charge. John sat uncomfortably on the edge of an overstuffed sofa. Stephenson winked at him, an old gesture from his Indiana days.

'You made a hell of an impression on someone last night, son.'

'Did I?'

'You never told me you spoke German.'

'Never thought I'd need to round here, sir.'

'Well, it looks like you were wrong. Your new friend Mr Himmler was greatly taken by you. Thought you talked a lot of sense.'

'I'm flattered.'

'You shouldn't be. He doesn't flatter. But he likes a man who talks his own language. I believe you met Hans Geiger last night as well.'

'That's right.'

'You know he's the Police Attaché? It gives him an interest in legal matters. He's asked if he can use you as a sort of liaison. Pass on any questions they've got, that sort of thing. You like to do that, John?'

John felt panic rise in him. This would upset all his plans.

'It's not exactly . . . what I'd in mind, sir. I was looking forward to working here with you.'

'This isn't a job. You work for me as before, but every so often something lands on your desk from one of their legal types. You go over to the embassy maybe once a month, listen to their problems, tell them what you think they want to hear, and get back here in time for coffee and doughnuts. It's a formality. I'd like you to take it on.'

John nodded.

'OK. If it doesn't get in the way.'

Stephenson looked at the clock. It was almost half past.

'I hear you finally got to meet Shirley last night.'

John nodded.

'She's a lovely child. You must be very proud of her.'

'You bet. She's Daddy's girl. It's time you found yourself a wife and had a child. It makes a difference. Teaches you we're all little children at heart. She'll be joining KidsKlan soon. We're going to start a chapter right here in the White House.'

Just then there was a knock on the door and a secretary

entered. She was a pale woman with frightened eyes, another staffer, but without the confidence of the man who had been in previously. She approached the President diffidently and handed him a file.

'You said you wanted this the minute it was finished, sir. It's the report on the Jews, the pair who killed President Lindbergh.'

Stephenson snatched the file from her and opened it. He glanced over a couple of papers, then hurled it back at her. It burst, scattering loose papers everywhere.

'What the fuck is this?' he bellowed. 'I asked for psychiatric profiles. This is just forensics. What are you, stupid?'

The secretary got on to her hands and knees and started picking up the papers.

'This is all there was, sir. Nobody had anything else on them.'

'Then make it up. For Chrissake, leave those alone.'

Suddenly, he bent down and grabbed her, yanking her harshly to her feet and pushing her to the door.

'I want a full psychiatric report on my desk by three o'clock. If it isn't there, there'll be somebody else at your desk in the morning. What do you think I'm running here, a goddamned kindergarten?'

He slammed the door and returned to his seat. It was as if nothing had happened. He just looked at John and smiled and asked, 'Where was I?' John, still shocked, said nothing.

'KidsKlan. That's right. We're starting a chapter. The Shirley Stephenson chapter, for her and the other staff kids. Great idea, ain't it?'

John nodded, still thinking it prudent to say nothing. He had started to understand Laura and her fears a lot better.

'You're too old to have been in KidsKlan yourself,' Stephenson went on. 'But how come you never joined the regular Klan? Man like you, you'd have made a lot of good connections.'

John looked round sheepishly, as though proud of where he found himself.

'I guess I haven't done too badly without them, have I, sir?'

Stephenson grinned. His choler had subsided as quickly as it had come.

'Maybe you're right. But you haven't answered my question. You just a college boy who felt ashamed to hand over fifteen dollars for a white robe and a hood? Or maybe it just plain embarrassed you? All those Kleagles and Kligraphs, and Goblins.'

'Well, no, sir . . . just, I was never much of a joiner. I'll take out membership if you like, but . . .'

'Hell, no, that ain't necessary. We're all Klan now, boy. All us white Christian folk anyways. I was just asking. Sam Hoskins – you know Sam?'

John nodded.

'Well, Sam was just wondering. He likes a man to belong. Watch your step with him, John. Old Sam misses nothing.'

There was another knock on the door, and a second secretary entered. She looked terrified.

'Colonel Sutter's outside, sir. Shall I send him in?'

Stephenson nodded, and John got briskly to his feet.

'See you get to Hoover's place on time,' Stephenson said. 'Don't worry about lunch. I'll explain to Ms Cordell that you're tied up. When Edgar says one o'clock, that's what he means, believe me. He doesn't like people turning up late. Be nice to him. If he asks you to suck his dick, just get on your knees and open your mouth.'

At the expression on John's face, the President guffawed again.

'Hell, no, son, he ain't one of those. It's just my way of putting it. The fact is, if he asks you to suck his dick, just be sure I'm the first to know. I've been trying to get something on old Edgar for some time now.'

A man in military uniform appeared in the doorway. John shook Stephenson's hand and hurried from the room.

200

PART 7

FBIS

From *The Kolumbia Encyclopaedia* (Kolumbia
University Press/Aryan Alliance Publications
Committee, Second edition, 1944)

FEDERAL BUREAU OF INTERNAL SECURITY
(FBIS)

A division of the US Department of Justice, charged
with monitoring, forestalling, and policing all forms
of seditious activity within the boundaries of the
United States of America. The Bureau has a wide
responsibility for the enforcement of Federal law
in respect of over two-hundred-and-fifty seditious
or potentially seditious acts, including the publication of anti-government or anti-American sentiments, radio broadcasts, acts of terror, assassination of public officials, and public statements
of discontent. Created (1908) as the Bureau of
Investigation, its original work was restricted to
investigations on behalf of the Justice Department.
After J Edgar HOOVER became (1924) director,
Kongress gradually added to the Bureau's powers,
and in 1933, one year after the election of Charles
LINDBERGH as US President, it was reorganized,

and in 1935 renamed the Federal Bureau for Internal Security. The investigation of ordinary criminal activity at the Federal level became the responsibility of a newly-created Federal Office of Investigation (FOI). Under Hoover's direction, the FBIS became the most powerful and the most feared arm of the state, protecting the freedoms of ordinary Americans from numerous plots by Bolsheviks, Jews, and Katholiks, including the **Highbury Conspiracy** (1937) and the **Missouri Kiwanis Incident** (1940).

Following the outbreak of WORLD WAR II, the FBIS became closely involved in the defence of the state from foreign, mainly British, intrigue. Kongress conferred on the Bureau the right to operate as a counter-espionage agency. This led on occasions to clashes with other state intelligence agencies. It was Hoover's personal initiative that led (1941) to the uncovering of a British espionage network in New York city. During this period, the Bureau borrowed many of its investigative techniques from the German GESTAPO, with which it had entered into a close partnership. The January 1940 **Heidelberg Conference** organized by Gestapo chief Heinrich MÜLLER was followed in April by the **Chicago Security Konvention**, when a formal pact of cooperation was signed by the two organizations. Hoover was made an honorary SS-Gruppenführer, and Müller an honorary FBIS Chief-of-Staff.

Relations between the FBIS and the Klan's own security apparatus (see KLEXTER, KLOKANN) were sometimes frosty. Hoover believed that Klan investigators kept a file on him and his senior officers, and a burglary at Klan Headquarters in 1937 was widely believed to be the work of FBIS agents.

CHAPTER TWENTY-SEVEN

The monolithic building on 9th and Pennsylvania towered over John like something from a bad dream, high, menacing, and seemingly impenetrable. He'd seen it before often enough, but always out of the corner of his eye, with a glance that turned elsewhere before it had time to linger. FBIS Headquarters was not a public monument. Tourists did not stop to admire and take pictures outside it. Pedestrians quickened their step as they passed it.

He stood looking at it from the other side of the avenue, and it was like a cold shower drenching him. This was the true face of the beast he had come to fight. It told him more about the New Republic than a million posters ever could.

Set like a fortress in the heart of the capital, it soared storeys above everything around it. There were no real windows in its walls, just long, deep slits like machicolations in a medieval castle. At any moment, John thought, molten lead might pour from its gutters, or fire belch from some hidden crevice. A stone eagle, its wings spread and its claws extended, was the only visible indication that this was a government building.

He crossed the street, weaving through the morning traffic, and started to walk up the long flight of shallow steps that led to the entrance. As he climbed, he felt his every movement watched, as though untiring eyes were gazing out at him.

A guard in the uniform of Hoover's elite bodyguard unit,

the Watch, checked his ID and let him through into the lobby. From here, a single door led into the heart of the building. On the wall facing him hung a giant photograph of David Stephenson, flanked by the Stars and Stripes.

He gave his name and was told to wait. Minutes passed in a profound silence. The footsteps of passing staff were cushioned by rubber floors. The door opened and a man came through, bald-headed with wire spectacles on a sharp nose. He introduced himself to John and led him back through the door.

A hum of intense activity filled the interior. Men moved purposefully from room to room, carrying files or wheeling trolleys on which sat mountains of stamped and labelled papers. The bald man, whose name was Lark, walked side by side with John along a corridor that seemed to stretch the entire length of the building.

FBIS HQ was the Mother Temple of the religion of death. John sensed that all lives ended here, that every citizen was already trapped behind these walls, his name and most intimate details catalogued, filed, cross-referenced, and permanently stored. As Lark took him to the room where his meeting was to be held, he caught glimpses through half-open doors: bank after bank of filing cabinets were tended by battalions of grey-coated clerks. It was all bloodless and painless, and he felt himself suffocated by it.

'What's down there?' he asked at one point, indicating an elevator that served half a dozen underground floors and no others. Lark smiled discouragingly. Behind the lens of his glasses, his eyes did not smile at all.

'Out of bounds,' he said. 'You need a special pass to go down there.'

'You got one?'

Lark shook his head.

'My work keeps me up here. I've no call to go anywhere else, not unless I'm sent for. This place is run on a need-to-know basis. What I don't need to know, it's better I don't.

Same goes for everyone, yourself included. Call it the first rule of survival.'

John kept his questions to himself from then on, but he also kept a careful watch. Something told him this place was more than just a secret police headquarters. The heart of the Aryan Alliance state lay within these walls. If he wanted to penetrate and destroy it, this was where he had to come.

The meeting passed without incident. Three men in navy suits and black ties introduced him to the arcane realm over which they presided. A thin man with a prominent Adam's apple spoke first, setting the tone for what was to come.

'One of our biggest problems is habeas corpus. The constitution makes it clear it can't be suspended except in cases of rebellion or invasion. Article one, section nine. So far, we've just tried to ignore it. But with what we've got in mind, it's got to go.'

John nodded. He was beginning to understand their thinking. As long as it looked legal, their consciences were clear. As he listened to them talk, shifting, weaving, constructing an artificial world out of clauses and amendments and sub-clauses, he realized they were as frightened as anyone else. Now they were top dogs, tossing aside other men's liberties like so many bones. But they knew that what they decreed today might rebound on themselves tomorrow. In the world they inhabited, no-one was safe.

'Just what do you have in mind?'

'Just putting people in camps isn't enough. Camps cost money to run if the prisoners can't be worked. Edgar thinks there may be other ways. Sterilization. Euthanasia for the unfit. Selective culling. But they all need legislation. It makes for a lot of work.'

'Why not just scrap the constitution?'

A man with a Hitler moustache and prominent blue eyes broke in. He was younger than the others and had about him an intensity that sent shivers of cold along John's skin.

'That's exactly what I've been recommending for over a year now, but these maggots won't hear of it.'

'It can't be done,' said the thin man. 'The constitution's sacred, everybody knows that.'

'You proclaim a new one,' said John. 'A real constitution, the first true American constitution. And you make it read whatever way makes sense. Hell, you're running the country anyway.'

From the constitution they passed to Congress, and from that to the powers of the presidency. The visit was amicable, John impressed them with his radicalism, and the basis was set for full cooperation. As he rose to leave, John turned to Cummings, the man with the moustache.

'You say you've got a unit handling the investigation into the conspiracy?'

'That's right.'

'Could I pay it a visit? If there's time?'

Cummings looked at the others. John's request seemed perfectly natural. There was no reason to take it at anything but face value. They shrugged.

'Sure, why not?' said the thin man. 'White House gives you a high security rating. Anything you'd like to see in particular?'

'Well, what I need to know is how the wider investigation gets tied back to the assassination proper. It's like ripples – the further you get from the stone, the bigger they get and the weaker they get. And that's where the legal problems are going to come in. Habeas corpus, the works.'

'You mean, we arrest some guy in Oregon, and folks ask, "What did he have to do with something happened back there in Washington?" That what you mean?'

John nodded.

'Imagine he's a bean farmer out in Nebraska. Never harmed anyone in his life. Never lifted a hand to his wife, never touched his kids. Good man to have as a neighbour. That needs some justification.'

'Not if he's a Jew.'

'Didn't know they had Jews out in Nebraska.'

'They got Jews every damned where. About fifteen thousand in Nebraska at the last count.'

'There's nearly a thousand in Wyoming. That's how come this conspiracy's so widespread. It's like a disease. Once it starts spreading.'

Cummings butted in.

'I'll take you down to the unit. Introduce you to a few people I know there.'

The unit was two floors up, set apart in a secure area of its own. Almost the entire floor had been given over to the investigation, which was officially headed by Hoover in person. He came in two or three times a day, spoke with the chief investigators, and told them to keep going.

The moment he set foot inside, John sensed something in the air – a buzz of barely contained excitement that was almost infectious. Nobody here was going about his job just because he had to. People scurried about, making marks on maps, drawing diagrams on blackboards set every ten feet or so along the walls, making phone calls, calling for files.

'John, this is Andy Schultz. Andy's unit chief for this investigation. He's spent some time in Germany, worked with the Gestapo, got some great insights.'

Cummings explained who John was and what brought him to the unit. Schultz listened like somebody who knows he has better things to do. He had a schoolboy's face and eyes that gave nothing away. His hair was slicked back to reveal a broad forehead. He seemed very calm, like a benign Buddha.

Cummings made his apologies and left.

'Ring down to the lobby when you want to leave. Lark'll pick you up.'

Schultz took John into the little cubicle that served as his personal office. In spite of the vastness of the building, space was at a premium here.

'What do you need to know?'

John told him.

'What can I tell you that hasn't been in the papers?'

'You can tell me exactly what happened. All I've read is that Horowitz and Rosen got themselves into the White House, surprised the President and his wife, and shot them. Everybody knows that.'

'Why do you need to know?'

'Because there are legal problems. In any criminal case, the details are important. I want you to prove to me there's a conspiracy here, because it isn't you who's going to have to prove it in court.'

'What makes you think any of this is ever coming out in a courtroom?'

'The President makes me think so. This has to look legal or it starts to stink.'

'OK, what do you need to know?'

'You already asked me that. I need to know how they got in to begin with. Did they break in, or did somebody let them in?'

'A guard let them in. Name of Peters. Has Jewish connections through his sister. She married one five, six years back.'

'He let them in where?'

'There's a small service entrance on the south side of the main building.'

'I know the one you mean.'

'They must have known their way around. Peters stayed downstairs while they went upstairs. There's no lock on the President's bedroom.'

'Aren't there guards up there?'

'There are now, but Lindbergh wouldn't have any, not up there, not anywhere in the presidential suite. So Rosen and Horowitz just sauntered on up, cool as you like, opened the door, switched on a light, and started firing.'

'How many rounds?'

'I'm sorry?'

'How many rounds did they fire?'

'I'm not exactly sure. It's in the autopsy report. It's hardly important.'

'No, I don't suppose so. What happened next?'

'There was a maid, Conchita. She was sleeping a couple of doors away. She heard the shots and rang down on her telephone, alerted the main guard post. That's when the Marines went in. They caught Rosen and Horowitz on the stairs, saw the guns, and opened fire. The gunfight didn't last long.'

'Did they get off any rounds?'

'Who, Horowitz and Rosen? I don't think so, it all happened pretty fast. Had their guns on them, though.'

'OK. And what was Peters doing while all this was going on?'

'Look, why do you need to know all this?'

'Is Peters under arrest? Can I speak to him?'

'I don't know, yes. He's in a cell in this building. His wife too. And we've got his sister and her husband, and a heap of his friends. They're still being interrogated.'

'This is how you found the conspiracy, through Peters's brother-in-law?'

'Some of it, yes. Horowitz and Rosen had their own connections. This is big. It has bits that go off everywhere.'

'That's the way with conspiracies. Was it Peters's regular night on duty?'

'That should be on file. Look, Mr . . .'

'Ridgeforth.'

Schultz looked at the clock on the wall opposite.

'Look, Mr Ridgeforth, I've got a lunch break coming up, then I have meetings all afternoon. Why don't I show you where you can get the files on the shootings? Leave you with them. You'll find everything you need in there. My men did a good job, a thorough job.'

'I appreciate that. And, yes, I'd like to see anything you've got. I'd like to focus on the assassination. It's where the ripples start.'

'Ripples?'

'Peters, his family, their friends. They're all ripples in what looks like a very big pond.'

'You said it. Big. You could drown in it, nobody'd notice.'

'I don't intend to. I just want to take a look round the sides.'

CHAPTER TWENTY-EIGHT

Howard County Concentration Camp
Florence
Maryland

Jim Jackson never left the camp, except to pay official visits to Federal Camp Administration HQ, something he did once every quarter. Anything else could be taken care of in the camp itself. If he wanted a woman, one was brought in (and sometimes two, when he was in the mood). If he needed food from a good restaurant, a car was sent to pick up the chef. If he had a hankering after the latest movie, there was a small cinema in the administrative block for himself and his senior staff. He regarded the camp as a world separate from the world beyond the wires, and considered it his duty to remain where he was, on call day or night.

There was a reason for such single-mindedness, of course, though it was unlikely that Jackson had ever recognized it. Doing what had to be done in the camp meant cutting yourself off from some of the values of the outside world. In here, men and women had to be beaten and whipped and cudgelled, had to be fed starvation rations, had to be worked like animals, sometimes had to be killed. Not everything that went on in the camp was legal, at least not according to the rulebooks they used on the outside. But that was the whole point about the camps: they were a world apart, they existed in and for themselves, and the real laws were made and administered by men like Jim Jackson and his staff.

Hence his worry about the phone call he'd received that afternoon. It had come from a man called Ridgeforth, a flunkey at the White House glorying in the title of 'Presidential Advisor on Constitutional Law'. According to Ridgeforth, he'd just come from a meeting with Edgar Hoover, where they'd been talking about constitutional amendments that would affect the camps. He'd like to interview Major Jackson, and could the governor please make himself available that evening at nine? It was to be a private meeting, known only to his driver and himself.

Jackson had double-checked, of course. It turned out this Ridgeforth wasn't just a legal pain in the ass, but some sort of blood relation to the Queen of Hearts. Jackson hadn't got where he was by making mistakes. Offending potential heirs to the throne wasn't one of them. He'd rung straight back. Of course he'd come, he'd be only too delighted. Was there anything he needed to bring? No, just himself.

He sauntered to the gate while Barnes brought the Chrysler round. It was a chilly night. From the towers, spotlights moved like the legs of giant spiders, crossing and crisscrossing the perimeter, illuminating the grey dormitory blocks one after the other. A sound of agonized coughing rose from one of the huts. Jackson frowned. Now the cold weather had set in, they'd started going down like flies. It was a devil of a job, keeping the work quotas at their proper level. A good thing there was going to be such an influx of Jews tomorrow. He wanted to be back early to see everything was in order.

Barnes waited for him in the driving seat. He stepped into the back, and was joined by Crosby, his bodyguard.

'Cold night, Major.'

'That it is.'

Crosby was a big man with small features, as though the head of a child had been grafted onto an adult's body. He thought little and reflected less, but he was quick and

214

strong and incomparably loyal, and Jackson trusted him with his life. He was never more than a pace away when the governor made his tours of the camp. Jackson had once seen him snap a prisoner's back with a single, wrenching action, and throw the man down, broken, on the muddy ground.

The car snarled briefly, then hurried into the night, throwing the camp and its unnatural lights behind it like something extra-terrestrial from which it fled. Half a mile further, they joined the little road out of Florence down to the state highway, just after the Patuxent Bridge. Jackson settled back to enjoy the ride. Thinking about it, it might not be such a bad idea at that, getting to know this Ridgeforth kid. Maybe he'd ask him on out to the camp, show him a good time. Not all the women prisoners were kept starved. Not all the men either.

The bridge was closed. A large sign said it had been declared unsafe. They'd have to head back up to Lisbon, then on down through Cooksville. Barnes cursed and started to make a three-point turn. As he did so, the wheels jammed in something, trapping the car, and leaving the tyres spinning helplessly.

'What the hell?'

Barnes engaged another gear and tried again. At that moment, a shadow came out from behind the parapet of the bridge and walked up to the car window. Jackson opened his mouth to say something, but before he could speak there was a loud report, the window shattered, and Barnes jerked sideways, leaving part of his head behind on the seat.

Crosby yanked his gun from its holster, but he was already too late. An unseen hand pulled open the door while another grabbed his arm and pulled him through the opening. He lifted the pistol, trying to bring it round to an angle from which he could fire, but his assailants were still a step ahead. The man holding the arm brought it back quickly in a curving motion, snapping it, with a brittle sound that reminded Jackson inside the car of a snapping spinal cord. As Crosby bellowed, the second man brought a sharp blade from behind and passed it almost gently across the bodyguard's throat. The bellow became a gurgling sound in harmony with the running of the river fast beside them. Even in death, the big man struggled, for his loyalty and his desperation knew no bounds. He reached out with his good arm and found a man's hair, and he tried to pull the man towards him. But a second trick with the knife brought him to his knees like a bull, his quick blood invisible in the darkness, his breath already gone for ever.

Jackson made no attempt to run. Living and breathing death all day, he knew better than to try to outrun the inevitable. When they had finished with Crosby, the two men got into the back with him, while a third, tossing Barnes onto the road, climbed into the front and took the wheel. The road sign had already disappeared from the bridge.

CHAPTER TWENTY-NINE

John made sure he stayed late in his office. There was nothing unusual about that, most people had taken to staying on two, three, or more nights a week. All the new brooms wanted to be seen sweeping America clean. These were early days for the new administration, and everyone hoped to make a good impression. John made himself out to be happy to be one of the gang. And if Jackson by any chance missed the ambush and turned up after all, he'd be at his desk ready to welcome him.

While he watched the minutes tick by, he went over again in his head the plan he was devising for the assassination. The thought of tomorrow's meeting at the German embassy had implanted in him the notion that he might be able to pin the blame for Stephenson's death on Germany. It was a twist that had already been discussed in London. The problem then, as now, was motive. A political reason seemed out of the question: Germany wanted Stephenson where he was and would do anything to keep him there. But John remembered what he'd been asked to do at the embassy. Stephenson was interested in Hans Geiger and his staff, and in all likelihood he already had a dossier of some sort on them. Supposing there was something incriminating in a file like that. And supposing Geiger or some other guilty party got to hear of its existence. For a brief moment John thought he might not even have to pull the trigger himself.

He looked at his watch again. He'd give Jackson another

ten minutes before deciding everything had gone according to plan. The meeting with Hoover and his cronies had been a stroke of luck. They'd talked about methods of forcing through legal change that would allow them to pack the concentration camps with Jews, eventually intern the whole Jewish population. That had given John the chance to work Jackson's name into the conversation.

'I might give him a ring,' John had said. 'Sound him out. Get a grass roots opinion. I hear he's a hardliner, likes to get things done.'

Hoover had nodded.

'Jim Jackson's one of the old gang. Joined the Klan back in '22 or so. Made a name for himself lynching niggers down in Georgia. Runs that camp like a battleship.'

He stuffed a few papers into his briefcase and was about to switch off the desk lamp when Laura appeared in the doorway.

'I noticed your light was on,' she said. She seemed shy tonight, like a little girl, the society hostess of last night's reception buried somewhere out of sight.

'I was just leaving. Shouldn't you be at a banquet or something?'

'David has a meeting at the Imperial Aulic.'

'What the hell's that?'

'It's where the Imperial Wizard has his offices. I know, it all sounds like a joke. Until you meet some of those people. They aren't remotely funny. Anyway, the President meets the Wizard and his cabinet once a month. I should have been there too, to meet the wives, but Shirley has a temperature and a sore throat. I think she caught something last night.'

John came round the desk and joined her. They stepped into the corridor. John nodded to other late workers as he passed their open doors. They'd remember he'd been around.

'She wants to see you.'

'Me? What on earth for?'

'You're her cousin, or my cousin anyway. You made a big impression last night.'

'I did? I thought I made a mess of it.'

'Believe me, you went down fine. Come on, she'll tell you herself.'

They passed through to the main building and upstairs to the presidential quarters. Shirley was sitting up in bed reading. She looked up when John entered, smiling as if he was an old friend.

'You don't look too bad,' he said. 'Your Mom told me you were very sick.'

'I have been. But I had some chicken broth and I feel a lot better.'

He crossed to the bed and bent to kiss her, but Laura waved him away.

'I wouldn't kiss her if I were you. I think she's still harbouring germs.'

John sat on the edge of the bed and pinched Shirley's cheek instead.

'Your Daddy tells me you're going to have your very own KidsKlan here in the White House.'

He'd expected her to be pleased, but she looked back at him glumly.

'I'd rather do something else. I don't like those hoods they make people wear. They frighten me.'

'You don't have to wear hoods in KidsKlan, do you?'

'The older kids do. They have initiation ceremonies with blood. Lucy Hillerman told me.'

They talked on about hoods and ceremonies and friendships, all the delicate areas of childhood. Then, seeing Shirley yawn, Laura looked at the clock.

'It's way past her normal bedtime. You go into the next room, I'll tuck her in.'

John patted Shirley's cheek goodnight and went out. He was joined a few minutes later by Laura.

'She'll be asleep soon. It's been a tiring day for her. I'm worried the throat may still turn into something.

You shouldn't have mentioned KidsKlan. It upsets her. Her father thinks it's terrific, but the costumes really do frighten her. I wish they'd think of something less lurid.'

'Well, I'm told it's her chapter. Maybe she can ask for something different.'

'Maybe you're right. Can I get you something to drink?'

'I'd better go. It's getting late.'

'David won't be back till well gone midnight.'

'All the more reason for me to go.'

'This is perfectly innocent. You were visiting Shirley.'

'Yes, but it mightn't look that way to someone else. You can't afford gossip.'

She took a step towards him.

'John, last night, when I came to your apartment . . . I'm sorry I was angry.'

'You had good reason. Even if what you thought wasn't true, you were right to be suspicious.'

'Afterwards, when you held me . . . No-one's ever held me like that before.'

She was close to him now, closer than was wise. Her hair had fallen forward, and he reached out a hand and lifted it and put it back in place.

'Hold me again, John.'

He tried to stop himself, but she moved in towards him and her arms went round his waist, and he reached out for her and drew her close.

'I didn't mean for this to happen,' he whispered.

She stroked his cheek.

'For what to happen?' she asked.

'To fall in love with you.'

She looked at him at last, drawing her head back to see him better.

'Do you? Do you love me?'

He kissed her, gently at first, then with a growing passion that would have risked anything. His hands moved across her body, tentatively to begin with, then with mounting conviction. Bit by bit, he lifted her skirt with his fingers, raising it a handful at a time until he reached the waistband, and then he brought his hand inside and touched her belly and her lower belly, and slid his hand between her legs, gently, more gently than he had ever touched a woman before, and beneath the silk of her panties she was soft and moist, and he wanted her desperately.

Suddenly, she pushed him back, shaking her head.

'No, John, not here, it's too dangerous.'

'Where, then?' He still held his arms round her, as though afraid she would vanish.

'Go back to your apartment. I'll come there in an hour.'

'How can you get away?'

'Trust me. This isn't Fort Knox. I'll be there, and I promise I won't be followed.'

'You have to be sure.'

She kissed him hard again, then escorted him to the door.

'I'll be sure. Don't worry.'

From *A Child's History of the United States* by Holly Lee Bobbs (Saginaw Books, Grand Rapids, Michigan, Second edition, 1940, pp 90–91)

Did you ever hear a black boy laugh? Hee-haw, hee-haw, just like a donkey, that's right. Or did you ever see one dance? Hop-two, hop-two, up and down like a jack-rabbit, yes, sir. And did you ever hear a bunch of them together singing like they were fit to bust? Lordy, Lordy, pick a bale o' cotton, you know what I mean.

The thing is, blacks were never meant to laugh or dance or sing like white folks, for they haven't the means of civilization in their souls. The good Lord just didn't put it there. He didn't forget – He doesn't do that – He left it out on purpose, because some people (the white people) were put on earth to make it a place fit for salvation, and others (the blacks and coffee-coloureds) were set here to labour for those the good Lord placed over them. That's the natural order of things in the world, and that's the way they were in this country when it was first set up. Everybody who could afford it had a slave, and even the poorest white man was a step above the nigger.

Ask your Daddy to take you to a movie called *The Birth of a Nation*, made by a man called D W Griffith. It's an old movie now, what's known as a 'silent film', but it tells the tale of this country honestly and fairly. It shows how, after the Civil War that came near to tearing this great nation of ours apart, things in the South got out of hand. Some people in the North were misled into thinking there was no difference between blacks and whites, that God wanted us to treat everyone equally. They started to pass laws that would give niggers the vote and who knows what else.

The result of all this was that niggers everywhere started breaking the law, stealing, raping, and killing just for the love of it. It's hard to imagine what it must have been like back then. People who'd fought hard against the savage Indian suddenly found themselves hemmed in by even fiercer savages, some of whom they'd reared in their midst, and fed, and given homes to. The negro isn't by nature given to gratitude, and never was that more obvious than when he got a whiff of freedom and thought it was time to lord it over his truer masters.

You've all heard of General Nathan B Forrest. If you haven't, ask your Daddy to show you the front of a dollar bill. That's right, General Forrest is the man with the beard looking out at you as though he's asking, 'What have you done for America today?' I hope you can answer him with an open face and a clear conscience.

It was Nathan Forrest who founded the Ku Klux Klan back in 1865, at a place called Pulaski, in Tennessee. He was the first Grand Cyclops. He told his followers to put on white hoods and white robes, and to ride to the defence of good white folk set about by negro rebels.

The Klan wasn't alone: there was a White League, an Invisible Circle, and the Knights of the White Camellia out in Louisiana. But the Klan led them all, and it has gone on to this day, waging its Kristian struggle against lawlessness and injustice. We should never forget that it was set up 'to protect the weak and relieve the injured and oppressed' and organized 'to protect and defend the Konstitution of the United States'.

223

So, next time you see a black boy trying to laugh or sing or dance, next time you see a black girl trying to make herself look pretty with ribbons in her curly hair, next time you see a bunch of nigger men and women dressed in their finery and walking down the street like they owned it – remember Nathan Forrest and the battles he fought to keep those black folks in their place. Ask yourself where America would be today if there'd been no Klan, and where you'd be if the niggers had been allowed to run wild and take control. When you're in Church this Sunday, think about General Forrest and his Knights of the Ku Klux Klan, and say a prayer for them and the great country they went out to serve.

CHAPTER THIRTY

The place they brought him to was dark and damp-smelling. He'd been blindfolded on the ride there, a long journey over rough tracks, never once touching a proper road. Only God knew where he was, but he doubted if God cared. They'd hauled him out of the car at last, white with fear, like a ram in some demon-infested outback, quivering before a god of briars and nettles.

Someone removed the blindfold. His eyes shook in the sudden, tremulous light. His hands were still tied behind his back, making it impossible for him to rub his eyes, so he just stood blinking long enough to let him see. And wished he had not.

They were wearing hoods like Klansmen, but their hands were black. He had come into a world reversed.

'You'll pay for this, you sons of bitches!' was all he could shout. It was banal, and he knew it was as empty as hell was full, but it was all he could respond with.

No-one said a word. He could see the noose now, hanging from a rafter. The building was a disused barn, its floor made of compacted earth, its walls flecked with straw. It reminded him of barns he had been in as a young man, far to the south. Several times to make love to women too shy or shrewd to risk his open bed, and after that to sit on hooded juries that had adulterers whipped and blacks castrated.

A man came from behind him, one of his abductors, and touched him, making him flinch. His arms were untied and he was stripped of his coat and jacket. A second man ripped his shirt open, then pulled his trousers down to his ankles, followed by his underpants. He shivered in the dense cold of the unheated barn, and felt his testicles shrivel. No-one moved. No-one sang or danced. He wanted to cry out, but he dreaded to break that tightly wadded silence.

His heart sang out with terror. He'd spent time in his youth on a sheep farm out in the mid-west, before going back to the south. Maybe his captors knew that, knew he'd recognize the instrument one of them carried. It was a long forked metal device with cups in the centre, and it was used for castrating sheep. It didn't cut the testicles. Sometimes an animal would bleed to death when operated on. This crushed the testicles instead, in a single, violent movement.

The stranger brought the instrument up to Jackson and, with the delicacy of a physician, lifted his penis away while he placed his testicles in the cup and brought the other half close up.

'Oh, Jesus, God, just kill me and get it over with!' Jackson bared his teeth. To his horror and shame, his penis had begun to swell tremendously, as though a woman had touched him and not bare metal. They were holding him on either side now.

'At least tell me what I've done to deserve this.' But even as the words left his mouth, the answers were evident.

The man on his right-hand side leaned towards him and whispered in his ear.

'I can have this stopped right away. You just have to say the word. Even if you can take this, there's worse. Believe me. Just say the word and it will stop.'

'Word? What word?'

The voice came again, still in a whisper, as though they were part of some conspiracy.

'Think back a while. You had a Jewish boy in your camp. Name of Danny Horowitz. Recognize the name?'

That was when he knew he was dead, whatever he said

or didn't say. That was the moment he knew it was simply a matter of making up his mind which way to die, and how long to take about it. He looked down at his engorged penis, at the crushing tool encircling his balls. He looked up at the silent ring of hooded men. And he made up his mind.

CHAPTER THIRTY-ONE

She took his penis in her hand and cradled it, flaccid and lazy now, like a small dead animal that she had loved and wanted to bring back to life. He held her close against him, and his hand touched her hips blindly while he looked at her face on the pillow beside him. It confused him that he should be this happy and this sad at once.

'This is very dangerous,' he said. 'You could have been followed, or recognized.'

'I know what I'm doing. Trust me.'

'You've done this before, then?'

She shook her head softly, and her hand moved to his thigh and rested there.

'An affair, no. But I've often needed time away from David. I've found ways.'

'But you're the President's wife now.'

'It makes it easier in a way. There's so much going on round me, I just disappear. But don't worry, I'll take care. I promise.'

'You mean you want to come again?'

'Of course. Don't you?'

He laughed and pulled her to him.

'You don't feel guilty about this?' he asked.

'About cheating on David? No. We don't sleep together. We have sex from time to time, when he's in the mood and there's no-one else around. I moan a bit and pretend I'm enjoying it, but the truth is, it disgusts me. We sleep in separate rooms.'

She paused and rolled over on to her side, facing away from him, as though what she wanted to say precluded intimacy. It belonged to that other world she inhabited, a cold, ambitious world where nakedness had no charms, and where people only touched one another in order to leave their mark.

'Shall I tell you about our President?' she asked. 'What he thinks of women, how he treats them? He was married twice before he met me – did you know that? I didn't think so. Not many people know, it's a well-kept secret. They weren't long marriages, a couple of months each. He ran out both times. The divorces came much later, when he got worried about a bigamy charge.

'Later still, when he was elected Governor down in Indiana, his ex-wives got in touch. They reckoned they could screw a few more dollars out of him, threaten to tell what they knew to the press if he didn't cough up. I found some letters in a drawer, that's how I know. I don't know if he paid anything, but I doubt it. About a month after he got their letters, they ceased to exist. Nobody knows what happened to them, nobody's seen them since.'

'How do you know this?'

'I hired a detective. He cost a lot of money, but he did a good job. It's solid information.'

'Maybe he paid them off after all. Maybe it was part of some deal: take the money, get a new name, start a new life in Canada.'

'Maybe.' She held his hand, troubled by thoughts she had never shared with anyone before. 'And again, maybe not. Did you ever hear of Madge Oberholtzer?'

He shook his head.

'She worked in a government office in Indianapolis. This was back in 1925, when David was still just Grand Dragon of Indiana. A couple of years before he was made Governor. He started seeing Madge, not in any very serious way at first. They went out a few times together. Then something happened. He was going to Chicago for some meeting or other, and he decided she was going with him. Except that she didn't want to. He sent a couple of his men over to her house to get her. They dragged her to a car, drove her down to the railroad station, and handed her over to David and the staff who were travelling with him. He had a private compartment where they kept her hidden.

'They . . . drugged her to make sure she stayed quiet. When they got to Chicago she was moved to David's hotel room. She'd already been raped on the train, now they beat her and . . .'

She paused, squeezing John's hand out of pity for a woman she'd never met, and fear for herself.

'And she was bitten. He . . . he bit her badly in several places. Later that night, she took an overdose, something caustic, I'm not sure what. It burned up her stomach, but it didn't kill her right away. They got her back to Indianapolis, dumped her outside her house. She died three days later. But before that she made a full statement to a lawyer friend.'

'You've seen this statement?'

'No, I've read a summary. The original's been destroyed. Every copy that ever existed. It was the principal evidence at his trial.'

'He was tried?'

'For murder in the second degree. Tried and acquitted. He claimed she'd been neurotic, made the whole thing up. He just walked away from it.'

'But death-bed evidence.'

'That meant nothing. The Klan took over. There was a Klan judge, a Klan jury. It was a walkover. Two years later he was Governor. Now he's running the country.'

She rolled over again and their faces met. He looked into her eyes.

'Has he ever hurt you?'

She did not answer at once. A tear rolled from one eye onto the pillow. Another threatened to follow it, but she wiped it away. He did not press her for an answer. She took a deep breath.

'Yes,' she whispered, so softly he could scarcely hear it. He did not ask for details. It was something he would prefer not to know.

He rolled across and knelt astride her, looking down at her as though from a great height. Her vulnerability astonished him.

'I will never hurt you,' he said. 'Do you understand that?'

She nodded.

'Or let anyone else hurt you.'

'There's nothing you can do. Nothing anyone can do.'

He reached out with one hand and stroked her cheek.

'He isn't God,' he said. 'I'll find a way.'

CHAPTER THIRTY-TWO

The German Embassy
Washington
Wednesday, 31 October

Pieter Werfel hesitated before knocking on Geiger's door. The station chief was in a bad mood this morning. Heinrich Himmler and his party had left the night before to fly back to Berlin. Geiger had spent the previous day shut up with his boss, and he'd looked in a foul temper at dinner. He'd gone in an hour ago to talk something over with Friedrich von Schillendorf.

Werfel had never liked the baron, he represented the old Germany, the Germany the Führer and his party had come into being to destroy. Unfortunately, Von Schillendorf had influence, and a mere functionary like Werfel was powerless to have him displaced. He'd never been able to work out exactly what Von Schillendorf's function was, who he reported to, what he held responsibility for. In the new Germany, you didn't cross someone unless you knew exactly who was on the other end of his telephone.

He knocked and received a curt 'Come in' in Geiger's voice. Schillendorf and Geiger were standing at a table on which lay a heap of documents. Geiger glared at him.

'Yes?'

'I'm sorry to interrupt, sir, but you told me to show this to you the moment it came through.'

He held out a green folder.

'Leave it on my desk.'

'It probably needs some explanation, sir.'

Von Schillendorf got to his feet.

'It's all right, Hans. It's time I got on my way. I've taken up enough of your time.'

He clicked his heels, made a perfunctory *Hitlergrüss*, and left.

Geiger turned to Werfel.

'I hope this is important.'

'I think it is, sir.'

He laid the folder on the table.

'This is a report I've just received from my contact Loomis. He came up with several dozen police incidents for the night in question. I've gone through them carefully. Some of them are interesting, but there's one in particular which attracted my attention. Here.'

He showed Geiger the report from Halifax county.

'Vomit? That's not a lot to pin an investigation on.'

'No, sir. But a policeman was killed. I had Loomis get hold of the autopsy report. The neck was snapped. Professionally, I'd swear to it. A couple of black hoodlums didn't do that. This has a feel about it. He was there, I'd stake my reputation on it.'

'You may have to stake far more than that if a pool of vomit and a broken neck are all you've got. Supposing he did kill this policeman. You can be sure he isn't hanging around down there in – where was it?'

'Halifax, North Carolina. No, sir, I don't suppose he is. But that isn't all we've got. There was something else in the police report, something out of the ordinary.'

'Go on.'

In spite of himself, Geiger was getting interested. If enough unexplained factors came together he might have a trail after all.

'It seems there was a hanging that night, in a field just off the road where the policeman was murdered. Since it was a perfectly legal affair, there was no problem about getting

233

the names of witnesses from among the crowd who'd turned up. A lot of them knew the dead policeman, volunteered information. Some said they'd seen these black boys on the road. That's probably true, but even a first-day recruit would notice the discrepancy in the times.

'But there's a nugget in here, something the police overlooked, or chose to overlook. A group of Klan members went to the lynching in a pick-up truck. They say they passed a smart car, a Duesenberg, not long before they got to the spot where the hangings took place. It was a bit peculiar, so they thought, seeing a car like that out on a road in the middle of nowhere.

'I thought it was worth looking into, so I asked Loomis to mention it to his informant.'

'Who was that?'

'A policeman, a man called Harkins. He went to Loomis over his sheriff's head. Claimed he'd never been convinced by the evidence against the boys they hanged for the crime.'

'That does him credit. And what did he tell you?'

'That he had a friend, someone who couldn't be named unless there was a court case. Loomis assured him this was strictly between law-enforcement officers. It seems this friend was in a car down on the road while the hangings were going on. He was with a woman.'

'Then he can't have been paying much attention to anything.'

'Maybe, maybe not.'

'So, what did he see?'

Werfel told him. Geiger's eyes darkened. Like a beast of prey, he sensed the nearness of his objective.

'A Duesenberg with Massachusetts plates,' he said. 'That still leaves a lot of ground to cover. We don't even know what direction he was travelling in.'

'I think we do, sir. If we point the car away from the murdered man and the hangings, it takes it north. He got to a main road not long after. You'll remember there were road blocks that night, on account of the curfew. Loomis traced him through them. A Duesenberg with Massachusetts license plates entered Washington through the Hoover Checkpoint at five minutes past midnight. You'll find the details on that pink slip at the bottom.'

Geiger retrieved the slip and unfolded it. He glanced at it for a couple of seconds, then folded it again slowly, very slowly, and closed the folder on top of it. When he looked up, his expression had changed entirely.

'You've done extremely well, Herr Sturmbannführer. Please leave the folder with me. And be sure you say absolutely nothing to anyone about this matter.'

'Yes, Herr Major. Will that be all, sir?'

'For the moment, yes. I need to think about this.'

Werfel saluted and headed for the door. As he reached it, Geiger called him back.

'Werfel, did it mean anything to you, the name on the slip?'

'No, sir. Should it have done?'

Geiger shook his head.

'No, I just wondered.'

PART 8

The Search

CHAPTER THIRTY-THREE

'Have you seen this little girl?'

Agent Johnson held out the photograph as though offering it – or the child in it – for sale. He had grey skin and unattractive eyes, dull, aching eyes that seemed to have no purpose, and he couldn't have sold dollar bills for dirt. But, then, he wasn't in the business of selling anything. Beside him, his companion restrained a yawn. They'd been at this for three hours now, door to door, and they weren't getting anywhere. It didn't help that the photograph was blurred and sloppily printed. And, in any case, who was going to admit anything to the FBIS? 'Yeah, sure, I know her' – what could that lead to? A beating, a spell in prison, maybe a one-way ticket to the nearest camp?

The woman in the doorway frowned, shook her head, and closed the door politely, but firmly. If they'd just run a film in a loop, door opening, head shaking, door closing, it would have saved them shoe leather. Johnson put the photograph back in his pocket. He was thick-set, and his grey face proclaimed a permanent scowl, as though life had dealt him an irreparable blow even while he was waiting in his mother's womb. They walked down the steps and on to the next house. Ferney, the tall gangly one, the one with bad acne, the one who preferred killing to any other sport, rang the bell, and the film started rolling again.

It was forty doors and nearly an hour later before anyone

rewrote the script: an old guy with liver spots and rheumy eyes, in a stained sweater.

'Ain't she the one whose father . . . ?'

Johnson nodded. They'd got this far several times before. Anna Rosen and her parents had been known in the neighbourhood. There'd been a time when they'd been liked, even valued. Now it was just 'that filthy Jew', 'that murdering kike', 'that stinking pervert Hebrew'.

'She was a good girl.'

'I'm sorry?' Ferney leaned forward into the doorway, bringing a shadow six feet high with him.

'I said she was a good girl. You deaf or something? She ran errands for me. Did it for anyone who asked. Lot of us old folks hereabouts, we relied on her. Nothing's been the same since she left. Pity about the father. He was a nice man. Hard to believe he killed Lindbergh.'

'Don't worry about that. He killed him. You seen the girl around since then?'

'Since when?'

'Since Rosen went off the rails, killed the President. When we picked up the wife, the kid was missing. Now we're looking for her.'

The old man snorted.

'You think she's in this thing too? Some big Jewish conspiracy, they're all in it? That the idea?'

'We're concerned about her welfare. She's a minor. State's got responsibilities.'

'First I heard of it. Funny thing, though. I saw your people at the Rosens' the night before Lindbergh got killed. Some coincidence. They took the Rosens away in a car. Must have released them later. What do you reckon?'

Johnson and Ferney exchanged glances. Ferney cleared his throat.

'Listen, Mister . . .'

'Carter. Name's Carter.'

'Can we step inside for a moment, Mister Carter. Be more neighbourly than standing out here on the stoop.'

240

The old man hesitated, but to no avail. Johnson and Ferney were already pushing inside. He closed the door slowly and followed them to the living-room.

'You saw these men take the Rosens?'

'Sure I did. It was dark, but the streetlamps were lit.'

'And the kid. What about her?'

'She was here with me. She'd been doing some errands for me, down at Kaufmann's deli. Salami, I think, and bread. He does great rye. I can get you some, it's good.'

'We're on duty. You're telling us Anna Rosen was in here with you that night?'

The old man nodded. The room was shabby, an old man's last refuge, its furniture battered, its carpet threadbare. But Carter and the room fitted. He belonged there. Looking at Johnson and Ferney, he wondered where they belonged. Their leather coats hung round them like flags of mourning.

'And you said nothing to anybody?'

'Who wanted to know?'

'We want to know now. What happened to her?'

'She saw your guys picking up her parents. Through the window there. I told her to stay put. She's a bright kid. She plays the violin – did you know that?'

'No, we aren't in the music business. What next?'

'I wanted her to stay here. Wait to see what happened, see if they'd come back. But she wouldn't. Said she had to go see somebody, get some help.'

'Did she say who this was?'

The old man shook his head. His little remaining hair straggled across his scalp like a disease. Johnson kept his distance. He feared old age and its associations more than he feared death or injury.

'She didn't say, I didn't ask her. But I remember she said something about walking to Georgetown, to the university. Her mother knew some teachers out there. She was musical. Had a lovely voice. But you should have heard the kid play the violin. It brought tears to your eyes. When you

241

find her, make sure she gets her violin. Bring her over, I'll ask her to play something for you.'

'About what time did she leave?'

'It was shortly after that, when things quietened down. Maybe half-eight, nine o'clock.'

'And you haven't seen her since?'

'No, sir. The poor kid must be frantic. Is her mother OK?'

'I couldn't tell you.' Johnson looked at Ferney.

'Mr Carter,' said Ferney, 'you've been a big help. We owe you something. Had you anything special in mind for your funeral?'

'Funeral? I got that fixed up with Winslow. They do a proper job. Won't be much of an affair, though. Nobody much left. All gone before me.'

'That's a shame,' said Johnson, loathing what had to be done. In a tired and tawdry room, without devices.

He stepped up to Carter and took the old man's head in his hands, one hand on each temple. Unnoticed, Ferney stood behind and clasped the old man round the waist. Johnson's movement was quick, expert, and, in its fashion, almost kindly. They rang the police when they got back to headquarters. An expected death, but sudden. An old man. In a tired and tawdry room.

242

John spent the afternoon at FBIS headquarters. At his request, his boss at the White House had increased his security rating. After all, if he was working as a sort of liaison between the President and Edgar Hoover, he'd need fuller access. And there was the inconvenience to consider if there was a call from FBIS archives every time John wanted to look at another file.

The constant bustle in the Assassination Investigation Unit allowed him to go about his work like a rodent gnawing his way through the foundations, unnoticed by anyone. Nobody had the time or the inclination to stop and ask what he was doing, nobody asked twice when he requested a file or a sheaf of papers. He got to know the filing clerks, Doris and Fay, and by the second hour they'd stopped crosschecking his withdrawals. He was digging deep, but made sure to cover his tracks at every stage by taking out files unrelated to the line he was pursuing. If anybody checked up later, they'd see a random sifting of documents, nothing more.

The night of the assassination had not been Peters's regular. It should have been his shift off, but a phone call to his quarters earlier that evening had asked him to cover for a colleague who'd been taken suddenly ill. John made a note of the colleague's name.

After the Marines had finished pumping the bodies of Rosen and Horowitz full of lead, they'd dragged them off the stairs and thrown them in a heap in the guardroom. No chance there for scene of the crime officers to do a proper evaluation. The President's doctor, a man called Reilly, had been called to the bedroom, where he'd examined Lindbergh and his wife and pronounced them dead. His name did not appear on any further documents.

The bodies had been shrouded and taken by ambulance direct to the mortuary at the Walter Reed Hospital, where they were examined later that day by a team of six pathologists led by Professor Murray Stanton. They produced two reports: one, a short, one-page statement summarizing the injuries to the Lindberghs; and a second, forty-eight-page document, setting out their findings in full. The short statement was the 'autopsy report' made available to Congressmen, State governors, senior party officials, and the upper echelons of the Klan. An amended version was subsequently passed on to the press in the United States and abroad, and formed the basis for most news reports on the actual slayings.

John requested a copy of the full document. It took Doris over ten minutes to return, only to say that the forty-eight-page version had been entered under the highest level of classification within half an hour of its signature. In effect, its circulation was restricted to the President, the Imperial Wizard, and Hoover. John thanked Doris and made a note of the names of all six attending pathologists.

He returned to his desk to look more closely at the files relating to Rosen and Horowitz, the alleged perpetrators of the double crime. The main file contained a statement by Jim Jackson, governor of Howard County Concentration Camp, alleging that Horowitz had escaped from the camp earlier the day before. In a separate document, it was recommended that security measures at the camp be beefed up.

A report by a team of FBIS investigators claimed that Horowitz had made his way straight to Washington, where he'd contacted his former 'criminal partner', Moshe Rosen. Rosen's wife Miriam had later confessed under questioning that Horowitz had told Rosen about his wife's execution, 'a legal hanging inflicted for a serious infringement of camp regulations'. The two men had decided to put their plan to kill the President into immediate action. They'd contacted Peters, found he was on duty that night, and gone in at a time when the White House would be least alert.

The weapons used had been provided by a Jewish underground quartermaster, Abe Stein, now in custody. These had been British-made handguns, an Enfield No 2 Mk 1, found on Horowitz, and a Webley Mk 4, found on Rosen. Both had been reloaded after the assassination. The autopsy report maintained that Horowitz had killed Mrs Lindbergh, while Rosen had shot the President, this being based on the bullets taken from the bodies.

John looked hard for a record of Rosen's arrest, all those hours before the assassination, but could find none anywhere. There was, however, a sheet made out for the following day, showing that Miriam Rosen, his wife, had been picked up within an hour of the killings and brought directly to FBIS headquarters. An accompanying sheet noted that the Rosens' daughter, Anna, had not been at home when agents called to arrest Miriam.

John closed the file. They'd be looking for Anna – they couldn't afford to leave her on the loose, spreading the news that her parents had already been in the hands of the FBIS hours before the assassination.

CHAPTER THIRTY-FIVE

Edgar Hoover crumpled up the report and hurled it across the room. It hit the wall and fell to the floor.

'The damn fools,' he murmured. He'd have hauled the old man in, questioned him until he'd squeezed the last drop of information out of him, and then dropped him in a stretch of the Potomac his agents had popularized as 'Dead Man's Bend'.

Still, they had got something. It looked as though the kid had taken refuge with somebody on the Georgetown faculty. There were several professors there already under surveillance, and his first impulse had been to pull them all in and get a team of interrogators to work. On second thoughts, he'd realized it might not be that easy. There was no guarantee the man in question would be on their list, and they could waste valuable time chasing a chimera. The moment word got around that faculty were being picked up, the man they were looking for would take fright and move the child elsewhere.

There was another way.

He picked up his internal phone and dialled three digits. At the other end a man's voice answered, hollow and spectral, as though transmitted over a great distance.

'Unit Five.'

'This is Hoover. Let me speak to Norris.' He felt the old weariness drift over him in a drab cloud. He was not a brutal man by nature, nor a sadist by training, but he understood the nature and cravings of the beast he served. It nurtured him, and he fed it in his turn. If the state was to survive, if law and order were to prevail, then somewhere at the heart of things there must be brutality. He did not think it could be avoided. Whether hidden or public, it was the means by which the civilized state might be reached. He would willingly tear one man's tongue out by the root, or excise another's penis, or cut another's head from his shoulders, if by so doing he could buy five minutes' peace for the Republic.

'Is the woman in the isolation cell still alive?'

'Which one? The Jew?'

'Yes, the Jew.'

'She's OK. She's a tough one. You want to see her?'

'Keep her there. I'm coming down.'

'She'll be here. Where else is she going?'

Anna set down the violin. The strings were still, but the music seemed to linger in the air all round them. She tried to smile, but the effort was too much for her. A tear started to roll down one cheek.

'What's wrong, sweetheart?'

Mabeline went to her and held her while the tears came. Once she had started, Anna found it almost impossible to stop. For just over a week now she'd bottled everything up: her fear, her grief, her horror. She had not cried once since first arriving at Miles's apartment.

It went on a long time, but Mabeline did not once relax her hold of the little girl. She and Vernon had never been able to have children of their own. In the nights, year after year, she'd told herself that God had made a space for something. Now, holding Anna, she began to wonder if the space had been for her. Nine years – it had been nine years ago the doctors had told her she could never have a child. Just around the time Anna had been born. Mabeline believed in God and Fate. She held Anna tightly until the tears subsided.

'You missing your Momma?'

Anna gulped in air. From somewhere she found her voice.

'The music . . . Poppa taught me that piece. We used to play it together. I didn't think, I just . . .'

'You played it beautifully. Believe me. I've never heard music like that in my life. Do you like the violin?'

'It's terrific. Better than the one I had before.'

'Good. Vernon looked real hard. All the people he knows are in the wrong side of the music business.'

'It's a wonderful violin. I'm so grateful. But you'll want it back when I move on.'

'Let's not even talk about that right now. You're safe where you are. When Vernon comes back, you can play another piece for him. Maybe you can teach him some.'

Mabeline had already decided that Anna wasn't moving on. Her own growing need for the child apart, there was the question of where Anna would be safest. After the assassination and the supposed involvement of Anna's father in it, it would be madness to expose the child by allowing her to live in an ordinary household. The hidden cellar lacked comfort, but for the moment it was the safest home for her.

Miriam Rosen stood in the corner of the cell, shivering like a flame on the verge of extinction. Her world was a stone box from which there could be no escape. A light burned all the time, far up, out of reach, blurring all distinctions of day and night. There was no window. No door. They'd lowered her inside through a hole in the ceiling and gone away again. Food – if it was food – came through a slot in one wall. Another hole, lower down, allowed her to get rid of waste. She was naked and cold and frightened to death. Her nose ran constantly, and she had no means of wiping it but with her bare arm. Her red nostrils gave her constant pain, a narrow focus for thoughts that would otherwise run crazy into the air and destroy her.

She never stopped thinking. That was the true horror of her situation. Without thoughts, she might have been comfortable. Without dreams, she might have slept. But every moment, waking or sleeping, or somewhere in between, the fear and the anguish were constant.

Sometimes she sang to herself: old, pitiful songs from her childhood. And she thought of Anna or Moshe, or both of them together, and her voice rose like the scent of flowers in a garden, and for a moment the stone and the cold and the fear would be blotted out, and she would imagine herself at home again, with her husband and child. But when the song ended and her voice faded away and she opened her eyes, it would all come screaming back again. There is no nightmare greater than one that does not end.

There was a sound of stone grating on stone. She looked up and saw a hole opening in the wall opposite her. She screwed up her eyes and tried to make out what was in the opening.

'Come here, Miriam. Over here.' A man's voice spoke to her through the opening. She felt frightened and did not move.

'It's all right, Miriam. I just need to speak to you.'

Perhaps it was Moshe, perhaps they would let her see him, speak to him. On all fours, like the animal she knew herself to have become, she crawled across the floor until her face was inches from the hole. A man's face looked through it from the other side. It was not Moshe. But perhaps Moshe was there, behind the other face, waiting.

'Miriam, my name is Hoover. Edgar Hoover. You may know my name.'

She knew the name, of course she did, everyone knew his name. And who he was, and what he did, and what happened to people who fell foul of him.

'What do you want? There's nothing I know, nothing I can tell you.'

She knew why they'd picked up Moshe. But her own

involvement with the underground had been slight. J Edgar Hoover couldn't be personally interested in her.

'There are some things I think you should know, Miriam.' He told her about Moshe and what he was supposed to have done, and what had happened to him. She didn't believe any of it for a moment, except the last bit. That Moshe was dead. Other than that, it was a nonsense.

'Miriam, you know it's my job to protect this great country of ours from people like you and your husband. I don't care whether you think I'm an evil man or a saint, it makes no difference to me. All I care about is doing my job properly. Part of that job at this moment is to find out just how wide this conspiracy was. I'm sure you understand the need for that.'

'There was no conspiracy.'

'There was an assassination. Your husband and another man were involved. But we think there was another person. Someone you know. A teacher at Georgetown University. Your daughter Anna knew him as well. I wonder if you can remember his name.'

'I know no-one at Georgetown.'

'Of course you do. You gave music lessons there. Unfortunately, you kept no records, you treated the lessons as a hobby. Who did Moshe know there? Who did you know?'

She tried not to listen, but she could not stop the voice any more than she could stop the light. It was safest to remain silent. He would lose patience and go away in time.

'Please listen to me, Miriam. The cell you are in has numerous functions. One of them is to act as a water tank. Water is poured in from a grille in the top, and slowly the cell fills up. A non-swimmer would drown once it reached their mouth. A swimmer would last longer, unless they used immense willpower to get it over quickly. Your records show that you are a strong swimmer, and I'm sure you'll last a long time in the water. It will rise higher and

250

higher until it reaches a foot or so beneath the ceiling. A tiny pocket of air will be left. When you have used it up, you will begin to lose consciousness. I would not like to die like that, Miriam. I am giving you the choice not to do so either.'

Still she did not answer.

'All I want is a name. Perhaps two or three names. Leave it to us to decide who is culpable and who is not. You only have to open your lips.'

Still she refused to speak.

'Very well. Let me tell you something else. Yours is not the only cell. There are several others, some of them occupied. Your daughter Anna is in the cell next to this. You remember her, don't you? Little Anna.'

This time she could not hold back the words. They tore out of her like hornets.

'That's a lie. You don't have Anna. She wasn't at the house when we were arrested.'

'She came back later. She'd been with an old man called Carter. Lives opposite where you used to live. We have him as well. My people were still waiting when Anna came in. I believe you taught your little girl to swim, Mrs Rosen.'

Carter. How could they have known about him unless what Hoover said was true?

'You're lying.'

'You're entitled to believe that. Perhaps it will comfort you. Death can come so slowly. You could save Anna if you wanted. Obviously you don't want to.'

The stone that had been taken from the opening was replaced. A terrible chill descended, filling the already freezing chamber. She sat beside the wall, and she wondered where the opening had been. The wall appeared seamless. No voice now, only the light and the silence in which it burned. And then, behind her, another sound. Water trickling from high up. Slowly she turned and looked. The trickle became a gush, and suddenly the floor was soaking wet. Within minutes her feet were covered.

Inch by inch, the cell filled, and the water crept up her legs. It reached her knees and continued to climb. It came to her thighs, freezing and dirty, and went on rising. She thought of Anna, remembered how small she was. Her daughter barely reached Miriam's breasts. The water touched her pubic hair, wetting it gently.

She shouted out then, not knowing if they could hear her. Her voice echoed in the hollow chamber, bounced back from the walls and the water, hurting her ears with its loudness.

'Vanderlyn!' she shouted. 'His name is Miles Vanderlyn.'

But the water went on rising and did not stop.

CHAPTER THIRTY-SIX

Back in the White House, John sifted through the notes he'd made before taking a walk along the corridor to the personnel office, run by a woman called Nancy Draper. He'd met her once, on the day he started work. She was a charmless woman, flat-faced, wooden, and rigid, and he'd heard stories of her facing down more than one President in her time. Today, she seemed angry about something. Stephenson's new intake were taxing even her powers of endurance.

'I'd like to consult your files on the guards here at the White House.'

'I can't see why.'

She looked down at him through gold pince-nez, as though from a great height.

'I'll be the judge of that.'

'Those files aren't White House property. They belong to the War Department.'

'We're not in the War Department. I don't have time to mess about over there getting the go-ahead. This is White House business, I'm working directly for the President, and I'm doing a favour for Edgar Hoover. Now, if you'd like to pick up the phone and speak to either of them about this, I'd be grateful. Because, Miss Draper, if you don't, I sure as hell will.'

Her anger deepened, and for a moment he thought she'd call his bluff and throw him out of her office. But even she was still unsure of her ground. Stephenson's people were clever and unpredictable, and John Ridgeforth was related to the President's wife. Prudence dictated a safer course of action.

'You can look at them here. But not one file leaves this office. And you can't take notes. If you want to do that, I'll need written permission from the military.'

It took him an hour to go through all of them. He imagined he was following exactly the same procedure as that used by whoever had chosen Peters as the fall guy. At the end of the hour, he closed the filing cabinet, smiled at Nancy Draper, and went back to his own office. His heart was beating. Eugene Peters, aged thirty-five, married, two children had been the only member of the entire guard detachment with even a remote Jewish connection.

He picked up the phone and asked the switchboard to get him an outside line. Moments later, he was answered by a soft man's voice.

'Reilly.'

'Dr Reilly, my name's John Ridgeforth. I'd like to speak to you.'

'What's it about?'

John explained who he was and why he was looking into the assassination.

'I'm sorry, but I can't speak to you about that.'

'Why not?'

'I've signed a paper. It has a confidentiality clause. Even if you subpoena me, I still can't answer your questions.'

'Tell me one thing. Was Charles Lindbergh still alive when you reached his bedroom?'

Reilly's phone clicked down. A silence filled the spaces where his voice had been, a cold, elaborate, and pristine silence that nothing could alter. John set down his own receiver gently and took his hand away.

CHAPTER THIRTY-SEVEN

'She's not with him, believe me.' Hoover took a handker-chief from his pocket and blew his nose vigorously. A cold wind ruffled his hair. Von Schillendorf looked away as though embarrassed.

'How can you be so sure? Where else would she have to go? A frightened little girl in such a big city. Take my advice: go in tonight. Break the door down. It's the simplest way. You'll find her in a closet.'

They were standing in the Lincoln Memorial. The empty room embraced them like a tomb from which all but the last mourners had fled. Hoover felt a sense of desolation grip his heart, and wondered what had brought him here, how much further there was to go. He was forty-five years old, and he felt twice that age. He had power, great power, and access to riches, but he felt no satisfaction in anything. Today, he had drowned an innocent woman, tomorrow or the next day he would kill her child. With the passing of time, it took longer each day to still his conscience. Above his head, the great statue of Abraham Lincoln brooded like the effigy of a God with whom he had long ago broken faith. He kept his eyes fixed on the Washington Monument, almost a mile away across still water. It rose, floodlit and stark, a symbol of all he could never attain.

'He couldn't keep her there,' he said. 'A cleaner comes in twice a week. Woman called McGill. He could never be sure. The walls are thin, someone might hear her. He'd have to smuggle in food, get rid of the rubbish. Believe me, she isn't there.'

'Where would he take her, then?'

'We're checking all his contacts. If we can narrow it down, see who'd take in a Jewish kid, we'll have a list of spots to hit. Without it . . .' He shrugged and folded the handkerchief as though concealing a great treasure in it.

'That will take too much time. We don't have time. Every day the girl is free the risk gets greater.'

'What would you do?'

'Pull Vanderlyn in. Make him talk. You can do that. You're good at it.'

Hoover shook his head. He felt cold out here, and exposed. Behind him, eyes of stone were fixed on him. He shivered.

'He won't talk. Take my word for it.'

'What do you propose we do, then? Watch him until he goes to her? Or wait for her to pay him a second visit? You know we don't have the time for that.'

Hoover hesitated. He looked at Von Schillendorf, contemplating him as he might have contemplated a work of modern art. The German was not truly human, not flesh and blood like other men. He was as emotionless and as cold as the chiselled monument out there, less human even than the statue at their backs. Hoover wondered how he'd come to be involved so intimately with such a creature.

'There is a way,' he said. 'I can't guarantee it, but if it's handled properly it may work. I've been looking at Vanderlyn's files. He's a very interesting man. I'm beginning to think there may be more to him than meets the eye.'

CHAPTER THIRTY-EIGHT

John finished work early. He paid a visit to Shirley, who was still confined to bed. Her throat infection had stabilized, but the doctor recommended further rest. John had bought her a present in Stacey's, a wind-up clown with a rotating head and enormous feet. She laughed at it so much, Laura feared for her throat.

'Tomorrow, sweetheart. If you hurt your throat you'll only have to spend more days in bed.'

There were tears, then hugs, and a promise of another visit if she was good.

As he kissed her goodnight, John noticed a couple of books on the bedside table. He picked one up, a large volume with a brightly coloured jacket showing girls and boys standing in front of the US flag. Above the flag ran the title in heavy block letters rimmed in black: *A Child's History of the United States*. He opened it at random and saw an illustration of the Knights of the Ku Klux Klan riding to the rescue of a white woman threatened by menacing blacks in the old South. On an earlier page, Abraham Lincoln was described as 'A good man who fought for the wrong cause'.

'Isn't this a bit too old for you?' he asked.

Shirley shook her head.

'Daddy reads it to me,' she said. 'He says the President's daughter can't afford to be ignorant of our country's history.'

John smiled at her earnestness and felt his heart grieve

for her. He remembered the history books he'd had as a child, the pride he'd felt that half of him belonged to a country that had fought a Civil War to make men free.

'When you're older,' he said, 'I'll give you another book. It's one I read when I was eight years old.'

'What's it called?'

'*Uncle Tom's Cabin.*'

'I didn't know you had an Uncle Tom.'

'Your Mommy will tell you all about him. Won't you?'

Laura nodded. She took the book from John and put it back in its place.

'That's enough books for tonight,' she said. She bent down and kissed Shirley on both cheeks, tucking her in.

When they left the room, she closed the door softly and turned to him.

'I wish we could spend every day in bed,' she whispered.

'Shhhh. Over in England they say walls have ears.'

'These ones have eyes as well. When can I see you again?'

'We mustn't take too many risks.'

'Don't you want to see me?'

'Good God, Laura, I can't stop thinking about you. It's just so dangerous.'

'What you're doing is dangerous already. Have you found out anything more about the assassination?'

'I'm due to see Vanderlyn this evening. He may have something for me. Maybe you can help. Can you get access to any of David's private papers?'

'I'm not sure. He keeps most of his paperwork in his office. But I know he has a safe in our country house in the Allaghenies, and I've seen him put papers in there or take them out.'

'How often do you go up there?'

'We used to go about once a month. Now, I don't know. I guess it's not going to be that often. Not now he's President.'

'Could you arrange to take Shirley out there to convalesce?'

'Sure, but how do I get into the safe?'

'I'll think of something.'

He glanced at his watch.

'Miles is expecting me.'

The room was silent. She bent forward and kissed him softly on the lips.

'Take care,' she whispered.

Miles was waiting at a small coffee shop near the university. It had been a hangout for the more radical students in the old days, before radical became synonymous with dead or watching the world through barbed wire. Miles sat at a corner table from which he could see the entire room. He cradled a large cup between his hands, watching steam rise without interruption from the congealing surface of the coffee. John joined him and ordered one for himself.

'Well? I presume your friends made their connection last night.'

'You guess right.'

'And learned what they wanted?'

Miles looked round. The café had been almost empty when he arrived, but now it was slowly filling with faculty and students.

'Let's go outside,' he said.

'I've just ordered a coffee. Coffees are the best thing there is round here. Where I come from . . .'

'Outside.'

Miles stood and put enough money on the table to cover the two coffees and a tip.

It was cold. They walked briskly along a tree-lined avenue, their breath white like milk poured out on the frosted air. On every tree was pinned a poster proclaiming a new crusade against the International Jewish Conspiracy: it showed a hook-nosed man with ringlets peering out from a Star of David and holding a smoking pistol behind his back.

'Jackson talked. He knew he was going to die whatever happened, it was just a matter of how long it took. It was common sense to take the easy option. He's been reported missing. You'll probably get a visit from somebody tomorrow.'

'Who asked him for the body?'

'He had a call from the Vice President's office. No question about it. He had the operator check the number.'

'Does he know who made the call?'

'Oh, yes. That was easy. David Stephenson in person. You can bet that's true. David wasn't going to let anyone in on his secret who didn't have to be.'

'But he can't have arranged it on his own. Somebody had to dump the bodies, kill the Lindberghs. Not even David Stephenson did all that single-handed. He isn't Superman.'

'No, he had accomplices. Jackson wasn't asked to deliver the body, it was picked up that evening. Jackson handed Horowitz over personally. The driver had a German accent.'

They walked on. Above their heads, the autumn trees shuddered in a stiff breeze. John pulled his collar up. They had almost made a full circle, and Vanderlyn's block was visible a little further down.

John told Miles about his investigation of the FBIS files.

'I made several more phone calls later today,' he said. 'Murray Stanton, the professor who headed the autopsy team, is no longer contactable. He's not at home, and he's on indefinite leave from the two hospitals where he works and the medical college where he teaches. I tried the other five pathologists. Same story.

'Miles, almost nothing holds together. They bungled the whole thing, now they're trying to patch it up. We have enough to go public, I'm sure we do.'

'Who pulled the trigger? Who actually killed the Lindberghs?'

'Is that important?'

'Of course it is. Is there any way you can get hold of the autopsy report? The full version.'

'I don't know. I'm not even sure where it's being kept. But I've asked Laura to find out more.'

He explained about the safe at the country house.

'I wish you hadn't done that.' Vanderlyn was angry. 'I didn't want Laura any more involved than she is. She's in far too vulnerable a position.'

'I agree. But she's involved already, and not just because of me.'

He told Vanderlyn about her visit on the night of the reception.

'You told her you'd been sent to kill her husband? I can't believe this.'

'I had to. It's hard to explain.'

'Like hell it is. Your people sent an imbecile to do a man's job.'

'Don't be simplistic. I've already told you – she thought I'd arranged Lindbergh's assassination. When I made it clear why I couldn't have done that, it didn't take a law professor to see the real reason I'd been sent.'

'You realize what you've done?'

'She won't talk. If she did, she'd be implicating herself.'

'So, you think she'll just stand by and wait for you to kill her husband?'

John did not answer at first. He watched an old man pass, walking a bandy-legged dog. The dog stopped to urinate against a tree, and the old man waited patiently.

'She detests Stephenson,' he said at last. 'She's afraid of him, so deeply afraid she can hardly speak of it. She won't stand in my way. What concerns her is the child.'

'Her daughter?'

'The little girl loves her father. She'd be devastated if anything happened to him.'

'So Laura has reason to stop you after all. To protect Shirley.'

'I've been thinking there may be a way round the problem.'

'It's not your job to think.'

'If we can make the plot public, Stephenson will be disgraced. He'll be washed up whatever happens. There'll be no need to kill him.'

'You really are a fool.'

'I don't see why . . .'

'Aren't you forgetting something? This isn't a democracy any longer. We may be able to destroy any hopes of an American–German alliance. But David Stephenson won't go down without a fight. We got you in, John. We put you close to the man. You owe us.'

CHAPTER THIRTY-NINE

'How's Shirley?'

David Stephenson threw himself onto the sofa, a whiskey glass in his hand. He'd come back earlier than expected from his evening engagement, a charity dinner convened by the Chamber of Commerce in order to launch an appeal for a Lindbergh Memorial Statue. He looked bored.

'She's sleeping.' Laura took a seat on the other side of the room. 'John was here. He brought her a present, a clown.'

'You're seeing a lot of him.'

'Hmm.' She picked up a copy of *Life* magazine and began to leaf through its pages. Klan meetings took up a large part of the current issue.

'Your father get back all right?' he asked.

'Yes, he rang earlier. He sends his love.'

'Pity he had to leave so soon.'

'I don't think he enjoyed himself too much. He didn't think much of your German friends.'

'Didn't he?' He took a sip of whiskey and let it sit in his mouth for a while before swallowing. 'What didn't he like about them?'

'He thought they were arrogant. It takes one bully to recognize another. He thinks we should stay out of their war. Come to think of it, so do I.'

'You're an expert on foreign policy suddenly?'

'It wouldn't do us any good to get mixed up in Europe again. What if Germany loses?'

'They won't lose. Not with us behind them.'

'So you're planning on going in?'

'You'll find out.'

'Maybe I should start a campaign. "First Lady says: 'Keep out of Europe'". People liked that about Charles Lindbergh. He kept us independent.'

David put his glass down gently and stood up. Four quiet steps took him to where Laura sat. He looked down at her, then, grabbing a handful of her hair, pulled her painfully to her feet.

'I'm going to warn you once. I don't expect to have to do it twice. Keep your nose out of politics. It isn't a business for nice people. Stick to women's affairs. Invite the Daughters of the Revolution to tea. You're the First Lady, not the President Elect. Be careful not to fuck with me, Laura. Because, if I fuck you back, I have a very long prick.'

Laura struggled against the hand holding her.

'You're hurting me, David! You'll pull my hair out.'

'I want you to tell me you understand. You leave the politics and the public statements to me. Is that agreed?'

'Yes. Yes, it is.'

'Say it again. Who makes the statements round here?'

'You do.'

'Good.'

He let her fall back onto her seat. As she put a hand to her scalp, frightened that he might have yanked some of her hair out after all, she looked up at him.

'Never do that again,' she said.

He shook his head.

'This is my room,' he said. 'This is my house, this is my city, this is my goddamned country. And I do as I please.'

Picking up his whiskey glass, he went out, slamming the door behind him.

John drank alone in a small bar near the university, thinking things over. Miles's reaction had shocked him. He was beginning to wonder if he really understood just what it was he'd got himself involved in. What if Miles should find out about Laura and himself? It would be better to bring the relationship to an end.

He drove back slowly and parked his car on the street opposite his apartment building. Everything was quiet. His footsteps sounded unnaturally loud on the footpath as he walked to the door. He looked round, thinking he was being watched. But the street was empty of both traffic and pedestrians. He shrugged and went inside.

Larry Loomis stepped out of the doorway in which he had been waiting for over three hours. He felt stiff and cold, but inwardly gratified. Walking up to John's Duesenberg, he stroked the bonnet with his gloved hand, feeling it smooth and shiny beneath his long fingers. He smiled and looked up at the building just as a light came on in John's apartment.

Laura could not sleep. Her head still ached from David's tugging. She sat up in bed, wishing she were anywhere but here. It was after one o'clock, but it might as well have been noon. It wasn't the pain in her scalp that was keeping her awake, it was the intensity of David's hatred. As the President's wife, she knew herself completely trapped. He would never let her go, never divorce her. Perhaps there was only one way after all. But she had to think of Shirley.

She decided to look in on her daughter. When she'd kissed her goodnight a couple of hours earlier, Shirley had been frettish, and her temperature had been slightly higher than earlier in the day. She put on a robe and slipped into the corridor. Up here, in the presidential suite, all was quiet. But if she stopped and listened, she could hear the faint buzz of activity that went on through the night. There was a light under Shirley's door. Laura turned the handle and went in.

David was sitting on the bed next to Shirley. The bed-clothes had been turned down. That was all Laura noticed at first. Then, as she adjusted to the light, she saw that Shirley's nightdress had been pulled up around her middle and that her pants were on the bed. David's hand rested on the child's pubic region. He looked round, and the expression in his eyes resembled that in the eyes of an animal disturbed in the act of procreation.

'She has a stomach ache,' he said. 'I was rubbing it better.'

Shirley looked at her mother, a look of bewilderment and fear. David's hand moved away, and he drew her nightdress down about her legs again.

'How long has this been going on?'

'This?'

'I'd like you out of this room. Now, please.'

'Laura, I think you're getting the wrong idea.'

'No,' she said. 'I have the right idea. We'll talk about this tomorrow. Right now, I want you out.'

He opened his mouth to protest, but all his bluster, all his machismo had evaporated. The bully had become something even more despicable. He could not tolerate Laura's gaze. With an effort he rose. Laura noticed that his pants were unbuttoned. He made no attempt to button them. She shrank back as he passed on his way to the door, as though he might strike out. But he did nothing, said nothing. She watched him go, then turned back to the bed. Afterwards, she wondered how she was able to summon up a smile. She spent the night with Shirley, watching her sleep and crying softly to herself in the semi-dark.

266

From Charles Maddox Crane's *A Brief History of the United States under the Klan Administration. Volume 3: Stephenson* (Arundel Academic Press, New York, 1992, pp 311–12)

THE JEWISH CLEARANCES

New York City (referred to in official documents of the time as 'Jew York') had a 1937 Jewish population of 2,035,000 out of a total urban population of 7,454,995. (The next largest Jewish populations were Chicago, with 363,000 out of a total 3,396,808, and Philadelphia with 293,000 out of a total 1,931,334.) The Klan leadership in the city had been agitating for several years in the hope of having all Jewish citizens either forcibly removed or packed into a ghetto outside Queens.

By 1939, numbers had already fallen by several thousand as a consequence of arrests and removals to concentration camps. In November 1939, all Jewish residents of New York over the age of seventy were given three days notice in which to pack a single suitcase and present themselves at Central Station. This staggered operation took place between the 8th and 15th of the month, and in that period a total of 58,543 elderly Jews were transferred from the city to camps close to the Canadian border. It was initially assumed that they were to be expelled into Canada, but on March 10th the Canadian government denied that any arrangement had been made with the US government and stated that it was not prepared to receive such a large consignment of Jewish immigrants.

A fire at Ogdensburg camp on the St Lawrence on 24th November resulted in the deaths of 875 individuals. The official report said that the fire had been started when a group of Jewish men lit candles for the Sabbath meal, but information later leaked out that the victims had, in fact, been attempting to burn bunks in order to provide heat. Between November and March, severe winter conditions resulted in the deaths of over 30,000 of the deportees.

In New York itself, the remaining Jews were moved in successive waves out of their main areas of residence and concentrated within the Williamsburg district of Brooklyn. Irish and German residents were moved out in order to accommodate this massive influx. The Germans were compensated by resettlement in better quality Jewish housing elsewhere in the area, while the mainly Catholic Irish were forced to look out for themselves. The Williamsburg ghetto eventually grew to accommodate almost 800,000 inhabitants under conditions of the utmost privation and overcrowding.

A second ghetto was created at Queen's. In the meantime, the Jewish population was further thinned by the deportation of all males between the ages of fifteen and thirty-five to labour camps in Maine, New Hampshire, and Vermont, where they were put to work on a variety of forestry and quarrying projects.

The ghettoization of New York's Jewish population was largely complete by the summer of 1940. With the rise to presidential power of David Stephenson later that year, the next phase began.

PART 9

Helena

CHAPTER FORTY

Thursday, 1 November
11.15 a.m.

Miles put down his briefcase and collapsed into the nearest chair. Sometimes he felt so tired he thought he would never get up again. He'd just given a class on the law governing constitutional amendments, and for the first time he'd seen behind the masks his students wore. None of them cared for the law, not really. And certainly not for justice. One particularly vile young woman, a leading light in the Kappa Kappa Kappa Sorority, had argued that the country could flourish only when the President stood above the law and the constitution.

'In Germany, Adolf Hitler is the Führer. He *is* the law. When things go wrong, he can put them right without wasting time. That's why Germany has become the strongest country in Europe. We can become even stronger if we get rid of this nonsense about democracy. David Stephenson is our leader, not the other way round. What would happen if a shepherd had to stop all the time to ask the sheep if they minded going this way or that?'

He'd argued that people were not sheep, that everyone mattered, that no-one could be infallible, not even a President; but nothing sank in, and he soon realized that the tide of opinion was set against him. They craved a leader, and in David Stephenson they'd found the man of their dreams.

He got up and went to the kitchen to prepare himself a

cup of coffee. It smelled good. At least some things hadn't changed.

There was a knock on the door. Odd, he thought. He wasn't expecting anybody. He put down the percolator hastily, hitting his cup and sending a stream of hot liquid across the worktop. Swearing, he hurried to find a dishcloth to mop up the spill. There was a second knock.

'I'm coming,' he shouted. 'Hang on.'

He wiped up as much of the coffee as he could, set the cup upright again in its saucer, and went to the door.

He did not know her at first. Nothing had prepared him, not even hope. For several moments, he only saw a strange woman standing awkwardly in his corridor, a waif crept in from God knew where, emaciated, shivering in a thin grey dress, her hair shaved back to the scalp, her eyes huge like opals set in two black hollows. He opened his mouth to speak, to ask who she was and what she wanted, and at that moment he understood.

'Helena! Good God, Helena, is it really you?'

She did not speak his name, as though names no longer held any meaning for her. He spoke her name again, whispering it this time.

'They let me go,' she said. 'They sent for me last night, after roll call. Let me out this morning.'

'I thought you were dead,' he whispered. He stepped up to her, and took her in his arms, and held her tightly as though she were no more than a phantom and might disappear again at any moment. That was when the spell broke, and she let herself fall on him, weeping as though her heart would break. But it had already been broken.

He took her in and made her sit while he fetched brandy. She waited until he brought her glass, and sat holding it, terrified, not knowing what was expected of her. He noticed the 'K' on her forearm, in a Star of David, and stroked it clumsily, as though afraid to hurt her.

'Take a little brandy,' he said. 'It'll make you feel better.'

272

She took a cautious sip, and coughed, as though she'd forgotten what brandy was.

He knelt down and put one arm round her and held her while she took another sip.

'What have they done to you?' he asked. 'You're so thin.'

She tried to smile, but her mouth would not follow the directions of her brain. He stroked her head, his hands remembering the long hair she'd had when they first married, the shorter cut she'd adopted from around the time she was forty.

'Scalped you as well,' he whispered, trying to make light of it. She nodded and put her own hand there, as though noticing her condition for the first time. Their fingers met, and he interlaced his with hers and held her hand.

'I tried to find you everywhere,' he said. 'Visited camps, wrote letters, asked people in the administration. Your name wasn't on their registers, not after the first camp.'

'Coxsackie,' she said.

'That's right. I think you were in Howard County after that.'

'Yes. Howard County. Not for very long. Maybe a month, I don't remember. They wanted me to work on a project.'

She looked at him properly for the first time. He'd aged, or was it just her faulty memory? She wasn't even sure exactly how long she'd been in the camps. Four years? Five years? After a while, you lost track of time. Summer ran into fall, ran into winter, ran into spring, ran into summer ... Her memory was a blur of seasons that meant nothing. Without freedom, time has no value.

'A project?'

'It was run by a man called Hopkins. He's a professor at Columbia. Or was.'

'This was a scientific thing?'

She nodded. The room looked familiar and unfamiliar

at one and the same time. He'd moved furniture around, turned the place into a bachelor apartment. She felt totally disoriented and wanted to burst into tears. But tears were part of the past, something she'd unlearned in order to survive.

'Please, Miles, I'd rather not talk about it now. It's too soon. There are things I need to tell you. About the camp. About what's going on there.'

He sensed the fear in her voice, how it edged towards terror. It was far too early to broach anything like that. She'd been in the camps, that was all anyone needed to know. He bent forward and kissed her softly on the forehead. For half an instant she shied away, as though expecting a blow.

'Why'd they let you out?'

She shook her head.

'I'm not sure. Someone said they were closing my section of the project down, that I wasn't needed any more. I thought they were just putting me back in the main camp. That's where I spent the night.'

'In Howard County?'

'No, Abilene it's called. Down in Virginia. They drove me back this morning. I spent the night in a dormitory block. They told me Lindbergh was shot.'

'That's right.'

'Hell of a thing. Lindbergh dead. Who's President now?'

'David Stephenson.'

'Of course. I should have guessed. Did he . . . ?'

'We'll talk about that later. First we need to find some decent clothes for you.'

'Aren't my things still here?'

'Some of them. I gave most of them away. I had to convince myself you were dead. I'd given up hope, you see. Oh, Helena, this is . . . it's unbelievable, you sitting there.'

This time the tears came, floods of them that seemed to go on for ever. And he held her like a small broken animal, and caressed her, and whispered things he'd almost forgotten he ever knew, things from their first days together, old, familiar words that seemed to belong to another lifetime.

There were a few clothes in a trunk, things he'd been unable to bring himself to throw out. She went to the bathroom and spent a long time inside, and when she came out she was a ghost haunting his memory of her. She was wearing a dark blue dress with silver buttons, and a scarf tied in a knot at the side, and little silver earrings that glinted brightly in the morning light.

'Do you remember when I wore this last?'

'At the Willard, at Ed and Norma's anniversary dinner. It fitted you better then.'

She managed to laugh. In spite of her best efforts with a needle and thread, the dress was still baggy.

'I guess I need a new wardrobe,' she said.

'We'll go out tomorrow. Today, I want you to myself.'

'I'm not ready for people yet. It'll take time.'

He'd already rung in to say he wouldn't be giving his state legislature class that afternoon. Something had come up, he'd told them, something important. He put together a late lunch, and they ate together at the kitchen table.

'This is like a banquet,' she said. 'I've never seen so much food in my life.'

'Yes, you have. You've just forgotten.'

'You've no idea what I've forgotten.'

'It'll come back. Wait and see.'

She lifted a forkful of pasta to her mouth. It seemed a tiny mouthful to him, but she ate it hungrily, chewing it as though there would be no more food all day. He closed his eyes, imagining her life in Abilene.

'Did you know Miriam Rosen is in Abilene?' she asked.

He looked at her, stunned.

'Miriam? No, I'd no idea. Did you see her?'

She shook her head.

'No, but I was told last night. You remember I said I spent the night in a dormitory?'

He nodded. His food lay untouched on his plate. Miriam Rosen alive? How was that possible?

'One of the people in the dormitory was Susan Frankel. Remember her?'

'Yes, yes of course. They arrested her – what? – two years ago.'

'I don't know. I'd no idea she was there at all. It came as a shock to me. She recognized me when I came in. Her bunk was in the next row. There was a little time before lights out. We talked a lot. She told me you'd been trying to find me. Then she mentioned Miriam. She said she was in another block, that it was absolutely forbidden to have contact between blocks during the night, but that she'd try to speak to Miriam before I left. Did you know Miriam was in there, Miles?'

He shook his head.

'No, but I knew she'd been arrested.'

He explained to her the circumstances of Moshe and Miriam's capture, and of Anna's arrival at his apartment.

'But that's wonderful. I was so sure she'd come to you. When Susan told me about Miriam, and that Anna hadn't been brought in with her, I knew you'd have done something. The next morning, Susan went across early to Miriam's block. There was just time for Miriam to write a quick note for Anna, then her dormitory was sent out on its morning assignment.'

'Miriam sent a note?'

Helena got up and went to the bedroom, where she'd left her camp dress. She came back with a crumpled piece of paper.

'It was all there was. Paper's like gold dust in the camps.'

She held it out to him. It had been scribbled hurriedly using a blunt pencil, but the handwriting seemed like Miriam's.

My beloved Anna, you must be a brave girl and wait until your Mummy is free again. I'm safe here and well looked after, and I'm sure they won't keep me here for long. Take care of yourself, and don't cry or fret. I'll be home soon.

'She wants me to take this to Anna. Susan said I should tell her I'd spoken to Miriam. What do you think? Is that an acceptable white lie?'

'I think so. But I don't think it's wise for you to see Anna, at least not yet. They're probably looking for her, and I'm sure they're watching you.'

'Surely not. They can't watch everybody they let out of a camp.'

'Well, there's still a risk. I don't want to put either of you in danger. Give me the note. I'll see it gets to Anna along with your news about her mother.'

'You may be right. She is safe, isn't she?'

'Who? Anna? Yes, of course she is. I took her to the James's. They're looking after her. I'll take the note round there myself after dark.'

She passed the note to him.

'I'd like to see Anna, once it's safe enough. What about Moshe? Where's he?'

He told her. And she left her food untouched and wept, knowing she had not left the evil behind her in the camp, but that it had followed her, that it was everywhere.

CHAPTER FORTY-ONE

Abilene Concentration Camp
Virginia
Thursday, 1 November
3.15 p.m.

They'd been called back early from the fields, just after lunch. Susan Frankel felt impatience rising in her like a fever. They'd told her she would be released later in the day. It was already early afternoon, and soon it would be dark again. She was afraid to ask, knowing that to do so might do more harm than good. What they'd asked her to do had been simple enough, and she couldn't see how it could harm anyone, not Miriam, not Helena. But they'd offered her her freedom in exchange for doing it, so she guessed it must have some importance for them.

Harrison, the woman guard with a face that might have been transplanted from Mount Rushmore, had tramped them back without a word and stabled them in their block. She'd been gone about half an hour now, and people were starting to get nervous. Any break in routine brought people out in the shakes. Bad things happened when routine was altered. Susan wondered if it could have anything to do with her deal, and reasoned that they'd hardly take the entire block off work over a matter that involved herself alone. She'd mentioned to one or two close friends that something must have happened to

Miriam Rosen, that she'd had to pretend she was in the camp; other than that, not a word.

The door opened and Harrison came in, accompanied by Torrance and Revel, all of them armed.

'We've got a fresh job for you up by Crocket Woods,' snapped Harrison. She never said anything in a normal tone of voice, as though the etiquette of the camps demanded it of her.

'Ain't it too late to be thinking of new work today?' someone asked. 'It's going to be dark in an hour.'

'Shut up and move out,' shouted Revel. She looked human, as more than one of them had thought to their undoing. Her humanity was a freak of nature, nothing more.

They marched out in pairs, as they did every morning, and they all feared they would be kept at work until well into the night. A job that started mid-afternoon wasn't going to be over much before midnight.

They walked sullenly through the deserted camp. Susan had started to panic. Surely they hadn't forgotten about her, surely they weren't going back on their promise? Luckily, she still had the written letter the governor had handed her the day before, setting out the terms of their agreement. She fingered it as she walked, knowing it might be her only guarantee of the freedom she'd been promised.

Once outside, the march to Crocket Woods was less than half a mile. As they reached the woods, they noticed two large trucks drawn up. FBIS trucks by the look of them, without numbers or lettering. A group of men in grey uniforms stood in the lee of the trucks, smoking cigarettes and telling jokes. As the women approached, an order was barked, and those with cigarettes threw them down. The company came together. Susan noticed they were all armed with sub-machine guns.

A path led into the woods. Light and darkness speckled it as if it was a leopard stretched beyond all reason between

279

the trees. At the gate, the three camp guards handed the eighty women over to the officer in charge, then turned and headed back to their barracks, relaxed now, and chatting between themselves like three teenagers returning from a barn dance in the light of early evening.

They were at once flanked by guards.

'Head on down the track in double file,' shouted the officer, a meaty-faced man from the Mid West, a herder of cattle who'd become a drover of men.

In the camp they were guarded by women most of the time. It disconcerted them to find themselves again surrounded by men, and to sense that the men treated them, not as women, but as two-legged cattle.

Someone brought spades from one of the trucks and handed them round, one to each woman. The sky above them started to lose colour as the sunlight weakened and dipped below the trees. They set off into a rapidly growing darkness, hustled down the long dappled path. Coming beneath the trees, the dappling gave way to deep shadow, and they were half blinded. There was no opportunity for escape. The men hemmed them in on all sides. Anyway, they'd all seen failed escapes in their times, heard the guns stutter, seen dying women jerk their lives away on mattresses of mud and stone.

The path led to a clearing. All around it battery-driven lamps had been set up, filling the empty space with a queer pearl-like radiance. It seemed to them as though they'd been marched on to some other-worldly theatrical set, with trees for a backdrop. Even here, protected as they were, the chill was penetrating.

'I want a hole dug right here,' said the officer, pointing to where stakes had been set to mark out a rectangle thirty feet by ten.

They started work, eager to bring some warmth back into their limbs. It was only as the digging progressed that the truth began to dawn on them. No-one said anything. No-one needed to. One by one they were overcome by an understanding that seemed to pass between them by telepathy. And, indeed, living as they did in such proximity, among so much death and suffering, they had developed some form of unearthly communication among themselves.

Susan broke away from the group, setting down her spade and drawing the governor's letter from her pocket. She walked up to the officer, holding it out as an Indian, facing his first white man, might have held out a talisman of wampum. He glanced through it, threw back his head, and laughed. The laugh rang through the clearing, but no-one looked up. They all continued their digging as though, by doing so, they might hold off the inevitable for ever.

He tore the letter in two and tossed it into the edge of the growing pit.

'Get back to work,' he said. 'You ain't goin' nowhere.'

She looked at him for as long as she dared, for as long as it took to sink in that she wasn't going home after all, that she was as dead as any one of her friends. Without another word, she walked back to her spade and resumed digging. The sound of spades cleaving earth echoed back and forward among the trees. She looked at the faces of their guards, bored and uncaring. No-one worked fast, no-one dared work too slowly. They just dug as if it was what life was all about.

One woman started to weep. Another started to sing an old song, a hymn that slaves had sung in days gone by:

Swing low, sweet chariot, coming for to carry me home,
Swing low, sweet chariot, coming for to carry me home . . .

CHAPTER FORTY-TWO

Miles stroked Helena's face gently, tracing her features with a blind man's fingers, as if unable to accept what his eyes saw. They had gone to bed late in the afternoon, not to make love, but to lie in one another's arms, for the comfort of it, to put an end to loneliness. The touch of flesh against flesh was nothing more than a conjuration against the darkness out of which Helena had come. It was too early for passion. Or too late.

'I don't understand why they moved you from Coxsackie.'

'They moved several of us at the same time. Jewish scientists. They needed our expertise for their project. Some were sent to Abilene, others to different camps. I've heard that a few went to Germany.'

'Why Germany?'

'It's a joint project. They're working on certain aspects of the problem, we're doing the rest. I only know that because they've sent some of their people over here.'

He sat up. This might be important.

'Why are they basing a scientific project in concentration camps?' he asked.

She shook her head.

'Only some of the work's being done in camps, the rest goes on at regular laboratories. They've split the whole thing up, so nobody knows more than they should. You're meant to work on your own tiny area, ask no questions, show no curiosity. But security isn't perfect. If you've been in this field long enough you know how to put two and two together. Things start to add up. We all know more than we're supposed to.'

'I still don't understand why some of the work's done in camps.'

'It's mainly a security thing, where they're using people like me. Plus they get free labour and . . .'

Her voice died away. He looked down to see her face close up against some inner pain.

'What's wrong?' he asked. 'What else do they get?'

'Guinea pigs,' she said. 'At Abilene, they wanted to see the effects of high doses of radiation on human subjects. Men, women . . . children. You can't imagine.'

She moved up until her head was level with his. He put his arm round her and rested his hand on her breast. Shudders passed through her, but she was past tears now.

'What do two and two add up to?' he asked her after a while.

She did not speak at once. Her thoughts were elsewhere, not in the camp, but in another, abstract world. She had nothing to go on but hints and allusions, a chance remark overheard here, a note in a paper there. But it added up, she knew it did.

'They're building a weapon,' she said. 'Some sort of bomb. A bomb powerful enough to wipe out an entire city.'

'Is that possible?'

'I think it could be. And I think they're near. The project was set up by Stephenson eight years ago. The year before that there'd been an immense breakthrough at the Cavendish Laboratory in Cambridge. They smashed atoms using accelerated protons. A couple of our people saw the potential and started working along similar lines here. You've met Ernest Lawrence, the one who built the cyclotron. He really speeded things up.'

'How'd Stephenson get involved?'

'A man called Brewster. He knew Stephenson in the old days in Indiana. He was working with Lawrence for a while, then set up his own lab in New Mexico. When the Klan got into power, he paid a visit to his old buddy, David. I don't know exactly what they cooked up between them, but a lot of money got syphoned off into the project. The Germans were already working on something similar, but we were far ahead of them. I don't know how their research and ours got tied up, but they did.'

'How long?'

'Before they have a bomb? I don't know. Most of this is just guesswork. I do know they've gone a long way with uranium fission. Some of the results I saw recently . . .' She hesitated and looked round at him. 'I think they could have a prototype ready in two to three months.'

'And a working weapon?'

'Not long after. By the spring.'

'With a weapon like that they could just walk over anyone who tried to stand in their way.'

He held her more tightly, as though she might turn to vapour before his eyes. She rolled over until she lay on top of him. Looking into his eyes, she kissed him on the lips, gently at first, then harder.

'Make love to me,' she said. 'Like you used to.'

'I've forgotten how,' he said.

She smiled, and she lifted herself so that her thin breasts swung against his chest. He looked at her. She had grown so thin and so weak, he feared to love her lest she break in two.

'Let me teach you,' she said. And she shut out everything from her mind, everything but the room she was in, and the bed she lay on, and her husband's body beneath hers, and the rhythm of their breathing. Kneeling, she moved her hands across his skin, and slowly memory returned, and pain, and longing, and the long desperation of loneliness.

'I love you,' she whispered.

His cheeks were covered with tears. He could not speak. But his lips opened and closed, and he reached up for her, to draw her down against him again. And he entered her slowly, as if for the first time, and she opened her eyes for him, and gazed at him, and cried out for the happiness that washed over her.

'Vernon? This is Miles. Is it safe for me to come over?'

'No reason to think it ain't.'

'Good. I'll be there in twenty minutes. I'll take a cab.'

Miles put the receiver down and smiled at Helena.

'You're sure you don't want me to stay?'

'I'd like nothing better. But that child needs to hear news of her mother. She has to see that note. You've got to take it to her.'

'I won't be long. We'll have an early night.'

She laughed.

'I thought you'd forgotten how to do that.'

'I'm relearning fast. Seriously, though – you're tired. You need a proper sleep.'

'I've forgotten what that is.'

'It'll come back.' He bent down and kissed her. As he left, he looked back and smiled. For a moment, as he closed the door, he felt young again.

Anna had not yet gone to bed. Vernon and Mabeline were clearing away the dinner things when Miles arrived.

'We've got some corn cobs left,' said Mabeline. 'Take no more than a couple of minutes to heat some up. Did you know she's got us cooking kosher?'

Miles shook his head.

'Thanks, I've already eaten.'

'You look happy 'bout something,' exclaimed Vernon, popping his head round the door.

Miles told them about Helena. They'd never met her, but he'd often spoken of her to them, and they were overjoyed at the news of her release.

'She told me something important this afternoon,' he said. 'Stephenson has people working on a new weapon.'

Briefly, he told them what he knew of the project.

'I need you to make contact with Bill Costello,' he said.

'Tell him it's urgent, say he has to speak to Helena, then see what he can find out on his own.'

'OK. I'll go over there later.'

'There's something else,' Miles said. 'It concerns Anna.' He took the scrap of paper from his pocket. Anna was sitting at the table, starting the homework Vernon was giving her in an attempt to keep up with her schooling.

'Anna, I've got some good news for you.' Miles held out the note.

She looked up, her eyes widening, scared even to think the unthinkable.

'Is it Mamma? You've found her?'

He nodded.

'This is from her,' he said. 'She gave it to my wife. Your mother's alive, but she's still in Abilene. Don't worry, we'll get her out. She's done nothing wrong.'

He spoke with a heavy heart, knowing how unlikely it was that Miriam Rosen, the wife of a President killer, would ever be released. But what could he tell Anna? Your mother's in a concentration camp, she's never coming out?

Anna had just taken the note from Miles when Vernon froze. He looked round at Mabeline.

'Mabeline, take Anna and Miles down to the cellar!'

'Vernon? What's wrong?'

'You heard me. Take them down.'

Miles turned to him.

'What's the matter?'

'Something's wrong. This time of night, the street outside's usually still pretty busy. People, cars, there's a lot of noise. Now listen.'

Silence had fallen like new snow. Miles nodded. There'd been normal activity on the street when he'd arrived.

Mabeline had already rolled back the carpet and opened the concealed hatch that led down to the cellar. Anna was with her, the note still in her hand, unread.

286

Miles insisted on staying with Vernon. Together, they went to the front room.

'Get down,' said Vernon. On all fours they made their way to the window and looked out.

The street was filled with FBIS vans, heavy black-painted rectangles that sat squat and sullen in a ring facing the house. Armed men had already been disgorged from them and were awaiting orders.

Someone hammered loudly on the front door. The pounding resounded through the house, as though it had become a drum. Miles turned to Vernon.

'Is there a back way out of here?'

'Don't even think about it. They'll be there already. Our only chance is the cellar. There's a tunnel leading down to the creek. It takes a while to crawl through, though. If they break in, they'll find it quickly enough.'

'We'd still be ahead of them.'

They ran back to the kitchen. As they reached it, there was a crashing sound. Some sort of battering ram was being used on the front door. Vernon hurried to a cupboard, swung out a false shelf, and pulled a Thompson sub-machine gun from a hidden recess. He tossed it to Miles, then pulled out another.

'There's no time for all of us to get out,' he said. 'You take Mabeline and Anna. I'll hold them off here as long as I can.'

He lifted out a square metal box and tore off the lid to reveal a nest of hand grenades. There was a second, louder crash at the door.

'Door's reinforced,' he said. 'But it won't hold them back long. You've got to get moving now.'

Miles hung back. Vernon was an old friend, a good friend. He couldn't just abandon him to the beast.

'I'll hold them back here with you. That'll give Mabeline and Anna longer to get out.'

'Like hell you will. The Good Lord put you on earth for one thing, me for another. You're more danger to the cause if they take you alive. Get the hell out of here while you can, and take Anna and Mabeline with you.'

'Somebody talking about me?' Mabeline appeared behind them, in the entrance to the cellar.

Vernon turned. Miles caught the look of mingled horror and relief on his face. 'I thought you were out of here already.'

'I can't get her to go into the tunnel. She says she's afraid of narrow spaces.'

'She's got to go. They'll kill her if they find her.'

A crash heavier than the others brought the door down. Vernon dashed into the hallway in time to catch sight of the first armed intruder thrusting through the rubble. He pulled a pin from a grenade and lobbed it at the dark-suited figure before ducking back. Seconds later a loud explosion ripped the doorway to rubble.

Mabeline snatched the second gun from Miles's hands.

'I'm not leaving him,' she said. 'You get Anna out. Hurry, you don't have time to hang around.'

Miles still hesitated. If he indulged in false heroics, Anna would die anyway. And Helena . . . What would become of Helena if he did not return?

'God bless you,' he said, embracing Mabeline quickly. 'God bless you both.'

'Make sure Anna doesn't forget us,' she said, her voice on the verge of tears. Suddenly, reaching across the table, she picked up Anna's violin. 'Here. Give this to her. Tell her it's hers to keep if she makes it through that tunnel.'

A roar of gunfire came from the hallway. Mabeline looked round.

'I've got to help him. Get in there and I'll block up the entrance.'

Miles hesitated a second longer, then climbed down into the cellar. The hatch closed over his head, and he bolted it from underneath. There was a sound of furniture being moved on top, then silence. And then more rapid bursts of gunfire, followed by a second gut-wrenching explosion.

Anna was standing in one corner, shaking. Behind her, a section of wall had been pulled out. A hole led down into utter darkness, from which there seemed no escape.

CHAPTER FORTY-THREE

Helena could not rest. She'd tried reading, listening to the radio, playing a recording of chamber music that normally relaxed her – all things she'd dreamt of doing while in the camp. But after a few moments, she'd fling down the book or switch off the radio or lift the arm of the phonograph. She felt free and confined simultaneously, and to her horror she experienced a dreadful homesickness for the camp, and a terror of this dream-world in which she found herself.

She switched on the radio again and spun the dial until she got NBC. A news broadcast was under way.

' . . . until tomorrow.

'And now for more on that earlier, unconfirmed report that President Stephenson may be getting ready to put his signature to an alliance between the United States and Germany. Recent rumours suggested that the alliance was on the agenda when he met in the White House with high-ranking German officials following the funeral of President Lindbergh. Until this evening, both the State Department and the Aryan Alliance Office for American-German relations refused to comment on these rumours. However, there has now been official confirmation that informal discussions did, in fact, take place.

'We have just learned that the President plans to meet with the German leader, Adolf Hitler, sometime in the next two weeks. A suitable venue for their meeting has yet to be arranged, but there is already speculation that a Latin American state may provide facilities. Should these bipartite talks prove positive – and all indications are they will be – David Stephenson's long-standing dream of American-German unity will be set to become reality.

'The terms of such an alliance remain to be thrashed out, but it's thought unlikely they'll be restricted to trade and cultural relations. In their time of peril, the Germans need our military strength and know-how. We, on the other hand, stand to benefit immeasurably from the markets their armed forces are opening up throughout Europe and beyond. News of the upcoming talks raised prices on Wall Street today, with German firms like I G Farben benefiting from strong share bidding.

'One thing is certain: never have the forces of world Communism and international Jewry faced a greater threat. The commissars and the hooked-nose brigade must be shaking in their boots right this minute. Their time's up, but our hour is coming. And when it comes . . .'

Helena reached forward and switched off the set. Her hand was shaking, as if she'd just managed to turn off a cyclotron before it got out of control.

She went to the window and looked out into the street. It seemed quieter than she remembered it. Or had her imagination populated it with thronging crowds as compensation for her despair and loneliness? She wished Miles would get back. He was already much later than he'd said he'd be. Out of nowhere the despair and the loneliness flew back, surrounding her with their dim, nauseating wings, breathing their fetid breath into her open nostrils.

CHAPTER FORTY-FOUR

'Just keep your violin in front of you. Pretend it's a lamp, that it'll lead you out.'

'What if there's no way out? It could be a dead end, we'd never get out again.'

The barely-contained panic in Anna's voice worried him. If she lost her head he might not be able to calm her, and the consequences could be disastrous.

'Vernon says it leads to the creek. You don't think he'd lie, do you?'

'No, of course not, but he could be mistaken. Somebody might have blocked it up.'

'Don't even think that. This is a secret tunnel: nobody else knows it's here. Just keep crawling. It isn't far.'

It was pitch black inside the tunnel, and foul-smelling, and damp. The entrance to the cellar had been pulled tight shut behind them, leaving no visible mark in the outside wall. No sounds came to them from anywhere. Miles had never been in such total darkness. Had it not been for the rough touch of soil on his hands and knees, and the rasping of his breath, and Anna's voice ahead of him from time to time, he might have thought himself dead. The reality was worse, of course: for all he knew, he was buried alive.

He lost track of time. They might have been in the tunnel five minutes or an hour. Fighting down her terror of the dark, Anna crawled forward inches at a time. But it was harder work for Miles, whose adult body almost filled the available space. A larger man might have stuck halfway.

In spite of himself, he felt a sense of panic growing in his chest. Once he stopped and tried to crawl backwards, just to see if it could be done. Within seconds he realized it was pointless: he'd give in to the claustrophobia long before he got halfway back to the entrance. He shut his mind off and kept moving forwards.

'I never got to read the message you gave me, the one from my mother. What does it say?'

He hesitated. The darkness made it easier to lie, and harder to accept the fact of doing so.

'She says she's fine, that she's in Abilene camp, and that she's hoping to come out soon. Something like that. She says you have to be a brave girl.'

'I'm trying.'

'I know you are.'

'What's it like in there, in the camp?'

'I'm not too sure. You can ask Helena when we get back.' He'd told her all about Helena, and how she'd come home.

'Yes, I'll do that.'

Her voice sounded charged, carrying some burden at which he could not guess. A long silence followed, then, softly at first, he heard her crying.

'What's wrong, dear? It won't be much further. We're under the park by now.'

She did not answer at once, but when the words came they were controlled and almost without emotion.

'It's not her handwriting,' she said.

'What?'

'I looked at it quickly, just before Vernon said we had to leave. It's like somebody imitated it.'

'Anna, you're just a child. Handwriting is difficult. Even grown-ups find it hard to tell a real signature from a fake.'

But in his heart he knew she was right. It made sense suddenly. Helena's unexpected release, the coincidence of finding Miriam in the same camp. He was sure more than

293

ever that Miriam was dead. They'd been after Anna, and he'd led them to her.

'There's something here!'

Anna's voice shook.

'It's the end of the tunnel,' she said. 'But there's no way out.'

He sensed her start to panic, felt his own heart go cold.

'There has to be an exit. This tunnel wasn't cut for nothing.'

They tried everywhere: in front, on top, the sides, the floor. Just bare soil shored up by struts, as it had been all along. Frantically, they pushed and shoved, but nothing gave. They were shut in by solid earth on all sides.

'It won't give way! We can't get out! We're trapped in here!' Anna's voice rose rapidly in pitch as the panic within her mounted. 'I told Mabeline, I said I didn't want to get in here.'

Miles struggled to control his own terror, telling himself that Vernon would never have sent them into a trap. He got hold of Anna as best he could, and held her and whispered to her through the all-encompassing darkness.

'Keep calm. There is a way out, we just have to find it. Don't stop looking.'

He moved awkwardly, afraid of hurting her, and as he did so his elbow touched something hard. Gently easing himself back about a foot, he reached out. His fingers touched a metal object – a trowel.

'This is it,' he said. 'This is our way out. If they'd left a proper entrance, there was always a chance of somebody stumbling on it. Vernon left the last few feet intact. All we have to do is dig our way through it.'

He handed the trowel to Anna.

'I can't reach from here,' he said. 'You'll have to do the honours.'

Stifling the sobs that kept pushing their way to her lips, she took hold of the little tool and started scraping at the

294

wall in front. The soil was soft and came away in clumps. Soon, she was knee-deep in it.

'Push some of it back, I'll do the same.'

They cleared as much of it away as they could, then Anna started again, stabbing viciously at the invisible wall in front of her.

'Why won't it break, why won't it open?' She fell against it, sobbing.

'Pass me the trowel,' he ordered. Numbly, she handed it to him. Angrily, he began to slash at the sides of the tunnel, widening it. After about ten minutes of this, there was enough room for them to pass. He told Anna to get behind him, then crawled forward to the tunnel head and started to dig.

Five minutes later, he sensed that something was wrong. In the darkness, it was not obvious at first, then he felt an unmistakeable rush of wet across his hand. Water was seeping into the tunnel.

'It must be the creek,' he said, and as he spoke he realized what must have happened. Vernon must have designed the exit to come out in the bank just above the water. That way somebody escaping could hope to avoid being seen as they crawled out. They'd get wet, but that was better than a bullet in the head. Unluckily for him and Anna, there'd been heavy rain for two days. The level of the creek must have risen.

'I'll have to dig higher. Help me get more of this soil out of the way.'

But even as he spoke the small hole became a bigger one, and more water flooded in, widening the breach even more. Within seconds the earth in front was breaking apart as streams of ice-cold water flowed into the tunnel.

He turned to Anna.

'Can you swim?'

'Yes.'

'Take a deep breath. Then swim up. It'll only be a foot or two to the surface.'

She was silent for a moment, as though the flooding water wakened a memory in her.

'My mother's dead, isn't she?'

The water ran into the tunnel in an unceasing stream now, a stream nothing could staunch.

'Yes,' he said, saying it to the darkness as much as to the child, as though all words spoken now were spoken to the dark.

He took a deep breath and crashed against the wall in front of him, breaking the last of it down, bringing the water in on them without hindrance. And he kicked forwards and upwards and felt himself taken into the water and into the darkness.

CHAPTER FORTY-FIVE

She arrived shortly after ten o'clock. Shirley was asleep, David was at a meeting of the Party elite, and her own reception with a bevy of wives from the Japanese military mission had ended on time. He took her straight into his arms, and she clung to him for a long time without speaking or moving.

'What's wrong?' he asked.

'Nothing. I'm just tired. Those women were just awful. You don't know what it's like.'

'Let me get you a drink.'

She followed him to the living-room, and he put on music, a slow jazz recording one of the guys in the office had slipped him the day before. There was more than one jazz fan among the White House staff, and smuggled records did a roaring trade. He'd heard Billie Holiday a couple of years earlier, before she was finally banned. This was an old recording, a little scratchy, but melodious and sad, and he played it for her with the sound turned down, so no-one in the next apartment would hear.

He turned it over and played the other side. The high voice drifted like smoke through the dimly-lit room, poignant, almost breaking. He went back to her, where she sat drinking her vermouth and watching him.

He leaned forward and kissed her, and her lips parted like ripe fruit beneath his own. She put down her glass on the floor, and he held her more closely, stroking her left breast with one hand while he supported her neck with the other. Her breathing grew tight, and her tongue flew into his mouth, and he held it there and stroked her nipple until it rose beneath his fingers.

She was wearing the dress she'd had on for the reception, a long silk gown that clung to her body now like a flag blown about its pole. He moved his hand down to her leg and ran it slowly up beneath her skirt, along her silk stockings to her naked thigh, pausing there for a moment to draw back and look at her. He smiled and she reached out a hand and drew him close again, kissing him harder, breathing him into her as though he was breath itself. His hand moved higher and he touched the edge of her pants, and he slipped his fingers inside and rested them on her.

She froze. He felt her body go tense beneath him, then she pulled her face away and put her hands against his chest and pushed him back.

'What's wrong? Laura? What did I do? Did I hurt you?'

She shook her head, not answering, and he reached forward as though to caress her, but she drew back again, shaking her head.

'I'm sorry,' he said. 'I don't understand.'

It was a long time before she could begin to speak.

'My father . . . He used to . . . From the time I was twelve.'

'I thought you said . . .'

'That he never raped me? In a way that's true. He frightened me into a sort of consent. No, that's not true either. I never consented. I just learned to keep my mouth shut. It was years before my mother found out. That's what finally broke her.'

'Why tonight? Has something happened to make it fresh? When he was here, did he . . . ?'

She shook her head. Slowly, in words she dug out of herself, she told him. About David. About Shirley. About herself. He listened, horrified. When she finished, she lay in his arms, not a lover merely now, but part of him, and was quiet. And when he kissed her again, it was not as a lover, nor as a friend, but as someone beyond those things, and part of her.

'You can kill him now,' she said. 'It doesn't matter. Better for Shirley if you do. Maybe she'll forget in time. They say children do.'

'You understand what you're saying?'

She nodded.

'There's something else,' he said.

She looked at him, not afraid any longer.

'I'll need you to help me.'

She did not answer at once. Then she reached out for him and drew him close again.

'Yes,' she said. 'Yes.'

And he kissed her then, and she closed her eyes, and her whole body lifted for him.

'Yes,' she said. 'Yes.'

Outside, in the dark and cold, Larry Loomis waited in the shadows. He knew it would be a long wait, but something told him it would be worth it. She'd come out again, she had to, and this time he'd be prepared. He'd done plenty of this sort of thing in his day – divorces, pre-marital checks, routine marital suspicions. He'd learned how to use a camera, how to dig deep without making the guilty parties suspicious. But until tonight all his prey had been small fry. Now, as he watched the door of John's apartment building, the sturdy ghosts of dollar bills began to drift through his mind.

CHAPTER FORTY-SIX

By chance that seemed to Miles like providence, they stumbled on an encampment on the west side of the park, between Bingham Drive and the Military Road. Or had he noticed it before in passing, and now remembered it unconsciously, and led them there? It hardly mattered. The tents – rickety constructions thrown together from branches, cardboard, and rags – were inhabited by homeless blacks whose presence was tolerated only because they served as a warning to others.

Anna and he were bitterly cold, and the water on their clothing had started to freeze. He was frightened that the child might catch pneumonia if they remained exposed much longer.

A woman saw them coming out of the darkness. She was sitting by a struggling fire, trying to keep warm. Her thin clothes and thin body gave little protection against the cold. Behind her in the shadows, other eyes shone in the firelight.

'My granddaughter and I fell in the creek,' said Miles. 'Could we warm ourselves at your fire?'

The woman came forward, limping, frightened of this man and child appearing from nowhere.

'We ain't supposed to let no white folks in here,' she murmured. The curfew was being rigidly enforced, and mixing with whites after dark was a punishable offence. She'd heard of people being hanged for it.

A man came forward, a large man with a shaved head.

'It's all right, May, can't you see they're both in a bad way?'

He brought them to the fire, and had someone go in search of fresh wood.

'You're gonna die if you don't get those things off,' he said. 'Why don't you come in my tent? One of the women here'll take the child.'

Miles was led off to a low tent a few yards away. Everywhere, he picked out groups of wretched-looking people huddled round struggling fires, everywhere he saw children clutching their mothers' skirts, everywhere he smelled the fear and the degradation. This was the bottom of the line. There was little enough to choose between this and the camps.

'In here,' said the man. 'Strip off your wet things while I fetch something for you to put on.'

Miles put out his hand.

'Thank you for helping us. I know you're taking a risk.'

'Living's a risk, mister. But you're white, you wouldn't know.'

'White isn't everything, believe me.'

Something in Miles's tone arrested the other man. He took Miles's hand.

'My name's Pete. Pete Rawlings.'

'Miles Vanderlyn. I'm pleased to meet you.'

'Get those things off, now. I'll be back.'

Miles stripped slowly, shivering uncontrollably. The tent offered scant protection against the elements. On the floor lay some bundles of torn rags that probably served as Pete's bed. A winter here would pick off all but the strongest.

Pete finally returned with items of clothing he'd scrounged from friends, and a couple of thin blankets.

'Let's get you back to that fire,' he said, leading Miles out again into the darkness.

The fire was brighter now. Miles guessed that people had given up pieces of wood they'd been holding back.

'They hang you if they catch you cutting down wood,'

said Pete, as though reading Miles's thoughts. 'We gotta make do with what we can pick up. Ain't much.'

But it was enough to keep Anna and him warm while their clothes dried out. A cluster of women had gathered round the little girl, fussing over her and rubbing her to keep her warm.

'How come you're both out here after dark?' asked Pete. 'Ain't a lot to see in Rock Creek Park come nightfall.'

'We tried to take a short cut,' said Miles. 'Came the wrong way. Anna here slipped and fell into the creek, and I jumped in after her. She'd been at a music lesson.' He pointed at her violin, which she had managed to keep with her through everything.

'You hear that shooting and stuff earlier?' Pete asked, not quite innocently Miles thought.

'We heard something. Couldn't work out where it came from, though.'

'Over the other side of the park, past the creek, I reckon. I'd steer clear of there for the moment. Which way you folks headed?'

'Back home,' said Miles, making it clear that was all he was willing to say.

'That's the best place to be, a night like this.' He asked no more questions

When their clothes were dry enough to wear, they dressed. Anna had on only what she had been wearing when the raid began. They still had over four miles to walk, with the constant risk of being stopped by a curfew patrol. Anna's papers had been left behind in the James's, and all it would take to destroy her would be a suspicious policeman with an arrest quota to fill. Miles realized he'd come out without money.

'I'm sorry to ask this,' he said, 'but I badly need to make a phone call. Can any of you spare a nickel? I can pay it back.'

Pete burst out laughing. His world had just turned upside down. Here was a middle-class white man dressed in damp but expensive clothes, asking if poor nigger trash could spare him a nickel. He went to his tent and came back with two nickels.

'Here. You may need to ring more than once. And I don't need paying back. Just see this child gets home safe.'

Miles thanked him and prepared to go. As he did so, Pete came closer.

'What do I tell them when they come askin' questions? Some of these folks here ain't gonna say they never saw you. They're frightened. They don't want trouble.'

'Just say I had a gun. Say we stole some of your things. You're just a bunch of scared niggers, no match for a young white man like me. They'll believe that.'

Pete nodded and shook hands.

'Maybe I'll leave out the bit about "young",' he said. 'Take care.' Behind him the fire had burned down almost to nothing. There'd be no more wood for the rest of the night. The cold returned with the dark. Dawn was a long way away.

CHAPTER FORTY-SEVEN

The phone rang eight or nine times before John picked it up. He'd fallen asleep beside Laura. She shook him awake, and he answered. She watched him nervously, wondering who could be ringing so late. He listened for half a minute, and when he spoke his voice sounded tense.

'Where are you?'

Laura could hear a thin voice crackling through the receiver, but could make out nothing.

'OK, stay where you are. I'll be there in fifteen minutes.'

He put down the receiver and turned to her.

'That was Miles. He's in some sort of trouble. I said I'd pick him up. Can you let yourself out?'

She nodded.

'I'll be all right.'

He kissed her gently, then drew her to him, holding her naked body against his as though they would never meet again, and kissing her harder. She responded briefly, then pushed him away.

'You've got to go. If Miles is in trouble you shouldn't be wasting time.'

Larry Loomis meditated on his piles, much as a Buddhist monk might have pondered the mysteries of ahimsa. Sitting was bad, but standing for a long time had its own effects. He had known long vigils that had turned into nights of torture. For comfort, he ate a succession of candy bars. He knew he'd regret them in the morning, but with luck his regret would be overlaid with triumph.

So deep was his concentration on his own discomfort that he almost missed John. His target was out of the building and almost in the Duesenberg before Loomis realized. He panicked momentarily and craned forward to check. No, the woman wasn't in the car. As John started the engine, his watcher debated within himself what to do next: follow the man he was being paid to keep tabs on, or wait for the woman, who might turn out to be a prize beyond understanding?

He opted for the latter. If she was who he thought she was; confirming it would be balm to what he'd suffered waiting for her to come out. He watched the Duesenberg pull away from the kerb and reasoned with himself that he could always check tomorrow's police records: if lover-boy passed through any checkpoints, he'd leave a trace.

As John's taillights disappeared down the street, Loomis turned his gaze back to the door of the apartment building. Somewhere, a voice sang, very low and tremulous, casting the half-remembered words of a love-song into the cold air and the darkness and the restless city, then faltered and broke. In the silence that followed, Larry Loomis watched and waited.

Miles and Anna were waiting near a call box at the east end of Utah Avenue. They were both shivering uncontrollably. Miles had left his heavy overcoat in Pete's tent: it had been thoroughly saturated and would have taken days to dry; and he reckoned Pete needed it more than he did.

John drew up at the box, opening the door as he did so, and they came running towards him from the shadows. In the distance, a siren could be heard howling.

'Get in. Hurry up, we can't stay here.'

They started to get in, but John shook his head.

'You said on the phone that Anna has no papers. I'd a

lot of trouble getting here. The streets are crawling with cops and FBIS. She has to go in the trunk.'

Anna at once shook her head violently. All the emotions of being trapped in the narrow tunnel surfaced again.

'I can't go in there. Please don't make me.'

Vanderlyn turned to her.

'Sweetheart, you've been a brave girl right through this. I'm proud of you. You've done things not many grown-ups could do. But John's right. If they're out looking for us, just seeing you sitting here would be enough. They'll kill you, they'll kill me, and they'll kill John.'

She stared at him, hurt by his harshness, yet knowing that what he said was true. In the new world she'd lived in since that dreadful night when they took her parents away, they killed people out of hand. She knew now that her mother and father were both dead, that Vernon and Mabeline, whom she'd begun to love, were dead, and that Professor Vanderlyn was risking his own life to save her.

'OK,' she said. Then, turning to climb inside, she looked back at him. 'Will I be able to breathe in there?'

'We'll stop as soon as we can. I'd reckon there's enough air in there to last a couple of hours. We'll be back long before that.'

She nodded and he helped her into the trunk.

'Will my violin be OK?' she asked. 'It got real wet back in the creek.'

'It's a good instrument. I know a man who repairs them. We'll take it to him first thing tomorrow. Now, I'm going to have to shut you in. It's time we were moving.'

He closed the trunk and felt himself shudder as he did so. It was almost as if he was shutting her inside her coffin.

Once he was in the passenger seat, they drove off.

'They're looking for you,' said John.

'How do you know?'

'I've got a pass that says I'm a special advisor to the President. My security authorization gives me high-level clearance at the FBIS. All I have to do is ask the first policeman I see "What's going on tonight?" and I get an answer. They have your name and description, they have Anna's name. Now, what papers are you carrying?'

'My own. It's usually the safest thing.'

John put his foot on the brake. They were on Nevada, heading south-west. The first check was five or six blocks away. The Duesenberg came to a halt.

'Hurry up. Look for a drain and throw them in. They can see our headlights already.'

Miles opened the door and started to get out. John put a hand on his arm.

'Wait. Let me have the photograph from your ID card. Be careful not to tear it.'

Miles walked under the nearest streetlamp and carefully removed the photograph. Then, searching along the street, he found a storm-drain and tossed his papers down it.

Back in the car, he handed the photograph to John.

'It's damp. What have you been doing?'

'I'll tell you later. Vernon and Mabeline are dead. The FBIS raided the house. I think I led them there.'

John nodded. He'd already taken a set of false papers from a hidden recess in the glove compartment. From his pocket he retrieved a small tube of glue. Working quickly, he covered the photograph of himself with that of Miles. Just down the road, he could see the slowly-rotating lights of the police cruisers that formed the roadblock. Without waiting for the glue to dry, he handed the card to Miles.

'Your name's Greg Lawrence, you're a high-school teacher from Vermont. I guess you must be on vacation here.'

'In term-time?'

'You just retired.'

'How do we know one another?'

'You're a friend of the family. You're down here on vacation, I'm showing you the sights.'

'And what have I been doing in this end of town? There aren't too many sights to see up here.'

'We've been driving round the park. I came here on Connecticut, then across, these guys won't know I was on my own.'

Miles glanced through the ID, memorized his supposed home address, and his Klan membership number.

'Let's get moving,' he said. 'I'm anxious to get home.'

John's pass worked even better on the way back. They only asked for Miles's papers at one checkpoint, and that was as a formality. For all any of them knew, John himself might be supervising the entire operation.

As they drove, Miles explained what had happened, from Helena's appearance to the raid and his escape with Anna.

'If they're looking for me, they'll be at my apartment. What about Helena? Jesus, they'll arrest her again.'

John drew up at a phone booth at the corner of Van Ness. Getting out of the car, he turned to Miles.

'What's your number?'

In the booth, he dialled it, praying Miles was wrong, that they'd leave the apartment alone in the hope Miles might go back there. The phone rang several times, and he'd almost given up hope when a woman's voice answered.

'Vanderlyn apartment.'

'Is that Helena?'

'Yes, who is this?'

'You don't know me. I'm a friend of Miles's. Listen, I can't talk now, but . . .'

'Is Miles all right? Has anything happened?'

The fear in her voice seemed magnified by the impersonality of the wires along which it reached him.

'Miles is with me, but it's better he doesn't come to the phone. Look, can you leave the apartment by the rear?'

'Yes, I think so. But what's . . .'

'Can you get to the National Cathedral?'

'It's about a mile from here. Give me half an hour.'

'We'll wait for you there. Don't worry – Miles'll explain everything when he sees you.'

CHAPTER FORTY-EIGHT

They hit a large checkpoint at Ward Circle, just where Nebraska crossed with Massachusetts. Traffic along Massachusetts was heavier than usual – John later learned there'd been a Klan dedication at Falls Church – and there were long delays in processing cars moving in their direction. When they finally reached the checkpoint it turned out to be a lot tighter than the others they'd come through. For one thing, it was manned entirely by FBIS agents, which meant harder questioning and greater attention to detail. John began to worry about Anna, how long she could stand being shut up in that confined space, how long before the air in the trunk started to grow stale.

A grey-faced agent with narrow lips and an Adam's apple carved from granite handed John's papers back and saluted.

'Sorry about this, sir. We won't hold you up much longer.'

He turned to Miles.

'Can I see your papers too, sir?'

John leaned over.

'What the hell's all this about? The President's going to ask me about it in the morning. Can I tell him you guys have got it under control?'

'Yes, sir. All under control. We're looking for a man called Vanderlyn. He's mixed up in the Lindbergh assassination.'

'I've heard of him. Law professor, is that right?'

The agent nodded and gave a brief description.

'I know him,' said John. Suddenly, he glanced at the dashboard clock. 'Hell, I've got a meeting at the White House. Can you run me through?'

Forgetting Miles's papers, the agent waved them on, and John made a left on to Massachusetts, heading down to the cathedral, a mile further on. Still unfinished after thirty-five years of building, it rose up on Mount St Albans like a work of medieval craftsmanship, though most of its stones had been laid by living hands. Set atop the east roof, visible from far off, stood a great cross wreathed in everlasting flame.

'I knew Bevins,' said Miles, looking upwards. 'He was a good man. He had integrity.'

'Bevins?'

'Bishop Bevins. This was his cathedral. The Klan wanted to take it out of the hands of the Episcopalians, make it a national church headed by a Klan bishop. Bevins held out for three years, ran rings round them in the courts. They wanted a cross like that one put up there – he wouldn't hear of it. So they sent men in to get rid of him. Shot him while he was praying, up by the altar. Blamed it on the Catholics, but everybody knew. There's a new man now, name of Teller. Wouldn't know the Bible from the Book of Mormon. But he had the cross put up the first week he put on purple.'

They crossed Hamilton Circle. John turned into Wisconsin and drew up facing the unfinished west end of the cathedral. He switched off his headlamps and the partly-lit body of the church took a step further out of the darkness surrounding it. The vast edifice stood alone and silent, like a web of stone woven by the earth itself. It did not really belong here. Not in America, not in this century, not in this warped empire of wizards and goblins and hydras. Up close, the garish cross on its roof was invisible. At eye level, the stone and coloured glass proclaimed a different message.

Miles got out. There was no sign of Helena.

'She's not here yet. I'll wait at the curator's office where she can see me. You'd better stay here: seeing someone she doesn't know might frighten her off.'

311

He went through the gate and walked down the path. John watched him go, then got out of the car. He opened the trunk and found Anna curled up like a baby, cradling her violin and crying gently to herself.

'You can get out now, sweetheart. I'm going to open up the rear seat. Miles is waiting for his wife to come.'

She climbed out slowly, her limbs cramped by cold and confinement.

'You remember me, don't you?' he said.

She nodded.

'You're Professor Vanderlyn's friend, the one who picked us up when I went to Vernon's.'

'Miles told me what happened tonight. And he told me about your mother. I'm really sorry.'

She hung her head, and her fingers brushed the strings of the instrument in her hand, sending a tiny, vibrating note out into the darkness.

'You don't have to be sorry. Everybody dies sometime. They'll kill me too. You're just wasting your time.'

She looked up at him, and in what little light there was he saw the despair in her eyes, the invasion of adulthood that had laid waste all hope.

He took her into his arms and held her pressed there, knowing nothing of how to comfort a child. And she was like wood, like unseasoned timber, neither responding nor caring that she did not respond.

He looked up and caught a movement on a side path running towards the west facade. A woman was walking towards Miles. He saw Miles detach himself from the doorway of the curator's office, a tiny figure dwarfed by the immensity of the building in whose shadow he stood.

'Helena!'

The woman quickened her pace and Miles stepped onto the path, walking to her with his arms open.

At that moment someone opened fire. It was a handgun, an automatic pistol of some sort, and it stuttered its one and only word, repeating it again and again, then falling silent as Helena staggered forward and fell face down on the path.

Miles ran towards her, bending and picking her up in his arms, and from the road John heard him cry her name, 'Helena, Helena', as though it was the right word at last, the word the gun with its stammering persistence had been unable to complete.

John looked on in horror, frozen by the suddenness and emptiness of what had happened. Then, out of the shadows, he saw them move in, men in grey uniforms, their weapons visible, forming a circle around Miles and his dead wife. He bent down to Anna.

'Get into the car now, Anna. Don't slam the door, just push down the handle and pull it to.'

He slipped into the driver's seat and, when Anna was safely inside, switched on the engine but not the lights, and crept forward, slowly at first, then with growing speed. He kept on up Wisconsin only as far as Macomb Street, then made a right that brought him down to Connecticut and brighter lights.

When he was sure there was no-one following them, he looked down at Anna. She was crying softly, and on her lap lay her violin, broken beyond repair, its strings falling loose against pieces of shattered wood. And he realized he'd crushed it against her when the shots had rung out, pulling her to him as though to save her life. There was nothing he could say to her. If she asked him later, was Professor Vanderlyn alive, he'd say no, they'd killed him, he'd seen it in the mirror as they drove away. But that was a lie. They'd taken Miles alive, he'd already be on his way to FBIS headquarters. And that was when John understood there could never be true pity in the world. Miles had to die, and John would have to find a way to help him do it.

Extract from *Edict 513 (1935)*, US Department of the Interior, Federal Kommission for Kultural Change (FKKC), (pp 71–72)

Article 7:19 (iv)

The following changes in the spelling of proper names and common nouns beginning with a hard 'c' have been proposed and will become legally binding in grade schools, high schools, colleges, publishing houses, newspapers, federal government offices, Klan chapters, and state government offices from 12/31/1935. Failure to comply with these and related changes without good cause will result in fines not exceeding $100 in the first instance. Private firms wishing to make alterations to their published materials should make application for tax exemption directly to the US Board of Tax Appeals.

Old Style	New Style
Cadillac	Kadillak
Cagney	Kagney
Calamity Jane	Kalamity Jane
California	Kalifornia
Calvary	Kalvary
Calvin	Kalvin

Old Style	New Style
Camp Fire Girls	Kamp Fire Girls[1]
Canada	Kanada
Cape Cod	Kape Kod
Capitol	Kapitol
Captain	Kaptain
Carnegie	Karnegie
Carolina	Karolina
Carpetbagger	Karpetbagger
Carson, Kit	Karson, Kit
Catholic	Katholik
Catskills	Katskills
Christ	Krist
Christian	Kristian
Christmas	Kristmas
Christopher Columbus	Kristopher Kolumbus
Clam Chowder	Klam Chowder
Coca Cola	Koka Kola

[1] In most cases, it is appropriate to replace this name with KidsKlan.

Old Style	New Style
Colorado	Kolorado
Commerce, US Dept. of	Kommerce, US Dept. of
Communist	Kommunist
Concentration Camp	Koncentration Kamp
Coney Island	Koney Island
Confederacy	Konfederacy
Congress	Kongress
Congressman	Kongressman
Connecticut	Konnektikut
Constitution	Konstitution
Continental Congress	Kontinental Kongress
Convention	Konvention
Coolidge, Calvin	Koolidge, Kalvin
Copperheads	Kopperheads
Cornell University	Kornell University
Cotton Belt	Kotton Belt
County	Kounty

Old Style	New Style
Court	Kourt
Crockett, Davy	Krockett, Davy
Crucifixion	Krucifixion

CHAPTER FORTY-NINE

All the way home, Larry Loomis debated with himself in an attempt to decide on his next course of action. He had a hard-on as he drove, a massive erection he'd had from the moment she'd walked out the door and passed the streetlight near which he'd been hiding. Pure rapture had flooded him, bringing his whole life into focus, transforming him in an instant from a skulker in doorways to a national hero, a lottery winner, Babe Ruth hitting it out of sight. A woman, a gorgeous woman, a babe: but he'd seen gorgeous women before and they'd left him cold. This was something else. This wasn't just any woman, this was fifty per cent of the biggest act in town, and he had her where he wanted her. Who wouldn't have had a hard-on?

The erection, brought on by an excess of excitement and greedy anticipation, was making him uncomfortable. His trousers rubbed against it and his thoughts inflamed it. He wasn't thinking about sex, he was way beyond that: he was getting off on a presidential handshake, a wad of money thicker than his belly, or maybe . . . He drew in to a side street and found a spot away from the street lighting. Smiling beatifically, he unbuttoned his trousers and slipped his hand inside. Her face danced in front of his unfocused eyes, and he concentrated on it as his hand gave him his hero's reward.

Relaxing afterwards, he continued the debate. There were three men he could tell, but if he made a mistake and chose the wrong one the whole thing could go sour.

Stephenson might be so upset about the revelation, he'd have Loomis sacked or shot as the bearer of ill tidings. Hoover would be all gratitude and congratulations – this was precisely the sort of information he loved to squirrel away for rainy days ahead. But short of a promotion, he wasn't likely to pay an employee one extra cent, not even for handing him the earth. He made up his mind. Right now, the thing to do was go straight to Geiger, collect more money than he'd ever dreamt of, and hold everybody else in reserve. Maybe they'd all pay up. He'd heard her family had a lot of money. Maybe her father would cough up, and keep on coughing till he spat blood.

Footsteps sounded in the street outside. A policeman was approaching the car. Hurriedly, he replaced his flaccid penis in his pants and buttoned his fly. When the man came to the window, Larry wound it down and held out his FBIS card. The cop saluted nervously and went on without a word.

He went to Werfel's first and told him he needed a new Magnetophon and fresh tapes. The machine still knocked him out. AEG Telefunken had been making them for years, so Werfel had told him, but they didn't send them outside Germany. The Gestapo used them to eavesdrop on suspects, and Werfel had shown Larry how to install and run a unit connected to several microphones.

He'd moved out the woman in the apartment underneath Ridgeforth's and set up a Magnetophon in her living-room. That day, while John was away, he'd broken in to his apartment and installed a microphone in the living-room, bedroom, and kitchen, drilling holes through which to bring the wires downstairs.

That night, after he'd watched Laura leave, he'd gone back up and played the tape, the one he'd left running while they'd been in there together, the one he now had in his pocket and which he planned to copy once he got home. He didn't need to play it again, he could remember it almost verbatim.

'You can kill him now. It doesn't matter. Better for
Shirley if you do. Maybe she'll forget in time. They
say children do.'
'You understand what you're saying?'
'Uh-huh.'
'There's something else. I'll need you to help
me.'
'Yes. Yes.'

There'd been a pause after that, and sounds he couldn't
quite make out, then her voice again, different, using the
same words, but with a different meaning.

'Yes. Yes.'

As he left Werfel's, he played her words back in his own
head, savouring them in their finest detail. *Yes. Yes.* He felt
roused again.

'Is that Mr Geiger?'
'Yes. Who the hell's this? It's after one in the morning, I
hope you've got a good reason for waking me up.'
'I think I have, Mr Geiger. My name's Loomis. Larry
Loomis, you remember?'
'No, I don't remember.'
'I do jobs for you from time to time. Through Mr Werfel.'
'Yes, I see. I understand. That still doesn't give you the
right . . .'
'Why don't you just listen, Mr Geiger? This is a sample.
There's more, much more.'
He pushed up the lever marked 'Play' and held the
telephone receiver against the Magnetophon's speaker.

'He was . . . Oh, God, John, I can still hardly believe
this. This is the President of the United States I'm
talking about. I just . . . He had his hand on her

320

belly, he was . . . putting it inside . . . Oh, God, I feel sick.'

'It's OK, it's OK. Jesus, I'm sorry, Laura.'

'His own daughter. How could he do a thing like that? He made up some excuse, but I knew what he was doing, and he knows.'

He pressed the 'Stop' button.

'There's a lot more, Mr Geiger, but I guess that's enough for now.'

'Where was this recording made?'

'I'll tell you that when I see you. I take it you're interested in seeing me?'

'Yes, Mr Loomis, you know very well I am.'

Geiger opened the side door of the embassy himself. The duty guard watched impassively as he let Loomis in and led him upstairs to his office.

'Make yourself comfortable, Mr – I'm sorry, I've forgotten again.'

'Loomis. Larry Loomis.'

'Of course. You were responsible for tracking someone down for me recently. An excellent job. You showed initiative. It's something your people have. No doubt some would say it is a benefit of democratic freedom. And it seems your initiative has paid off again. You have the tape with you?'

Loomis produced it from his pocket.

'There's a machine on my desk. Give me the tape, I'll put it on. Don't worry, I won't steal it. Is this the only copy?'

Loomis shook his head.

'Do you think I'd just hand my only copy over like that? That tape's worth money. A lot of money.'

'We shall see. Now, tell me where it was made and how you came to make it.'

When Loomis finished his account of Laura's visit, Geiger played the tape from beginning to end. They listened together, and sometimes Geiger would ask Loomis what this word or that phrase was, and he would play back that section of the tape once, two, three times, just to fix it in his mind. No sounds of traffic came from the street below. They seemed the only living creatures in a dead world, and with them the voices of ghosts. The tape crackled to its close.

'Where are you?
'OK, stay where you are. I'll be there in fifteen minutes. That was Miles. He's in some sort of trouble. I said I'd pick him up. Can you let yourself out?'
'I'll be all right . . . You've got to go. If Miles is in trouble you shouldn't be wasting time.'

'I guess,' said Loomis, shifting in his chair, 'I guess a man like you could do a lot with a thing like that. They sure are clever machines your people make.'

Geiger nodded and removed the tape, winding the stray end back onto the reel and securing it.

'Yes, of course, we make the best machinery in the world. That goes without saying. You say you want money for this tape?'

Loomis nodded.

'How much?'

'You decide. Make an offer. If it's good enough, the tape's yours. If not . . . ?'

'Who else knows you have it?'

'Werfel gave me the machine: he doesn't know what's on the tape. You're the first person to hear it besides myself. I know how to keep quiet. You can trust me. But if you don't want it, I know one or two other people.'

'Yes, I'm sure you do. Unfortunately, I have a moral problem. You were working for me when this tape was made. The tape itself, and the machine on which it was recorded, are property of this embassy. You see, you have no true legal right to the recording. And I'm sure you'd hardly be keen to test your claim in an American court of justice.'

'I don't think the other people I have in mind will worry too much about that.'

Geiger shrugged.

'No, I don't suppose so. However, I really don't have either the time or the inclination to haggle over something that already belongs to me. You are evidently an admirer of German craftsmanship. Let me introduce you to another example of our industrial skill.'

From the drawer of the desk Geiger lifted a Luger automatic pistol. Sighing, he pointed it at Loomis.

'Look, mister, if you think you can just shoot a US citizen and get away with it, you'd better think again.'

Geiger shook his head.

'That's all history, Mr Loomis. US citizens no longer have rights, any more than German citizens. Nobody knows you're here. And, frankly, nobody cares.'

The sound of the shot echoed down an empty corridor and rolled away into silence. Geiger put the Luger away carefully and closed the drawer. The tape went into his pocket snugly, as though it had always been destined for it.

CHAPTER FIFTY

'Why do you want to see him?'

Hoover was not in a good humour this morning. They'd picked up Vanderlyn, but the girl had slipped their clutches. Now she could be anywhere again, warned of their intentions, and better hidden than ever. Getting information out of Vanderlyn would be neither easy nor pleasant, and it might not lead anywhere much in the end.

'I know him,' John said, his face a mask of perfect honesty. On the walls, dozens of photographs of Hoover looked down on them. Hoover with Lindbergh and Stephenson, Hoover with Grand Wizards and Dragons, Hoover with Himmler, Hoover with a man John guessed must be Bishop Teller. The Great Spider with his flies.

Hoover looked down at the pad of paper in front of him. He'd been drawing aimlessly on it, lines and squiggles without apparent meaning. But now, looking again, he saw a pattern in them. Eyes, monstrous eyes, stared back at him from the page. And in one corner, as though it sought to hide, a tiny figure cowered. Not a little girl, but a man very like Hoover himself.

'I already know that. Why do you want to talk to him?'

'He may tell me things he won't tell you. Of the people he knows, I reckon I'm the only one with the security clearance to ask him difficult questions.'

'And what makes you think he'll answer any of them?'

John shrugged.

'He probably won't. But I want to try. He fooled me. He took me in. I feel kind of bad about that. I feel bad because I thought he had integrity, and now I find he's mixed up in a conspiracy to shoot the President.'

'So are a lot of other people.'

'I don't know them. I know Vanderlyn. Give me an hour with him. He may let something slip.'

Hoover let his pen run through the eyes, scribbling and scribbling until he'd all but obliterated them. The little figure remained where it was. Carefully, he drew a circle round it, cutting it off from the rest of the page, from the whole world.

'You can have half an hour. Lark will sit in to make notes. Anything Vanderlyn tells you stays within these walls. It only goes to the President on my say-so. Is that clear?'

Miles had not been treated well. Several of his teeth were missing, there were bruises on his face, one eye was black, and blood had caked on his neck. He sat on the floor in a circular, white-tiled cell, trying not to think, without much success. That he would die was certain, and that he would suffer greatly before he did so was inevitable. He feared the suffering, but, with Helena snatched from him again, not the dying. More than the suffering, he feared talking, knowing that, if he did so, he would betray men and women in several cities. The floor on which he sat was spotted with red, where drops of blood had spattered the white tiles. He counted the drops, but each time gave up after one hundred.

A door opened in the wall and two men entered, shutting it behind them to recreate the illusion of a seamless room. Miles registered with only mild surprise that one of the men was John Ridgeforth. He could guess how John had obtained admission, but not his motive in being here.

John and the stranger had brought folding stools to sit

on. They faced Miles across the tiny room, only feet away, yet somehow conveying a notion of great distance. The man with John eyed Miles fastidiously, disdain written on his face as though his mother had mixed it with his milk. High eyebrows, hollow cheeks, eyes like glass. He would never smile unless to create an effect he had planned long before. He sat down and took a notepad from his pocket, and a pen to write with. John sat beside him, glancing unhappily at the evidence of Miles's beatings.

'Professor Vanderlyn,' he started, not knowing yet how to get into the rhythm of this, 'you don't have to answer any of my questions. I'm not an official investigator, I don't work for the FBIS, I've no good reason to be here. There are other people to do this job better, other people who will hurt you very badly. I think you know that, and I see you've met some of Mr Hoover's boys already.

'But if you decide to speak to me, you may be able to avoid some of the unpleasantness they have waiting for you. I'm here because I know you, because I used to admire and respect you, and because I'd like to see you hanged.'

Miles looked into John's eyes. He saw no irony and no compassion in them. For a moment he was seized by the chilling thought that John might not be who he said he was, but an imposter planted on Miles in order to draw him out. He'd made the arrangement for Helena to meet him at the cathedral: who else could have known about it, who else could have informed the FBIS?

'You've disgraced yourself and your profession,' John continued. 'I'm a former student of yours, so now I'm branded with the possibility that I took in heretical ideas from you, that I'm not quite safe to be around the President. I could lose my job because of you.'

'You could do worse,' retorted Miles, stung against his better judgement. 'The law isn't about advising corrupt Presidents, or selling yourself to the highest bidder. You can stop worrying about being tainted with my ideas. It's pretty obvious you never listened to a word I said.'

'I listened. I thought what you said used to make sense. And now I realize you were lying through your teeth. You don't give a damn about America or the constitution, you just care about yourself.'

'It's because I care about America that I've done the things I've done. You wouldn't understand. Whatever makes scum like you tick, it isn't patriotism.'

'What are the things you've done, Professor? Tell me about them. Maybe you haven't done anything too terrible. Maybe I can help sort things out.'

'Go to hell.'

Lark turned to John.

'You're wasting your time here. He's not talking. Not to you, anyway.'

'Just make your notes. Let me handle this.'

'He's right,' said Vanderlyn. 'I've got no reason to talk to you.'

'Who are you going to talk to, then? One of those bully boys who roughed you up last night? Lark here? Do you know what he does? Have you any conception of his enormities? Of his capacity for pain?'

Miles shook his head.

'None of this frightens me.'

'I don't seek to frighten you. I seek to reason with you. Tell me, do you love your wife?'

'My wife is dead.'

'I'm aware of that. Do you know what they did with her in the camp?'

'She told me a little, yes.'

'Did she tell you she was a prostitute? That the prison guards used her for sex? Eight, nine, ten times a day. Imagine that.'

'That's a lie.' Despite himself, Miles felt the anger surging through him.

'You can check. I can show you papers. It's all documented. Believe me, all this loyalty's misplaced. Everyone's for sale. Everyone cheats. They gave Helena a few privileges, and she opened her legs. Your precious wife was a Jewish whore.'

'Shut up!' bellowed Miles. The beating had been nothing compared to this. He was convinced now that John had been a plant, that he really was an FBIS agent.

'You make this big thing about protecting your Jewish friends, and all the time your wife is in there sucking uncircumcised cocks. Does that sound stupid or what?'

John watched him come, as he'd known he would, watched him unwind and raise himself from the floor like a cat suddenly roused from sleep. Lark looked on impassively, not really caring if anyone got hurt.

Miles hurled himself with all his strength on John, throwing him off the chair, crashing back hard against the wall. He wanted to kill him, he didn't care what the consequences might be, he'd gone past consequences in here. The breath was knocked from John's lungs, and he had to struggle to keep moving. In his fury, Miles was proving stronger than John had anticipated. His fists pummelled into John's body, their force barely broken by the arms he put up to defend himself.

Suddenly, Miles's hands were round John's throat, throttling him. Their faces were only inches apart, and John could feel the older man's breath in his nostrils. He leaned up and whispered, 'Forgive me, Miles, but this was the only way.'

At that moment, the door opened and an armed guard forced his way into the room. Lark put up a hand, wanting to see the outcome of the fight.

Miles relaxed his grip, understanding at last what this had been about. John pushed up and back, bringing his hand down against the other man's neck, making it look like a flailing gesture of defence. But the blow did what it was intended to do. He felt Miles go suddenly limp, felt his body roll away from him.

The guard bent down to examine Miles as John struggled to get to his feet.

'He's dead. You must have hit him awful hard.'

John said nothing. He got up and went to the door. Lark followed him. In the corridor, row upon row of cell doors ran away in both directions. There was a stench on the air. John bent down on all fours and threw up. When he got up again, Lark was standing a couple of feet away, watching without emotion.

'I think we'd better have a word with Mr Hoover,' he said. 'He isn't going to be too happy about this.'

CHAPTER FIFTY-ONE

'Werfel, come in here and sit down. And for God's sake, take that silly grin off your face.'

'Sorry, sir. It was something Heinz just told me.'

'Another one of his obscene jokes, I suppose.'

'Well, sir, you know the way the Führer holds his peaked cap against his belly, like this, when he's reviewing a march-past?'

Geiger nodded. He hoped Werfel wouldn't go too near the edge this time. He'd had to reprove him often enough before.

'I don't suppose you know why?'

'I've no idea. It seems as good a place to keep it as any.'

'Actually, according to Heinz, he's protecting Germany's last unemployed.'

Werfel broke into a grin again. Geiger gave a wry smile.

'You will go too far one day. Now, sit down and listen. I have a job for you. An important job. If it goes well, I guarantee you a promotion.'

'I'm all ears, sir.'

'I've got a package here that has to go to Germany. Never mind what's in it. The thing is, I don't want to risk it to the diplomatic bag or any of the usual channels. I want you to take it over personally, and I don't want you to let it out of your sight from the moment you leave this office to the moment you make delivery. When you're asleep, it stays chained to your wrist. I'm wholly serious. The package does not leave your sight.'

Werfel's earlier levity had gone. He nodded gravely, setting himself in tune with his superior's mood.

'I understand, sir. You can rely on me. May I ask exactly where I'm to deliver it, sir?'

'Not "where", Werfel – "who". You're to take it to the Führer in person.'

'The Führer?'

'Don't look so gormless. The man you've just been making jokes about. I trust you'll be more careful with your tongue when you meet him.'

'But how . . . ?'

'He's staying in Berchtesgaden at the moment. I'll give you a briefing on the channels you're to go through. By the time you're in Germany, I should have cleared them all. But be very careful. When you get to the Berghof, some of them will insist on seeing inside the package, others will say you have to leave it with an adjutant or a secretary or whatever. It's imperative you stand firm. This is for the Führer's eyes alone. Is that absolutely clear?'

'Absolutely. But what if they won't let me past?'

'They will. I'm sending a coded message to Berchtesgaden this morning.' Geiger glanced at his wristwatch. 'I've arranged for you to fly to Ireland on a Pan-American plane. There'll be a Luftwaffe plane waiting to take you on to Berlin.'

He stood and took a small package from his desk. Passing it to Werfel, he saluted.

'Good luck, Sturmbannführer. And take great care. What you hold in your hands may decide the fate of this country. And perhaps even that of the Reich as well.'

Werfel returned the salute and made to leave. As he reached the door, Geiger called him back.

'Before you go – did you take care of that other matter?'

'Loomis? Yes, sir, it's all been taken care of.'

'And the tapes?'

'All accounted for, sir. He hadn't hidden them very well.'

331

'Did you listen to them?'

Werfel shook his head.

'No, sir. I always follow orders, as you know.'

'Very good. See you leave them with me before you go.'

PART 10

Mary

CHAPTER FIFTY-TWO

That afternoon, John received a phone call from a woman. The White House switchboard put the call through to his office at 3.13 p.m. He did not recognize the voice.

'Mr Ridgeforth?'

'Speaking.'

'You don't know me, but we have mutual friends. I think you know Victor, for example.'

He let a few seconds pass before answering.

'Who is this?'

'I'll let that be a surprise. When are you free to meet?'

'Not till I finish work. What about six o'clock?'

'I'll meet you in the foyer of the Willard. I'll be near the piano. Carry an umbrella, it may rain.'

'How will I . . . ?' The line went dead. He continued holding the receiver as though it might come alive again and answer his questions, but half a minute later the switchboard operator asked him to hang up. 'Victor' had been the codename used by him during his voyage in the *Torque*.

At half-past five he collected a folding umbrella from a stack in the main office, and headed into town. It was a cloudless day, and the umbrella made him feel like the man who never listened to good advice.

He reached the Willard with a few minutes to spare. The foyer was already crowded. Well-dressed men and women were drinking fruit juice, flirting very, very discreetly, and pretending to have a good time in the absence of most of the things necessary to it. But John knew this was only the start of the evening. Those who weren't dining in the hotel had the sort of money you needed to buy booze and dice and women, and they knew where to find them. He recognized a couple of White House staffers, accompanied by women considerably younger than their wives. And he recognized one of the women: it was the girl in the red coat who'd called out to him on the corner of K Street. She seemed sad and lost, scrabbling to cling to whatever thin hold she had on life, knowing that the drop beneath her was voracious and bottomless and utterly black. And for the first time he realized that he himself hung there, suspended over the blackness on a cord as thin as a spider's leg.

She was waiting by the piano, a large, short-haired woman of about fifty, carefully dressed, but not elegant. She wore well-tailored trousers and a somewhat shapeless top. He guessed who she was at once. An intelligent, unemotional face showed signs of strain. He approached her guardedly.

'I think we spoke earlier on the phone.'

She stretched out a hand.

'I'm pleased to meet you, Mr Ridgeforth. I hope you approve of my choice of place for an assignation.'

'Is this an assignation?'

'Of sorts. Let's sit down over here. It's out of earshot.'

He followed her to a sofa on the other side of the piano. A waiter detached himself from the wall and glided towards them.

'Can I get you anything?'

John asked for lime juice, his companion said she'd have a large soda.

'You still have the advantage on me,' John said as the waiter moved away.

'First of all, I need some proof that you really are John Ridgeforth.'

He showed her his ID card, with its flat but recognizable photograph.

'My name's Mary Laverty,' she said at last. 'I was a friend of Miles Vanderlyn. Or perhaps a colleague would be nearer the mark.'

'You say "was". What makes you . . . ?'

'Let's not beat around the bush, Mr Ridgeforth. Miles was arrested last night and taken to FBIS headquarters. I do not expect to see him alive again.'

He breathed in deeply.

'Miles is dead,' he said. He noticed her flinch, then recover herself. The waiter reappeared with their drinks. Mary looked at hers as if it was poison.

'How do you know that?' she asked.

'I think I would prefer it if you told me who exactly you are, how you knew Miles, and what you know about our friend Victor.'

She reached inside a large handbag and took out a brown envelope.

'Miles left this with me. I was told to open it in the event of something happening to him. I did that this morning after I heard he'd been taken in. Here, read it.'

The envelope contained a lengthy handwritten letter. John still had the constitutional notes Miles had passed to him on their first night. He compared the handwriting. It was identical. In the letter, Miles had set out details concerning John and his mission. The plan was for Mary to take Miles's place as John's liaison with the resistance. An accompanying note for John recommended that he trust Mary and put himself entirely in her hands.

'He took a great risk, giving this to you.'

'It was safe where I hid it. Don't worry.'

'We have to talk. This isn't the best place. And just in case somebody asks, how do we come to know one another?'

'You're taking flying lessons. This is our first meeting, to discuss terms. You go up for the first time on Saturday. I've got a little biplane out at the airport.'

'That's what you do?'

She nodded.

'I follow in the footsteps of the late Mr Lindbergh. Try to anyway. Whatever else you may have thought of him, he was a great flyer.'

'Why do I want to take flying lessons?'

She shrugged.

'Search me. Something to add to your accomplishments. A way to impress young ladies. You've always wanted to be a pilot. I don't know – you think of something.'

He smiled. Something about this unusual little woman appealed to him. And something about the airport rang a bell in him.

'I need access to a radio. To transmit as well as receive. I assume there are a few out there at the airport.'

'I knew you were going to think of that.'

'And?'

'I think you should come out to see my biplane. When are you free?'

'I'm not free. But I need that radio.' He finished his drink and put down the empty glass. Taking a billfold from his pocket, he left enough to cover the drinks and a generous tip. 'I think we should go now.'

As she got up, he noticed for the first time a walking stick beside her chair. She retrieved it and followed him with a limp. Noticing his glance, she bent and knocked her lower leg.

'Came all the way from a forest in Maine. Don't worry, I can still handle a plane.'

'How'd you get it?'

'Used to teach. Up your way, in Harvard. Had a run-in with some of my students. This was about six years ago.'

'What did you teach?'

'Philosophy. I was telling them about a book by someone called Thomas Paine. You may have heard of it. It's called *The Rights of Man*.'

'I think someone told me about it once.'

'Yes, it had a certain reputation, didn't it? You may remember a little section in which he talks about religion.

338

He says "All religions are in their nature kind and benign, and united with principles of morality". They didn't take too kindly to that. They said the Jews were cruel and vicious, and their religion was a vile parcel of heathen practices. And they liked even less the sentence lower down the page, where Paine says: "In America, a Catholic priest is a good citizen, a good character, and a good neighbour". That got them hopping mad. One of them took hold of the book and ripped it up. Then a bunch of them – I think they belonged to the football team – a bunch of them got hold of me and threw me down the stairs. My leg was broken. Actually . . .'

Her voice fell away, an almost silent thing among the tinkling voices and raucous laughter and braying outbursts all around her.

'Actually, I didn't notice the leg at first. My heart was broken much more. The doctors never set the leg properly, and it had to be cut off a year later. But I have a new one, one I like, one I can walk on and fly with. It's my heart I worry about. They don't grow trees in Maine that fit in here.'

And she pointed to her chest and smiled. He took her arm then and led her out to the street, where it had started to rain after all.

CHAPTER FIFTY-THREE

Anna felt a sneeze coming on. She did everything possible to stop it, from pushing a finger against her nostrils to snorting down them, but nothing worked. The sneeze came, followed by several more. She was frightened she had caught a cold, or something worse, like pneumonia. Her fear stemmed only partly from a natural dread of illness. Its real source was the risk attached to going to a doctor or hospital, not to mention the danger of discovery if her sneezes should alert John's neighbours to her presence. He had no basement in which to conceal her, no soundproof walls to shut out her voice or her nasal explosions.

She tried to read, but John had no books she could enjoy. She felt restless without her violin, and fretted that, without daily practice, she would rapidly lose her facility and never make it up again. Safe for the moment, her mother's death preyed on her mind terribly. But she could not let herself give way to tears, for tears could turn to sobs and sobs to howls, and pretty soon a neighbour would ask questions. She'd heard the man on the left-hand side several times: once coughing, once singing to himself, once speaking to someone at the door. These were expensive apartments, but the walls were thin.

John had warned her to keep away from the window, otherwise she'd have sat there looking out into the street below. The sounds of feet and passing cars came up to her as though from an abyss, tempting her to peep out and join, however vicariously, in their life. She thought a great deal about Vernon and Mabeline and Uncle Miles, and cried silently for them too.

John puzzled her. He said he worked at the White House, that he advised the President. And yet he'd helped her escape from the FBIS, he'd tried to save Miles, and he'd driven her to the James's that first evening. She felt she could trust him, but she wished she knew how he'd come to be mixed up in all this.

There was a sound of a key turning in the lock. John hadn't said he'd be home this early, but it was a relief to her. If they kept their voices low, maybe they could talk for a while before bedtime. She got up from her seat and hurried to welcome him home.

Laura put down her book. It was entitled *Absalom, Absalom!* The author was a little-known southerner called Faulkner, and she'd only started it out of curiosity, having heard it was banned. There'd been a copy in the White House library, which she'd sneaked out. She thought she'd like to meet Mr Faulkner. Maybe she could start literary soirees and invite him to attend under another name.

Shirley was much better, and the doctor said she could get out of bed tomorrow. Laura had not asked her about what she'd seen that night, and the longer she put it off the harder it got. She wanted to know if it had been the first time, though it seemed unlikely. That would have been too much of a coincidence. This would have been a good time, while David was out at some sort of military reunion and likely to be back late.

There was a knock on the door. A maid came in carrying a note on a small tray.

'This just came for you, ma'am.'

Laura took the letter and opened the envelope.

'Do you know who left it?'

'It was a special messenger, ma'am. He said it had to be given to you personally.'

The note was typed. It read:

'Something has come up. Please get over here as soon as you can.'

John's signature had been scrawled hastily across the bottom.

CHAPTER FIFTY-FOUR

Mary drove over the Arlington Memorial Bridge onto Columbia Island, then crossed back on the Mount Vernon Highway, turning off it just before they reached the Highway Bridge.

'I found a break in the fence back here,' she said. 'I use it when I don't want anyone to know I'm around. The guards they post on the gate are regular pains in my irregular ass.'

The breach was not the result of accident. It was invisible from the road, and John guessed Mary had made it herself. She held part of the fence back while he climbed through, then followed him, letting the wire mesh fall back into place. Her car had been left well-hidden among trees, and would only show up if someone made a full-scale search in that area. There was a scent of burning leaves in the air, and behind that the river smell, like rotting vegetation, and above them both an odour of engine fuel, medicinal and faintly nauseating.

The airfield appeared deserted. The last flight of the day had taken off an hour earlier, and Mary said nothing was expected in until the mail flight from New York shortly before midnight. A few lights shone outside the main buildings, and the entrance was floodlit. Otherwise, silence, darkness, and an air of inexplicable melancholy hung over everything.

'You feel it?' She sensed his mood, understood its cause. 'Airfields are like sea ports, time weighs heavy when the ships are out at sea. There's no connection to anywhere else, everything's sort of suspended. Like waiting for the world to come back to you.'

They crossed a stretch of wild grass and weeds, then a flat bed of concrete laced together with strips of tar. Laverty's Flying School was a hangar out on the west end of the field, not many yards from the railroad tracks. On the other side of the tracks lay a government experimental farm, and beyond that was Arlington cemetery.

Mary let them in through a side door secured with a heavy padlock.

'Often wonder what they grow on that farm,' she said, nodding back over her shoulder. 'Guess they're experimenting with fertilizer. They say bone meal's good for roses.'

She switched on the lights to reveal a sand-coloured biplane.

'I call her Sandy. She's a Focke-Wulf 44C, built as a trainer back in '33. This one was made in Brazil under licence. It should be a two-seater, but this one was modified to take three. That comes in handy sometimes. I bought her four years ago with some money my Uncle Henry left me. He wouldn't have approved. Didn't think women were fit for anything but peeling potatoes and rolling about in bed. When I was about thirty, he asked me why I didn't think of becoming a prostitute. "The money's good, you get to lie in late, you meet a wide variety of interesting people, and your overheads are low. Think about it."

'I asked him "How interesting are these people I could meet?" and he said, "Interesting is the wrong word. Sexually voracious would have been better." I just told him I didn't think I had the looks for a career in that field. Guess what he replied? "Looks you don't need. What you need is stamina. And an interest in meeting new people."'

'A nice man, your uncle.'

'He was nice. Somewhat strange, though. But he had a lot of money.' She snorted. 'I made the right choice, though. Can't imagine a wooden leg would have attracted many customers.'

'Well, I'm glad you never made it. It would have been awkward for me having to visit a brothel every time I wanted to see you.'

'You like some coffee?'

'Why not?'

Her office was a little room at the back, an afterthought that seemed to have been built from leftovers, painted in a revolting shade of green, and left to warp slowly through the seasons. On the wall hung three photographs: one of Mary among a group of academics, all wearing robes; one of her in a leather jacket and goggles, grinning and holding aloft her pilot's licence; and one of a little boy in baggy trousers clutching a fishing rod.

'You have a son?'

Her face clouded over. She shook her head.

'Had. He died soon after that was taken. Polio. Don't know why I keep it there. Too much of a reminder.'

She made coffee on a gas ring, in a steel percolator that had lived a hard but useful life. Pouring two cups, she fished in a cupboard and brought out a large bottle of bourbon.

'Top you up?'

'No thanks.'

'I'll oblige myself then. This is going to be difficult.'

'You like to drink?'

She shook her head.

'I like to forget. Keep my mind on the things that matter. Like getting you to a radio. Which, as I said, is going to be difficult.'

'What's the problem?'

'Security. Anywhere with a radio has to be guarded on a twenty-four hour basis. FBIS orders. They're strict about it.'

'Then why bring me here?'

'You need to transmit to where? London? Well, then, you don't have a lot of choice. I can get you a receiver, no problem. I can get you a small set that transmits over a few hundred miles. But if you want to speak to London, your best hope is over there in the control tower.'

'Do you have access?'

She shook her head.

'That's restricted to long-distance operators. Mainly they fly out of National, but Washington handles a few long-range flights as well. I don't count.'

She looked at a clock on the wall.

'Nothing's going to happen round here till the mail flight comes in. Most of the airport staff have gone home. I reckon this is your moment.'

She drained her coffee and banged the cup down on the table among a heap of stained and torn flight maps. John took a few more mouthfuls to be polite, but to be honest, it tasted vile. When he finally put his cup down, she smiled.

'You should have had the whiskey. It doesn't make it taste any better, but it helps you not to care. Come on, I'll take you outside and show you what's what round here.'

There wasn't much to see. A central block housed the administration, waiting areas for the public, toilets, a cafeteria for staff, and a newspaper stall. Beyond it lay six hangars, a fuel depot, and a garage for the fire engine. On the other side of the railway tracks, near the Columbia Pike, a short control tower looked down on everything else. In the darkness, a few lights shone out like fireflies. A freight train went by, dragging its endless cargo through the night, headed on a long journey from nowhere in particular to nowhere in particular.

They walked slowly across a weed-encrusted tarmac. The night hung loose above them, baggy, and full of nameless stars.

'There's one guard in a little box outside the control tower. You already saw the two men on the gate. They all have machine guns and dogs. What you won't have seen is that they have alarms they can set off in case

346

of trouble. There's an FBIS post at the National Airport, with a permanent contingent of fifteen men and a direct telephone contact to base. Takes them about a minute to get across here.'

'How many shifts?'

'Three. Guys on duty now came on around four. They stay till midnight. Same routine at National, only they don't rotate the whole unit at the same time. The guys here will sleep at the post tonight.'

'You've been watching them.'

'Some. Never know when it might come in handy.'

'Meaning?'

'You don't think I keep that Focke-Wulf just to train bored citizens in the noble art of flying, do you? It's surprising what you can put on board a quality airplane.'

'How far can you go?'

'She's got a range of three hundred something miles, but that gets you most places. Set down for fifteen minutes, refuel, go up again. I go to Mexico a lot. Bring in plenty of things that go bang. Surprising what you can get down there.'

There was a sound of cars a little way off. Mary glanced round.

'Lot of traffic on Route One tonight.'

There had been no checkpoints on their way out to the airfield, but John reckoned they'd still be looking for Anna. She'd be getting worried back in the apartment on her own. He should have telephoned her, made sure she was all right.

A light mist had come from nowhere. Around the top of the control tower, the light bounced back, creating a dim halo. John shivered involuntarily. He knew they'd have to kill the guard, they had no choice. Mary would talk to him, reminding him of something, distracting him while John crept in, a shadow with a knife, and slit his throat – quickly, efficiently, elegantly.

Out on the highway, the snarling of cars and trucks grew

in volume. There was a sound of running feet nearer at hand. John froze, thinking they'd been seen, but the feet moved away from them, towards the main gates. A man's voice barked out orders gruffly in the distance. Moments later, a grinding sound drowned his voice as the gates swung inwards.

'Something's up,' said Mary. 'Quick, down here!'

She pulled him down behind a large sandbox, a sturdy concrete block whose contents served to keep the runways clear of ice in winter. John reached out to steady himself, grazing his hand against the rough surface of the block.

Lights went on in the main building, one at a time. At the gate, more floodlights picked out the guard hut. A military jeep came roaring up the road from the city and swung in at the gate.

'Is this normal?' John asked.

'The hell it is.' Mary squinted from behind the block, straining to see just what was going on. The sound of motor vehicles on the road grew louder. Suddenly, bright headlights cut through the mist and darkness. Seconds later, a convoy made up of civilian and military trucks turned through the open gate and drove down to the main building. Lights went on in the control tower. The air was filled with the snap of orders, then the crash of boot leather on concrete as soldiers piled out of the larger vehicles and ran to form lines at the front of the building.

Car doors opened and slammed shut, dim figures emerged and were saluted, at the gate another car arrived, sleek and black and powerful.

'Looks like somebody important's flying out,' whispered John.

Mary shook her head.

'They'd have the plane ready. If he's a VIP, they'd have been crawling all over it for the past two hours. No, they're expecting someone. But why here? Why not at National?'

Even as she spoke, she heard it coming, faint still and far

away. She paused to listen. The throb of the engine grew until there could be no mistake.

'It isn't one of ours,' she said. 'It's an engine I don't recognize.'

Steadily, the vibration overhead grew in strength. John looked towards the scene at the terminal. He sensed that everyone there was fixing his attention on the sound of the incoming plane. An unexpected silence, broken only by the humming of the engines far above, rose up from the ground like another kind of mist, silencing first the footsteps and crashing feet, then the slamming of doors, then the shouting of orders. All was still, and John saw men turn and look skywards.

Two rows of lights outlined the runway. The approaching engines changed pitch.

'We won't be able to see a thing from here,' said John. 'We've got to get closer.'

'It's no good going straight across, we'll be seen. Let's double back round the perimeter.'

They slid away into a darkness that deepened rapidly. With it and the mist to hide them, it was not hard to creep all the way round and emerge at the rear of the main building. As they approached it, the roar of aero engines filled the sky, and they looked up and saw the lights of the aeroplane itself as it came swinging in over Arlington and dropped in a steady arc to the waiting ground.

The landing was smooth. As it ended, the pilot turned and taxied forward to the disembarkation area, where the welcome party waited. John crept along the side of the building until he was in a position to see almost the entire scene. Bright lights turned the reception dock into something resembling a stage set. Men in military uniforms flanked a group of officials in civilian dress. Just then, the plane approached, and several of the party turned their heads to watch it come.

'That's Norquist, the Secretary of State,' whispered John.

'The man beside him is Hoover. Stephenson's next to him. And that's . . . I know him, he was at the reception – Von Drexler, the German ambassador.'

'Who's the big man, the one in the tan hat?'

'That's Speight, the Secretary of Defense. Look how he's leaning on that cane. I've heard he has cancer, that Stephenson's thinking of replacing him.'

The plane drew up facing them. It was a long machine with a narrow fuselage and massive wings. A swastika on the tailplane proclaimed its country of origin.

'It's a Messerschmitt 261,' exclaimed Mary. John could hear the excitement in her voice. 'I've only seen photographs before. They developed it last year for long-range use. The wings are employed as fuel tanks. Gives them a range of several thousand miles.'

A ladder was wheeled forward and set against the door of the plane. John felt his heart slap hard against his side. He had a premonition, and he prayed it was false.

The door opened and a figure appeared. John let out a sigh of relief. He'd been mistaken after all.

'That's Ribbentrop,' he said.

The German Foreign Minister slowly descended the steps, clearly uncomfortable after hours on board. As he approached the welcoming party, Von Drexler stepped forward and saluted, then introduced him to each of the Americans in turn. They were just finishing when a second figure appeared.

'Goering,' whispered Mary.

Resplendent in a large grey greatcoat with broad lapels, Hitler's Reichsmarshal was greeted enthusiastically in his turn. Von Drexler showed him round like a trophy, or a specimen of an exotic master race come among savages. John's heart was in his mouth now, he could taste it, bitter and thick with gristle, an indigestible lump. He looked up at the door of the plane. As he did so, he realized that the murmur of introductions had subsided, that the stillness broken earlier by the aeroplane engines had returned, more intense now and replete with an expectancy that was almost menacing.

A third figure appeared in the opening and started down the steps. Not too fast, not too slow, but at a proper pace. David Stephenson detached himself from the crowd and walked forward to the steps. His greeting was soft, but in the silence it carried.

'Welcome to America, Herr Hitler. It's an honour to have you with us at last.'

CHAPTER FIFTY-FIVE

The front door was already open when Laura got to John's apartment. The mysterious message lay in her pocket, smouldering there like a rag snatched from a bonfire. She pushed the door all the way open and tentatively stepped inside.

'John? Are you there?'

There was no answer. Something told her to turn and run, but the thought that John might be in danger held her fast.

'John? It's Laura. Are you all right?'

There was a sound from the living-room, a muffled call that might have been John's voice. Inside her head, another John called to her, urging her to get out. She hesitated, then the door in front of her opened.

A man she did not recognize came out. He was holding a little girl tightly round her shoulders. The girl's eyes were wide with fear. Her cheeks were chalk white, her lips thin and bloodless. The barrel of an automatic pistol was pressed hard against her temple. The look on the man's face said he'd pull the trigger at the least prompting.

'Thank you for coming, Mrs Stephenson,' he said. 'My little friend here is tired. I think it's time you and I had a talk. Please close the door behind you.'

The last car slipped through the gate, its taillights twinkling briefly. One by one the lights were extinguished. Later that night, when the mail plane arrived, there would be nothing out of the ordinary for its pilot to see. In the morning, the sun would rise on a sleeping airfield, with no trace of the night's visitation.

The Messerschmitt was towed to Hangar 6, the largest on the field. A detachment of six FBIS guards was deployed at front and rear, while the German aircrew remained inside with the plane. They were all members of the Führerkurierstaffel, Hitler's personal transport unit. Once they were inside, heavy locks were placed on all the doors.

'I need to get to that radio,' said John. 'More than ever now.'

'Leave it, John. Don't even think about it. If they know someone's been here, that they've been seen, the little man in the moustache will just hightail it back to where he came from. I'd prefer him to stay. I want to know what he's up to.'

'Another radio, then. This can't be the only one.'

'As far as I'm concerned, it is.'

'Then I have to use it. London has to know about this.'

'At the moment, I couldn't care less what London has or hasn't to know. Let's get out of here. You can come back tomorrow night.'

'By tomorrow night, anything could have happened. We're in this thing together, don't make it hard for me.'

She hesitated. She wanted to help him, but knew the consequences if doing so alerted the authorities. In the past few weeks, the underground had lost Moshe, Vernon and Miles, along with their wives. Mary had to keep her loyalties limited.

'Okay,' she said, 'on one condition. You pass on any information London gives you about this Hitler visit. You keep nothing back. Understood?'

'That's a deal. Come on, I want this over with.'

John came out of the shadows as though he was strolling down Constitution Avenue, casually walking towards the guard, like someone who steps up to a policeman to ask the way. The echoes of his footsteps sounded unnaturally loud, clicking away among the concrete and glass of the little airfield, and vanishing somewhere in the uninhabited reaches of the night. The guard raised his sub-machine gun.

'Who's there?' he barked.

'White House security,' John answered. He held out his pass. The guard unclipped a flashlight from his belt and shone it towards John. He let the light rest on the pass; John gave him enough time to read 'White House' and 'First Class Security Rating', then whipped it away.

'We had a report some of the Krauts were still on the field.'

'They're in Hangar Six along with their plane.'

'Report said they weren't all inside. Can you open the control tower? I need to look through it.'

'I'd need authorization for that, sir. The guys at the gate can contact base for you.'

'Sorry, but this goes higher up. I don't have time to waste. Are you opening the door, or am I putting you on a charge?'

The guard was young, maybe eighteen or nineteen, and totally in awe of authority, especially authority that said 'White House'. He'd been within touching distance of the President that evening, he'd seen Adolf Hitler shake his hand, he'd watched them all drive away into the world's darkness. The man asking him to open the door spent his working life in close proximity to the centres of power: to refuse him would have been a denial of what he'd been so briefly linked to.

'It's your call, mister.'

He took a set of keys from his pocket, fumbled until he found the right one, and slipped it in the lock. As he did so, a shadow to his right shifted and moved forwards. He made to look round, but it was already too late. The wire was over his head and about his neck before he had time to open his mouth. John snatched the gun away from him quickly. He stood awkwardly beside the man he had helped to kill, waiting for Mary to finish the job. The wire was too thick to cut through flesh, but it dug deep into the guard's neck. John wanted to stop his ears, to shut out the horrid gurgling sound that was all the young man had left to say.

Mary lowered the dead man to the ground.

'You've got ten minutes,' she said. 'Make the most of them. I'll drag him back to my hangar. My leg's a nuisance, but I try not to let it stop me doing what I want to do. I'll take him up in the morning, drop him somewhere out at sea. If there's no body round here, they'll think he's deserted.'

John opened the door and went inside, taking the flash-light with him. As he climbed the stairs, the sound of gurgling seemed to follow him.

CHAPTER FIFTY-SIX

Laura was waiting when he returned. He found her sitting in the living-room, facing the door. A single light burned above her. She was very still.

'How'd you get in?' he asked. 'Did Anna let you in?'

She shook her head. It was then he noticed how distressed she was.

'What's the matter, love? What's wrong? Where's Anna?'

She told him. About the man with the gun, about the little girl whom he'd taken away. He listened, struggling to hold back his fear.

'His name's Geiger,' she said. 'Hans Geiger. He works at the German embassy, which means he has diplomatic immunity. I don't know what position he holds.'

'He's their Police Attaché. That means he's station chief for their foreign security service. Go on.'

He sat down beside her and slipped his arm round her shoulders, but she did not respond.

'He knows you're a British agent. He knows about us and . . .'

It poured out of her. Geiger had played a tape, a long tape featuring their voices, and at the end he had asked for money, a great deal of money.

'If I don't pay, part of the tape goes to David. Geiger knows what will happen. David will have us both killed. He'll do what he likes with Shirley.'

'What about the rest of the tape? What's he plan to do with that?'

'He didn't say. Does it matter?'

'I'm just curious. I'd guess he could do a lot with it if he could get it into the right hands.'

Even as he spoke, John remembered the secret landing at the airfield. The right hands were here in Washington.

'The little girl,' Laura whispered. 'What was she doing here?'

John explained.

'What does Geiger want with her?'

'Maybe what everybody else wants, I'm not sure. He may have his own agenda.'

'He'll expect you to come after him. It's what he wants.'

'Yes, I've thought of that. But it makes it difficult for him. If he releases his recording without getting his money, the most he gets is a pat on the back from someone. More likely, your husband will put a bullet in his brain, diplomatic immunity or no diplomatic immunity. David will hardly want Geiger around to tell tales out of school.'

'Surely Geiger's taken that into consideration.'

'Oh, I think he has. I imagine he's confident about getting his money from you, then using his information elsewhere. He has no intention of going to David, not unless he's pushed. And it's not in his interest to kill me. Like yourself, I'm more use to him alive than dead at the moment.'

She leaned against him, and for the first time responded to his attempts to soothe her.

'How long before you have to pay?' he asked.

'Day after tomorrow.'

'How much?'

'Half a million dollars.'

He whistled.

'Have you got that sort of money?'

She shook her head.

'Not really. My father could carry an amount like that in spare cash. David's worth God knows how much. But that doesn't make me rich. I've got money of my own, but most of it's locked up in trust funds and things like that. I could get my hands on a hundred thousand or so.'

'It's still a lot. It could keep him happy. But once he starts he's likely to come back for more.'

He looked at the clock on the mantelpiece.

'It's late. You'd better go.'

'I'm frightened to go back. What if David already knows?'

'David has other things on his mind at the moment. You'll be safe for a couple of days. Believe me.'

'What makes you so sure?'

'Your husband has important visitors. This is not the time for a domestic tragedy. He may not even be home when you get back.'

He took her to the door. As he put his hand on the knob to open it, she put her arms round him and kissed him hard, a kiss so full of fear and need that they were lost in it for a long time. While it lasted, there was nowhere else to go, no home, no country, no altar. The kiss was everything. But it finished at last, and he opened the door.

'Laura, how did he know? How did Geiger know I'm an agent?'

'He wouldn't say. But that's why he put a microphone in your bedroom. One thing, though. He referred to your car several times, said how beautiful it was. I think you should get rid of it. It draws too much attention.'

'I'll take care of it. And, Laura . . . don't breathe a word about visitors. Let him mention them first, if he does so at all.'

She looked back at him.

'I want to get out,' she said. 'Out of the White House, out of this country. Can you get Shirley and me back to England?'

'I'll do my best,' he said, but the words stuck in his throat. It was something he'd never bargained for. The decision would not rest in his hands, but in those of politicians; and he knew in his heart that, if he succeeded in his mission, the last thing they would want would be him returning with the widow and daughter of the man he'd killed.

CHAPTER FIFTY-SEVEN

Geiger kept the apartment for no other purpose than to see women in. A great many of the embassy staff did the same thing. He shared it with a young staffer from SS Hauptamt, Adolf Eichmann, who'd been sent to the embassy as an advisor on the Jewish problem. Eichmann had recently married, and hardly ever used the apartment now; Geiger knew that a discreet word in his ear tomorrow morning would keep him away for as long as he needed to keep the child there.

One of the apartment's former occupants, a rotund and jovial Bavarian called Walther Kaufmann, had entertained his own young ladies in unusual ways. Recalled to the Reich a year ago for breaches of some obscure diplomatic regulation, he'd left behind a cupboard full of unpleasant-looking equipment, all of it bought in a notorious shop in Hamburg and imported under diplomatic cover. Geiger found it revolting, and ever since moving in he'd intended to throw the lot of it into the bin. But he and Adolf had enjoyed a good laugh more than once, displaying Walther's whips, hoods, studded belts, and chains to various of their amours, and somehow it had all stayed in the cupboard like a sexual talisman. 'You see, my dear, I may be a Nazi, but I don't myself go in for this sort of thing.' It had cheered up more than one of their tender recruitees and made for a certain bravado.

The chains and handcuffs now came in unexpectedly handy. He knew Anna would have escaped the apartment the moment he left her alone, so he chained her to the bed and gagged her efficiently with a large red handkerchief, a 'bandana' he'd bought on a trip to Texas.

He'd guessed right away who the child must be, though he couldn't for the life of him work out how she'd come to be in Ridgeforth's apartment. The manhunt for Moshe Rosen's daughter had been too large for Hoover and his elite to keep to themselves. Geiger had caught wind of it and asked himself why there was so much fuss about one little girl. He'd concluded that she must know something her pursuers would have preferred her not to know, and he suspected it had to do with her father's part in the Lindbergh assassination. But that was as far as he could get.

He had not been altogether surprised to find her holed up in the apartment of a British agent; but he was sure she had not been there long: his recording of the goings on between John and Laura were enough to show that.

He ran himself a bath. He was tired, and a long, hot soak would help his brain recover its flexibility. It had been a difficult evening, but rewarding all the same. Love-sick Mrs Stephenson had fallen for his note and run straight into his waiting arms. The recording had scared her shitless. And having the child to point a gun at had proved an unexpected bonus. She'd said she couldn't get money like that, but he knew better. As he undressed, he luxuriated in the thought of what five-hundred-thousand dollars could buy.

He'd known about Von Schillendorf's project for some time, but the secrecy surrounding it had been so tight that he'd been able to do little more than guess. Now, from the same recording that had given him so much else, he had a much clearer picture. All he needed was evidence to link the good baron with Stephenson.

Preparing to climb into the bath, he was reminded of good times he'd enjoyed with one or the other of his regular sweethearts. He usually came in here with them first, to take a bath before proceeding to the bedroom for other pleasures. It gave him a chance to look them over first, to make sure they were clean, that they had no skin conditions or other blemishes. That's why he stuck to regulars, he knew they were what he wanted. Deep down, he had a dread of disease, of germs passing from one body to the next in the heat of intercourse.

He thought of the last girl he'd had in here, a foreigner called Marta, Dutch or Belgian, he wasn't sure, a pretty little thing all the same. She'd been on a corner along K Street, standing there forlornly in a red coat and scarlet shoes, and he'd taken her home with him, something he didn't often do. But she'd appealed to him, she'd possessed a sad fragility that was already disappearing, and he'd wanted to capture it before then. Besides, she'd come a lot cheaper than the usual. And she'd responded to his love-making with an almost innocent enjoyment. She'd lose that along with the fragility, he reflected. Maybe he'd look out for her again.

The thought aroused him, and he realized he was in the mood for a woman tonight. It was too far to K Street, and he didn't want to leave the apartment unattended, so he put on his robe and rang the usual number. Nothing was too much trouble for 'Herr Schmidt': Patty, one of his favourites would be along in fifteen minutes.

He'd have to move the kid. The apartment was tiny, and he didn't have much choice about where to put her. In the end, he decided the kitchen would do. Going to the bedroom, he unfastened the chain that held Anna to the bed. He removed her gag, after warning her of the consequences should she try to scream or shout for help.

'Tell me, Anna, why is the good and gentle Mr Hoover chasing you so hard?' he asked.

'I don't know anybody called Hoover, and I don't know who you are either. I just want to be left alone.'

'Maybe I can help. If you tell me what it is they're looking for, I'll do what I can to help you.'

'You didn't help my father. You didn't help my mother. Why would you help me?'

'I had nothing to do with your father and mother. That was Mr Hoover. He and I don't agree. If you tell me what you know, I'll see he never gets his hands on you.'

'I don't know anything. My father and mother are dead, my friends are dead, and now you're all trying to kill me as well. I don't know what to do.'

There was a knock on the door.

'Come on, I've got to get you out of this room.'

Hurriedly, he gagged her again, then, taking her by the wrist, dragged her from the bedroom.

'Wait a moment,' he shouted as he passed the front door.

He got Anna into the kitchen, a tiny area fit for little more than preparing snacks, and chained her to the handle of a cupboard.

'I'm sorry I have to keep you like this,' he said, 'but I don't have any choice.'

It was what everyone said. Anna, who had no choices of her own, would not have disagreed with him. He patted her cheek in a mockery of paternalism, and shut the door.

'Patty, I'm so glad you could come.'

'Already? That's quick work.'

Patty was popular with the embassy staff. Most of them had had their fill of the statuesque *jungfraus* whose nude images populated Munich's House of German Art, the blonde-haired, large-breasted Rhine Maidens of the Hitlerian imagination. Patty was small, slim, and dark-haired, with little breasts a man could cup in one hand.

She stepped inside and kissed Geiger lightly on the cheek.

'They said you needed me straight away. You men are all the same. You don't even ask after a girl's health for weeks, then it's "Come over right now, I'm feeling horny."'

'As a matter of fact, I did ask after you a couple of weeks ago, but you weren't available.'

'Well, I am now.'

He helped her out of her coat. Underneath, she was wearing a skin-tight black silk dress that clung to her like seaweed to a rock.

'I haven't seen you wearing that before.'

'Honey, it's brand new. One of my clients – one of my *generous* clients – bought it for me yesterday. You like it?'

'It suits you . . . what's the phrase?'

'Down to the ground?'

She reached one hand behind her back and unzipped the dress in a single flowing movement. It unfolded like a spent chrysalis and fell snaking to the floor. Under it she was wearing stockings and a suspender belt, nothing else. He drew his breath in sharply.

'Bath-time?' she asked.

He shook his head.

'Let's skip that tonight.'

She stepped across the yard or so that separated them and put her arms round his neck, pressing her body hard against his.

'I'm sure Mr Hitler must be proud of you, Hans. Such a hard-on.'

He put his hands on her buttocks, pulling her even harder against him, delighting in her softness, then bent his head down and kissed her. Not all his girls let him do that, but Patty made no objections. Her tongue worked its way slowly through his mouth while her right hand started its gradual descent to his groin.

She lay with him afterwards. It was too early for her next job, and she felt indolent and free. These were her best moments, when she knew a man would demand nothing more of her than conversation or a gentle hug. It was at times like these she regretted not being married; then she thought of her one attempt and decided she had the better deal.

'Looks like your folks and mine are going to be allies before long,' she said. 'They won't haul you back over there if that happens, will they? They won't shut down the embassy or anything?'

All his thoughts lay in that direction, but he shook his head.

'No, even allies need embassies in one another's capitals. Bigger ones. There'll be more trade, more cultural exchanges. You don't have to worry. You can go on doing your bit for American-German relations.'

'Did you like tonight's contribution?'

'Mmmm. I liked it immensely. We should do it that way again.'

'Like this?' She mimed what had happened earlier. He stroked her breast and smiled, but it was too early for a reprise.

'I guess all this alliance stuff would never have happened if Mr Stephenson hadn't become President. They say Lindbergh wasn't crazy about the idea.'

'That's probably true. We got lucky.'

'You said it. You guys didn't have him polished off, did you?'

'Who?'

'Your Gestapo or whatever it's called.'

'The Jews killed Lindbergh. You know that.'

She leaned away from him and took a cigarette from a box beside the bed. Lighting it, she leaned back against the pillows and bent one leg.

'I'm not so sure.'

'Really? Why's that? Everyone knows Rosen and his buddy were caught in the act.'

'That's just it. I'm not sure they were.'

He watched her inhale slowly from the cigarette and blow the smoke out again through tight lips. She amused and lightened him, and her body drove him mad. She

365

wasn't the sort of person he'd have thought likely to have opinions on something like this.

'You know something that says they weren't?'

She looked uncomfortable.

'It's just something I heard.'

'A rumour?'

'Sort of. From one of my clients. Look, he told me this in confidence. I don't go blabbing what clients tell me.'

He was alert now. This didn't sound like a mere rumour doing the rounds.

'You needn't worry. I'm a professional as well, I don't repeat things I shouldn't. Who told you about this?'

'Just a Joe. It was late one night. We'd had dinner and stuff, we went back to his place afterwards. He's kind of a regular. Says I give the best blow job in the trade. You think that's true?'

'I'd say so, yes.' He leaned closer to her and laid a hand on her hip. She blew a long stream of tobacco smoke into his face and laughed when he choked.

'What did this Joe tell you?'

'He's a doctor of some sort. A path . . . Whatever. Does autopsies.'

'A pathologist. Yes.'

'I don't like that. You know, him touching all these dead people, then putting his hands on me. But I guess he doesn't touch them with his dick, so it's not all bad. And he's a nice guy. Never caused me any trouble.'

He slipped his hand between her legs as though to caress her, but she rolled away and crossed them.

'He said he'd examined them. You know, Rosen and the other guy . . .'

'Horowitz.'

'That's right. The two kikes that are supposed to have killed Lindbergh. Only Murray . . . my Joe said they couldn't have. He said they'd already been dead some hours when they got to the White House.'

'Is that so? Surely he must be mistaken.'

She shook her head.

'He's not the type to make a mistake. A careful guy, the sort that takes care. Like, when we go to bed, he always folds his clothes up real careful. And he likes to sort out what we're going to do and stick to it. He'd tell me things like, how many times he was going to stroke my nipple, and how many times he'd like to stroke my pussy before I came. He does things like that. It could drive you mad, the way he counts everything. But I'm kind of worried.'

'Worried?'

'He didn't show up last time. He'd see me once a week, real regular. Never missed. Then he didn't call. I rang him the next day, just to check he wasn't ill or something. This is like any other business, you gotta treat your clients well if you want to keep them.'

'Like you treat me.'

'Well, sure. Anyway, he didn't answer, not then, not since then. So I'm worried maybe he told the wrong people his ideas.'

'Why are you telling me?'

'I don't know. Maybe you can help. You know a lot of people. You could ask around. Casual like.'

He nodded thoughtfully.

'I'll do that. But you'll have to give me his name. His first name's Murray?'

'Murray Stanton. Only, be careful. And don't say anything about what I told you.'

'What do you take me for? Now, what do you say about having that bath after all?'

She stubbed out the cigarette in an ashtray on the bedside table.

'Okay, but I have to go soon.'

'You've got time for a little splash and maybe some more of what we did earlier. I'll pay double.'

Her eyes widened.

'Let's go.'

He followed her, admiring her naked back, the slope of

her backside, the length and suppleness of her legs. She'd given him a lot of pleasure, he was very fond of her.

The water he'd run earlier had gone cold, so he emptied the bath and refilled it. They chatted while it ran, and he began to feel aroused again. He sat on the edge of the bath beside her and stroked her nipples, making them stand erect. She teased him, touching his penis tentatively, then taking her hand away.

When the water came to over half-way, he helped her in, then climbed in himself, facing her. The water rose until it covered her breasts, then she lifted herself slightly, so he could see them better, as she knew he liked to do.

'Why don't you stroke your nipples for me?' he said. 'Put yourself in the mood?'

She put her tongue out and softly licked her lips. Her smile as she did so was infectious. He smiled back. Bracing herself with both legs against the bottom of the bath, she took her arms from the sides and put her hands on her breasts.

'What are you going to do?' she asked.

He put his hands on her knees, then stroked her thighs, then ran his hands back to her knees from behind.

'I'm sorry about this,' he whispered. And the smile left his face at the moment he pulled back. She kicked and struggled as her head vanished beneath the water, but he had her in a firm grip with her knees against his chest, and it did not take long before her desperate struggling became weak and spasmodic, and finally came to an end. He looked down at her as he climbed out of the bath. She seemed so pretty and fragile beneath the water, like a drowned mermaid or a water nymph, and her hair spread out from her head like the fronds of a mysterious underwater plant. He sat on the edge of the bath, watching the water grow still around her.

CHAPTER FIFTY-EIGHT

The White House was silent, bleak, and dark. As Laura entered, she grew aware of something in the atmosphere. The usual guards were on duty, the usual cleaners were doing their rounds, the usual late-night hum came from behind the doors of offices where administrative staff were working late. But nothing felt as usual. Her own fears elaborated the sense of strangeness, and she crept upstairs expecting the floor to open at any moment and engulf her and the guilty secrets she carried with her.

A light was burning in the living-room. Hilary, her maid, was waiting up.

'Hilary, I thought I said you shouldn't stay up. You should be in bed.'

'That's all right, ma'am. Ma'am, I . . .'

'Is something wrong?'

'It's Shirley, ma'am. She . . . Mr Stephenson . . .'

Laura had already turned and left the room. She ran to Shirley's bedroom and flung the door wide open, thinking to find him there again, doing God knew what. But there was no-one there. The bed was empty.

Hilary appeared in the doorway behind her.

'I tried to tell you, ma'am. Mr Stephenson took her.'

'Took her? Took her where?'

'I don't know, ma'am. I asked him, but he wouldn't say. Just that he'd be away for several days and he wanted her with him. I . . . I couldn't do anything to stop him, ma'am. I tried, I really did, but . . .'

She burst into tears.

'All right, Hilary, all right. No-one's blaming you. I couldn't have stopped him either. He gave you no idea where he was going?'

'None at all, ma'am.'

Laura hurried back to the living-room and picked up the internal phone. It rang for half a minute before anyone answered.

'Hayter? Where the hell is my husband?'

Lynn Hayter was David's social secretary.

'I'm not at liberty to tell you that, ma'am.'

'Not at liberty? Who the hell do you think you're speaking to?'

'I'm sorry, ma'am. I really am. But I have strict orders to tell no-one. The President's whereabouts are above top secret. I only have a telephone number in case of emergency.'

'At least tell me if he's in Washington.'

'I can't say.'

'Damn it, Hayter, this is my husband I'm asking you about. He's got my daughter with him. Don't I have any rights? Doesn't Shirley have any rights?'

'I couldn't say, ma'am. You'd have to ask somebody in the legal department. I'm sure they'd be happy to advise you. But if you're willing to make do with my personal opinion, I'd just drop the whole thing. Let it go. He'll be back in a few days. Your daughter will be with him. Why make a fuss? Why do something you could live to regret?'

Something faintly resembling warmth had crept into Hayter's voice. But Laura knew when she was being warned off. Maybe even threatened.

'Thank you, Hayter. I'm sorry I disturbed you.'

'It's no trouble, ma'am. You know I'm at your disposal any time of day or night.'

Laura slammed down the receiver. Hilary was still standing beside her.

370

'Go to bed, Hilary. There's nothing more you can do. Thanks for staying up to tell me. It's nice to know somebody round here thinks I should know what's going on.'

'Will you be all right, ma'am?'

'All right? I don't know. I expect I'll be fine. I'm going out again.'

'Out? Where can you go this time of night?'

'Nowhere. Somewhere. I don't know. I just like to walk around.'

Hilary tried to argue, but Laura overrode her protests and ordered her to her room. When the maid had gone, Laura sat on the sofa. For a long time she sat there, staring at the wall, thinking things over. Her life had become a torment and a confusion. Even John, whom she loved so desperately, was part of that confusion, and now Shirley had been dragged into it. Thinking did not help. Nothing helped. She got up and put on her coat again, and headed for the stairs.

A marine guard was posted at the foot. There'd been one there ever since the Lindberghs had been killed. He had his back to Laura as she came down, but hearing her footsteps he turned.

'I'm sorry, ma'am,' he said in a clipped West Point accent, 'but I've got orders not to let you past.'

'Orders? Whose orders?'

'I had them from my commanding officer, ma'am. I really can't tell you who passed them to him.'

For a moment, she thought of brushing past him, just to see what he would do. Surely he wouldn't use force to stop the President's wife doing as she pleased in her own house? And then she looked into his eyes. They were cold and unflinching, and she knew her first assumption had been wrong: he'd shoot her in her tracks if she tried to pass him. He had his orders – that was all that counted.

She took a deep breath and started back up the stairs. At the first landing she looked down. The guard was still there, still watching her.

CHAPTER FIFTY-NINE

Removing Patty's body from the apartment proved no more difficult for Geiger than making Loomis's disappear from his office. The embassy employed two men whose full-time task it was to make good any indiscretions committed by members of staff. The idea was to nip in the bud anything that might embarrass the mission, or anger or upset the host community, and so bring the wrath of public opinion or the scorn of journalists upon the Reich. Hjalmar and Gregor were both ex-Gestapo men, slim, heavenly creatures with blue eyes and the faces of newly-fallen angels, whose hushed and calming manner soon set troubled souls to rest.

Their work ranged from neutralizing parking tickets to removing cadavers. Geiger personally knew of two cases where they had created the corpses before carting them away. One had been the indiscreet and politically insensitive mistress of a former First Secretary (now repenting his lusts in Sachsenhausen concentration camp), the other the patriotic husband of a valuable informer.

Hjalmar and Gregor never kept distressed callers waiting. Geiger had not sounded in the least distressed, but they were at his apartment within fifteen minutes, smiling and easing themselves past the door with the suppleness of old hands.

'Some trouble, sir?' one of them asked. Geiger did not know how to differentiate between them.

'There's a woman's body in the bath. A most unfortunate

accident. She must have lost her grip and slipped under the water. If I'd been there, I could have saved her.'

'No doubt of that, sir. Saving lives is a thing we'd all like to have in our power, but seldom do. A young woman is it, sir?'

'Young, yes. But as old as she'll ever get. However you look at it.'

'It is a matter of perspective, yes,' said the other. Geiger decided he must be Gregor. He asked himself if they were lovers. If they were, they were discreet: it was in the nature of their trade. And, in any case, they had long ago made themselves indispensable. They knew America, they knew the law and the police force and the FBIS, they knew how to dance in the Washington ballroom, how to perform the jigs and reels and waltzes it required.

'You must be Gregor,' Geiger said.

'No, sir, I'm Hjalmar. We're often taken for one another. Some think we're twins. As a matter of fact, I'm from Dresden and he's from Düsseldorf, we've nothing in common except for the job.'

He smiled and Geiger shuddered. Without saying a word, Hjalmar had conveyed the certainty that, should they find it advisable to remove Geiger along with the woman in the bath, they would have no qualms about doing so.

'This woman, sir,' Hjalmar continued, 'is she connected? Does she present diplomatic problems of any kind? Family, a husband with influence, you know the sort of thing I mean.'

Geiger shook his head languidly, despite his nervousness.

'Nothing like that,' he said. 'She's one of Rosie Lamont's girls.'

'Fine. That should cost about five-hundred dollars. We'll put it on your account. Did she have a name?'

'Patty. I don't know the second name.'

'Makes no difference. Now, sir, if you'll make yourself scarce, we'll see she's out of here in a jiffy. Would you mind signing this form – here, that's right – and here. Thank you, sir.'

Geiger saluted, raising his arm with an intense serious-ness that brought him and his companions into a wordless and unpremeditated harmony. The Reich was a world of gestures, cautious signals men sent out to one another, as animals and birds do, to convey reassurance or warn of danger. Geiger marvelled at the silent power of these men, who could make not only corpses but whole cities vanish – for he sensed he was no longer in Washington, but Berlin.

'I'll make myself scarce, then,' he said. Hjalmar nodded, and Gregor smiled, then headed for the bathroom.

'I've left her clothes on the bathroom floor,' Geiger said, but they went inside as though they had not heard him. He sighed and went to the kitchen.

Anna was sitting as before, quietly disconsolate on her stool, her arms in front of her, one hand clasping the chain that bound her to the cupboard. She looked up sullenly as he entered, terrified of what this man could do, yet determined to reveal nothing to him of her fear.

He walked up to her, and for a moment she thought he was about to strike her. He lifted his hand, and she flinched from him, but he merely laid it on her cheek and caressed her.

'I think you know more than you pretend,' he said. His voice was a whisper, but penetrating for all that. 'I think your father had nothing to do with the shooting of Charles Lindbergh. And I think you know that. Isn't that so?'

She said nothing. In her heart, she wished he would go away. Deeper still, in her heart of hearts, she wished she could die.

'Tell me,' he said, his voice coaxing and mild, 'what would you do to leave this little place of mine? Mmmm? I'd like to help you. All I want from you is the truth.'

'I don't know anything,' she answered, aware that the truth was not what counted here.

'Of course you do. But we'll come to that in time. I'm in no hurry. As I said, I want to help you. You're only chained up for your own good. If you got out of here, how long do you think you'd last? That man Ridgeforth is no use to you, not any longer. His time's nearly up, he'd only drag you down with him.'

She stared into his face, and he could see the blankness in her eyes, like a cloud over stars. He had to bring her back to life, arouse whatever sentiment or self-interest hung on in her.

There was a knock on the door. Geiger went to it and stepped into the corridor. Hjalmar and Gregor were standing in the corridor side by side. A large box marked 'Laundry' stood on the floor.

'Just to let you know we've got everything packed up, sir. We'll be on our way. Unless you've got more here for us to do.'

Geiger shook his head.

'Thank you, no. You've been very good about this. I'll make sure you receive a commendation. I'm sure it won't be the first.'

'That's kind of you, sir. We'll let ourselves out.'

Geiger went back to the kitchen.

'If you were free to choose, what would you do? Tell me what you wish you were doing at this moment.'

At first he thought she would not answer. Perhaps she was beyond his reach. Perhaps he should just hand her over to Hjalmar and Geiger, let them take her along with the thing in the laundry box, dump one with the other – who would know or care? The front door opened and closed. But there was still time.

'Playing my violin,' she said.

He stared at her.

'You're a musician?'

'My father was a musician. A great musician. I want to be like him one day.'

'What do you like to play?'

She told him the names of her favourite composers, her favourite pieces. He was impressed. They had much in common. The child's knowledge far surpassed her years. He would have liked to hear her play.

'I'll buy you a violin,' he said, 'if you tell me what you know.'

But his attempt at bribery went astray. She clammed up again.

He reached for her right hand and took it gently between his fingers. Like a lover, almost, caressing and modest. His fingers were long and brushed with rows of fine hairs. The nails were carefully clipped and immaculately clean.

'Such a pretty little hand,' he whispered. 'Such delicate fingers. Perfect for the violin.'

He smiled, and she tried to smile back at him. Perhaps she could trust him after all. He lifted her hand and kissed it, ever so softly, his lips barely touching the skin. He lowered it and put both hands on it and bent her little finger back, snapping it clean in two. She screamed and he clapped a hand over her mouth, stifling the sound.

When she had grown quiet again, he dropped her injured hand and picked up the other.

'The left hand, now,' he said. 'This is the one that counts. A violinist needs the fingers of her left hand.'

She struggled to master the pain, to drive it back down into the dark cave from which it had leapt out at her. But wave after sickening wave of it ran through her finger and up her hand into her wrist. Tears flooded her eyes. She looked down and saw her left hand in his grip.

'You'd never play again if I broke these fingers, would you? Don't you think you're being silly, saying nothing? Don't force me to do this. I'd like to hear you play one day.'

She told him everything he wanted to know. He listened, smiling, caressing her injured hand, from time to time wiping away her tears. And he thought of Friedrich von Schillendorf and the plot he'd woven with David

376

Stephenson and Edgar Hoover, and he smiled again, more inwardly than outwardly, knowing he had them both where he wanted them. When her story came to an end, he bent across and patted her cheek.

'Let's get you back to the bedroom. You can have a sleep. In the morning, you'll wake up feeling much better.'

'My finger hurts. How can I sleep with a broken finger?'

'I'll bandage it. You can have something to kill the pain.'

He reached in his pocket for the key to release Anna's chains. The telephone rang.

'Herr Oberführer? Werfel. The embassy gave me this number. Is it possible to speak?'

The line was bad, but Werfel's voice was clear enough.

'When did you arrive?'

'Two hours ago. Sir, we have a problem.'

'I told you, be firm with them. You have a right.'

'No, sir, it's not that, sir. There's something else. Something we didn't expect. The Führer – he's not in Berchtesgaden. Not in Berlin either. The fact is, nobody knows where he is, or else they just won't tell me. But I think . . .'

A rush of crackling flooded the line, as though the sea-bed had suddenly devoured the cable. Geiger held the receiver away from his ear until it cleared again. There was silence at the other end. Geiger wondered if anyone was listening. It was best to assume they were.

'I didn't get that, Werfel.'

'I said I think I know where he's gone. One of his adjutants made a funny remark. Regretted it the moment it was out of his mouth. I said I'd come all the way from America to deliver your package, and I wanted to be treated properly. He just laughed and said "You're wasting your time, Mahomet – the mountain's already gone."'

'I don't understand.'

'"If the mountain won't come to Mahomet, Mahomet must go to the mountain", sir. I think he's in America. In fact I'm sure of it. I'll find out what I can here, but I think you'll have more success at your end.'

Geiger let the receiver drop back on its rest. He'd sent Werfel on a fool's errand. And yet it seemed as though Fate had chosen to step in, bringing the Führer to him. He smiled and went back to the kitchen. It was more important than ever now to see the child was kept alive and well. What a present she'd make. She'd tell the Führer everything. She'd make Hans Geiger all the things he'd ever wanted to be.

CHAPTER SIXTY

The night passed without further incident. Everything that happened, happened in Laura's mind. She was possessed by her loss of Shirley, and her fear of what David might do to her. And possessed too by the most terrible feelings of guilt. She'd left her daughter alone in order to run to her lover's apartment. It didn't matter that the message had been false, that she'd been tricked and used. Her very willingness to drop everything and go there had been a base betrayal, and now she would have to live with the consequences.

Sleep would not come, and the harder she tried to summon it, the further it receded. She lay in bed, bolt upright, weeping or staring into the darkness, and there was nothing familiar or consoling in her surroundings. There were times in the small hours, when it was dark through and through, that she thought of death. Only the thought of Shirley and an overpowering need to be with John again took her through those moments and out to safety again.

Dawn came at last, a pale and anxious reality superimposed on the city and its pale and anxious dreams. It made no difference to Laura. Night or day, it was all one to her. She dragged herself from bed and went to the window. The White House grounds were empty, and for a moment she thought there was nothing that could stop her walking out alone, as free as any other citizen. But at that very moment a guard passed below her window, his white cap caught like a halo in the insipid sunrise, and there was a glint like dew on his bayonet. She drew back from the window and sat on the edge of the bed and felt very close to panic.

Fighting her fears back, she picked up the telephone and was answered within seconds by the switchboard. She gave a foreign number, one she knew by heart, and asked to be put through. The operator hesitated, and for a moment Laura thought her husband had left orders that she could not ring out. But the woman had only been checking the time at the other end.

'It's lunchtime there, Mrs Stephenson. Is that all right?'

'That's fine. It doesn't make much difference.'

It took a long time for the call to go through. The situation in Europe didn't make telephoning easy. But Laura did not hang up. She knew there would be an answer. Suddenly, there was a crackling sound, and a woman's voice came on the line, thin and fluctuating.

'*Demandeur, vous êtes en ligne.*'

'Hello? Hello, can you hear me?'

Another woman's voice, clearer than the first.

'Sanatorium Handelsmann.'

'Hello, I'd like to speak to my mother, please.'

'Yes, of course, Madame. What is she called?'

'Cordell, Harriet Cordell.'

'Ah, yes, of course. You must be Mrs Stephenson. The wife of . . .'

'Yes, I am. Can my mother come to the phone?'

'Yes, certainly. It is an honour to speak to you. I'll ask one of the nurses to bring your mother. It won't take long.'

A button clicked, and Laura was left stranded on the line. Silence dripped through it like sea-water, dark and bitter. Her life and her mother's life joined by little more than sentiment. But they had this thing in common now, they were both prisoners of men without love.

'Who's that?'

Her mother's voice sounded alien, transformed by distance and insanity into a phantom's voice. But at least she was alive and able to come to the phone.

'Mother? Mother, it's me, Laura.'

'Laura? Laura who?'

'Your daughter Laura. Or have you forgotten me already?'

'I know who you are, you don't have to tell me. You were here yesterday, I haven't forgotten. I don't forget easily.'

'"Here"? What did you mean, "here"?'

'Here in my thoughts. What did you think?'

The voice stopped abruptly, and the silence returned, like threads to a loom. It was weaving something shapeless between them.

'Why are you calling me? You don't call that often.'

'Sometimes I call you, Mother, and you aren't able to speak to me. Sometimes they tell me you're ill.'

'Who could be ill in this place? It's got everything anyone could want. You should come and see me sometime.'

'I have been, Mother. Once a year since I was eighteen.'

'Then come again.'

'It's very hard. I . . . I can't . . .'

This time she let the silence come of its own accord. Warp and woof, it filled all the spaces between them. How could she get through it, how could she break through to her mother?'

'Did you know that David was made President? Did they tell you that?'

'David? Who's David?'

'My husband, David. He became President after Lindbergh was shot.'

'Was Lindbergh shot? I hadn't heard that. Nobody tells me anything. Was he in his airplane? Did they shoot him down in it? The Spirit of St Louis they called it. He flew to the house in it once.'

'No, Mother, he was shot here in the White House.

That's where I'm calling from. They killed his wife as well.'

'That's bad. She was a good woman, I liked her. Her husband was . . . What do they call them over here? A Fascist.'

'Everyone's a Fascist now, Mother. He wasn't the worst. But I didn't call to talk about this. You haven't told me how you are.'

'I'm alive. Does it matter how I am?'

'Yes. Yes, it matters to me. I'd like to get you out of that place.'

'How would you do that?'

It was no longer silence, but the ocean in its entirety, a great swelling between continents, a chasm filled with the roaring of Leviathan. How would she free her mother, when she could not even walk out of her own home into the open street?

'I don't know, Mother. I could speak to Dr Handelsmann. I'm the President's wife. He'd listen to me.'

'You're a woman. I'm here at your father's request. It wouldn't matter if you were the Pope's wife, you still couldn't get so much as my little fingernail out of here.'

Waves of silence, like waves of sickness, overpowering her.

'Mother . . .'

'You're wasting your time, Laura. He pays the bills and he gives the orders. Dr Handelsmann told me I was perfectly well six months after I arrived here.'

Waves of silence, waves of sickness, waves of loneliness. As black as Atlantic waves, and as cold.

'Mother, he . . . David's been interfering with Shirley. I don't know how long. I caught him several nights ago. I don't know how long he . . . Oh, Jesus, what can I . . .'

'Keep her away from him. Laura, you have to stay with her. The way I should have stayed with you. Sleep with her, don't leave her alone for a moment.'

'It's too late. She's with him, I . . . don't know where.

He took her away. I . . . They won't let me leave. There's a guard on the stairs. Guards everywhere.'

'Surely they won't stop you.'

'He said he'd shoot me. He meant it, believe me.'

'Where are you now?'

'In my bedroom.'

'Stay there.'

'Mother, I . . .'

The phone went dead. Laura jiggled the rest a few times, but there was nothing, not even the raw silence that had been there so short a time before.

CHAPTER SIXTY-ONE

John lay sleeping, trapped in a dream from which he could find no escape. He was back in the *Torque*, at the bottom of the Atlantic, far below the submarine's normal operating depth. The boat was empty, and its engines dead. He ran from section to section, desperately seeking someone who could bring the *Torque* back to the surface and continue its journey. But there was no-one anywhere. The air was stagnant, and the rooms and corridors were filled with a dim red light that stained everything the colour of blood. He felt as though he was walking in blood, while remaining dry and unstained himself. The hull of the submarine groaned and creaked under the fearful pressure of the sea outside. But no-one came to raise it, and John did not know how.

The telephone rang ten minutes after Laura's mother had disconnected herself or been disconnected.

'Laura? This is Christina Rivadavia. Are you feeling all right, dear?'

Christina was the wife of the Argentinian ambassador. Laura's mother and she had been close friends ever since they attended a finishing school in Switzerland together. She had been one of the first people introduced to Laura when she arrived in Washington, and in spite of – or perhaps because of – the difference in their ages, had become a good friend.

'Yes, I . . . I'm fine, Christina. Why are you calling?'

'Your mother rang. And she said you are not all right.

That you are having a little difficulty. Is that true, my dear?'

Laura hesitated. Christina was a good friend, but . . . But nothing. Becoming paranoid would not get her out of the jam she was in.

'Yes,' she said, 'it is true.'

'In that case, I would like to come over. I think we should go for a little drive together. You're not doing anything in particular, are you?'

'No, I'm free, but I don't think a drive . . .'

'Expect me in fifteen minutes.'

She arrived earlier than that. The sticker on the windshield of her K-Series Lincoln took her past the guards on the gate. Expensive clothes, panache, and long familiarity with official residences took her the rest of the way to Laura's quarters. A tall woman with jet-black hair, her elegant features and upright bearing shouted aristocrat at anyone who cared to look. Her family had come to Buenos Aires from Asunción with Juan de Garay, and she had never taken no for an answer from anyone.

She kissed Laura on both cheeks, leaving a faint smear of lipstick on one, and pushed her into the nearest chair.

'Tell me what's going on.'

Laura explained as best she could. She made no allowances for David, but said nothing about her fears for Shirley.

'I've heard all I need to,' Christina said. Laura's story had galvanized her. 'Have you got a coat?'

'In the wardrobe. But I told you, the guard . . .'

'I'll deal with the guard.'

Christina bundled Laura into a warm coat, thrust her handbag into her hands, and pushed her through the open door. The guard was waiting for them at the foot of the stairs.

'I'm sorry, ladies, but Mrs Stephenson can't be allowed past.'

'Not allowed? Well, suppose I tell you Mrs Stephenson and I are going for a drive?'

He shook his head.

'Sorry, ma'am. I have specific orders.'

'Not as far as I'm concerned. Are you capable of making a telephone call?'

'My instructions are to wait here and ensure the safety of the First Lady.'

'Young man, I asked you if you could use a telephone. And let me tell you that, if you refuse to do so, you'll regret it every single day of your wretched life, starting today.'

West Point had trained him well, but not well enough to stand up to someone like Christina Rivadavia. There was a telephone in the guard-room near the door. Satisfied that Laura could not slip past, he went there with Christina and dialled the number she dictated to him.

'State Department. Mr Norquist's office.'

The guard looked dumbfounded.

'Pass the phone to me,' Christina ordered. 'Hello, this is Christina Rivadavia. Is Mr Norquist free?'

'Just a moment, I'll put you through.'

'Alan? Hello, it's Christina here. I'm very well. How's Norma? Good. Listen, I have a young man here, a Marine lieutenant. I'd like you to explain to him the consequences of shooting me or anyone in my company. Yes, I'm perfectly serious. No, I've no intention of telling you what this is about. I just want you to make the position clear to this young man.'

She handed the receiver to the guard. He listened for about half a minute, then handed it back to her. His face had gone ashen.

'Thank you, Alan. Give my love to Norma. We must have you both over some evening. In the New Year.'

She put down the receiver.

'Come along, Laura, we're late as it is.'

They walked out together, watched by the Marine lieutenant and his companions.

As Christina drove out of the main gate, she glanced in

her mirror. A long black car had fallen in behind them. Two men sat in front, FBIS men by the look of them.

'Hold on to your seat, Laura. I want to leave these gauchos behind.'

Losing a tail on the neatly-planned streets of Washington wasn't easy, but Christina had learned to drive in the traffic of Buenos Aires and honed her skills in more than one South American capital. The Lincoln's engine packed a punch that could not be matched by the Ford behind.

Christina's driving skills and the power of the Lincoln were outweighed at first by the sheer impossibility of racing flat out along the tightly-guarded streets and avenues that ringed the White House. She swung onto Constitution Avenue, pulled hard right, and put her foot down, turning sharply at Dupont Circle onto Massachusetts, then gunning the car forward through a red light.

'Where the hell did you learn to drive?' Laura exclaimed, grabbing her seat by the edge.

'My father taught me. He kept racing cars. Good ones. Fast ones. I drove a Bugatti when I was six.'

'I don't believe you.'

'Ask my father.'

A quick dodge through Mt Vernon Square took them onto New York Avenue and a straight run towards the open areas round Brentwood Park. The Ford was still behind them, but labouring to keep up. They'd be radioing ahead, but Christina hoped she could outsmart them. She wanted to get enough space between them to make her final manoeuvre. They crossed the railroad track just where it split between B & O and Pennsylvania, sped past the park, and seemed set for a race down to the junction with Montana, but at the last moment Christina braked and made a hard right into a side street called Fairview. That let her twist back to West Virginia, and from there to Maryland. For the first time the Ford was out of sight. She pulled off before reaching Station Square, and started to work her way more sedately through the grid until they drew up outside an elegant Colonial mansion in Corcoran Street that Laura recognized as the Argentine embassy.

'Keep your head down,' advised Christina as they drove past the police guard at the gate.

They slipped inside while an attendant took the car round to the rear.

Christina took Laura straight to a room on the third floor.

'This is my dressing-room,' she explained, throwing the door open to reveal what was little more than a large cupboard, one wall of which was covered by an enormous mirror surrounded by naked light bulbs. The wall beside it rolled back to give access to a walk-in wardrobe bigger than the room itself.

'I use it when I'm in town, if we have to go straight on to a reception or the theatre. You've no idea the time it saves me. Now, we've got to do something about you. Clothes will be the real problem. You're the wrong size entirely.'

Christina looked Laura up and down, moved her head from side to side, raised her eyebrows, puffed out her cheeks, and finally threw up her hands.

'Stay here,' she commanded. 'I won't be long.'

She came back fifteen minutes later with an armful of clothes, wrested from God knows which unfortunate member of staff.

'They aren't very elegant, but I'm sure that doesn't matter. See if they fit you.'

Once Laura had found a skirt and top that looked like they belonged to her, Christina sat her down in front of the mirror and took a pair of scissors from a drawer. She lifted one side of Laura's hair in one hand.

'I'm sorry, dear, but it has to go.'

'I was afraid you'd say that.'

Five minutes later, much of her long hair lay on the floor.

'It's not a very good cut, but it should do. Now, let's wash it and see if this dye is any good.'

A huge bottle of black hair dye was produced from nowhere, and Christina proceeded to turn her friend from a Nordic blonde to a very good facsimile of a pale brunette. Once the dye had dried, she patiently bobbed and parted and pinned Laura's hair into a very respectable version of the latest style.

'Why are you doing this, Christina? It could be dangerous.'

'I'm an ambassador's wife. What can they do to me?'

'Christina, I'm married to the President. No-one's safe in this country.'

'Just like home. If you want to know, I'm doing this because I don't like what happened to your mother, and I don't want to see the same thing happen to you. Now, let's do your eyebrows and lashes.'

By the time Christina had finished, only a clairvoyant could have recognized Laura. Christina took a small make-up bottle and filled it with some dye.

'You'll need this in a week or two. The dye won't run in the rain, but try to keep it dry all the same. And take my advice: once you get a bathroom to yourself, use it you know where. If you were picked up and strip-searched, it's the first thing they'd notice.'

'How come you know so much about this sort of thing, Christina?'

'Put it down to experience. Life in a South American embassy gets very interesting at times. You're not the first person I've had to smuggle out of a country in a hurry. Now, where do you want me to take you? I can't put you up at our place, Juán would never stand for it. If he knew about this, he'd go loco.'

'You've done enough already, Christina. I'll find my own way.'

'You're going out of here in the back of an embassy car. Not even your FBIS numbskulls would dare search one of those.'

'All right. I'll tell you where to go. But from then on you can wash your hands of me.'

'Don't worry, my dear, I fully intend to.'

No-one saw them leave. Laura directed Christina to John's apartment. As she prepared to get out of the car, Christina turned to her.

'I don't mean to pry, dear, but are you having an affair? Is that what this is about?'

Laura slumped back in her seat.

'An affair? Funny, I hadn't thought of it as that. I'm in love with someone, and I've been to bed with him. But it's only an affair if you betray your husband. David betrayed me long before I met anyone else.'

'Does he know about your new friend?'

'I don't know. I don't think so.'

'Well, you should take care anyhow. I've had five affairs, two of them with the same man. Juán never knew about any of them. He'd have killed me if he'd found out. I think David could be jealous. Jealous and violent.'

'It doesn't matter any longer. I never want to see him again.'

Christina looked grave.

'He is the President. This is his country, and you are his wife. Do not forget that.'

The hull split apart and all the dead Atlantic rushed in, drowning him, and as he drowned a bell rang, and he rose up from sleep like a corpse long laid in water, and there was darkness for a time, then sudden light, blinding him awake.

CHAPTER SIXTY-TWO

The Führer, reflected David Stephenson, spoke English about as well as a drake pretending to be a rooster; but at least he tried. From the outset they had known they would be discussing matters too sensitive for a regular interpreter. It was fortunate that Friedrich von Schillendorf was not only fluent in both languages, but knew almost as much as anyone about why his leader was in America.

Hitler stopped in mid-pace, as though he had suddenly reached a decision. He put his hands behind his back and looked hard at Stephenson.

'*Wieviele werden umkommen?*'

Von Schillendorf turned to Stephenson.

'He wants to know how many would die.'

'I'm sorry, what exactly does he mean?'

Von Schillendorf asked for clarification.

'*Kann man mit dieser Waffe eine Kompanie, ein Regiment, oder gar eine Division vernichten?*'

'This weapon. Will it destroy a company? A regiment? A battalion?'

David shrugged. The little man next to him had dandruff. Hard to believe he was ruler of half of Europe. He smiled and addressed his answer to the baron.

'It's hard to say. The truth is, we don't really know until we try it out. Your scientific team has been shown our team's estimates. We think it may be possible to destroy a town, perhaps a small city.'

The Führer's composure deserted him for a moment.

'*Eine Stadt? Das ist erstaunlich.*'

David smiled. The other man's face told him everything. From now on, he had the Reichsführer in his hands.

'Later,' he said, 'when it's been further developed, we hope to increase the power considerably.'

'*Kann man damit eine Stadt wie London oder Moskow von der Landkarte ausgradieren?*'

'He asks if you could destroy a city like London or Moscow.'

The President shook his head.

'Not at this stage. But in a year or so, who knows?'

A military plane had brought them overnight to their destination. The place they were in now was not like any other place. Overhead, the winter sun looked down from a cloudless sky. On the horizon, a plume of dust spiralled as if dancing to music only it could hear.

'Why is there a delay? Has something gone wrong?'

'I'm sorry about that. You know these things happen when something's in the experimental stage. It may be a day or two before they're back on track. But I think it's worth waiting. I'd rather this was a complete success. In the meantime, I think we both have a lot to talk about.'

Von Schillendorf conveyed David's reply. Hitler nodded. They were walking together, away from everybody else. For a long stretch, they continued walking in silence. The German leader wore, as always, a double-breasted military jacket with a single medal, an iron cross pinned to the left breast pocket.

'*Warum haben sie uns belügen?*' he asked, trying to regain the offensive.

'He asks why you lied to us.'

'About the stage we were at?'

'Yes.'

'I was worried about Carmichael, about his going to Lindbergh. He didn't know. The real work was kept a secret from him. The only reason I had him there in the first place was to avert suspicion in case there were leaks. And then . . . Well, you know what happened.'

Von Schillendorf explained as best he could, leaving out details of what had happened to Carmichael. Hitler nodded slowly.

'Wenn wir ihnen Zugang zu allen Unterlagen gewähren, wie lange brauchen Sie, um eine grösserer Bombe zu produzieren?'

'If we give you full access to our findings, how long before you can manufacture a larger weapon?'

'A month, two months. I'm not really sure. I'd have to consult my advisors. But if we make this our top priority . . .' He shrugged, and Von Schillendorf murmured a quick translation.

Above them, a spotter plane circled, keeping a careful watch for anyone not permitted to enter the designated area.

'And what will you do with it?'

Stephenson breathed hard.

'I would be willing to make it available to you. One weapon, perhaps two.'

'Large enough to wipe out London and Moscow?'

'If all goes well, yes.'

Hitler nodded. He was finding it hard not to show the elation he felt. Having prepared himself and his people for a war that might last years, he was suddenly being offered total victory within months.

'Und welche Gegenleistung erwarten Sie von uns?'

'And in return?'

'I would expect a great deal.'

'Natürlich.'

'A free hand in the Far East. Canada and South America. Australia and New Zealand.'

'That is a great deal.'

'You will have Europe, Russia, the Middle East and India.'

'And Africa?'

'We will divide. The north for Germany, below the Sahara for ourselves.'

'This would need very careful planning.'

'Of course. When we get back to Washington, you can examine my proposals. I think you'll find them acceptable. They include detailed suggestions for trade agreements, joint intelligence operations, scientific cooperation, and the movement of labour between continents.'

'*Und die Juden?*'

'And the Jews?'

'Full collaboration in an extermination programme.'

For the first time the Führer smiled. He looked all round. Open desert stretched on every side, white and pitiless.

'London,' he said. 'And Moscow. Together we will bring the British and the Soviets to their knees.'

They shook hands, like two middle-aged businessmen embarking on a programme of mutual benefit. There were no witnesses but Von Schillendorf, and the dry white sands, and the spirits of the Anasazi dead. A sand devil rose up out of nowhere, and performed a dance, and died. And in the air, far out of reach, a bird with long wings dipped and soared, dipped and soared, and vanished beneath the lacquered gentian dome of the waiting sky.

CHAPTER SIXTY-THREE

Saturday, 3 November

'John, can I come up? I need to see you. We have to talk.'

'Laura? What are you doing here? It's eight in the morning.'

'Just let me in. I'll explain face to face.'

He pressed the button that controlled the lock downstairs. Half a minute later, he heard her footsteps in the corridor. When he opened the door, he saw a stranger walking towards him, a woman with short dark hair. And then she smiled and he understood.

'Laura? Good God, what on earth have you done to yourself? I didn't recognize you.'

'That's the whole idea. Can I come in?'

'Yes, you'd better.'

He drew her inside and closed the door behind them.

'I was worried you might have gone in to the office,' she said.

'No, I rang in sick. There's too much to do. I have to find some way of covering myself in case Geiger decides to play the good citizen.'

'That isn't likely.'

'No, but accidents happen. First of all, I have to find Anna, after that I'll see what I can do about Geiger. But what are you doing here? Shouldn't you be at the White House? What have you done to your hair?'

She explained as well as she could.

'I don't know where David's gone,' she said. 'Maybe our country house, I don't know.'

'That's possible. He has guests he'd prefer to keep under wraps.' John told her what he'd seen the evening before.

'Adolf Hitler? In this country?'

'London may know something about it, maybe even where they've gone. I'm waiting for a reply. In the meantime, I want to get Anna back. That means finding Geiger.'

'He'll be at the embassy.'

'Yes, but he must keep an apartment somewhere. I've asked Mary to come over – she may know how to find out.'

As if on cue, the doorbell sounded again.

'I said I don't know.'

'And I'm telling you you do know. I have urgent information for the Führer, information which must be placed in his hands directly.'

The ambassador shook his head, but he knew he was already out of his depth. Julius von Drexler would have preferred his old life of hosting parties and collecting antiques to the task of running an embassy, but the post had been his passport out of the Reich and its pressures, and he wasn't going to give it up now. Geiger was technically his subordinate, but it would have taken a will of iron – or bottomless stupidity – to cross the man beyond a certain limit. As their little chat progressed, it was growing abundantly clear that the limit was about to be transgressed.

'Perhaps if you were to hand this information over to me, I'd be delighted to . . .'

'I said "personally". I don't wish to seem impolite, sir, but you are a third party in this. I only wish to know where the Führer has been taken.'

'Look, even if he was in this country, he'd have more important things to do than visit me. I'm telling you I know nothing of his whereabouts.'

Geiger reached inside his jacket pocket and drew out an envelope.

'Then perhaps this will remind you.'

From the envelope he took a small black and white photograph. Without a word he laid it on the desk and slid it across until it lay directly beneath Von Drexler's gaze. The Count looked at it for a few pained seconds, then stared at Geiger. The limit had indeed been passed.

'Where did you get this?' His voice was choked, the words formed in that tiny fragment of his brain that was not gagging over the photograph.

'That's not important. I have the negatives. But then you'll already have guessed that. You don't have to worry, Ulrich is in no immediate danger. No one would wish to embarrass either him or you. But you have to admit that his behaviour in these photographs is somewhat bizarre, even for an aristocrat's son. He seems to have known some very unsavoury people. Well, you needn't worry about that either. Those that aren't in camps are dead, they won't trouble him again. But Ulrich himself is getting along fine. A future Count – people are nice to him. I wouldn't like to see that change, I wouldn't wish to hear people had started being unpleasant to him. Would you?'

Von Drexler took a leaf from a notepad in front of him and scribbled a short sentence on it. He passed it across the desk without a word. Geiger put it in his pocket without even looking at it. He removed the print from the desk and returned it to the envelope.

He clicked his heels and bent his head forward ironically.

'You may have done more than save your son's worthless life, dear Count. You may have made the Führer a happy man.'

As he reached the door, Von Drexler lifted his head.

'How much?' he asked.

Geiger raised his eyebrows.

'The photographs? You could never afford them. Not now. I'm out of your league, way out of it. I'll hold on to them for the moment. Never know when they may come in handy.' He paused. 'By the way, I wouldn't telephone him, if I were you. It would be a waste of time. I'm sure you understand.'

He went out, closing the door behind him, slowly and, above all, politely.

Mary found him through a contact in the Italian embassy.

'He says Geiger has two addresses. One's his usual apartment, where he lives. The other's some sort of love nest. He shares it with somebody called Eichmann. But Eichmann isn't around much at the moment.'

'Then that's where she'll be,' John said.

'If you get her back, where are you going to keep her?' Mary asked.

'I was hoping you'd help with that.'

'Yes, I rather thought you were. All the same, it's something of a risk. Have you any idea why he took her?'

'I've thought about it. They're all looking for her for the same reason: she can blow the whole thing about Lindbergh's assassination. Geiger may be involved.'

'If he is, she's dead by now. To be honest, I think he'd just have killed her on the spot. If he's keeping her alive somewhere, it means he's found a use for her.'

'Where's the love nest?'

'On Florida Avenue. I'll take you there.'

'What about Laura? She can't stay here, it's too dangerous. Geiger knows about this place.'

'I agree.' Mary turned to Laura. 'You'd better come with us. Then we have to figure out what to do with you.'

The apartment building was situated near the railroad

tracks, in a row of low, shabby houses, chiefly made up of rooming houses, cheap rentals, and low-price hotels. It crossed John's mind that, if he'd been looking for a place to hide out in the city, this would have been as good as any.

Laura waited downstairs in the car while John and Mary went up. With her dyed hair and a pair of dark glasses Christina had given her, it was improbable that any passer-by would recognize her.

The caretaker was a deep-fried greaseball who seemed to be wearing the same clothes he'd had on when the last war ended. Any stains they'd had then had acquired the patina of paint on an ancient canvas, but they'd been added to so many times that his shirt and trousers had become a palimpsest of tastes and odours, mainly hot-dog sausage, onion, and tomato ketchup.

'You've got a tenant called Hans Geiger. Has a small apartment on the third floor. Know if he's at home?' John tried his best to be intimidating, but the greaseball showed no sign of having noticed.

'Whaddya mean "tenant"? Ain't got no tenants here, mister. People come here are passengers, they come an' they go. Who are ya anyway?'

John used his pass, and got the reaction of someone who'd spent a long time smelling himself and saying to hell with everybody else. He sniffed at the pass and handed it back, faintly smudged.

'Ya got a reason to see this guy?'

'I don't need to have a reason. But you'd better have a good one not to cooperate.'

'Who ain't cooperating?'

'You aren't. I'm not police. I'm not FBIS. Now, make up your mind where you want to spend the rest of your life.'

'Don't go so fast, mister. Whaddya say his name was?'

'Geiger. He's a German. Works at the embassy. He and another guy rent an apartment in this crummy place.'

The greaseball scratched his belly, pulling aside an expanse of unlaundered shirt to reach a hairy navel. Maybe it was grateful for a rare chance to breathe, thought Mary.

'Go easy with crummy,' he grumbled. 'There's no need to be insulting. Maybe where you come from this is crummy. Down here it's top quality.'

'You supply the girls?' asked John, keeping up what little pressure he could bring to bear. 'Boys maybe?'

'I supply rooms, mister. What people do in their rooms ain't my business. Loddaguys rent rooms here. Lodda foreigners. Whaddya say the name was?'

'I told you already.'

'So tell me again.'

'Geiger. Hans Geiger.'

'Waidaminit. Let me get my books.'

The fat man got up and walked across the room. It wasn't much of a room, it had never been much of a room. The wallpaper seemed coeval with the caretaker's shirt, and it seemed to have shared many of the same meals. John averted his eyes from the carpet: it looked like a lot of the meals had ended up there. The caretaker pulled a ledger from a shelf and opened it, leafing through with the patience of someone for whom life has ceased to hold any surprises.

'Howdya spell that?'

John spelled the name out letter by letter. More leafing. A stifled yawn.

'Yeah, yeah. Here he is. Number thirty-six.'

'He has a number?'

For a moment, the fat face went blank, then revived.

'No, not him, the apartment. It's number thirty-six.'

'Is he at home?'

The unshaven face moved sideways several times.

'How the hell should I know? You think I spy on my tenants?'

'I think it's time you started.'

'This is a free country, mister.'

'It was. Now we're in charge. You ever see the inside of a concentration camp?'

'Concentration camp? What the hell . . . ?'

'Because you are talking very like someone who has a hankering to be given a guided tour of one. A man like you could get privileges, be allowed to spend some time there. A man like you would come out very different to how he went in. If he came out at all.'

'Geiger left this morning just after seven. Might be days before he comes back. Weeks even.'

Mary stepped forward.

'Let me have the key.'

'I don't keep the keys here.'

'You're the caretaker. You have a key.'

The fight had gone from him. He went to a desk with three short legs and pulled a ring from the drawer. Counting along it, he drew off a key and handed it to Mary.

Laura read a newspaper Mary had left in the back seat the day before. It gave her something to do and let her keep her face covered. The *National Kourier* wasn't the most informative paper in the world, but it was almost all that was available in the country. This issue ran a lengthy piece from Henry Ford's *Dearborn Independent*, devoted to the international Jewish conspiracy against American interests. Laura read it, thinking about the little girl she'd met so briefly the night before, whom they'd come to rescue.

There was a knock on the car window. Laura put down the paper, expecting to see either John or Mary, but instead there was a policeman peering in at her. She leaned across and rolled down the rear window.

'Can I help you?'

He was a potato-faced Irishman, a Northerner by the accent, not long ago arrived in the land of opportunity. Men like him, staunch Presbyterian Ulstermen and desperate Scots, had been recruited to fill the ranks left vacant when the Catholic Irish had been drummed out of police forces across the country.

'This car's parked illegally. You the driver?'

She shook her head.

'No, but my friends won't be long. They've just gone inside to fetch someone. It's a child. She's sick.'

'Not a very nice place for a kid.'

'That's why they're taking her out.'

'She your kid?'

'No, but she's kind of a relation.'

'Okay, but they'd better be quick. As it is, I could issue a ticket.'

'I'm sorry, it was quite urgent and they didn't notice the sign.'

'If you're still here when I come back, I'll have to make out that ticket.'

'Don't worry, we'll be gone.'

He saluted and made to leave, then turned as Laura started to wind up the window.

'Anyone ever tell you you're the image of Mrs Stephenson, the President's wife? 'Cept for the hair.'

'Lot of people. But it's just superficial. I'm not really like her at all.'

'Coulda fooled me.'

He saluted again and continued on his beat. Laura wondered how long it would be before the White House put out an alert.

Upstairs was silent. Nobody moved here much this time of day. A long line of anonymous doors filled the corridor like the entrances to a series of rabbit hutches. All anyone wanted in here was anonymity. There'd been clean-ups and clamp-downs and raids, but a few weeks passed and they all came back, pimps and hookers and liquor merchants. A smell of cheap booze hung over the corridor, and beneath it an odour of cheaper perfume. John knocked on the door of number thirty-six.

He knocked again. Still no answer. Mary took a gun from her pocket.

'Don't take anything for granted,' she whispered. 'Not in a place like this.'

John put the key in the lock and turned it. The door opened without resistance, and they stepped inside.

They went through the rooms one by one: bedroom, living-room, bathroom. Nothing.

'This must be the kitchen through here,' said Mary.

She pushed open the door and was about to step inside when something stopped her. John almost crashed into her from behind. Her hand went up to stop him.

'What is it?'

She could not bring herself to answer. Instead she stepped aside and let him look for himself.

The chain with which Geiger had fastened Anna had been long enough to give her ample freedom of move-ment. He'd left her in the kitchen that morning in order to allow her access to food. A bucket saw to her other needs.

John went to her and picked her up gently and cradled her in his arms. She seemed to smile at him. He laid her down again and ripped the chain from the cupboard to which it had been attached.

An open drawer showed where the knife had come from, but God knows where she'd found the courage to use it. Her blood had run across the floor and gathered in small pools everywhere. It was impossible not to step in it.

John picked her up a second time and carried her to the bedroom. Part of him wanted to talk to her, to reassure her that everything was fine, that she was in safe hands now. But no-one's hands were safe, not even her own hands clutched round the handle of the knife.

He removed the knife and wrapped her in a sheet from the bed.

'You should leave her here,' said Mary. 'It's too much of a risk.'

He shook his head.

'I told her she could trust me,' he said. 'I told her I'd look after her, find her somewhere safe. This is what happened. I'm not leaving her here. We have to find a place to bury her properly.'

He folded the sheet over her face and raised her gently in his arms and carried her out like that to the waiting car.

CHAPTER SIXTY-FOUR

Mary knew the Rosens' rabbi, a man called Hershel Rabinowitz. They drove to his house in silence and left her body with him, but they said nothing about how she had died, and he did not ask. If he recognized Laura, he said nothing. The burial would be performed that night in secret, at the Jewish cemetery. It would not be the first of its kind. As they left, he raised his arm in a gesture of farewell, and the yellow armband with its double letter 'K' in a Star of David seemed to John like an emblem of their common grief.

'I don't think Laura should go back to my place,' said John.

'She can stay at my house for a few days. My husband Pete has taken himself off for a vacation in Florida. I believe he has serious interests down there. Their name is Valerie. They get good weather when they don't have hurricanes, so he won't be in any big rush to leave.'

She lived out at Bladensburg, on the north-east edge of the city. Like all the commuter suburbs, it was quiet during the day, emptied of its cohort of government employees and teachers. She and Pete shared a little Georgian house in the centre.

'I never pictured you in a place like this,' said John.

'Where'd you think I would live?'

'I don't know. Somewhere tough. A tough neighbourhood in town.'

'Mister, I've done that. That's why I married Pete: I

wanted a place with roses round the door where I could grow old disgracefully. Didn't work out, but it wasn't the fault of the house.'

'I think the house is charming,' said Laura.

'It's not much compared to where you've come from.'

'That's a matter of opinion,' Laura ventured.

Mary made coffee and a late breakfast. They sat round a large pine table, trying to talk about anything but what most concerned them. Always the conversation kept returning to Anna. None of them really knew her, but she connected them to one another and to people they had never met.

There was a knock at the door. Mary came back with a sheet of paper.

'That was a friend from out of town. He's the radio operator for a group in Virginia. I asked him to monitor your wave-band. He says there was a problem with reception. Not all of it came through.'

John took the sheet from her and examined it. There were as many gaps as letters, and he wondered if he'd be able to make any sense of it. Mary had already suggested he bring his one-time pad with him, and he now opened it and started work on deciphering the message. When he put his pen down at last, he shook his head in defeat.

'That last part's gibberish,' he said. He held it out to Mary.

YOUR MESSAGE OF YESTERDAY RECEIVED
INTACT. INFORMATION ON ST GEORGE
INCOMPLETE. REQUEST FURTHER DETAILS.
CONFIRM REPORT ON ARRIVAL OF —— RAZMOTAL
FG QWNBV —— YOUR PARACAL —— ER TYO TO
B. UNCONFIRM —— SABOGHARE PM. LANDED
ROVO ALAMOGORDO —— ACTIVATED CVCG ——
GZ TRINITY —— YOUR RESPONSIBILITY. REPLY TO
FDGHYEX ——

She looked it through and handed it back to him.

'You'll have to request a retransmission.'

'We don't have time. Wherever Hitler's been taken, he won't stay long. I have to find him. I may have to risk a transmission in clear.'

'Just a minute. Let me see that again.'

He handed the sheet back to her. She scrutinized it for several seconds, then smiled and patted the paper with the air of someone who has just solved a difficult clue in a crossword puzzle.

'It's not all gibberish,' she said. 'Look. This is a place name.'

'Which one?'

'Here. Alamogordo. It's a real name. I've flown over it more than once on my way down south. There's an Air Force base there. Right on the edge of a desert called White Sands. I reckon that's where our birds have flown.'

CHAPTER SIXTY-FIVE

'I can't leave until I find Geiger.'

John sat in the front of the car next to Mary, his eyes fixed on the road, his mind elsewhere. Laura was in the rear.

'That's ridiculous,' protested Mary. 'What are you planning on doing? Walk in the embassy with a gun and shoot him? Some sort of cowboy thing, maybe? You know, Roy Rogers walking into the Last Chance Saloon and calling the bad guy out. You could have a shoot out in Massachusetts Avenue. Hell, you might as well hang a placard round your neck saying "Foreign Agent, Please Shoot".'

John contemplated the highway. Thoughts drifted in and out of his head like floating leaves.

'He has to pay,' was all he said.

Laura broke in.

'John, try to be reasonable. I'm sorry about Anna's death too, but she was only one person. There are far more lives at stake in all this, tens of thousands, maybe more. We've got to find David.'

He shook his head. Mary made a right onto Maryland Avenue.

'I don't know the tens of thousands,' he said. 'I did know Anna Rosen, even if it was for a short time.'

He told them about the incident on the *Torque*, when he'd left nearly a hundred to die without hope of rescue, just to protect the security of his mission. That mission now seemed to have unravelled, and the one that had taken its place was still nebulous in the extreme. But the bodies in the wreck of the *Hyperion* were real flesh and real blood, and they would never forgive him. Perhaps Anna would.

'Pull over at that phone box.' He pointed to a public booth ahead of them. Mary swore beneath her breath, but drew in.

The embassy switchboard put him through to an unpleasant-sounding man called Feder.

'The Herr Sturmbannführer is not in his office. He's not expected back today.'

'Where is he?'

'First, I would like to know who I am speaking to.'

'My name's Ridgeforth. I'm legal liaison between the embassy and the White House. I need to speak urgently to Herr Geiger.'

'Ah, yes, Mr Ridgeforth, of course. Just a moment, I'll find out where he is.'

There was a bumping sound as the receiver slammed down, then a protracted silence. John fed a second coin into the slot. A couple of minutes passed before Feder returned.

'I'm very sorry, Mr Ridgeforth, but I've just been told that the Herr Sturmbannführer left for the airport about an hour ago.'

'Which airport?'

'I'm sorry?'

'Washington or National? Or was it one of the military airfields?'

'His secretary says he went to the National Airport. That's the big one, yes? Where they filled in the river.'

'Yes, the big one. Was he getting a plane or meeting someone?'

'To catch a plane.'

'Can you tell me where to?'

'Yes, just a moment. It was to . . . I'm sorry, this is not a word I can pronounce well. Albu . . . Then is a letter "q" and a "u" . . .'

'Albuquerque. Albuquerque, New Mexico. When does the plane leave?'

A riffling of papers. Then Feder's voice again.

'It was due to take off five minutes ago.'

The DC–3 banked, and Geiger braced himself against the turn, like an angel falling from grace. He was not a good flyer and avoided aeroplanes whenever he could. But today was different, today he'd climbed aboard joyfully, knowing the plane was carrying him to his destiny.

On the rack above his head sat a case containing a Magnetophon and a bundle of magnetic tapes. They were all he'd brought with him, all he needed to bring. The Rosen girl would have been nice, but he'd put her out of his mind.

He'd slipped on the blood, and been forced to change into another suit. That had held him up, and almost caused him to miss the flight. Thinking it over, it would have been difficult to take her with him, but he'd have liked to have had her available, as a special prize, to show how clever he'd been. If the caretaker was to be believed, he'd arrived no more than ten minutes after the others had gone. He'd no idea who they were or what they'd done to her. There'd been a lot of blood, and she'd been a small child, so maybe she was dead. That was a pity, but it wasn't the end of the world. He patted his case and smiled to himself.

The Focke-Wulf took off at a steep angle, forcing them back against their seats. Mary sat beside John in the front, Laura was in the rear again. As they climbed, Mary started a slow turn that took them back over Arlington Cemetery. For a heart-stopping moment, John thought they were about to stall, then the plane flattened out a little and gained height more slowly. There was some turbulence, then even more as they hit a patch of low cloud. Laura

410

clutched the edge of the cockpit, terrified that the wind would snatch the little plane like a paper cup and toss it, spinning, back to earth.

And then, as though by some miracle, the clouds parted and they were levelling out under a clear blue sky.

'Do you do this with all your new pupils?' asked John, frantically wondering where he had left his stomach.

'Only the ones I think will be difficult.'

At a maximum air-speed of one-hundred-and-eighteen miles per hour, the little plane would take twenty hours or more to make the journey to New Mexico. If there were too many headwinds, it could be held back considerably. John had received a basic pilot's training as part of his instruction with the SOE, and this would allow him to assist Mary at the controls every so often. Even so, they'd need to make a lot of landings just to refuel, and John had no experience whatever of night-flying. They could not reckon on reaching their destination much under a full day.

It was difficult to speak above the roar of the engine and the noise of the wind. John wished he could see Laura, and touch her. She'd been the first to guess what Geiger was up to. He'd have his precious tapes with him, and maybe some sort of transcript or a German translation of what was on them. Armed with his revelations, he could make Adolf Hitler the most powerful man in the world.

The DC-3 hit a patch of bad turbulence as they lifted to clear the Ozarks just outside St Louis. They'd landed there and in Cincinnati before that, and a third and longer stop was scheduled at Oklahoma City, where all remaining passengers would spend the night before flying on to Albuquerque in the morning. Geiger resented the stopover, but there was nothing he could do about it. The plane pitched and tossed, and when he looked through the window, he saw only mountains, stretching in every direction. It occurred to him that he might be able to hire a private plane when he got to Oklahoma. He could not bear the thought that he might reach Alamogordo only to find the Führer had been and gone.

From *A Child's History of the United States* by
Holly Lee Bobbs (Saginaw Books, Grand Rapids,
Michigan, Second edition, 1940, pp 44–45)

If you ask your Daddy and Mommy nicely, they'll
tell you just how bad things were in this great
country of ours back around the time when you
were born. They'll tell you how white people were
starving, while Jews and niggers were living off
the fat of the land. And they'll tell you how
good folk were being thrown off their farms in
places like Indiana and Oregon, while trouble-
makers called Reds were travelling the length
and breadth of the country, stirring up unrest
wherever they went.

Back then, the President of the United States
was a man called Herbert Hoover. Mr Hoover was
a rich man from Iowa, who'd rather send food and
money to foreigners overseas than give them to
his own people, who needed them more. Ask your
Daddy what he did to the Bonus Marchers when
they came to Washington asking for bread.

That's right, he set the army on them and
ran them out of town. That wouldn't happen
nowadays, because America has a President who
cares for the ordinary men and women of this
country, and who listens to them whenever they
bring their troubles to him. When you grow
up, maybe you'll go to Washington and see the
President, and maybe you'll get to shake him by
the hand.

Well, the only people who got to shake Mr
Hoover's hand were Jews, because they had the
money and wanted to make sure it didn't go to

anybody else. They ran the banks and they ran the big businesses, and not even the President of the United States could lift a finger without asking their permission. What was worse, the Jews in America had rich friends in places like England, France, and Germany, who wanted to rule the world.

Things just couldn't go on like that, and in 1933 the American people got their chance to tell Mr Hoover and the Jews just what they thought of them and the mess they'd got this country into. That year, an election was held, and Herbert Hoover was given his marching orders and sent packing from Washington, just like he'd sent the Bonus Marchers on their way.

And that was when the most wonderful thing happened to this country. When your Mommy and Daddy woke up the day after the election, they knew everything was going to be all right after all. There'd be food to put on the table, and clothes for the children, and a job for Daddy to go to every morning.

Everybody loved their new President, and when he spoke on the radio that first morning, the country came to a standstill. You've already read about how Mr Lindbergh was the first man in the world to fly across the Atlantic Ocean on his own. He was that sort of man. An American, a hero, and a patriot. The people wanted someone they could trust, someone they could turn to in their time of need, someone they knew wouldn't let them down. That was Charles Lindbergh, a man sent by God to be the leader of the American nation in its time of trouble.

PART 11

Jornada del Muerto

CHAPTER SIXTY-SIX

'Honey, say hello to Herr Hitler. You remember me telling you about him, don't you? About how he's saving Germany from the Jews and is putting all the bad people in camps to make things better for everybody else?'

Shirley nodded. She'd been tearful all morning, waking in a strange place without her mother. She loved her father, and she knew he loved her, but last night had been the first time in her life she'd been separated from her mother, and it hurt.

The Führer bent down gravely and took her hand. He liked children, and he felt they liked him in return. This blonde-haired American child disconcerted him. Back home in Germany, children learned to say 'Mein Führer' before they lisped *'Mutti'* or *'Vati'*, and many a fond mother's first instructions to her offspring were *'mach hübsch dein Hitlerchen'* – 'now, do your Heil Hitler-kins nicely'. They couldn't help but love him. Shirley, however, had no such preconceptions, and seemed not in the least in awe of him. Still, it seemed politic to make a favourable impression on her.

'How are you, Shirley? It's a great honour to meet you.' He'd practised the words until he could speak them in his sleep, but they still sounded stilted.

'Es geht mir gut,' she replied. *'Un Ihnen, Herr Reichsführer?'* Hitler's eyebrows went up.

'Sie sprechen Deutsch?'

'It's being introduced into all our schools,' explained

Stephenson. 'If we're going to be allies, we should know one another's languages. Shirley doesn't go to school yet, but she has a tutor. I make sure she studies a little German every day.'

As the interpreter translated, the Führer's eyes lit up. He nodded and congratulated her on her mastery of the language, then reached out to stroke the top of her head. She flinched. It was a slight movement, but discernible. He wondered what it meant.

'Now, say goodnight, Shirley,' Stephenson broke in. 'It's time for your bath and bed.'

'But it's only six o'clock.'

'It's eight o'clock back home, and you're tired. Don't worry, I'll give you your bath and put you to bed. You'll enjoy that, won't you?'

She shook her head, then, remembering who she was with, nodded.

Hitler shook her hand again and patted her cheek.

'*Auf Wiedersehen*,' she said.

'*Auf Wiedersehen, meine Liebchen*.'

Stephenson took the Führer's hand and made his apologies.

When they had gone, Hitler sat down at his desk and started to work on a heap of telegrams that had been transmitted that afternoon. Conditions in the desert were Spartan, but that was more to his taste than any luxury hotel suite might have been. Only the heat made him uncomfortable.

There was a knock on his door.

'*Herein!*'

His Luftwaffe adjutant, Nikolaus von Below, came into the room.

'There is someone who wishes to speak to you on the telephone, Mein Führer. I thought I should speak to you before deciding whether to put him through.'

'Yes, who is it?'

Hitler took off his glasses and yawned. He was still

exhausted after the long flight from Germany, and the one that had followed it from Washington a few hours later.

'His name is Geiger: Sturmbannführer SS Hans Geiger. He's the Police Attaché at the Washington embassy. Heydrich's man.'

'Naturally. What does he want?'

'He says he has something to show you, something of great interest.'

'Couldn't he have shown it to me while I was in Washington?'

'He didn't know you were there, sir.'

'Then how the hell does he know I'm here?'

'Von Drexler must have told him.'

'Let's hope he had a good reason. What is this something that he thinks I should see?'

'He won't say, sir. I pressed him, but he says it's for no-one else's ears or eyes but yours. Top secret.'

It was tempting to dismiss Geiger's impertinence and to have him severely rebuked for bypassing proper channels. But Hitler knew that, as national station chief for the Ausland-SD, Geiger was more likely to be informed of what was happening in this country than most. Better find out what he was after.

'Tell him I won't speak to him until he's prepared to say what it's about.'

'He did say one thing, sir. He thinks that the information in his possession will make your negotiations here go a great deal more smoothly. In fact, and I quote, sir: "By the time you've finished, David Stephenson will be happy to clean your toilets." His own words, sir.'

'Well, what's the point of all this? If he's got something to show me, how's he going to do that while he's in Washington and I'm out here?'

Von Below looked uncomfortable.

'Ah, that's just the point, sir. He isn't ringing from Washington. He's in a place called Albuquerque. That's only a few miles from here. It seems he just arrived on the afternoon flight. He wants permission to come out here. Whatever he wants you to see, he's got it with him.'

CHAPTER SIXTY-SEVEN

The cold at five-thousand feet was intense, even dressed in the thick flying suits and fur-lined gloves Mary had passed out at the airfield. It wasn't just that the air at that height was unbelievably cold, but the slipstream running back from the propeller sent an icy blast straight across their heads. Unprepared and unaccustomed, John and Laura shivered like puppies in their kennels, desperately shifting their cramped limbs to keep a minimum of blood flowing in their veins.

They'd landed and taken off again more times than John cared to remember. He'd come to dread that awful whining of the engines as they raced down yet another runway and started to lift in a steep, sickening climb towards the clouds. Laura was exhausted past all measure now; the only thing that kept her going was the thought of Shirley, and their coming reunion. But just how a reunion was to be accomplished without David's cooperation she still hadn't the faintest idea.

Even with its engines full out, the little plane had made slow progress. Constant headwinds held it back, dragging its speed down and down. It was late on the second day when they took off from a lonely airfield outside Childress, not far from the west Texas border. The light was already fading from the sky ahead of them, and Mary started to have second thoughts as soon as they were airborne.

'Hold on tight,' she said, 'there's some bad weather up ahead. The report they gave me back there says there's a storm moving this way fast. I'm going to try to get above it.'

The wind was already strong. As gust after gust swept past, the tiny plane started to buck and rear like a horse being broken in. Its light wings and flimsy body were no match for the forces of Nature. A fierce gust took them at an angle and threw the biplane up over one-thousand feet in a matter of seconds. Suddenly, the updraught vanished and the plane juddered, struggling to get its balance. John grabbed hold of the side of the cockpit just in time to stop himself being kicked out by the force of the jolt.

Seconds later, a heavy downdraught caught the plane and sent it plummeting back down again in a dizzying descent that John never thought they'd pull out of. The needle on the altimeter spun crazily, trying to keep track of the fluctuations in height. Another jolt sent John's knees crashing against the rim. Behind him, Laura cried out in pain.

'Look,' cried Mary, pointing ahead.

A wall of black cloud lay across the horizon, stretching in either direction for twenty miles or more. They could not hope to outrun it. Mary did everything in her power to gain altitude, but the storm was advancing at an alarming rate. They'd be well inside it before they could make the height they needed.

'Can't we turn back?' shouted John above the roar of the engine.

Mary shook her head.

'They say it'll last for hours. We'd lose too much time. I'll go back down if you prefer, but I'd rather risk it.'

'How many times have you done this sort of thing before?'

'Couple. Came out alive both times. Don't worry, we'll be all right – she's built for worse than this.'

But up ahead 'this' looked absolutely terrifying. The wall seemed to plunge towards them, growing larger and more frightening every moment. Mary had to struggle to hold the plane roughly horizontal, fighting the steering column as though it had come alive in her hands.

'How far back does it stretch?'

'No idea, honey. Could be a mile, could be more. I want to get well above. In weather like this, you can drop a few hundred feet before you know it.'

They hit the storm, and were plunged into semi-darkness. John lost sight of the wing tips. Ahead of him, the luminous instruments on the dashboard glowed as if it was night-time. They were drenched in blinding rain, thick, freezing rain that ran in rivulets across the taut fabric exterior of the plane and hammered water down into the cockpits, building slowly into pools that rose above their feet and ankles. John turned and called to Laura, huddled up behind them in her separate box of hell.

'Mary's trying to get above this. Just a few more minutes.'

He smiled, but he knew she'd seen nothing, maybe heard nothing. In the storm and half-darkness, the few feet separating them had become an unbridgeable gulf.

Something kicked the plane hard, sending it rolling sideways like a ball. The propeller was caught half-on by a second blast, and the engine misfired, coughing and stuttering blindly as it struggled to reactivate. They started to lose height rapidly. Laura screamed. John felt as though his stomach had been ripped out of his body by a giant hand.

Mary opened the throttle lever. Nothing happened. She opened it again. Four-thousand feet and dropping. The engine kicked once and died completely. Three-and-a-half thousand, dropping like a stone.

'Come on, damn you!' Mary struggled to keep the craft's nose up, but the wind pushed them down again. The next huge blast would simply toss them out of the sky like a leaf, or send them spinning fast out of control.

A squall came out of nowhere and the plane turned over, tumbling now, and still falling fast. Mary opened the throttle. Nothing. Another spin. They were at two-and-a-half thousand feet, dropping faster than ever. The engine coughed and spluttered and burst into life. Two-thousand, still losing height. Mary pulled back with all her strength. The stick wouldn't come. John reached out with both hands to help Mary pull back. It gave a little, then a little more. The spinning began to ease.

Reluctantly at first, the plane started to fight back. Its nose lifted and they began to rise, an inch at a time, or so it seemed. The spin flattened out, and they were climbing again, but still not fast enough.

'Any hills ahead?'

'Not when I was here last. Keep an eye on the altimeter for me. We're going up, no matter what this bastard wind says.'

But the bastard wind could prove a friend as well as an enemy. A sudden updraught lifted them as though an Arabian Nights hand had taken them from underneath. They rose and continued to rise. Five-thousand feet, six-thousand, seven-thousand. And suddenly, as if a curtain had been ripped aside, the clouds parted and they lifted into the last light of the fading day, among rose petals strewn across a sky of pearl and milk.

The storm lay below them now. There was nothing ahead of them but an empty sky, and below them a bank of cloud stretching to the dim horizon and beyond. Even as they watched, the sun began to slip away from them, and the world grew red, then purple, then black, and they were engulfed in darkness again.

They landed at a place called Dora, a one-runway field south of Portales, just west of the New Mexico state line. A grizzled old man sat in the little corrugated iron shed that served as the airfield's crew and passenger terminal, baggage depot, waiting hall, radio communications room, and restaurant. He was chewing tobacco, and it looked as though he'd been chewing it all his life, that all he'd ever done had been to chew tobacco. First he'd chew a wad, then spit it out into a basin he kept on the floor. His hair was as white as the water in the basin was dark.

Mary asked for petrol, and he complained that it would have to be brought out from the depot two miles down the road. Why didn't they just wait till morning? the old buzzard asked. Jesse would be in around nine or ten o'clock. Mary swore at him, using words even he had not heard in all his years of tobacco-chewing and juice-spitting. He picked up the telephone and turned the crank. Maybe there'd be a line, maybe there wouldn't: he grumbled and turned the crank again.

John and Laura huddled at the only source of heat, an ancient wood-burning stove. The stove gave out plenty of smoke and fumes, but precious little warmth, and they continued to shiver. The old man didn't seem to care.

'You get a lot of out-of-state planes passing through here?' Mary asked.

The old man stared at her as though she'd asked if they handled a lot of ships.

'Nope,' he said. 'Not much call to land here.'

'We could do with some heat,' said John.

'Reckon you could. Gets cold in these parts this time of year.' Abruptly he turned his attention to the phone. 'Jesse? Harvey here. Think you could get down here, bring some gas with you? Got some folks lookin' to refuel.'

While they waited, Harvey reluctantly got the stove burning more brightly. It still didn't give out a lot of heat, but there was enough to take the chill off the air. Jesse arrived over half an hour later, in an ancient pick-up. He could have passed for Harvey's son; he probably was.

They filled the tank again with petrol from four-gallon cans. The cans were marked with the Klan Petroleum Konsortium symbol and letters, but Jesse wasn't willing to take the fixed dollar price. When Mary argued, he threatened to siphon the whole lot out again.

'Look, lady, ya ain't doin' me no favours. You drag me out here when I should be in bed asleep, you haul me outside on a night fit for no Christian creature, an' you 'spect me to take Klan rates. What the hell d'you take me for?'

Mary handed over a wad of dollar notes and got back into the plane. A light at the end of the runway was turned on. They took off again with inches to spare. John turned and looked down. He saw for a fleeting moment the light of the runway twinkling beneath them, then the lights were switched off, and darkness swallowed them once more. They had come to the last stage of their journey.

CHAPTER SIXTY-EIGHT

They'd made him wait at the airport all night. He had not been comfortable, and to make matters worse he thought he'd caught a cold. When Von Below appeared shortly after six o'clock, he didn't know whether to berate him for leaving him alone for so long or welcome him as his redeemer. For his part, the adjutant was hardly well disposed towards the intruder. Geiger's presence at the airport could not have gone unnoticed, and it sounded as if he'd made no effort to conceal his status as a senior official at the embassy.

'The Führer's waiting for you at Los Alamos,' said Von Below as they made their way to the Chrysler outside. 'It's taken until now to get security clearance for you. Los Alamos is a top security site. The very fact of your turning up here uninvited has caused serious alarm in some quarters.'

'Don't worry. What I've got here will be worth it. Wait and see.'

Their driver was an army sergeant, a German speaker, though they didn't know that. There was no glass between him and his passengers, and he listened carefully to everything they said to one another. It wasn't much.

The scenery through which they passed was like nothing Geiger had ever seen. Indian reservations, fenced in and guarded, proclaimed the aboriginal nature of the place. This was the old country, the land of the Anasazi and the Zuñi, Hopi and Navajo, the preserve of Blue Flint Girl, and

Big Snake, and First Bluebird. But the two Germans were blissfully unaware of all this, unaware and uninterested.

Thunderheads had formed high up above the Sierra Nacimiento to the west, as though a great bruise had formed across the face of the sky. To the east, the Sangre de Cristo mountains rose up, lavender coloured, with snow on their brows. Along the roadside, tanned faces looked out from adobe houses at the passing car. Clumps of chamiso and cholla cactus grew from the red earth, and the wind caught balls of tumbleweed and rolled them across the road. They were rising now, high into a world of eroded buttes and flat-topped mesas, vast fields and sprawling forest.

The car came to the first gate, where Von Below presented the documentation he'd been given before leaving. It still took ten minutes and two phone calls before they were waved through. The adjutant sat smugly silent through the entire process, as though to say, 'Look at the trouble you've put us to.' But Geiger was not put out. He knew what he knew.

They passed through a second fence into Los Alamos proper. The town was a cluster of log cabins, adobe houses, and jerry-built army huts built around an old ranch school. The driver pulled up outside Fuller Lodge, the main guest facility, now given over in its entirety to the German delegation.

Geiger was hurried inside and taken directly to the Führer's quarters. Von Below went in briefly and came out more stone-faced than ever.

'He's expecting you now. You'd better go straight in.'

As Geiger prepared to enter, the adjutant seemed to soften.

'Take my advice,' he said. 'Keep it short. He's in a foul mood.'

Hitler was standing at the window, gazing out at a view of the Jemez Mountains. He was thinking of Berchtesgaden.

428

This was magnificent, but in no way a match for the Bavarian alps. At the sound of Geiger's footsteps, he turned round.

Geiger snapped his feet together and saluted smartly. Hitler returned the salute with a tetchy motion of his hand.

'You realize I could have you shot?' he snapped. 'Your impertinence is beyond all limits. Not only do you pry into matters that do not concern you, you involve yourself in them. You place my security at risk. If you don't have a very good reason for all this, you'll spend the rest of your miserable life in Auschwitz.'

'I understand your feelings, sir. Believe me, nothing but the gravest concern for your position and the safety of the Reich would have prompted such an intrusion. Now, if you will give me a few minutes, I have something I would like you to listen to.'

CHAPTER SIXTY-NINE

It looked like snow at first, but low-lying, where there should not have been snow, and raised up in strange formations, more like sand dunes than snow drifts. As they flew closer, John saw that that was exactly what they were – dunes of gleaming white sand.

'That's not really sand,' said Mary, pointing down. 'It's pure gypsum, give or take a bit. It comes down out of the Organ Mountains back there, then it's deposited into Lake Lucero. When the sun dries it, the crystals get blown up into dunes.'

Gypsum or not, the official name for the desert was White Sands. It had been made a National Park about seven years earlier. The Klan had talked about making it a shrine of some sort, a symbol of racial purity. In the meantime, David Stephenson was planning on giving it another destiny.

'What's at Alamogordo?' asked John.

'It's a biggish town, but I don't think we're interested in that. I guess we're looking at the airforce base. They do a lot of test flying out here. It's open desert for quite a stretch, they can play about much as they like. Don't reckon they'll be too pleased to have us pass by.'

She'd hardly spoken when she caught sight of a fast-moving object at one o'clock. It was joined moments later by a second.

'Some sort of aircraft headed our way,' said Mary. She wasn't too surprised.

The black dots darted towards them at high speed. Mary made no attempt to change course: she could never hope to outrun them, but she hoped they'd just fly in, take a look, and fly away again.

Two Corsair fighters appeared. As they approached, they split and flew towards the Focke-Wulf from different directions. One lifted until it was above them, then flew in fast, firing a burst of machine-gun fire in front of them. The other moved in on their tail, crowding them. Mary knew they wanted to force her down. She waggled her wings to indicate compliance, then started a slow descent. The plane that had been behind now moved in front, and the pilot lifted his arm from the cockpit and jabbed a finger to the right, making a slow turn as he did so. Mary followed him.

Alamogordo Airforce Base came into sight three minutes later, a clustering of green-painted huts strung out around a network of runways, right on the desert edge. Mary followed the lead plane down, bumping along the runway and taxiing behind it until they were near what looked like a command post. Within seconds they were surrounded by soldiers carrying M1 Carbines. An airforce officer strode up to the biplane.

'All three of you, down. My men have orders to shoot if there's the slightest sign of trouble.'

They climbed down slowly and dropped the last few feet to the ground. All three were exhausted and half-frozen.

'Just what the hell did you think you were doing overflying this base? Don't you know this area's been declared an exclusion zone?'

The officer was a captain in his early forties, an experienced man who'd been given this job because he was good at it. The Focke-Wulf didn't look like trouble, but if it was, he'd see it went no further than here.

'I'm sorry, captain,' Mary began. 'We didn't know the base was off limits. We got caught up in the storms back east and pushed down this way.'

The captain held out his hand.

'Papers.'

Mary fished about in a pocket of her flying suit and pulled out a sheaf of crumpled documents.

'All of you,' said the captain, holding his hand out to John, then Laura in turn. They passed over their papers in silence. Laura's hand shook as she handed hers over: John and Mary had been working on them at every available opportunity during the flight, taking five minutes here and ten minutes somewhere else to transform the blank sheets Mary had brought with her into something resembling legitimate IDs.

The captain scrutinized the papers closely. When he came to John's, he looked up in surprise.

'What exactly are you doing out here, sir? You're a long way from Washington, if you don't mind my saying so.'

'I just got my pilot's licence – you've got it in your hand there. Mrs Laverty and I thought we'd fly my wife out to California. Seemed like something good to do. Kind of a tribute to Mr Lindbergh, if you see what I mean.'

'Yes, sir, I do see what you mean. All the same, it's giving me a headache, you being here.'

'I don't understand.'

'I'm not at liberty to explain, sir. Maybe you'd all like to accompany me to the guard-room.'

While two stony-faced airmen guarded his prisoners, Captain Lee Delaware hurried to his office. His mind was spinning. Just that morning he'd been given responsibility for the security detail covering the arrival of the President and his guests in preparation for the test that afternoon. Now he found himself guarding a stranger carrying a top-security pass from the White House. Just what the hell was going on?

He picked up the phone and asked the operator to put him through to White House security. It took over ten minutes to make a connection.

'Secret Service. This is Major Liddey, can I help you?'

'My name's Captain Delaware, USAF, fifteenth fighter squadron. I'm based at Alamogordo, New Mexico. The Holloman Base. Sir, I've just grounded a civilian plane with three crew aboard. One of them says his name is Ridgeforth. He has a security pass that describes him as a presidential advisor on legal affairs. Do you have someone matching that description working at the White House?'

'What's his first name?'

'John.'

'Let me check that.'

A few minutes passed. Captain Delaware looked out of his window onto the flat white sands beyond the base. They were planning something terrible out there, a dreadful new weapon that sounded like something from science fiction. What if it all went wrong? What if it destroyed everything within miles, even as far down as the base?

'Captain, you still there?'

'I'm here.'

'What you've got there ain't some fruitcake from Minneapolis. That is the President's cousin or some such thing. A note here says he rang in sick a couple of days ago. He look sick to you?'

'Looks right as rain.'

'You care to give me a description?'

Delaware had already committed to memory a detailed picture of the man claiming to be John Ridgeforth. He spelled it out down the phone.

'Sounds like the man in question. He giving you any trouble?'

'Not in person. I don't like his being here is all.'

'Sounds harmless to me. He's got a high security rating. You can trust him.'

'Thanks. Oh, just one thing. Is he married or single?'

'Let's see . . . Says bachelor down here.'

'Thanks.'

Delaware hung up. His commanding officer wasn't going to like this.

For the first time in his life, Colonel Brandon J Cutter's hand shook as he put down the telephone. The President hadn't sounded in the least bit happy to hear his wandering cousin had arrived in town. What was more puzzling, he'd asked if Ridgeforth had a woman with him. When Cutter had answered yes, the President had gone into a tail-spin.

He turned to Delaware.

'Lock them up. All of them. And keep the key in your pocket. The President's coming straight over. He wants to pay a visit before the countdown starts.'

CHAPTER SEVENTY

He could have strangled them all with his bare hands. That scheming bastard Hitler, his runty little henchman Geiger, that two-timing bitch Laura, and her so-called cousin, Ridgeforth or whatever the fuck's name was. He couldn't believe it: his wife had been screwing around with a British agent, she'd actually plotted to have him killed. As for Shirley, sitting in the back seat with him now like ice cream wouldn't melt in her pussy, he'd strangle her with one hand if he got the chance. Teasing him the way she did, egging him on, giving him a hard-on every time he undressed her for bed, waggling her little butt like she meant it.

'You wearing your underpants, Shirley?'

'Of course I am. I don't forget.' Not like Amy Turtle, and that stupid Lua Dafoe. She'd seen them do handstands with nothing on underneath.

'Let me see.'

'Aw, no, not in the car.'

'Let me see.'

She lifted her skirt. Little pink pants. He'd kill her, then her mother. Or maybe both together. Come to think of it . . .

Hans Geiger felt fulfilled for the first time in his life. Not only had the Führer listened to his tape and clapped his hands with glee as he began to understand just what it was he had, but he'd acted on it at once. Stephenson had been called in, the tape had been played, and the information concerning Ridgeforth had been laid out on the table like a deck of cards. Only this hadn't been a gamble, it had been a certainty, like betting on the only horse in a one-horse race. You could say it was bound to win or it was bound to lose, but if you laid your bets both ways, you'd make a killing.

He was in the Führer's car now, smiling at Von Below and his old chum Friedrich von Schillendorf, and generally making himself at home. Great things awaited him. He wanted to be back in Berlin, enjoying his new-found status as the Führer's right-hand man. The war would be over in a couple of weeks now, and Germany would rule the world. It was hard to imagine how the Fatherland would reward the man who'd made it all possible.

The door of the guard-room crashed open, and David Stephenson strode in, accompanied by two enormous Secret Service men in dark suits. John was halfway to his feet when Stephenson's fist caught him hard against the cheek, sending him reeling sideways.

'You little fuck. You think you can fuck with me, you fuck? You think you can fuck that whore without my knowing about it? Fuck you. You fuck. You'll regret it, believe me. I fuck back, you know that? I fuck back hard, I'll fuck you so hard your brains'll leave through your eyeballs.'

The President pushed John, sending him crashing to the floor, then kicked him hard in the side. Something broke. Laura ran forward, shouting and grabbing for her husband. Stephenson thrashed out, flailing with his right hand and catching her hard across the jaw, knocking her down.

'Take her out!' he shouted to the Secret Service men in the doorway. 'Take the bitch out and put her in my car. Put her with the kid. Keep them both in the car.'

Laura scrambled to her feet, cowering. Stephenson drew

back his arm as though to strike her again, then reached out and grabbed her by the hair.

'You think this is funny?' he asked. 'You think this is some big joke, cutting your bitch hair like this, turning it black? You don't want to look like the President's wife any longer? Fine. Fine. It doesn't matter, because you just stopped being my wife. I don't have no wife, I don't have no daughter, and you don't have no fucking life no more.'

He shoved her hard into the arms of the nearest body-guard and gestured to the door. Mary remained sitting on the chair she'd been on when he came in. He ignored her completely. Whoever she was, she didn't matter in David Stephenson's scheme of things.

A final kick to the groin sent John into a ball. Stephenson looked down at him. He'd have taken the bastard out with Laura and the kid, but he had to keep him alive, find out what he knew, why he was here, who'd sent him. In a world fast disintegrating, he wanted to know who his enemies were. He might have to make a sudden alliance with the British. But when all that was over, he'd kill the fuck himself, and take his time over it. It didn't matter if it took days or weeks, he'd make every moment count.

Stephenson drove the car himself. He didn't want anybody else to know what he'd done with them. Laura and Shirley sat in the back, terrified to the point where they could barely comfort one another. Shirley was too terrified even to whimper: her father had said what he'd do to her if she did. In a matter of moments he'd turned from the kindly father she loved and adored into a monster that would devour her and her mother if she wasn't good. She'd been good before, and she'd be good again, but she didn't think he was going to give her the chance.

The land they drove through frightened her almost as much. It was white and empty and uninhabited. Huge hills of sand, some as high as three-storey buildings, reared up as though set there to fall on the car and bury it. In other parts, the emptiness seemed to go on for ever, unbroken but for a thrusting plume of Spanish Dagger or a clump of saltbrush. It reminded Laura of a trip she had made to Alaska, so cold and so white she'd felt afraid to breathe.

The test site was sixty miles from the air base, out in a stretch of desert called the Jornada del Muerto – the Journey of Death. David reckoned on a couple of hours to get out there and back. He'd have a lighter load on the return journey. They'd hold off the countdown while he was out there, restart it once he gave the word.

They came to a small concrete bunker, one of the ten-mile posts. A soldier stepped out into the track and put up his hand. Stephenson slowed and lowered his window. The soldier took one look, realized who was in the driving seat, and pulled himself up straight, saluting.

'I'm going out to see this thing for myself,' Stephenson said. 'Stick here. I'll be back.'

They reached the bomb tower soon after that, a monstrous derrick one-hundred feet high. The huge metallic sphere of the bomb had been hoisted to the top, where it now hung in silence, waiting for the electrically-generated signal that would transform it into a fireball capable of wiping out a small city and its inhabitants.

He drove right up to the tower and braked to a halt, sending up a spray of sand. With a snapping gesture, he switched off the engine, and instantly the silence hurried back to reclaim its ancient possession. It had been there millions of years before man appeared, and it would be there long after he had wiped himself out. None of that mattered to David Stephenson. *He* was here now, and *he* was in charge. He got out of the car, slamming the door as if to make his point.

Laura refused to get out. He reached in and grabbed her by the hair and pulled her screaming to the ground. Then he reached in for Shirley and dragged her out as well and threw her beside her mother.

Leaving them there, he went to the trunk. When he

came back, he was carrying a golf club, a number ten iron with a broad head and a sturdy rubber grip, the very same club with which he'd despatched Leroy Carmichael. It still bore traces of the dead man's blood on its wedge-shaped head, ineradicable little grains of the substance that had embedded itself in the grooves of the blade.

Laura looked at him in horror, guessing what was on his mind. They couldn't outrun him here, certainly not Shirley, and Laura would not leave her daughter.

'David, take Shirley back with you, please. Don't hurt her. I betrayed you, but she's done nothing wrong . . .'

'Shut the fuck up!'

He knew what he wanted to do, he felt a need for it in his blood. Beat them to a pulp, dead or as near dead as made no difference, leave their bodies here for the bomb to wipe away for ever.

But even as he lifted the club to strike the first blow, the anger left him. It drained away from him in an instant, as though the silence had taken possession of his soul.

He walked across to Laura. She was sitting on the sand, cradling Shirley on her lap. The terrified child whimpered as he approached.

He knelt in front of her.

'Why, Laura? I don't get it. Why'd you do this to me? We had something good. I was President, you were First Lady, what the hell is worth giving that up for?'

Laura went on staring ahead of her. She couldn't bear to look at him.

'You wouldn't understand,' she said. Her voice was faint and unsteady.

'Try me.'

'David, you're beyond understanding the sort of person I am. You don't care about people, you don't care about how they feel. Look at Shirley. She's your daughter, but you've got her scared to hell. I'm your wife, and you've got me so I can't bear to look at you. Do you want to know why that is? It's because you aren't really human. You don't have feelings.'

'I care for you and I care for Shirley. If I didn't, I wouldn't be so angry.'

'Forget it, David. You don't treat people you care for this way. You don't care for little girls by jerking off in their beds.'

'Who the hell are you to speak to me like that? You go to bed with a foreign agent, you make plans to kill me, you come out here with him to do God knows what.'

'David, I don't know how you know all this, but I don't intend to waste my breath saying it isn't true. I could say it isn't personal, I could pretend I did it all for love of my country. But it is personal. I did it because I think you are the most despicable human being I have ever met, because you are, God forgive me, unfit to live, much less govern a country. You can do what you like with me, but Shirley doesn't deserve to be treated like this. Take her back with you. Give her a chance.'

The anger did not return. He was past anger now, past fury, past rage. More than ever, he wanted them dead, but not like this, not bludgeoned to death. He got to his feet and looked down at them, a wife who was no longer a wife, a daughter who meant nothing to him.

He would turn his revenge into something beyond description, make it echo down the centuries, transform it into a monument to himself. His wife and child would be his sacrifice to the God that was about to be born.

He lifted the club high above his head. Laura bent over Shirley, trying to protect her from the blow that was about to fall. But he wasn't aiming at Shirley, and he wasn't aiming at Laura's head, as he might have done a couple of minutes earlier. Instead, he brought the club down hard on Laura's right leg, smashing her shin.

The scream that followed seemed to fill the expanse of

sun-baked sand. He stood and watched her writhe in pain, but it gave him no satisfaction. Only when her cries had subsided into racking sobs did he turn and head back to the car.

CHAPTER SEVENTY-ONE

The interrogation had gone on for over two hours without interruption, but they were getting nowhere. John had been handed over to Captain Delaware, whose job was to soften him up before the FBIS boys arrived. Delaware wasn't keen on the FBIS taking over. Security on this base was his responsibility, and he wasn't about to give that up to a bunch of grey-suited Hoover clones from out east. The prisoner had invaded *his* air space, he was sitting in *his* office, and he was breathing *his* oxygen.

'Look, mister, you're wasting your time. Once this test is over, they're going to wheel in some big shots from DC. They'll knock you about a bit, put you on board a plane, and ship you back home. You'll talk. The thing is, you already know you'll talk. Those guys know what they're doing, you've probably seen low-lifers like them at work. So why hold out on me? If you start talking to me, you give me an edge. I can argue you're airforce property, have you sent to one of our debriefing centres. You can be kept there indefinitely. Hoover's hellraisers won't be able to lay a finger on you.'

He waited for an answer. Couple more years and his chances of promotion would be gone for good. A few words from the man in the chair would amount to gold braid and a fatter pension. He kicked the chair out from under John, leaving him sprawling on the floor.

'Just so you don't think I can't hurt you.'

John picked himself up and righted the chair. Delaware watched impassively.

'All I need is your real name and the names of your chief associates here in America. Or let's keep it real simple: are you an American or a Brit? You must know the answer to that. Won't hurt to tell me.'

John just kept on looking at the floor. Delaware wasn't going to break him. But he feared those faceless men in Washington. He'd been inside their cells, and he had no illusions. They'd break him there if he didn't find a way to cheat them.

The door opened and David Stephenson entered. His hair was dusted with white sand, and his shoes were coated in it. He looked cold, and he walked as if he was in a trance. Delaware turned and snapped to attention. Stephenson stepped into the room and closed the door.

'Relax, Captain. I want to speak to your prisoner.'

'Yes, sir.'

'Alone.'

'I think someone should stay with you, sir. Make sure you're not in any danger.'

'I said I wanted to speak to him alone. That's the last time I'll ask.'

Delaware, trained to obey orders, and frightened out of his wits to find himself face to face with the most powerful man in the country, clicked his heels together and saluted again. As his hand went to his temple, John took his opportunity, knowing there would not be a second one.

He jumped from the chair and took Delaware from behind, locking his neck with his left arm while he snatched his revolver from its holster with his right hand. He did not make the mistake of pointing it at the captain's head: Stephenson would just have turned round and walked out. Instead, he aimed it straight at the President.

'Nice and easy, Mr President. Just walk on over to the chair and sit down with your hands behind your head.'

'This is a waste of time.'

'I'll be the judge of that. You just need to concentrate on staying alive.'

'Anything you say.'

Stephenson sat in the chair and folded his hands behind his head. He wasn't too worried. He'd left two Secret Service agents outside.

John struck Delaware hard above the right temple with the butt of the pistol. He dropped like a bull in an abattoir, without a sound.

'Is Laura safe?' There was no time to lose. John wanted answers right away.

'Safe from you, I guess. Safe from scandal.'

'That doesn't answer my question. Is she still alive?'

'I guess so. Yes.'

'Where is she?'

'Why should you want to know?'

'I'm taking her out of here.'

'The fuck you are. It's time you wised up to what's going on down here. I'll tell you exactly where she is. No, let me correct that: where *they* are. Shirley's out there with her. The big whore and the little whore. Where they are is a place called ground zero. You heard of that? That mean anything to you?'

John shook his head. He sensed that Stephenson was playing games with him.

'Didn't think so. Meant nothing to me at first. Just some damn fool science jargon. It's the name they have for the dead centre of the blast.'

He looked at his watch.

'Countdown restarted half an hour ago. Reckon that leaves them about an hour. If you care to hang about, I'm told we'll see it all from here. They say it's going to be one hell of a fireworks show.'

John pressed the gun hard against the side of Stephenson's jaw.

'Get to your feet very slowly and walk to the wall.'

The President complied. Too late, he realized that what he'd just told Ridgeforth was likely to make the man reckless. On the wall was a large map of the region covered by Captain Delaware's security operation. It showed the base and a sweep of territory far to the north. There were two perimeter lines, one clearly intended to mark the ordinary limits of Holloman Airforce Base, the other running through a much wider radius that took in part of the Sierra Oscura and San Andres Mountains.

John jabbed a finger at the map.

'Show me where she is.'

'You're wasting your time. There's nothing you can do for her.'

'Let me be the judge of that.'

'You don't understand. This isn't some Chinese fire-cracker we're planning to let off here. This fucker is going to blow your balls through the back of your head. Ground zero isn't some adobe hut back of the base. It's sixty miles away. You hear what I'm saying? Sixty miles. Took me two hours to get out there and back.'

John felt as though Stephenson had punched him again, only harder this time.

'I don't believe you.'

'Believe me.'

'On the map. Show me on the map.'

Stephenson raised a stubby finger and brought it down on a spot to the north-west. A name had been scrawled on it with a red pencil: Trinity. John wondered where he'd seen it before, then it came back to him. It had been part of the radio message he'd received from London.

'She's dead,' said Stephenson. 'Or as near as makes no difference now. You're dead too. Why don't you just drop the gun, Johnnie? It ain't doing you no good.'

The two Secret Service agents had come in at last. John looked round from the map and saw them in the doorway, a dark man and a fair man, facing him, pistols in their hands.

'Don't presume to know what's going through my head,' John said to them. 'Whatever you imagine, you will get it wrong. And if you get it wrong, this man will be dead or badly hurt. Put your guns on the floor and kick them to one side, then walk to the side of the room.'

Neither man moved.

'Tell them,' John said quietly to Stephenson. 'Tell them I have reason to kill you, and that I will at the very least cause you unendurable pain for the remainder of your miserable life.'

He heard it in John's voice, a thing so far beyond hatred or petty revenge that he had no adequate word for it. His vocabulary did not embrace an emotion of such calm desperation.

'Put the guns away,' he ordered, 'and do what he says. Just let him do what he wants to do.'

They put the guns on the floor and kicked them gently away. John picked them up and put them in the pockets of his flying suit.

'Move aside from the door.'

They looked at one another, then back at John, and moved to one side.

Carefully, keeping the gun hard against Stephenson's head, John manoeuvred his way to the exit. He almost expected to find himself looking down the barrels of thirty or forty rifles when they emerged, but so far no-one had raised an alarm.

John breathed a sigh of relief. The Focke-Wulf was still standing where it had been left. He hoped Mary had not been harmed. If there'd been time, he'd have taken her with him; but there was none.

With Stephenson as his cover, keeping the pistol low and out of sight, John pressed forward to the plane. Everyone was getting ready for the test: the airfield was almost deserted. There were faster aircraft on the field, but most of them were single-seat fighters. Only the Focke-Wulf offered a chance of getting them all out.

As they drew near the plane, he hit Stephenson hard, knocking him to the ground. Cries came from Delaware's office, armed men started running in his direction, shots rang out from several places at once. John leaped onto the lower wing, then clambered up and into the cockpit.

The engine started at the first attempt. He opened the throttle wide, running for a quick take-off. The biplane spun along the runway, pursued by bullets flying past like hornets. Several struck the fuselage, one punched a hole in the tailplane.

The next moment he was aloft, lifting at a steep angle towards an ominous grey sky. Mary would have been proud of him, he thought. And as the ground fell away, he lifted his arm and glanced at his watch. There was barely time.

'Are you all right, sir?'

The Secret Service men helped the President to his feet.

'I'm fine, I'm all right.' He brushed their fussing hands aside and straightened himself.

'Don't worry, sir. They'll bring him down. He's no match for the Corsairs in that thing.'

Stephenson shook his head.

'No, tell them to let him go. He doesn't stand a chance out there.'

He looked up at the fast-disappearing speck of the Focke-Wulf. It gave him a warm glow of satisfaction to know that, when he pressed the button to detonate the bomb, Laura's lover would be there, arriving or leaving, it made no difference.

CHAPTER SEVENTY-TWO

Shirley had refused to leave Laura, despite her mother's repeated and tearful entreaties. She did not understand the deadly danger that hung over them, although she sensed a spirit of evil in the place; but even had she known she would die there, she would not have left.

Laura's broken leg gave her astonishing pain. She lost consciousness more than once, and drifted back each time to see Shirley's face hovering before her own. It happened again. As she re-emerged, she felt the pain first, then saw Shirley bending solicitously over her, gazing at her with an expression of profound anxiety and love.

'Why did Daddy hurt you?' Shirley asked. 'Why is he being so bad to us? Did we do something wrong?'

Laura gathered her to her breast and soothed her as best she could. She'd lost all track of time, and wondered that they were still alive. She thought of her mother and her father, and wondered if they had ever loved one another in their earliest times together, for she knew David and she had not. But the moment she thought of that, she thought of John. These were her best thoughts, and she forced herself to remain conscious as long as possible, to think them, to die thinking them.

The buzzing of the plane meant nothing at first. There'd been one or two flights over them earlier, but none had landed. This one grew louder and louder, and then Laura looked up and saw it, no mere speck in the sky, but a plane coming lower and lower. Had David lied? Had it all been a sick joke? Surely no Airforce pilot would fly straight into the site for a bomb test?

The plane dropped until it was over the desert, then landed, rolling towards the tower, then coming to an abrupt halt only feet from them. A man climbed out of the cockpit.

'Quickly!' he shouted. 'We've got to get out of here. There are only minutes left.'

Her brain refused to work at first. It could not possibly be John. He ran up to her. No, it couldn't possibly be him.

'Laura, please. Help Shirley into the plane. The bomb's due to go off any time now. I don't know how far we need to go to get out of its range, but the nearest markers are about six miles from here.'

It was John. Not a mirage, not an hallucination.

'I can't move,' she said. 'He broke my leg.'

She lifted her skirt to her knee, and he saw what Stephenson had done. He wished now he'd killed him back at the airfield while he'd had a chance.

He turned to Shirley.

'Sweetheart, it's me, John. You remember?'

Shirley nodded.

'I need you to help me, honey. We've got to get out of here quickly, but your Mommy's hurt. I have to carry her and put her in the plane. Then I want you to get in beside me and hold on tight. Do you think you can do that?'

Shirley nodded again, her face smeared with tears, her mind numb with fear and confusion. But maybe it would be all right now, maybe the man from the aeroplane was going to help them like he said.

Laura grabbed John's wrist.

'John, I can't make it. You said yourself we don't have much time. Take Shirley and get her out of here. But leave me behind.'

'Like hell I will.'

He picked her up in both arms. She cried out with pain, and again and again as he helped her struggle into the rear cockpit. He knew that if he took the time to spare her the pain, they would die. Halfway through, she lost consciousness. He strapped her in and ran back for Shirley. Her mother's cries had re-awakened her terror, and she was sobbing loudly. He took her in his arms and ran for the plane.

As he did so, he looked round. Apart from the derrick, there was almost nothing here. It was an emptiness among a greater emptiness. Above his head, the metal sphere of the bomb looked clumsy and inert. Ground zero was the most ordinary place he'd ever been.

Hunka-no-zhe sat like an eagle on top of Thunder Butte, watching the sky. He'd been in the hills since before dawn, collecting simples. His *dah nidiilye'e'h* lay on a lump of rock beside him: a deerskin prayer bundle containing items with which to replace the plants he'd taken. A child in the village was sick, and they had called him in to perform the Hail Chant and burn herbs. He would go back down later, before it grew dark. But for the moment he preferred to sit and watch the sky move. There had been rain further to the north, and a rainbow that had stretched from Ladrones Peak to Albo, spanning the Rio Grande like an arch of coloured glass.

Something kept him waiting there, a sixth sense, a presentiment that a great event was about to take place. He gazed down on the river and the desert beyond. A flight of sandhill cranes lifted from the barren earth, their strange fluting cries sudden in the stillness. They made him uneasy. The pattern they made against the sky was ominous. Something had frightened them, but he could not see what it was.

He traced the line of the fence that had been put up two years earlier, cutting off whole tracts of land, some of them sacred places he'd visited as a boy. What were they hiding? What were they making?

The sky was darkening as rainclouds formed in the west

450

and started drifting in, thick and ill-omened, as though sent there by the White Thunder God. His heart was beating fast, against his will. The air up here was pure as ice, but he could smell the evil far below.

An aeroplane lifted from the ground many miles away, heading north towards Socorro. He watched it gain a little height, then travel forwards, much lower than was usual. The rest of the sky was suddenly empty. No birds flew. He felt his disquiet grow. His eyes were drawn back to the little plane, and he shivered. A minute or two passed. Hunka-no-zhe stood and gazed out across the valley.

Something happened then, something beyond all human understanding. He saw a white light, brighter than fifty suns, turning golden then red. The red became the colour of an orange pepper, then began to rise, a great orange ball, growing bigger and bigger as it lifted into the sky. A minute later it had turned black at the edges, then transformed itself into a lifting ball of smoke and ash. And then the roaring came, like thunder, except that it was not thunder, as though someone had slammed a door in heaven. As though God had walked out of His creation in anger, crashing the door behind Him, never to return.

When he looked again, the little plane had gone.

PART 12

Last Rites

CHAPTER SEVENTY-THREE

Saturday, 10 November

'Hello? Who is this? How did you get this number?'

'David, it's me, Laura.'

'Laura? I thought . . .'

'It's all right, David, I'm not a ghost.'

'Where the hell are you? How did you . . . ?'

'John got me out. We barely made it. David, I need to see you.'

'Me? What the hell for?'

'I need your help.'

'Help? My help? You don't need my help, you've got Superman.'

'No, David, that's just it. I don't. He's gone. He went back to England.'

'Without you?'

'He dumped me, David. He was just using me to get to you. He fooled both of us.'

'He fooled me, maybe; but you knew who he was all along.'

'Haven't you asked yourself why I would do that? Why I'd help someone like that?'

'Why the fuck should I ask? You wanted to screw him, so he screwed you. Tough.'

'They threatened to kill my mother, David. The British have agents in Switzerland. There was a man called Burton, and another one called Holloway. They made a phone call from my mother's room. They said they'd kill her if I didn't go along with it.'

'So, your fucking mother gets to live and you help them rub me out.'

'David, I'm frightened. I've got nowhere else to go. No-one else to turn to. You've got to help. Please. I've got mixed up in something I shouldn't have: I know that, and I'm sorry. But it won't happen again. I made a mistake, but I've paid for it. Jesus, David, you made me pay for it.'

'How's your leg?'

'It's bad, but it'll mend. Given time, anything can mend.'

'I hope it hurts. I hope that leg hurts you for the rest of your fucking life.'

'David, I've got Shirley with me. She really wants to see her Daddy. She misses you, David. She really does miss you. I'm sorry I said those things. I was out of line, I'm sorry.'

'Have you any idea what that cost me, you saying that stuff? Some crazy guy called Geiger . . .'

'I know about Geiger. Forget about him, David. He's got nothing he can use. I'll deny I ever said any of that. That isn't my voice on the tape, it's a fake. If I'm with you and Shirley's with you, who's going to say otherwise?'

'I don't know. This is . . . You're asking . . . what you're asking is a lot. Wanting me to take you back after what you did, I don't know.'

'David, please don't make this hard for me. I'll get down on my knees, I'll beg you like I'm begging you now, just don't push me out. I need to be with you, David. I need you to take care of me and Shirley.'

'I don't know. I'll think about it. This isn't easy. You've got to give me time. Maybe you're right. Maybe if you and Shirley stick with me, none of that stuff on Geiger's tape will count. I'll send somebody to pick you up. Where are you?'

'Please, David, it's you I need to see. I want to meet you on your own. So I know it's safe. No Secret Service, no FBIS, nothing like that, please. Just the two of us.'

'Shirley, too. You've got to bring Shirley.'

'All right; you, me, and Shirley. You're right, Shirley has to be there too. She misses you. She says she misses you tucking her up in bed. We'll be at the cabin tonight. Eight o'clock. Promise you'll be there.'

'I promise.'

'Alone.'

'I'll be there alone, for Christ's sake. I promise. But why don't you . . . Laura? Laura, you still there?'

'Sanatorium Handelsmann.'

'I'd like to speak to Mrs Cordell, please.'

'Mrs Cordell? Just a moment, madame. What was her first name?'

'Harriet. Harriet Cordell.'

'I'll have to check that, madame. Let me see . . . No, I'm sorry, we've got no-one of that name registered here.'

'But that's not possible. You must be making a mistake. Harriet Cordell's my mother. She's been at Doctor Handelsmann's sanatorium for several years now. I spoke to her only a few days ago.'

'But I am sorry, madame. There has never been anyone of that name here. Perhaps you should try Paris. There is another Handelsmann there. He has a clinic on the Rue Monceau.'

'Can I speak to Doctor Handelsmann?'

'Doctor Handelsmann has been called away unexpectedly.'

'Called away? Where to?'

'I'm afraid I don't know, madame. The doctor has many patients who prefer to remain anonymous.'

'Do you know who I am?'

'No, madame, of course not.'

'My name is Laura Stephenson, and my husband is the President of the United States.'

'Yes, madame. It was very kind of you to call us. And I hope you are successful in finding Mrs Cordell.'

'Listen, you can't . . . Hello? Hello? Operator? I seem to have been cut off.'

'Cordell residence.'

'Hi, this is Laura Stephenson. I'd like to speak to my father, please.'

'I'm sorry, who did you say was speaking?'

'This is his daughter, Laura.'

'Could you hold on a minute, please? Mr Cordell's attorney is here. He'll have a word with you.'

'Why can't I just . . .'

'Hello, Mrs Stephenson?'

'Yes, I'm Laura Stephenson. Look, I . . .'

'My name is Lester Agnew. I'm your father's attorney. Mrs Stephenson, I've been trying to reach you for a couple of days. I'm afraid I have some bad news. Your father had an accident. He was sailing the *Slocum* out to Block Island. We still don't know what happened. The weather was fair, maybe a little squally, but your father . . .'

'Is he dead?'

'Yes, that's what I'm trying to tell you. His body hasn't been recovered yet, but we have people looking right now . . . Mrs Stephenson? Hello, Mrs Stephenson, are you there?'

CHAPTER SEVENTY-FOUR

'Geiger here.'

'Mr Geiger, will you step to the window, please?'

'Who is this?'

'Just step to the window and look out. I'm in a phone booth right opposite. I'm sure your telephone cable will stretch that far.'

Geiger hesitated a few moments longer, then gave in and moved to the window as instructed. There was a booth facing him, with a man inside.

'Can you see me?'

'I can see someone. Perhaps it is you, perhaps it is someone else. How can I know? What is this about?'

'It's about you.'

'Who are you? I can recognize your voice.'

'That's not important.'

'It's Ridgeforth, isn't it?'

'Forget who I am. Who I am doesn't really matter. Just listen to what I have to say. Do you remember a woman called Patty?'

'Patty? Come to the point. What's this about?'

'You don't remember her?'

'No, of course not. I'm sorry, but this is a waste of my time. I'm flying to Germany this evening. I have important business to conduct.'

John looked up through the glass side of the booth. He could just make out Geiger's figure at the window.

'Patty would remember you if she were still alive. She'd

say, "Mr Geiger? Sure, I remember him: I sucked his cock often enough." That jog your faulty memory?'

'You're making a mistake. We have several Geigers in the embassy . . .'

'I think you've slipped up, Hans. What you did to Anna was stupid, but we both know that no-one round here would take it very seriously. A Jewish child, after all. But you made a mistake with Patty. You must have been aware she saw other men.'

'Patty – yes, I remember now. I knew she saw other men, of course. She was a whore, it was her profession.' He made no attempt at concealment now. If Ridgeforth knew something, he'd be better off knowing what it was.

'Didn't you think it might be wise to find out who she was seeing other than yourself? She was a popular girl, after all.'

'I don't see how that matters. A whore is a whore. I don't expect to exchange notes about her or make friends with her other clients.'

'She had powerful friends, Mr Geiger, friends who could do you a great deal of harm if they knew you were responsible for her death.'

'You're wasting your time. I have diplomatic immunity. I leave the United States this evening in the most powerful company imaginable.'

'I know exactly who you're planning to leave with. Nevertheless, I wouldn't like to put a bet on you reaching the plane alive. Your embassy wasn't the only large client to use the brothel Patty worked from. You must have known that.'

'*Natürlich*. I made no other assumption.'

'Would it surprise you to learn that one of their Corporate clients is the FBIS?'

There was a short gap before Geiger's voice came again, a fraction altered. John had guessed right: he hadn't known.

'No, but I don't see why that should surprise me. Maybe the President uses them as well.'

460

'I hadn't thought of that, but it's quite possible. I may look into it. In the meantime, the FBIS will do.'

'Does this really matter?'

'Patty was one of your favourites, wasn't she?'

'I don't know, perhaps. She was a pretty girl. And very skilful. Have you ever fucked a woman like that, Mr Ridgeforth? I doubt it. I can introduce you, if you'd like.'

'No, thank you. That isn't what turns me on. I'm told you saw a lot of her. Well, as you know, you weren't the only one. Edgar Hoover had a liking for her as well. In fact, he liked her so much, there's a rumour he was in love with her. Maybe that's taking it too far, but . . .'

'Look, Ridgeforth, this is all very amusing, but what makes you think this Patty is dead?'

'Oh, I'm pretty sure of that. I told you that what happened with Anna was stupid. She left a lot of blood. When we took her out of the kitchen, we didn't even try to clean up, there wasn't time. Seems the caretaker came along after that, just to see what we'd been up to. He didn't like what he saw. You see, he knew Patty had been with you the night before. This guy isn't the deadbeat he makes out to be. He looks out for the girls, finds clients for them, makes himself useful, gets a bit of extra cash for it. So, guess what he did. He rang a woman called Lamont. She runs the brothel – but I expect you know that already, I expect you've spoken to her often enough yourself. Anyway, she told him Patty hadn't come back after her session with you, even though she'd had other clients lined up.'

'All this means nothing. The blood won't match. You told me yourself, it was the child's blood.'

'Oh, that hardly matters. I spoke to the caretaker myself. He says you had visitors after Patty, a couple of men. He says he heard them speaking German. So I asked a friend of a friend to check who the cleaners are at your embassy, and I was given two names: Hjalmar and Gregor. I'm sure you know of them. But did you know who their special friend is? Someone you don't like at all, and who isn't very

461

fond of you. Freddy von Schillendorf. I don't think it will be hard to persuade Hjalmar and Gregor to explain what it was they took away from your apartment that night, or to say where they put it. But, to be perfectly honest, I don't think we'd have to go that far. Edgar Hoover will be very upset, and I don't think he'll think straight. Now, would you like to come downstairs on your own? You'll see my car waiting for you just outside. I think we should go for a little drive. We have to talk.'

There was a long pause. Geiger's voice, when it came again, had lost all its confidence of the past few days.

'Talk? What about?'

'About a lot of things. But more important, I want you to bring all the copies of the tape you made in my apartment. I consider them my property.'

'You're too late. The Führer has his own copy.'

'I'm not interested in that. I just want your copies. All of them. Otherwise I might as well put this phone down and dial another number. Would you like me to do that, Hans?'

This time the silence drifted like snow. John waited. He was in no hurry.

'Very well. I'll be down.'

'You have five minutes. Any longer and I take a short drive to Pennsylvania Avenue.'

Geiger put down the phone. John replaced his own receiver in its cradle. He smiled. Anna's revenge was sweet, and was going to get a lot sweeter.

CHAPTER SEVENTY-FIVE

They had not seen the blast directly, but its light had grown all around them, filling them with terror, and when that had faded, a wind had sprung up in their wake, ripping and tearing, throwing the plane about like a shred of paper. But that too had died away, leaving them abandoned in an empty sky. Laura had turned then, and looked back again, in spite of the pain in her leg, and she'd seen it, a huge pillar of smoke that rose into a dome, like a poisonous toadstool spread across the heavens. She would never forget the sight, for she knew she had witnessed the birth of something primitive and evil.

She limped to the window, using the stick they'd given her in the hospital at Albuquerque. The operation on her leg had taken a long time, and the doctors had wanted her to stay on for several days until they were sure everything was mending. But she'd checked herself out and wired for money from a trust fund in her own name. The following day they'd flown to Baltimore aboard a DC–3.

Now, she just wanted to get it all over with. The sharp beam of a car's headlights appeared on the road far below, then vanished again, obscured by trees. She watched it appear and disappear, now facing left, now right, as the car climbed the steep incline leading to the cabin. She'd arrived two hours earlier and sent the staff into town for a night off, saying she wanted the place to herself. She'd bought herself a blonde wig in Baltimore, just so there'd be no mistaking her for the First Lady.

The lights grew larger, and at last the car pulled up outside, its tyres crunching on the gravel driveway. She had not expected David to arrive unattended. The chauffeur and another man got out and came to the door.

'Stay here, Shirley,' Laura whispered. 'I'll go and speak to them.'

She opened the door to find two Secret Service agents.

'Mrs Stephenson, my name's agent Huntley . . .'

'I told my husband no agents. This is a meeting with me and my daughter. Will you please remind him of that?'

'Mrs Stephenson, there are national security issues here. You know very well the President can't just go into an empty house without having it checked out first. Will you let us do that, please?'

'All right, but as soon as you're finished I want you outside again, is that clear?'

'Perfectly clear, ma'am.'

They came inside, and went through the cabin from top to bottom. 'Cabin' was something of a misnomer for a country house with six bedrooms, a pool-room, a schoolroom, and a kitchen big enough for a small hotel. But it was among thick woods, high in the mountains, and David liked to think he was camping in the wilds when he stayed there.

It took them twenty minutes, checking each room in turn, to make sure there was no hole or crack where a crazed assassin might be lurking. They were in no hurry. Everything was checked and double-checked.

'Are you satisfied?' asked Laura when they finished turning over the last room.

'Not quite, ma'am. Can you tell me where the staff are?'

'Having a drink in Turvey's Bar at my expense. I told you, this is a family occasion.'

'Well, OK, but you really should have asked permission. Now, there's just one thing, ma'am . . .'

'Yes?'

'I wouldn't ask this ordinarily, but the President insisted. Just as a precaution, he asked you to be frisked.'

'By you?'

'Well, by one of us, ma'am. It won't take a moment.'

'Exactly what are you looking for?'

'A concealed weapon, ma'am. Please, I just carry out orders.'

She was tempted to say 'no', but that would make David nervous, and he might not come in.

'All right,' she said. 'Just don't make a meal of it.'

She closed her eyes and let him do it. He was fast, but he was thorough, and he left no part of her untouched. When he stepped back, she felt soiled and humiliated.

'I'm sorry about that, ma'am. I reckon everything's safe. We'll stay in the car, but if you need us . . .'

'I know the drill. Tell my husband I'll be in the den.'

David found her there, standing by the wide stone fireplace. Shirley was watching, wide-eyed and cautious, perched on a low stool beneath a wall of bookshelves.

'I asked you to come alone, David. How many more of those monkeys have you got posted round the cabin?'

'Don't get smart with me, Laura. Those monkeys have a job to do. I'm President of this country, for Chrissakes . . .'

'Watch your language in front of Shirley.'

'I'll say what I goddamned please in my own house.'

'David, I didn't ask you here to argue. You're frightening Shirley.'

David went over to where Shirley was sitting and made to pick her up, but she pushed him away, shaking her head and bursting into tears. Laura came over.

'Darling, I think you should speak to Daddy later. He and I have some things to talk about. David, do you mind? I think she should go to the next room.'

David nodded. The main thing was that Shirley was there. He could take her back with him afterwards. This thing with Laura shouldn't take long. In a way, he was pleased about what had happened. Laura could go to hell, he'd toss her aside as soon as he was done with her. Or maybe she'd make him angry and give him an excuse to finish what he should have finished that day in the desert. But he still had a soft spot for little Shirley, and he was sure that, once she got over her upset, Daddy's girl would shake her pretty little curls and sit on his lap and wriggle about the way he'd encouraged her to.

Laura opened a door leading into a room that was used in the evenings when they had guests. She switched on a light and found a pile of illustrated magazines.

'Stay here, darling. I won't be long.'

She closed the door and went back to David, who had seated himself in a thickly-padded leather armchair. It took all the strength she had left just to go back into the room, just to look at him and talk to him, just to listen to his hateful voice.

'Guess you're not up to sex tonight,' said David, looking her up and down as though assessing a filly at a race. 'What with your leg and all. It's a crying shame. You've got a great body, used to drive me mad the first few times I saw you naked. I've seen a lot of women in the raw, but you've got the best ass I ever saw. Why don't you come over, take your clothes off, show me what I'm missing? If you want to make me take you back, it's the best way, I guarantee it.'

'David . . .'

'Aw, hell, don't worry about Shirley. In fact, why not bring her back in? She could strip off too, we could have a family party, why not? It's time she learned what it's all about.'

'David, we have to talk.'

'So, talk.'

'David, I want a divorce.'

'What the hell? You said you wanted to come back to me.'

'I needed to see you face to face. We have to talk this

466

over. You tried to kill me and Shirley. I can't come back to live with someone who was willing to do that. I have plenty of money to live on my own, but I need you to agree to a divorce.'

'Not while I'm President. No President of this country ever got divorced, and I'm sure as hell not going to be the first.'

'I can't live with you, David. I can't put on a face and be First Lady. And I can't let Shirley live with you either.'

'Like hell you can't. Shirley stays, whatever happens. I don't really give a fuck what happens to you, Laura. I wish you'd stayed out there in the desert and let the bomb take care of you. Now, either you come back to Washington with me and make a show for the good people of this country, or I take care of you myself.'

She shook her head.

'There's no point to all this, David. I'm not afraid of you any more. I don't love you, I don't hate you, I don't even pity you. I just don't feel anything any longer. All I want from you is a divorce. Is that so hard to understand?'

He hit her. As he might have struck a fly or a wasp, with the back of his hand, hard enough to make her stagger. Her stick fell, and she lost her balance completely, reeling back against the desk. He came after her and hit her again, then pinned her down and slipped his hands around her neck. The plaster on her leg made movement difficult. She squirmed, fighting against his superior weight and strength, and she tried to cry out, but his fingers were like steel bands crushing the breath from her.

All across the desk, objects slipped and fell: diaries, photographs in silver frames, a clock, Klan emblems, an Aryan Alliance shield. Laura knew she was fighting for her life. She scrabbled about, trying to find something large enough to hit him with, but when she touched anything her fingers could not gain purchase. And then, just as she thought she was about to lose consciousness, she got hold of something, something she recognized – a large paperknife she'd given David two Christmases earlier. Its hilt was shaped like a burning cross. She took a firm hold of it and brought her arm back as far as she was able before plunging it forward, striking him hard in the side.

He reared up, roaring, and as he did so, she pulled the knife out. Next moment he threw himself on her again, but this time the knife was facing straight at him, and his own weight carried him onto the point. It penetrated his chest, plunging into the heart, as neatly and honestly as any dagger. His eyes opened wide, and he stared at her with a look of shock and indignation, incompetent to believe that a woman like Laura had defeated him. His mouth opened as though to cry out in pain or rage; but only blood came to his lips, and poured from his open mouth as he slumped against her.

She pushed him off and let him fall to the floor. With an effort, she straightened herself and stepped round her husband's body to retrieve her stick. She was choking and trembling, but she knew she could not afford to lose a moment.

A door led on to a patio at the rear of the house. She hobbled to it and opened it, staring into the darkness.

'John? Are you there? Hurry up, I think I've killed him.'

There was a rustle of foliage, then John appeared from the bushes in which he'd been hiding, pushing Geiger along in front of him. The German was bound and gagged, and shivering with cold and trepidation. He had no idea what this house was or why he'd been brought here.

'What happened?'

As he stepped inside and his eyes adjusted to the light, John saw the blood on Laura's dress.

'Are you all right?'

'I'm fine. It's David. He tried to strangle me. I stabbed him with that paperknife. Oh, God, John, I think he's dead. I think I killed him.'

468

John knelt down and laid a finger against Stephenson's neck. He nodded.

'Yes.'

'He tried to kill me. He had his hands round my neck. I only tried to . . .'

He went to her and put his arms gently round her, shaking with the knowledge that he had put her life so lightly at risk. Inwardly, he swore it was something he'd never do again, however compelling the reason.

'A stabbing's no good to us,' he said. He knelt again and drew the knife out. 'Here,' he said, handing it to Laura. 'Clean it and put it back on the desk.'

She took the knife reluctantly, with an unsteady hand.

'This ruins our plan, doesn't it?' she said. 'They'll never believe Geiger got close enough to stab him.'

'We can cover that up.'

He took a pistol from his pocket, a Walther P38. Crossing to where Geiger still stood by the door, he untied the cords that held the German's wrists, then unfastened the gag.

'What the hell is going on here?' demanded Geiger. 'Who is the dead man?'

'You don't have to know. This is just a variation on an old trick, one you know inside out.'

Laura had finished cleaning the knife. John took another gun from his belt and handed it to her. This was an American weapon, a Kolt KKK, a sturdy little gun much favoured by the FBIS and other government agencies.

'Keep him covered while I take care of this. If he tries to run, shoot him. It won't make any difference if it happens now or later.'

Turning back to the body on the floor, John took careful aim and pumped seven rounds into it, obliterating the stab wounds as though they had never been. Standing, he handed the empty weapon to Geiger.

'Here,' he said. 'This is a present from me.'

Geiger stood for a moment, clutching the Walther. There were running footsteps in the corridor outside. John took the Kolt from Laura and, as the door opened, he fired, three quick shots to Geiger's chest, and a fourth to his head. The German shuddered, still trying to understand what was happening, then his legs went from under him and he fell to the floor, and shook once, and was still for ever.

'Freeze!'

'Put your fucking hands in the air!'

The Secret Service agents crashed into the room, one to each side, guns held high, ready to shoot.

'Drop the gun! Drop it now!'

John did as he was told. Laura put herself between them, shouting.

'For God's sake, don't shoot! He's my cousin, he just saved my life!'

'Put your hands on your head, buddy. Move and I'll shoot.'

The door to the next room opened, and the first agent turned and pointed his gun at it. Shirley came out, her eyes bulging with fear.

'Mummy? Mummy, what's going on? I heard shooting.'

Laura ran to her and swept her up. She turned to the agents.

'Will you keep those guns down? Someone has shot the President, I don't want you morons shooting his daughter as well. Or my cousin.'

While one man kept John covered, the other bent down to examine the bodies.

'Both dead.'

The agent on his feet glanced at Laura.

'You okay, Mrs Stephenson? You've got blood on your dress.'

She shook her head, hugging Shirley as tightly as she could. All she wanted to do was scream and scream until her lungs burnt out and some sort of oblivion took her.

But her life and Shirley's and John's depended on her keeping her wits about her.

'I'm all right. I'm OK. It . . . the blood happened when he shot David. I'm not sure how, I think . . . I must have caught hold of David before he fell. Look, will you put your gun down? You're making me nervous. You're frightening Shirley.'

'Ma'am, there may be more assassins in the house. We've got to get you out of here. This was supposed to be a family thing, we weren't told to expect anybody else.'

'It was a family thing. I told you already – John's a member of the family. He's my cousin. He was here at David's invitation. John worked for him as a legal advisor.' She turned to John. 'John, show him your pass.'

John lowered one hand and moved it towards his pocket.

'Real slow, buddy. You can believe I know how to shoot this thing.'

'I believe you,' said John, and fished out the pass. He held it up so the agent could read it. One glance produced exactly the desired effect. For his part, John breathed a sigh of relief that his old friends from Alamogordo had not been on duty this evening.

'Good thing I was here,' he said. 'Otherwise he'd have killed them both. You guys can't have done much of a job securing the perimeter. He just walked in here like he owned the place. Jesus Christ, you and your partner are in bad trouble.'

Both agents wilted perceptibly. It was starting to sink in that they'd be held responsible for letting President Stephenson's killer past their guard. The consequences were likely to be terminal.

'Any idea who he is?'

'Oh, yes,' said John. 'I know exactly who this bastard is. His name's Geiger. Sturmbannführer Hans Geiger of the German embassy. I think you'd better get on the phone to the Vice President right away. And then I think you should phone the Secretary of State. We've got a long night ahead of us. If you guys want to come out of this alive, I think a little polite cooperation might do you some favours.'

PART 13

The Voyage of the Tadpole

CHAPTER SEVENTY-SIX

'Take her down, Mr Cunningham.'

'Aye, aye, sir.'

Jeffrey Wingate closed the cock on the voice pipe, slipped down and closed the upper hatch, securing it with clips and pins, and muttering the life-saving incantation as he did so: 'One clip on, both clips on; one pin in, both pins in.' A mistake could cost lives, and he wasn't about to start making mistakes on what might be his last voyage as captain of the *Tadpole.*

Below decks, the Chief Engine Room Artificer, Glyn Jones, shouted out orders. 'Out clutches, secure for diving.'

'Steer oh seventy, flood Q, eighty feet.'

Q tank was blown, and the planesman took the trim just below periscope depth.

They were under way.

Shirley looked round at the bearded men in the Control Room. In the dim red light, they looked like creatures from another world, but she was not afraid. They were taking her and her mother away to somewhere safe, someplace nobody could hurt them. Uncle John was with them too, to make sure they'd be all right when they got to England. The Navigating Officer, a Yorkshireman called Bill Worthington, looked up from his map and smiled at her. She smiled back.

In the wardroom, John took Laura's hand in his. It had taken two days of negotiation to get London to agree to her defection, but in the end they'd seen the sense of it. Love alone would never have won them over.

'It's going to be a long journey,' he said.

'I don't mind.'

'Not even with that leg?'

'I can celebrate getting to England by having the plaster removed. I'm afraid it isn't going to look very good by the time the doctors have done with it.'

'It'll look fine. As long as you can get about, what does it matter?'

'It matters to me. I had nice legs.'

'You still have.'

'Well, you can save that up till we get to the other side. There's about as much privacy on this thing as there is on Pennsylvania Avenue.'

'They've never had a woman on board one of these before.'

'Good, it's time they started. Maybe they'll teach me how to drive.'

'I don't think piloting a submarine is exactly what Mr Churchill has in mind for you.'

'Oh, to hell with him. I'm an American, I don't have to take orders.'

'You don't have to remain an American. If you married me . . .'

She stopped him with a look.

'No, you don't. I've said I'll marry you. But I won't take British citizenship. Like I said, I'm an American. That's important to me. When this war is over and the Klan is history, I'm going back. I'd like you to come with me, but if you won't I'll go alone.'

'That won't be necessary. You're forgetting I'm half-American too. But first we've got a war to win.'

He leaned forward and took her in his arms, and he kissed her, gently at first, then hard, as though she might slip away from him. She kissed him back, not without love, but thoughtfully, as though she could not bring her whole self into it.

He drew away, looking at her.

476

'What's wrong?'

She shrugged.

'Nothing. Not you. I love you. But I feel I'm only half here, as though I've left part of me behind and may never get it back.'

'That will change. You'll see.'

'Will it?' She thought of her mother's death, her father's murder, David's treatment of herself and Shirley, that terrible moment when she had turned the knife on David and finished the whole business. So many ghosts, they made her feel part-ghost as well.

'You mean hearts can't heal?' he said.

'Call it that if you like. It's more than that. I was somebody else before this all started, now I no longer know who or what I am. I could pretend David's death has freed me or given me a new lease on life, or something like that. Maybe it has. But I don't feel free. I don't feel a new person. I feel trapped by everything that's happened. It doesn't matter how long I live, I can never escape any of it.'

'Maybe you don't have to. Maybe you just have to take it with you and learn to live with it. I killed a policeman when I got to America. I don't know if he was a good man or a bad man, whether he had a wife or kids, whether he'd have been kind to his black neighbours if his parents had brought him up differently. All I know is, I had to kill him, and I have to live with it. And I had to kill Miles, and I had to leave Mary behind. And I couldn't save little Anna.'

Without warning, as though his own ghosts had ambushed him in a place where there were only shadows, he burst out crying. Not for any of the dead, but for himself and a world that deprived men of substantial hope. She took him in her arms and held him, knowing that all around them lay the deep sea and the darkness. They were carrying their pain with them to England. Perhaps it would never leave them, perhaps there was no comfort in the world. But that was no reason not to look for it.

The door opened and Captain Wingate came in.

'Mind if I come in?'

They drew apart. The captain held a sheet of paper in one hand.

'This just came through,' he said. 'I thought you should be the first to know.'

He handed the paper to John. He read it and handed it to Laura.

'It says Joe Kennedy's first act after being sworn in as President was to break off diplomatic relations with Germany. There'll be a fuller announcement later. The German diplomatic mission left Washington this afternoon.'

Laura looked at him. There were tears in her eyes.

'It's started, then?'

John nodded.

'Yes, love. It's started.'

Two days later, they arrived at coordinates 31 degrees 27 minutes North, 55 degrees 59 minutes West. All engines were stopped, but they did not rise to the surface. John and Laura were summoned forward to the Control Room. All the officers were there. There was a stillness throughout the boat. The crew remained at their stations and waited.

Jeffrey Wingate brought John forward.

'I thought you'd like to be here. I believe you were on the *Torque* when the *Hyperion* went down.'

'It was here, wasn't it?'

'Yes, as far as we know. I thought we should say some prayers.'

'Did you speak to the *Torque's* captain?'

'Peter Bosworth? Yes, we had a brief chat. He told me what happened.'

'He doesn't have a very high opinion of me.'

Wingate smiled.

'Don't be so hard on him. Or on yourself either. We've all had to do things we hate. I've put torpedoes into more than a dozen ships. They all had crew aboard.'

478

'You don't feel bad having me here?'

Wingate shook his head.

'No-one has more right to be here than you.'

The following year, on the twenty-second of October, on a night of storm, John Ridgeforth went alone to a small church in Liverpool. He'd paid for a plaque to be put there, bearing the names of all those who had died. Kneeling, he laid a spray of flowers at its foot, and though he was not much of a believer, he sat for a while in the empty building, as though listening for something, for a voice that would comfort or restore him.

Memories of his Quaker childhood came to him. Sunday mornings spent in Meeting, the long silence, the slow centring down, the moment of gathering, waiting through silence for the voice of God in him. But no voice came, and he left and walked back into the night.

Laura was waiting outside in the car. He got in without speaking, and they drove off through the darkness on the long journey home. Laura leaned against him, her head on his shoulder, and from time to time he'd turn his head and look at her and smile.

He brought flowers to the church on the same date every year, and every year he waited for the voice, or the comfort, or the restoration. In some measure, each came in its time. He memorized the names of the dead, and carried them with him everywhere, long after the church was demolished and the *Hyperion* no more than a footnote in someone else's history.

Each year, Laura waited for him in the car, and on the long drive home she'd put her head on his shoulder, and he'd turn his head a fraction, and smile.